Comes a Time for Burning

Books by Steven F. Havill

The Posadas County Mysteries
Heartshot
Bitter Recoil
Twice Buried
Before She Dies
Privileged to Kill
Prolonged Exposure
Out of Season
Dead Weight
Bag Limit
Red, Green, or Murder
Scavengers
A Discount for Death
Convenient Disposal
Statute of Limitations
Final Payment
The Fourth Time is Murder

The Dr. Thomas Parks Novels
Race for the Dying
Comes a Time for Burning

Other Novels
The Killer
The Worst Enemy
LeadFire
TimberBlood

Comes a Time for Burning

Steven F. Havill

Poisoned Pen Press

Poisoned
Pen
Press

Copyright © 2011 by Steven F. Havill

First Edition

10 9 8 7 6 5 4 3 2 1

Library of Congress Catalog Card Number: 2010932104

ISBN: 9781590588277   Hardcover
        9781590588291   Trade Paperback

Poisoned Pen Press
6962 E. First Ave., Ste. 103
Scottsdale, AZ 85251
www.poisonedpenpress.com
info@poisonedpenpress.com

Printed in the United States of America

For Kathleen

Special thanks to Zang Wood

Chapter One

The young man's arms were folded tight across his canvas coat, hands cradling each other as if he might be holding a baby bird. It was a position that Dr. Thomas Parks recognized instantly— pain clutched close to center, nothing else mattering. The man, perhaps twenty-two or three, sat astride a large, rangy mule, and he was accompanied by another young fellow who slouched in the saddle of a scruffy horse.

The injured man swung a leg over the mule's saddle without moving the position of his hands, and his companion stirred enough to reach over and take the abandoned reins. When the fellow's boots hit the ground he let out a little yelp, then walked around the mule with a big grin pasted on his face.

"Mornin', Doc," the young man called cheerfully, but his pale countenance confirmed that it wasn't an injured fledgling songbird that was the issue here. A few minutes before, Thomas had looked down the steep, rutted lane of Gamble Street and seen the two men rein up under the portico of the clinic, where they waited for his approach.

He had spent the last hundred yards of his morning walk to the clinic trying to imagine what injury the loggers—for that's surely who these young men were—might have inflicted upon their persons this time: the deep, clean chop of a four pound Plumb double-bit axe, the raking laceration of inch-long teeth from a eight foot ribbon saw, the hideous burn inflicted by one of the steam boilers, a hand crushed to pulp when a log kicked or the rigging tackle snatched the unwary. An occasional knife or bullet wound kept the mix interesting.

"Gentlemen, good morning," Thomas said affably. "You have something for me this fine morning?" He found the key for the front door and as he opened the lock and pushed the heavy door inward, the young physician watched the injured man shift from foot to foot, sucking quick breaths through his teeth.

"The animals are fine where they are," Thomas added, and the rider on the horse nodded without much enthusiasm. He turned in the saddle, looking this way and that, bending at the waist with his elbows close as if what he really wanted was a handy privy.

"Around behind the stables, if it's relief you're looking for," the physician said.

"He's got the shits," the first man laughed nervously, still dancing in little circles with the pain. "He'll be all right. You think you could take a look at this thumb here?"

"Let's see what you've done. Come in. Your name?"

"Buddy Huckla, Doc." Of medium height, the young man was dressed in clothes that smelled of the timber and hard work layered with camp smoke and tobacco, grease and alcohol. Thomas held the door wide and Huckla sidled in, keeping the injured wing away from any knocks or bumps. He stopped just inside the door, as if afraid to clump across the polished wood floor of the waiting room.

"Well, Mr. Huckla, you're out and about early this morning. You rode in from the mill?" Bert Schmidt's sawmill and shingle factory two miles south of Port McKinney on Jefferson inlet employed two of every three village residents.

"We're out at the Dutch." The young man referred to one of the many tracks of timber that surrounded Port McKinney.

"Ah." Thomas unlocked the door to the examination room. The supply of morphine and other opiates sometimes posed an attractive nuisance. All of the gas jets in the examination room and dispensary were turned up, and that meant Nurse Bertha

Auerbach was at work making her preparations for the day. The night nurse, Helen Whitman, would have already gone home, and Bertha would be upstairs, tending their single young patient.

Huckla hesitated again, perhaps struck by the characteristic odor of the pharmacy, perhaps by all the alien hardware. The young man kept flinching as if the very cabinets and tables in the room were reaching out to rap his injured member.

Thomas patted the end of the high examination bed and slid the rubber pad into place. "Sit yourself right there," he said. "What have you managed to do?" It was clear that Buddy Huckla didn't want to extend his arm, and he gritted his teeth in a comical grimace that was more theatrical anticipation of pain than the real thing. Slowly, as if presenting a gift, Huckla unwound his arms and held out his right hand.

"Well, well," Thomas observed. Three of the five fingers were straight and true. Huckla's right index finger appeared to be trying to point in several directions at once, and his thumb was grotesquely swollen at the base. "When did this happen?"

"Oh, last night, at the camp."

"There is assistance here at all hours, you know. You didn't need to suffer through to dawn, my friend."

"Thought it might be better by this mornin'," Huckla said, and Thomas worked hard to keep a straight face. In his seven months of experience in this place, he'd discovered that the rough loggers as often as not would go to considerable lengths—medically absurd lengths—to avoid appearing the sissy.

"Bones are remarkable things." He straightened. "But they don't heal over night. You work for Mr. Schmidt?"

"Sure enough do. You think it's broke, Doc?"

"Yes. You did a fine, workmanlike job of it, my friend. How did you manage?" He stepped across the small room and opened the door of the new gas clave. Sure enough, a full surgical kit had been made ready for the day. He removed a sterile hypodermic barrel and needle from the enameled pan. A half grain of morphine made a formidable injection, but Buddy Huckla didn't impress Thomas as the steely-nerved, leather strap-between-the-teeth backwoodsman who could amputate his own arm if caught in a bear trap. The lad's knees were bouncing, his face pale, sweat standing on his brow and upper lip.

In fact, Huckla's face drained of the last bits of color the moment he saw the hypodermic, and he swayed dangerously on the end of the bed.

"How did you manage this?" Thomas repeated. Huckla's eyes were locked on the needle.

"We was finger wrestlin'," Huckla said. He made a twisting motion with his good hand. "Had a dollar bet on it, too."

"A dollar? Really now, that's a lot of money, my friend."

Huckla nodded, his grin returning.

"But you didn't win, apparently. And perhaps what this is going to cost you will be a bit sobering." He patted the man's left shoulder. "Drop your shirt off your shoulder so I have some place to put this." At that moment, Nurse Bertha Auerbach entered the examination room, took in Buddy Huckla with a single, swift surveying glance, and walked around behind him to assist with the grubby flannel shirt. "Actually, all the way off, Berti. We're going to have to do some fancy splinting, and the shirt will just be in the way."

Huckla finally had something to eyeball besides the needle, and the nurse's familiarity at managing his wounded awkwardness hinted that they knew each other. Certainly, Bertha Auerbach's lovely face, with its dark features, riveting eyes, and flawless skin, took the logger's breath away. While he was thus captivated, Thomas jabbed the needle into the heavy muscle of the young man's shoulder, and the burn of the morphine brought a yelp.

"Jesus, Doc," Huckla protested, but he looked relieved. "I thought you was gonna stick that spike in my *finger.*"

"Just relax, now." Withdrawing the needle, Thomas then released the catch on the bed and folded the wooden foot rest upward for support as Huckla sagged happily backward. "Don't jerk away now." Closing his eyes, the physician used two fingers to trace the deformity of the patient's index finger. "Finger wrestling," he muttered for Bertha's benefit. "Medial joint is fractured and," he stopped without removing his own finger. "There's a large bone fragment right there, by the joint." He transferred his attention to the thumb, tracing the bone outline.

"Mr. Huckla, how are you doing?"

"I'm feelin' poorly."

"Hurts some, doesn't it."

"Oh, yeah. It hurts."

"You dislocated the thumb, I see."

"Doc, you shoulda seen it. It was stickin' out to one side." Huckla held up his other hand proudly and extended his unin- jured thumb. "All mangly. That damn Cooper just got a hold of it and God damn, I thought I was like to faint."

"I'm not surprised."

"Lost the buck, though," Huckla said dreamily. "That's too damn bad. Gonna have to get him back somehow."

"Who pulled your thumb back into joint, then?"

"Oh, Coop did that. I couldn't do it myself." He laughed weakly. "He pulled it out, so it seemed only fair game that he put it back."

"Thoughtful of him. He almost managed to do it…almost." Thomas straightened and regarded Huckla critically. "Let me tell you what we need to do, my friend. Your index finger is a mess, with several breaks. Now, the one that concerns me is right here, at your knuckle. There's a large, loose chip of bone right there, and if we just bandage you up with a splint, that finger is going to freeze utterly useless. The joint will have no hope of ever working properly, and you're going to end up walking about with one hand like this," and he held up his right hand, all the fingers clenched into a fist except for the index, which he extended rigidly.

Huckla looked across at Berti, and then at the Seth Thomas clock on the wall behind her. "They're gonna dock my pay," he slurred. "We're supposed to be out at the flume today."

"Well, I suggest that you won't be working *anywhere* today. Or tomorrow. Or for a fortnight, unless you can do so one-handed. We have to remove that bone chip and straighten things out."

"Can't do that. I mean, geez, Doc. I can't be laid up like that. You're talkin' about *cuttin'* me?"

"Yes." He gently lifted Huckla's hand at the wrist. "You see this?" He indicated a sharp lump just under the skin in front of the median knuckle, projecting sideways from the proper line of the finger. "That's a chip of broken bone, sir. We leave that, the finger is useless. You'd be better off having it amputated."

If it were possible, Huckla's face drained of still more color until his usually swarthy skin was the hue of flour paste.

"Can't you just throw a fix in 'er without all that?" he pleaded. "Just wrap it up or somethin'?"

Thomas laughed gently. "When a gear breaks in the guts of one of the steam donkeys out on the tract, don't you have to fix it? The break doesn't just go away, Mr. Huckla."

"Well, hell, no, *I* don't fix it. Them mechanics don't let us no where near the machinery," and the young man leered with morphine-stroked silliness at Berti Auerbach. "I ain't no steam donkey, Doc. Just do the best you can, no cuttin'."

"I can't *do* the best I can without surgery," Thomas said. "If I don't fix this properly now, I can guarantee that you'll be back here, and our problems will be just that much worse."

"I'm a bettin' man, Doc," Huckla said. "Just splint it up and I'll kind of favor it for a little while, and then we'll see." He leaned forward unsteadily and slid one leg off the high bed as if about to leave. "Thumb sure as hell is sore, though."

"That's because it's still partially dislocated, Mr. Huckla. This Mr. Cooper you talk about didn't finish the job. Do you want me to position that properly for you, or are we going to let that molder as well?"

"That's going to hurt like a bitch, ain't it." His voice had taken on a nice wistful tone from the morphine.

"With the nitrous oxide, you won't feel so much as a twitch, my friend."

"Don't know anything about that."

"It's a little bit of gas. You inhale it just like an Indian sucking on his peyote pipe or however they do it, and then you take a nice nap for a few minutes. You can dream about all the bets you're going to win from now on. You won't feel a thing during the procedure. Why, up in the women's ward, we have a ten year-old child who underwent surgery as bravely as any trooper. And she has recovered so well that she will be homeward bound tomorrow. So you see, there is nothing to worry about."

"You can do the finger at the same time? I mean, I won't feel it?"

"Absolutely. You'll wake up completely repaired."

"When do you figure to do this?"

"This very moment," Thomas said. "Without delay. We will tell your companion that he might as well return to work. There's no point in him waiting for you. Perhaps this afternoon, we'll be able to bundle you home. Certainly by morning."

"I gotta get out to the flume. I mean, you oughta see that, Doc. Ain't nothing like it."

Bertha patted Buddy affectionately on the shoulder. "First you take care of yourself, Buddy," she said. "If you don't have that hand fixed, you won't be any good to my brother on the next fishing trip." She caught Thomas' glance, and nodded. "Mr. Huckla and I are old friends," she said. "Last year he managed to catch a gang of fish hooks in one hand, didn't you, Buddy. It took some time for Dr. Haines to put that right."

"Then you're experienced at this," Thomas said. "Your friend's name? The chap outside?"

"That's Ben Sitzberger. Him and me share a tent out at the camp." Huckla grinned crookedly. "When he ain't shacked up with his lady friend, anyways. Him and me and Gunnar and Todd Delaney. We all share…" The morphine was taking a firm hold, and Huckla's voice drifted off.

"I'll speak with the young man," Bertha said. "And doctor… remember that Carlotta Schmidt is coming in at nine this morning."

"I do, I do." Thomas glanced at the clock, its loud ticking always a reminder that the day was far too short. "We shall hope for a simple answer for her."

"And a reminder that Dr. Hardy is expected today."

"Thank God for that. And we will do all possible to make sure his first hour in Port McKinney is less eventful and far more welcoming than mine." He grinned at his nurse as if the painful memory of his own misfortune the previous autumn was but a trifle. "And the Snyder child?" The three-story, brick clinic's only patient at the moment was 11-year-old Matilda Snyder, a delightful child easily coddled.

"Her parents are with her. She had a fair night, somewhat restless of course, but it helped to have her mother staying with her. I agreed to that. The ward is otherwise empty, and a child is apt to imagine all manner of ghosts and ghouls in the dark corners when left alone. And by the way, I should mention Howard."

"Yes?" At the mention of his clinic handyman and ambulance driver, Thomas looked at her sharply.

"I couldn't help noticing that his leg is giving him significant discomfort, Doctor."

"You think so?"

"I am certain. He does his best to disguise it, but on occasion, his discomfort is obvious."

Bertha Auerbach had a wonderful capacity for mixing sternness and sympathy in the same expression, Thomas thought. "He has said nothing to me about this."

"You're a busy man, Doctor." Bertha's smile was a ghost on her fine features. With no small chagrin, Thomas ducked his head in agreement. Busy or not, and despite his pride at his own skills and observations, he had found long ago that he was no match for Bertha Auerbach, whose sharp eyes and keen brain saw and recorded virtually everything in the world around her…so much so that Thomas had come to depend on her in a thousand ways. If Bertha Auerbach said that Howard Deaton was suffering, then he was. It was that simple.

Chapter Two

"I shall talk with Howard," Thomas said. "This very morning. Without delay." The previous autumn, Thomas had patched Deaton back together, but the injured man, a former teamster for one of the large freight companies, had lost the job that had nearly killed him. He had convalesced eventually into full-time employment with the Clinic. Deaton now drove one of the two white ambulance rigs, a man so dependable and resourceful that Dr. Thomas Parks gave that aspect of the Clinic's operation not a moment's thought, leaving it entirely in Deaton's capable hands. The six horses were always meticulously groomed and shod, the rigs kept clean of every speck of mud, dust, or blood.

"We'll have a moment right after I chat with Mrs. Schmidt," Thomas said. "So, let's be at it, then. Mr. Huckla, the boots, the trousers, the vest and shirt. You may leave on your drawers."

"Christ, Doc, it's just my *hand* you're workin' on," he protested.

"Indeed. And the cleaner, the better. I have no intention of working around clothing that hasn't seen the laundry for a month." He glanced down at Huckla's heavy, lace boots. "Those are a challenge with one hand, I imagine." He swiftly unlaced first one boot and then the other, grimacing at the bouquet as he slipped them off. "We're going to end up burning sulfur to fumigate this place," he muttered, but Huckla didn't reply.

A moment later, Bertha returned from outside and waved her hand under her nose. "That young man is having a fine time of it." She leaned over and looked into Huckla's eyes. "What did you fellows have last night for supper?"

"We had…what'd we have. Oh, Mike Curran, he had a bunch of that dried salmon from up the way. Eatin' on that all night when we was at cards."

"You might package some bicarbonate for him to take along," Thomas said. "For both him and his companion."

"I have done so." Bertha walked behind Thomas, who had drawn hot water piped from the Victor boiler in the basement. While he washed his hands in water so hot that it hurt, he had one of his anatomy texts open to a plate of the skeletal details of the hand, leaning sideways so he could peruse it without dripping on the pages.

"That's what it's supposed to look like," he quipped, and then nodded his thanks as she slid a pan with the carbolic acid drench near his elbow.

"Alvina is down at the barns," she said. "She said there was an issue with her horse…I'm not sure what."

"She's not riding anyway," Thomas groused, pushing back from the wash basin. "She said that she favored a short walk this morning, and I can't blame her for that." As his wife's pregnancy progressed, the confines of the large house at 101 Lincoln never seemed large enough for her. Regardless of the weather, Alvina Haines Parks toured her unborn child around Port McKinney, favoring the smooth footing by the inlet below the high tide mark.

"Is Prince with her?" The big hound, himself an off-and-on surgical patient, seemed to sense the imminent arrival of the child, and did not stray from his mistress' side.

"As always. She said that she will come inside when she finishes at the barns. She wanted to work an hour or so on the billing this morning."

"I won't discourage *that,*" Thomas said. "Were it left to me, we'd all be in the poorhouse." Preparations for surgery were simple and swift, and when Thomas was convinced that Buddy

Huckla's hand and arm up to the elbow were as sterile as they could be, he isolated the hand in linen. Donning a clean apron, Thomas rinsed his hands once more in the drench and, while Bertha Auerbach tended the small bottle of nitrous oxide and the face mask, Thomas took a moment to re-examine the fingers.

With Huckla relaxed in slumber land, Thomas first hauled the crooked thumb back into place, and felt a good, solid *pop* as the joint settled properly. Satisfied with that, he turned his attention to the index finger, selecting the finest bistoury in the collection.

"An interesting spiral fracture," he murmured, then sighed. "This joint will never work properly again. There's actually a piece of the phalanx process fractured clear. I can't envision how he managed that. Whether the ligaments will reattach after we clean this up…well, that's anyone's guess."

The lightest of raps on the door drew Thomas' attention. As soon as he looked up, Alvina pushed the door open the rest of the way. "You stay outside," his wife said to the enormous, gray-muzzled dog who accompanied her.

"Doctor Thomas, you have a young man determined to speak with you."

"Well, I can't just now, Alvi. And Bertha told him to go back to camp. His friend here will be detained most of the day."

"Mr. Sitzberger has taken his smelly carcass back to the timber," Alvi said cheerfully. "And taken the bicarbonate with him. The visitor is another fellow who brings word from Paul Bertram."

"Bertram? The timber foreman?"

"The same. They have an injury out on one of the bluffs. They've come to fetch you and the ambulance."

Thomas frowned, absorbed by the challenge under his scalpel. Alvi remained silent while he worked. Two tiny stitches helped to stabilize a torn ligament, and the physician allowed himself a deep breath. "What happened?"

"I don't know," Alvi said. "The fellow says that one of the high riggers is in desperate straights." Thomas had yet to spend sufficient time in the timber to boast familiarity with the myriad harrowing jobs, but he knew what a high rigger was and what those mad men did. Scaling the towering spruce or fir, working in the wet tree tops, every tool they handled was sharp and slick.

"If Howard will prepare the ambulance…"

"He is doing so as we speak. And Fats," she said referring to Thomas' gelding.

"That's good. Bertha tells me that Howard's leg is beginning to trouble him."

"I would agree."

"Give me ten minutes, then."

The door and the world closed around him as he worked, and by the time he had closed the small incision and helped Bertha with the bandages and splinting, half an hour had passed.

Huckla was already beginning to stir as they wheeled him to the ward and transferred the young man to one of the narrow beds.

"A quarter grain in an hour," Thomas said. "And then again if he needs it. But today only. It should be nothing more than a mild ache by this evening."

With his heavy medical bag in hand, Thomas hurried outside where the messenger awaited. The rider, a young man with peach fuzz where a beard might someday grow, drew the reins to the ready, and his bay mare looked at Thomas expectantly as the physician left the clinic. An oil slicker was rolled at the back of the man's saddle, but the lad ignored it, apparently preferring to drip instead. Thomas had never seen the youth before, but he was from the same mold as young Huckla—compact, confident, grubby and unkempt. The youngster obviously knew him.

"Doc, the boss man says that if you got the time, we could sure use you out on the Dutch Tract." The youth folded both hands on the saddle horn as if about to settle in for a pleasant conversation. He smiled, revealing a mouthful of wretched teeth. "Don't expect you've ever seen anything like this."

"And the 'like this' is what, my friend?" Thomas asked.

"We got us one of the riggers stuck up a spar." The rider smiled again.

Thomas laughed "Stuck? At the top of a tree? How does one accomplish that?"

"Takes some doin', I gotta say."

"He's hurt? Well, of course he's hurt," Thomas corrected quickly. "Else wise, you wouldn't be here. But surely he is out of the tree by now."

"Oh, yeah. He's hurt. But I don't think he's lit to the ground yet."

And bled to death by now, no doubt, Thomas thought. "How far, then?"

"South acreage of the Dutch, across the creek, Doc. Maybe eight miles."

Thomas frowned at the results of his automatic computations…eight miles meant an hour under the best of circumstances. "And can you give me some notion of the injuries?"

"Well," and the boy wiped his face and snapped the water off his fingers. "I ain't sure. He's too high up to see. Squished hands, I guess. That'd be a start. Don't know what else. Maybe got his noggin cracked open."

"I'll meet you right here in five minutes," the physician said. "Let me get my horse." He looked beyond the portico toward the stable. The rain, more a pervasive mist, wafted in ghostlike curtains between the two buildings, but Thomas could see that one of the ambulances had already left. "Howard knows the way?"

"Sure enough does," the young man replied.

He turned to see his nurse, Bertha Auerbach, standing in the clinic's doorway. "If you'll convey my apologies to Mrs. Schmidt…"

"Of course. I'll reschedule her for tomorrow."

Thomas pulled up his slicker and scrunched his soft hat down firmly on his head. He took no real joy in riding, and this day promised misery. In the barn, his gelding was bridled, blanketed, and saddled, reins looped loosely over one of the stanchions. The animal, a fifteen-year-old creature with impenetrable nerves and soft gaits the envy of any child's pony, stood stock still as Thomas lashed his medical bag to the saddle skirts. As he did so, a hand stole over Thomas' shoulder and stroked his cheek, and a huge, firm belly nudged against the small of his back. He turned to face Alvi, and before he could get a word out, his wife had taken his face in both strong hands, her characteristic gesture that said, "*I want your full attention, my husband, and I want it now.*"

"You be careful, Dr. Thomas." Her voice was a husky alto that matched her full-figured stature. Behind her, the gangly Prince had settled in a quiet corner well clear of horses' hooves.

"Oh, indeed. It's just a run up to the Dutch." He said it as if he'd been there a hundred times, rather than never at all.

"Howard took the harbor road with Sally and Ebbi, since there's some rough going otherwise. Taylor will be taking you straight across the ridge. That'll save you four miles."

"I hadn't even asked his name." Thomas glanced toward the portico where the young messenger waited.

"Taylor Simpson." Alvi grinned. "A good boy. That's the highest recommendation from Miss Bertha."

"She knows *everyone*," Thomas said. "I don't know how she does it."

"Twenty-five years living in the same tiny village, no doubt," Alvi said. She kept a hand on the gelding's bridle as Thomas led him out of the barn. When they were a number of feet away from the structure, she leaned close, pushing her fashionable canvas hat back until the mist settled fetchingly on her nose. Her breath was warm on his ear. "And she's right. Howard's leg *is* troubling him, Dr. Thomas."

The physician nodded. "I was coming out to fetch him as soon as the surgery was finished. And then the Simpson boy arrived."

"You'll watch over him." It wasn't clear to whom she was referring, but Thomas nodded.

"Of course."

"And watch over yourself, Dr. Thomas." She turned his head, heedless of who might be watching, and kissed him full on the lips, a long, passionate probing, hugging her belly against his.

"And you behave," he said, almost gasping for breath.

"Prince and I are planning a long, gentle walk. That's all."

"Keep it very gentle, and not very long, Alvi. Perhaps a couple of times up and down the front porch."

She laughed that characteristic little bubble that implied, *So you say.* "You can be so old-fashioned sometimes, Dr. Thomas. I am no invalid."

"I know you're not. But sometimes…" He caught himself. "Bertha reminds me that Dr. Hardy will arrive today."

"Then I'll give him a proper greeting and tour if you have yet to return," Alvi said, and patted her husband's arm. She stepped back as he swung up onto the gelding, the lingering stiffness in his own left hip forcing a careful, genteel mount. She reached out and squeezed his thigh. "Let the horse pick the way." She blew him another kiss and stepped away from the gelding, whose ears had perked in response to an excited nicker from Taylor Simpson's mare.

Chapter Three

Simpson pirouetted his horse around in the driveway. "It's about four miles goin' straight across the bluff. That'll save us some time. You mind that?"

Without waiting for a reply, the young man led them through the village, and then swung off on a side street that at first appeared to dead-end in a rocky bluff. Instead, the trail snaked through dense stands of rhododendron, cedar, and huckleberry bushes, and through forests of stumpage, the timber gone a generation before.

Thomas saw that the boy rode with his reins slack, letting the horse practically nuzzle the trail as he selected his footing. Thomas let the gelding do the same, and for the first mile, the physician focused on sitting erect but relaxed in the saddle. Each time he mounted a horse, apprehension still reared its ugly head, now almost nine months after a frightful wreck in which a mule had pitched him into a tidal pool and then rolled on top of him—all during his first hour in Port McKinney. His first months had been spent in painful convalescence, hardly the stuff of his medical school dreams. He had switched from crutches to cane for his twenty-seventh birthday in December, then abandoned even the cane by spring.

In twenty minutes they reached the high bluff lands northwest of Port McKinney. The land was scarred into fantastic patterns where the timber had been harvested, small strips left here and there where some feature of the topography made logging impossible. The stumps, some seven or eight feet high, stood as armies of silent giants, making a direct route to anywhere impossible.

In places, the timber was new growth, the majority of the stand little more than eight or ten inches in diameter, spots either harvested decades ago or regrowing after a lightning strike. The mist sifted through the trees in spooky swirls, the place dark and forbidding.

The footing made the gelding nervous, challenging him with downed timber, dislodged roots, or shelves of slick rock. Despite the chill, the animal worked on a froth under his cinch and along the flat plane of his neck. The tract was rarely flat, but rolled through ravines and across creeks, the path little more than a single deer-trail. There was no horizon, just an endless rumple.

"Spectacular country," he called to Simpson. The lad didn't reply to his jest, but as they jogged onto the broad back of the bluff where the land sloped sharply away, they intersected a rough and mucky trail rutted by the constant traffic of freight wagons. The youth nudged his mount faster and Thomas urged the gelding into a lazy gallop to keep up, the animal's over-fed gut releasing a veritable symphony of gassy complaint. Their hooves threw great clots of mucky sod above the riders' heads.

Across the bluff, the two riders eventually settled into a series of switchbacks that took them to a major stream bed. They splashed across twenty yards of water running two feet deep and the color of strong tea, colored by the continual soaking of saw logs rich in tannic acid. On the other side of the creek, the dense, mature timber blocked daylight, and Thomas could easily imagine that he was riding in the last moments of dusk.

They passed ever-increasing signs of the industry but saw no loggers, no riggers, no buckers. Smoke drifted up from a smokestack rammed through the roof of a rude slab-wood shack on log skids, and Thomas caught a glimpse of the steam donkey inside, its draw cables slack. Here and there, a deck of fragrant saw logs loomed out of the mists.

The bluff was narrow and ragged, the engineering problems of logging it explaining why its trees had stood for so long. Finally, far ahead through the trees, the physician saw the light of a precipice, and Simpson slowed his horse to a sedate walk. The gelding huffed, sides heaving.

"Right there," the lad called, and pointed off to the east. Sure enough, a crowd of men had gathered, the incident—whatever it was—dragging them out of the timber. For a moment, Thomas saw nothing that would warrant the men's attention. And then, silhouetted by the dim and curtained morning light, he saw a figure, a dozen feet below the top of an impossibly tall Sitka spruce spar. But the giant's feathery top hadn't plunged loose. Its uppermost limbs rested firmly in the crown of another neighboring spruce twenty yards away. The crown's bole, twenty-four inches in diameter, was suspended nearly horizontal to the ground, its butt somehow still attached to the spar.

Thomas craned his neck backward as he rode closer until he was looking sharply upward, so much so that the brim of his hat no longer blocked the fine rain. He blinked hard and rubbed his face and, just as he reined the gelding to a stand-still, he saw a second man right below the ragged and threatening tonnage of the skewed crown. Yet a third man was climbing steadily sixty feet below the pair, hitching his safety rope deftly, keeping on the side of the spruce opposite the threatening top. From his belt on a six-foot keeper hung both a double-bit axe and a short cross-cut.

"Take a look, Doc," a voice behind him said, and Thomas turned to see an older man with his gray hair tied back in a braid, a woolen sailor's cap pulled low. He didn't bother with a slicker, and as he stepped closer to hand a small brass spy-glass to Thomas, the physician could smell the rank odor of perpetually damp wool. "I'm Bertram," the man said. "I'm glad the kid could find you."

"Thomas Parks." Thomas extended his hand, and Bertram's grip was like iron, only the backs of his hands wet from the drizzle.

"Bert Schmidt speaks mighty high of you, Doctor. Thanks for comin' out. You can see for yourself, we got a fine mess up above. There'll sure as hell be some work for you in a few minutes."

Clearing the image took some finagling, but eventually the glass gave Thomas a view, the lens spotted with droplets…and the scene still made no sense. What appeared to be the man's safety rope hung from his trouser belt in two pieces, one half dangling past each leg. He was caught at least ten feet below the break, and sure enough, the tree's crown appeared to have been broken off, rather than sawed or axed cleanly.

"I don't understand," Thomas said. "The ride out here took the better part of forty minutes…I assume a little less for young Simpson to ride *into* town to fetch me…you're saying that this man has been caught up there for nearly two hours? Perhaps three?"

"Well…" Bertram said, and shoved his hands in his pockets. "We got us something of a problem. I'd just as soon discomfort him a little than have to bury him."

Discomfort him a little. Thomas marveled at those words as a man, apparently broken in some curious and painful way, hung a hundred and fifty feet above the ground, his safety belt useless.

"They've tried a couple things, but so far…" and Bertram shrugged. "We'll know more here in a minute."

Thomas stepped back to more secure footing, digging his boots into the muck. The spar was situated on the very rim of a steep incline, and certainly the view from on top must have been spectacular. Thomas knew that when the tree, stripped of all limbs and its crown, was rigged with a wonder of ropes and tackle for moving timber, it would command a large section of land so steep that oxen or mules couldn't skid the logs. The spar acted as an enormous, rooted crane.

"He appears to be hung up on something." Thomas lowered the glass. "I can't make it out."

"That's puttin' it one way, Doc," Bertram laughed and turned away, pulling out a pocket knife. In a moment the foreman returned with a small wand of limb wood. He shook off a geyser of moisture and then deftly nicked off the side twigs until he had a switch two feet long with a little fan top.

"See, this is what we got." He glanced up at the spar. The third climber had progressed to within fifteen feet of the pair above him. "He was cuttin' off the crown, right there where it's about two foot through. Maybe a little more."

He first held up the twig, matching against the huge spar to make sure that Thomas understood the model. Then, with a twist of the knife, he cut part-way through the switch just below the brush of remaining twigs. As he cut, his thumb bent the feathery crown over until with a snapping of fibers, it stood out at right angles from the stick, but not yet entirely separated.

"So she pitches over like that, see. The crown's supposed to break free, but she doesn't." Working the knife blade into the exposed end grain, he split the wand downward from the break of the crown, tugging a little on the top to widen the split.

"See, this is what we got," he said again. "And it looks like two things happened. After he lights the dynamite…"

"Dynamite?" Thomas stared incredulously at the foreman.

"Well, sure. He wants a banger. Wasn't *supposed* to do that, but he goes ahead and does it anyway." He made an imaginary circle around the stick with his index finger. "So he chops a girdle all around, see, right where he wants the top to separate. Maybe five, six inches deep. That don't take too long. Easy enough to lay the charge, packin' 'em in around the stick. Art thinks he used sixty or so."

He paused, amused by Thomas' thunderstruck expression. "Got a bit of light rope, stringin' them charges all together. Kind of a daisy-chain. All around where he wants the top to be blowed off. Then he cuts a good drop fuse. *Good* and long. Six, eight feet." He shrugged and looked skyward again. "On a good day, that should give him time to drop down—five, six minutes, something like that. Unless he gets hung up on something. Limb stub, just about anything. Sometimes just a stubborn scab of bark."

"But *dynamite?* Whatever for?" He gestured around him at the groups of men, all captivated by the drama above. "An *axe?* Saws?"

Bertram grinned at the young physician. "You ever run a one-man cross-cut through a couple feet or more of sappy knots? That spar's knot-studded like a stick of cheap knotty pine, Doc." He held his hand flat and made sawing motions. "One thing to do it on the ground. But sideways a hundred and fifty feet up? Hangin' by rope and spurs? You're fightin' it every inch you make. And an axe don't make it any easier."

"But *dynamite?*" Thomas repeated.

"Another thing," Bertram said. "Up here on the headlands, the wind will come up here pretty quick." He held up the twig and waved it back and forth. "That's a hell of a wand. That starts dancin'…why hell, you can sweep yourself an arc across fifty foot of sky. Hard to hang on, sometimes."

"So what happened, then?"

"My guess is that he had a skip or something like that. We've had some troubles with that if they don't pay attention. Now normally, Art Mabry…he's up there now…he's the one who sets the charges. But this time, Sonny Malone went ahead and did it."

"A skip?"

Bertram shrugged. "Most of the time, now, the fuse is long enough that after he lights it, he's got time to drop down as far as he can, see. Do it right, and don't get hung up, he can make it to the ground. That's what we want to see—him clear of the spar. But something goes wrong, and the charge don't go off. The fuse sputters out or something, or has a skip."

The foreman shrugged again. "Some of these fellas ain't got the patience God shoulda gave 'em, and that's where the trouble starts. That's what the boys tell me happened here. Sonny goes back up to see what's wrong. He's ten feet below the charge when off she goes. And this ain't his lucky day, see."

"I don't see."

"Well, first he got himself a goddamn serious hang-fire, and even then, some of them go off, some don't." He reached out and touched Thomas lightly on the shoulder as if the physician wasn't paying attention. He thumbed the top of his model tree to the side, the wood cracking but still attached. "So we got this. We got this split startin' to run down the trunk, see. And that's a lot of weight pitchin' off to the side. Then the trunk splits, bang." Bertram yanked at the top, and the split trunk yawned open where he'd started it with his pocketknife. "'Cept for that split, he mighta been okay. But the weight of the top just pried that trunk wide open. They'll do that sometimes. Now, as that trunk splits—and hell, it can gape a dozen feet before the top tears free and the split slaps shut—well, let me tell you, it don't take much *gape* before you're flat run out of safety belt, even if you're usin' every inch you got."

"And then?"

"If he don't cut the safety rope, it'll cut *him.* Well, it's going to crush him like a damn banana slug slapped with an axe handle. Saw a climber cut clean in half once up in Vancouver." He grimaced. "Weren't all that clean, neither."

"The safety rope won't break first?"

Bertram shook his head and spat. "Sure as hell better not. They got a steel core, you know. But I tell ya…old Sonny there is damn quick. He saw what was comin' and had time for one good swing with the axe. Cut the safety rope, then just hugged that tree and prayed, probably. See, it's small enough around up there that a man can hug it. Well, almost, it is. Trouble is, *when* he hugged it, he got both hands in the split. The crown settled in the neighbor tree, and the split slapped shut. You got about five tons of crown pushin' it closed now. Like a goddamn big rat trap, is what it is."

"My God."

"And there's old Sonny, up to his elbows in a stick of spruce that won't let him go. They've been doin' some thinkin', and we'll see what happens. Lemme see that again." He held out his hand for the glass. For a long time, Bertram watched the performance overhead. At first, Thomas thought he could hear one of the men calling, but then realized that the high-pitched keening, intermixed with a string of profanity so confused it sounded like jibberish, was uttered by the trapped man himself.

"What are they going to do?"

"Don't know," Bertram said. "I know what *I'd* do."

"I can send something up for the pain. Morphine would do it. Anyone can administer it."

"Got to have his wits about him," Bertram said. "What little wits he's got left after the dynamite."

"Hey!" The single word floated down from above.

Bertram took a couple of steps closer to the tree, craning upward. "What'd you decide, Art?" Thomas moved up beside the foreman, one arm over his head to shield his eyes. The light caught the individual droplets now, streaming downward like miniature diamonds, just enough air movement to slant them against the dark green of the timber.

"This crown's just got to come off." The man paused before adding, "There just ain't no other way around it." He was ten feet above the trapped logger, and with just a small effort could have drawn himself up to sit on the ragged, blasted pinnacle of the spar. "It's hung up real good in the neighbor."

"You're sure she's holdin' hard?"

"Got a couple limbs right through a crotch. It ain't goin' nowhere. Hell, I could walk across it."

"What's Sonny say?"

It took a while for the logger to ponder that…or perhaps to ask the whimpering Sonny.

"He ain't sayin' much, Paul. I guess he'd sure like to get down out of here. He can't hear shit. That the doc from Port McKinney you got there?"

"Yup."

"Well, if we got to cut Sonny's arms away, maybe you could rig the doc up so he can come up and do it. *I* sure ain't about to."

Bertram laughed. He stepped back, looking at the ground and shaking his head back and forth to take the kinks out of his neck.

"What will he do?" Thomas asked.

"Oh, Art will figure it out," Bertram said easily. "Nothin' we can tell him from down here. If it works, it works. That's all. If it don't, then old Sonny hangs there a while longer 'til we figure out something that does." He shrugged. "You see where that crown is hangin' fast? That's right over Sonny's head. So that's a complication. We don't want that goin' anywhere when the pressure comes off."

"And now?"

Bertram looked up as if what was happening far above was of no particular concern. "They think the best thing is to get rid of that crown that's hangin' there. That's puttin' just hellacious force against the split. Too much to wedge against. But," and Bertram wiped his face, "If Art cuts the crown too close to the spar, chances are good it could kick down and hit old Sonny, there. See, he's right under it, damn near. That would put him on the unhappy side."

"This Art fellow…"

"Art Mabry. He's the best we got. Been in the timber a long time."

"Lemme up there, and I'll get him," Taylor Simpson said. Thomas glanced over at him, having forgotten the lad who had guided him to this spot. Simpson had moved the two horses to a stump a hundred yards away and then returned, standing now with his hands in his hip pockets, the grin still lighting his features. Now and then he spat a huge, well-directed stream of tobacco juice into the duff and mud at his feet.

Bertram grunted something unintelligible and then ignored the boy.

"We got plenty of wood here holdin' the crown," Art called down.

"All right. It's your call, Art."

Art worked his way around the trunk until he was directly above the trapped man. He reached out over his head and patted the crown's trunk, then slapped it hard, as much effect as a slight breeze might have on the bedrock below them. Satisfied, he adjusted his climbing rope and then stamped each boot to reset his climbing spurs. For a moment he just rested there, then leaned back against the safety rope, his body almost horizontal. Sonny said something plaintive, and Art laughed good-naturedly.

"If this don't work, tell my ma I was a good boy," Art called down.

"If it don't work, I'll tell her that her boy was a clumsy son-of-a-bitch," Bertram shouted, and more laughter drifted down.

Art pulled up the small crosscut saw and then hung quietly for a moment, his full weight hard against his climbing belt. Thomas realized that, with the safety belt attached at the logger's waist, the young man was holding himself with belly muscles that must have rivaled the steel core of the safety rope. The logger twisted so that he could look out along the crown's length to the neighboring spruce tree where the limb wood was tangled. For another minute, he conversed with the third man, who appeared content to watch from the other side of the tree.

With a deft flip of the wrist, he swung the saw up and around, sinking its teeth into the top of the crown's bole at a spot nearly four feet out from the main spar. Even there, the crown's trunk was close to two feet thick. No matter how gymnastic he might be, the position was awkward, and he worked quickly. Sawdust drifted out and away on the light breeze, its white mixing with the diamonds of rain to float down to the ground.

Thomas watched through the glass, his breathing loud in his ears. It appeared that, where Art was sawing, the crown's trunk would sag, hopelessly binding the saw, upper limbs still caught in the neighbor, but still firm on the spar. Of course, Art *didn't* finish the cut. After cutting into the top of the horizontal crown's bole for ten inches, he slipped the saw out of the top cut. He hung motionless, feet braced against the spar's sides and one hand looped affectionately around the log above his head to give his belly and back some relief.

Then, shifting his position around the spar, slightly away from the crown, he hefted the double-bit axe and with his torso contorted so he could hit the target, made short work of the V-groove, relieving the notch as much as he could.

"WHOOOHOOOO!" he whooped, letting the axe's keeper slide through his hands until it hung free. "That'll work," he said, obviously more to himself than anyone else. Working his way back until he was beside the horizontal crown, he positioned the saw on the bottom of the trunk, sawing rhythmically for a full minute before stopping. He left the saw in the cut and drew himself back to the spar.

"That's a tussle," he said, his words again meant for no one in particular. He said something to the other logger, who immediately started down the spar. After another moment's rest, Art repositioned himself, the saw's soft voice resuming. Start, stop, start, stop. Progress was painfully slow, the awkward, twisted, laid-out position against the safety rope impossible to hold for long. Thomas recalled sawing firewood with his father in Connecticut, and he could imagine that this western spruce, fresh, knotty, and gummy, was actually far more difficult than cutting eastern hardwood.

The other logger reached the ground and unclipped his belt. "Need wedges," he said, and in a moment, he secured four heavy iron wedges to a draw line. He stood at the base of the spar, gazing up, then shook his head and walked toward Bertram.

"He wants me off it until the crown goes," he explained. "I told him that I needed to hang on to old Sonny, but he said he weren't goin' nowheres. He's got him belted and spurred in pretty good."

"How much wood do you got on either side of the split?"

The logger held his hands at least a foot apart. "Somethin' like that. Damn thing runs right down the center of the bole. It's got 'em good."

A shrill whistle jerked up a score of heads.

"You all stand there," Art shouted down, "and you're gonna be wearin' this thing."

"About where your horses are hitched," Bertram instructed Thomas. Then Art set to work, the sawdust clouding below his furious sawing. Thomas watched through the lens, and could actually see the saw cut, just a faint line against the bark at that distance, begin to gape. The top cut closed, and Thomas saw Art reach up with his left hand, hugging the crown on the stump side of the cut. Twisting like a contortionist, he drove the big saw hard, and then down below the spectators heard a single sharp crack. For an instant nothing happened, and then the saw dropped out of Art's hands as he hugged the stump with both arms. The crown popped and snapped and broke free, a giant, lazy candle of limb wood.

Because the logger had cut it off four feet out from the spar, and because its top was so securely snagged, it swung straight down to crash into its neighbor, a giant pendulum swinging away from the spar. Its top splintered and let go with a string of reports that sounded like rifle shots. Broken loose and falling, the crown's uppermost limbwood kicked back toward the spar, sweeping it like a giant broom half way down the stump. With an explosive crash, the crown settled in a storm of limbs, bark, and needles.

Art's cry of triumph rang across the bluff. The spar's arc of release snapped him and the trapped Sonny Malone through forty feet of open air. With the weight of the crown removed, the remaining stump stub above the dynamite line gradually eased upward to a forty-five degree angle. And as it did so, Thomas imagined, the split closed some more. Art released his hug around the bole and swung up, his axe and saw dangling. In a moment he was sitting on the sheered top of the spar, leaning an elbow against the stub of crown as if it were the back of an easy chair. He spread out both arms in victory. Sonny Malone let out a moan loud enough to be heard down below. He didn't sound victorious.

Chapter Four

"Need those wedges now," Art Mabry said, making no effort to raise his voice. "And a number two." Fetching things was apparently Taylor Simpson's forte, and he reappeared in five minutes with coils of rope and lightweight block and tackle.

For a moment he and the climber argued, the climber winning by snatching the rig out of Simpson's hands, and chiding him with a string of profanity. "God damn ignorant..." he finished off, and deftly adjusted his load on the end of the draw line—the block and tackle, a bundle of wedges, and a heavy-handled single bit axe considerably more massive than Thomas had ever used around the family woodpile in Leister, Connecticut.

The rigger headed heavenward again, trailing the slender draw line while Taylor Simpson, under continual but good-natured threats of creative deaths, minded that the draw line didn't tangle.

At the ground, the spruce was nearly seven feet in diameter, its trunk flaring out to enormous roots that Thomas imagined must surely sink to the center of the Olympic peninsula. The climber reached Art Mabry and the two of them conversed. Sonny remained quiet. Through the glass, Thomas could see that the injured man's head was slumped against the bark, jaw slack, a strand of drool hanging from the corner of his mouth. The physician moved to the nearest sapling, a runty big-leaf maple that had been struggling to find its way to the sun. He braced the glass against the inch-diameter trunk and found the image.

Sonny Malone was not just resting. His head hung against the trunk of the tree, the spruce bark pushing his eyebrow up into his forehead. It might have been a shadow from his cap, or the vagaries of the distance and light, but the rivulet of darkness below his ear looked to be hemorrhage. Thomas could not see the man's right hand, but his left was basically engulfed in spruce, as if the tree were trying to swallow him. Thomas walked a circle around the spar, finding another vantage point on the far side. Sure enough, Malone's right hand was also caught, this time just above the wrist bones. His right leg and boot hung straight down beside the tree, the climbing spur gleaming and free of the wood, while the Malone's left boot looked as if its spur was caught in the bark.

The draw line snapped taught, and the shipment of block and tackle, wedges, rope and axe jerked aloft. Feeling a presence standing beside him, Thomas lowered the scope.

"What do you think?" Paul Bertram asked. "Not gettin' much work done, are we." The crowd of onlookers remained, and Thomas supposed that the wagering was thick and heavy.

"There appears to be some discharge from his left ear. And he's clearly unconscious. So close to the blast…"

The logger thoughtfully dug the toe of his boot into the duff. "Don't know as a man can stand ten feet away from fifty sticks of dynamite goin' off and not end up with somethin' to show for it."

"It's incredible."

"What is?"

"I can't imagine how he could withstand the concussion and *still* have the presence of mind to cut his safety rope?"

"Cut it or get wrecked," Bertram said philosophically. "Sonny's been in the timber since he was sixteen."

"And how old a man is he now?"

"I think he's goin' on twenty-six, if I remember correct."

"You've had this happen before?"

"Nope. Well, let me see now. We've had a man or two killed by the dynamite, all right. And high riggin' in general has laid waste to a couple more. Never the two together." He looked almost proud of the accomplishment. "This is a first. Had crowns give a topper a good kick sometimes when they're not payin' attention. That's the most common thing."

Off to the left, Thomas' gelding uttered a long, heart-felt nicker, and the physician turned to see the ambulance threading its way toward them, sticking to the narrow trail through the stumps.

"Sure hate to see this. We're short handed as it is."

Thomas laughed. "And you'll be more so, Mr. Bertram. Does a young fellow named Huckla work for you? Buddy Huckla?"

"He's over on the flume gang. They're puttin' the last of the chute together, down to the bay." He turned and pointed off toward the north as if those directions were accurate enough. "Why?"

"He managed to ruin his right hand last night. Thumb wrestling, he says. You know how that's done, I suppose. One of his comrades fetched him in to the clinic this morning."

"A few wrenched fingers aren't going to slow *that* kid down none," Bertram scoffed.

"More than wrenched. I operated this morning. If he's very lucky, he may regain some partial use of his right index finger." He touched his own finger to his thumb. "I worked to give him some pinch. I won't know how successful we were for some time."

"Well, damn, then," the foreman muttered. "Can't work for a while?"

"Plan on six weeks. Maybe eight."

"Well, Christ. Who brung him into town?"

"A young chap named…it escapes me, but something German, I think."

"Sitzy," Taylor Simpson offered. He had once again drifted toward where Thomas and the foreman stood.

"Sitzberger. Yes. He's not feeling his best, either." He smiled at Bertram's puzzled expression. "Too much indulgence last night with rich food."

"Too much woman-friend, more likely. Huckla can use his left hand all right?"

"It's fine."

"Then he can tend one of the flume gates." Bertram turned and nodded at Taylor. "Does Huckla know his numbers and such?"

"Guess he does," Simpson replied. "He don't write as good as Sitzy does, but some, I guess."

"Well, then he can be a tallyman at the flume for a few weeks. That'll bore him silly, and maybe he'll heal faster."

Thomas turned to watch Howard Deaton take his time tying off the reins, then carefully lower himself from the rig. The fine white paint, touched here and there with elegant gold trim, was now showing a hundred pounds of the countryside, the rich muck welded throughout the undercarriage and splattered down each side. The driver moved two steps away from the ambulance and settled himself on a broad stump, the charging of his pipe requiring his full attention.

Up above, considerable discussion carried in only fits and snatches to those below.

Thomas handed the glass back to the foreman and then walked over to Deaton.

"What you got here?" the driver asked, calm as if asking the time of day.

"We have a man with both hands caught in the split trunk. And he was too close when a charge of dynamite went off. The crown got hung up in a neighbor."

"Well, hell." Deaton sucked on his pipe, the big match drawing and flaring, the cloud of smoke enveloping his head. "I tell you what, these boys think of more ways to ruin a day." He scanned the timber. "Whyn't they clear the close timber away from the spar first?"

Thomas shrugged. "Someone was in a hurry. The foreman said they weren't supposed to use dynamite anyway."

"Well, there you go."

One of the men topside shouted something, and Art let the single-bit axe hang loose. A moment of discussion followed, and they saw the block and tackle rigged, one end of the rope secured to Sonny's safety belt at the back of his waist. In a moment, a long coil dropped earthward.

"Couple of you get on that," Art called down, and Simpson jumped as if kicked. He and another logger secured the rope, tying the loose end to yet another coil with a deft series of hitches.

Up above, Art dropped down and drove a wedge into the split a foot or so above the trapped man's hand, then repeated the process on the other side. Still, the stubborn spruce refused to release its hold. More sawing ensued, this time three feet above the stricken man, and in twenty minutes—it seemed to Thomas to take hours—Art Mabry shouted again, and an off-side six-foot section of split trunk pirouetted away from the spar. It hit the duff below with a loud *whump*, driving a foot-deep wedge into the wet ground.

Now the rescuers had a flat seat half the width of the trunk, just above the man's trapped hands.

"Take the weight now," Art instructed the men below. Again the wedges were driven in. An excited shout greeted success. First the injured man's left and then his right arm flopped down, away from the tree. He made no move to lift them, his face still leaning against the bark. With his safety belt unclipped, Sonny hung like a large bean bag from the rope tied around his belt at the small of his back.

The two men on the ground fed rope upward to the block and tackle's rigging one hundred and sixty feet above their heads. Sonny Malone never moved a muscle as he was lowered. By the time his spurred boots touched the ground and half a dozen hands gently stretched Sonny out on his back, Howard Deaton had brought a canvas stretcher from the ambulance.

The group of loggers fell silent as they watched Thomas Parks adjust his stethoscope. Out of habit, he shut his eyes as he listened to the thin, thready pulse, then opened them to watch Sonny Malone's face as he counted again. The man had bled from both ears, and one eye was only partially closed while the right was squeezed shut.

"Gently now," Thomas ordered. Stripped of his safety belt, boot spurs, and an eight inch knife, the stricken logger was positioned on the stretcher and carried the few yards to the ambulance. "I'll ride with him." Thomas turned to see Taylor Simpson leading the physician's gelding across the clearing. "He'll trail the ambulance." Simpson nodded, tethering the gelding's reins to the ambulance's rear grab bar.

"You want me to come into town this evening to check on him?" Bertram asked.

"Someone needs to," Thomas said, situating himself on the side bench in the ambulance near Sonny Malone's head. The polished handles of the stretcher fit neatly into yokes, turning it into a secure cot for the trip to the clinic. "He has family somewhere?"

"Well, I suppose he does," Bertram mused. "Don't know for sure. Maybe one of the boys can tell us."

"That would be good. Someone needs to inform his mother and father. You could stop by and have a talk with Buddy Huckla at the same time. He's at the clinic, and I'm sure he's feeling sorry for himself right about now." Howard Deaton had already coaxed Sallie and Ebbie into a walk, and Sonny Malone made not a sound as the ambulance jerked forward.

Chapter Five

Dr. Thomas Parks stood in the clinic's dispensary, elbows leaning on the counter, head cradled in both hands. He stared at the printed pages in front of him, pages that he'd read a dozen times, searching. He could recite them by heart. The letters fused into fascinating patterns now, as elusive as a simple answer. The truth was simple—twenty-six year-old Sonny Malone lay comatose in the ward, unresponsive and dying. There was nothing to be done for him.

Thomas closed his eyes. Sonny Malone deserved to live, but he would not. It was really that simple. Fifty sticks of dynamite had detonated within a few feet of a human skull that protected a brain the consistency of gelatin. The shock had been as if Sonny Malone had been smashed with a giant sledge hammer. That ten sticks immediately over his head had *not* detonated might have saved his life for a few hours.

Careful examination had found no skull fracture, even with Sonny Malone's black Irish locks shorn and his skull shaven as smooth as a billiard ball. Little scars from past adventures here and there, but nothing else. Yet the damage to the fragile brain inside had to be immense. An ampoule of ammonia held under his nostrils or the prick of a pin on the bottom of his foot produced not the slightest twitch. With no obvious depression of the skull, no lesion, no laceration, there was no single, isolated spot that Thomas could point to and say, *"Aha! Here* lies the source of hemorrhage. *This* is where to begin. *This* is where we should open the doorway into the skull."

Thomas opened his eyes and regarded the textbook again, a current edition that professed the very latest in medical advances. But the author—and one of Thomas' favorite professors at the University of Pennsylvania—had been skeptical of treatment.

"The measures appropriate for the first few hours' treatment of contusion of the brain are diametrically opposed to the line of treatment required after reaction has been induced," Dr. John Roberts had written, then added—and Thomas could imagine that wry smile that he remembered so well from lectures—*"It is a nice question to know when the change should be made."*

A nice question indeed, since no discussion of initial treatment for blast injury had been mentioned. A contusion of the brain generally resulted from a blow, and a blow left marks that said, *"Open here."* Thomas had no such sign.

After reaction has been induced. But there had been no reaction induced. Sonny Malone lay comatose as his life's blood leaked from a thousand tears in his concussed brain—a thousand lacerations, the text called them.

Thomas snapped the book closed and pushed back from the counter. He glanced at his watch and saw that lunch had passed him by an hour before. He walked through the main ward to the three small rooms that had been partitioned off in the back. Sonny Malone lay in the first, curtains drawn over the single window and the gas light turned down to a tiny, quiet flame.

For a long time, the physician stood at the foot of Malone's bed. The "ice pillow" was in place, cushioning the patient's skull from the nape of his neck to his eyebrows, the chill of the ice helping to constrict blood vessels, slowing the deadly seep of blood that would suffocate the brain.

A nice question. At what point, then, should healing be encouraged by gentle heat or stimulation?

Should the patient be bled as a means of releasing pressure on the brain? The textbook had mentioned such a measure, but to be used with great caution. That meant that Dr. John

Roberts, despite his years of experience, was just not sure *what* would work. Yet Thomas could not bring himself to believe that draining the body's very life source would be anything but counterproductive.

Sonny Malone's bashed hands lay bandaged and splinted. The three great knuckles for the first, second and third fingers of each hand had been smashed by the spruce, but that was of little concern now. Thomas had rearranged the bones into a reasonably straight line and splinted them, but at this point, he would have considered it a triumph if Sonny Malone had howled out in conscious agony.

"Will you talk with Mrs. Schmidt now?" Bertha Auerbach's voice was a mere whisper, and he turned.

"Yes, I suppose so. When was the ice changed last?" He found it difficult to tear his mind from this case, to wash the slate clean, to direct his attentions elsewhere.

"Every twenty minutes, as you instructed. Twenty on, then rest for twenty."

"You've seen no reaction?"

"None. But the body has great resources."

Thomas sighed. "A daring rescue, and here he is, under our roof. And there's nothing we can do to save him. Nothing." Thomas ran a hand through his hair, pausing with his palm on the crown of his head. "What could we have done within the first few minutes? What if the rescue hadn't taken so interminably *long?* Should I have climbed up to him myself and tried to administer some relief? Sometimes I think that I should have insisted on that."

"What if," Bertha said, and Thomas glanced at her. "You can torture yourself all you like, Doctor. That won't change this young man's condition one iota. And if *you* suffered an accident doing something so foolish as climbing, who would patch you back together this time?"

"Yes, I suppose. I just can't help thinking..."

"Thinking is good. And of course there I go again, talking out of turn. You've spoken with Mr. Deaton?"

"I haven't yet had a chance."

Bertha managed to curb her impatience. "He's in the stables now. Carlotta Schmidt is also waiting for you. I asked her to wait in your office where she might be more comfortable, since I didn't know how long you would be."

"Ah." He brightened and held out a hand as if to escort his nurse. "If you please, then."

Carlotta Schmidt stood in front of one of the bookcases in the comfortable, over-stuffed office, her head cocked to one side as she read the titles. Her long auburn hair, now lightly streaked with gray, was captured up in a fashionable sweep, a small but stylish hat pinned to the bun. At the sound of their footsteps, she turned and offered a radiant smile. No wonder she was legend among the rough men who worked for her husband, Thomas thought.

"Mrs. Schmidt, please." He held a chair for her. It was a large, padded leather monstrosity, and Carlotta Schmidt appeared amused. She sat, perched well forward, one hand folded over the other.

"I'm loathe to take your time with such trivial matters." Her voice was a soft alto and she held a white linen kerchief to her nose. Thomas caught the delicate aroma of perfume water.

"At this point in my day, I welcome something trivial," Thomas said. It appeared that Bertha was about to leave the office, but Thomas beckoned her to stay. "You've met Nurse Auerbach, of course."

"Of course. We've had a moment or two to chat."

Thomas settled behind the desk. "Now, first let me apologize for not meeting with you earlier today."

"That's hardly necessary, Doctor." Carlotta held the white linen to her mouth, suppressing a small, shallow cough. The faintest flush touched her flawless cheeks, and her hazel eyes were bright but reddened, the conjunctiva swollen. Only a trace of darkness marked the hollows under her eyes, as if she had not been enjoying as much rest as she should.

"So," Thomas said. "Your complaint. From the beginning."

"I would not have bothered you..."

"It is no bother."

She smiled at the abruptness of his interruption. "A nuisance is all. I cough a little. And sometimes I think it bothers my husband more than it does me, especially when a fit strikes in the night." She smiled again, as if embarrassed at how silly and perhaps even indelicate the next suggestion might sound. "He is concerned...that I might have tuberculosis." At Thomas' frown, she added, "His mother and sister died of that affliction, so he fears..."

"I can understand his concern, and yours." That the disease sometimes favored families, even through generations, was well known. But Carlotta's blood relatives were not her husband's, and the woman who sat before him hardly was the definition of a tubercular patient. "In your family as well?"

"No one."

"That's good. Is the cough productive?" Her eyebrow lifted at that. "Does the cough itself relieve a congestion, a collection of mucous, or is it dry and *un*productive? We could call it a cough for no good reason."

"I feel as if the contents of my head are trying to run down my throat," she said, drawing two fingers down a velvety neck. "The cough offers some relief."

"And this is a recent condition?"

"Several weeks. Perhaps as much as two months. Perhaps longer."

"You've tried remedies?"

"This and that." She dropped her eyes. "I traveled to Portland some weeks ago to visit a cousin. I felt so much better while there. Upon my return..."

"Matters became worse."

"Exactly."

"So." Thomas leaned back. "Is there any pain? Especially around the ribs?"

"Only a little ache when the coughing is persistent."

"Well, to be sure. The rib muscles are assaulted. The discharge from the nose is clear, or of a color?"

"From time to time, colored. It is the itching that is most troubling."

"Your throat, you mean?"

She nodded. "The itching extends back into my ears." She made a claw of one hand. "Most irritating."

"And visiting Portland helped immediately. Is that what you feel?"

"Assuredly so."

"Have you been able to identify any *particular* thing that is irritating to you? That makes the nasal discharge more significant?"

She hesitated. "I'm not altogether sure."

Thomas looked thoughtfully at the journal in his lap. "I would like to listen to your lungs, to be sure. Shall we adjourn to the examination room?" He nodded at Bertha Auerbach, who turned to the door.

"Alvi…she is well?" Carlotta asked.

"She is wonderful, thank you."

"I thought I would stop by and call on her, if you think that would be appropriate."

"She would love to see you." He pointed toward the back of the examination room, where Bertha waited with a soft wrap. "If you'd step behind the screen, Nurse Auerbach will assist you."

In a moment, as Mrs. Schmidt returned and sat on the end of the examining table, Thomas noted how graceful and elegant she was, each movement so measured and careful. The nurse slipped a glass thermometer under Carlotta's tongue, and stood nearby to manage the decorous draping of the wrap as Thomas worked the bell of the stethoscope through its course. He listened, he thumped, he searched, but heard only one thing—the sound of healthy lungs moving air about—no rasping, no rales, no sounds of lung damaged or infected.

The delicate tissues lining the patient's throat were inflamed, her nasal passages swollen and painful, and the thermometer registered a scant 99.1 degrees.

After a time, Thomas relaxed back and regarded Carlotta Schmidt for a moment. "I think that we can reassure both you and your husband," he said. "Now…" but he interrupted himself at a subtle gesture by Bertha. Thomas assumed that she was reminding him that other patients were gathering. He could hear quiet voices out in the waiting room, one of them sounding very like his wife. But other visitors were not on the nurse's mind.

"Doctor, I'm sorry, but if I might be so bold?" Bertha didn't wait for permission from Thomas, but added, "If you would raise your left arm?" When Carlotta did so, the nurse re-arranged the wrap ever so slightly, at the same time stroking two fingers together down the curve of the left breast. She looked up at Thomas, waiting.

From a pace away, he could see the small irregularity, the ever-so-slight dimpling.

"If you please," he said gently, and Bertha stepped aside to give him room. He nodded at her thankfully, wanting her to be absolutely certain that he had forgiven her forward intrusion. Thomas had known professors who would have exploded in rage at such behavior by a nurse. To them, nurses should be cooperative, deferential pieces of furniture.

The tips of his fingers traced the soft, spongy outline of the tumor, an elastic mass the size of a walnut. He continued the examination with his eyes closed, trying to picture the perimeter of the mass, trying to assess the infiltration into surrounding tissues. He could feel nothing beyond the breast, nothing up in the arm pit. "Your age, Mrs. Schmidt?"

She didn't hesitate a heartbeat. "I am forty-one in July."

Thomas nodded. "Children?"

This time, Carlotta did hesitate, and for a moment Thomas thought that she might be considering the question a silly one. Thomas had met the Schmidts on more than one occasion, and had never heard rumors of a family. After a moment, she replied, "One who died in infancy. It was with my first husband. I was twenty."

"I'm sorry to hear that," Thomas said. "Mrs. Schmidt, you appear to have a small…perhaps we could call it a *knot,* here. You are aware of it?" A soft rap on the door interrupted them, and Bertha handed the corner of the wrap she was holding to Carlotta and then stepped quickly to block the door should the visitor enter. She held the knob and opened the door just enough to look through the slot. Thomas recognized his wife's voice again.

"It will be but a moment," Bertha said, and then added, "Oh? For heaven's sakes. Well, a moment."

"You are aware of it?" Thomas repeated, ignoring the interruption.

"Yes."

"It pains you?"

"No."

"When did you first notice its presence?"

"Some weeks ago."

"Weeks." He frowned at her in mock vexation. "Lie back, if you please."

When Bertha had assisted her and tended to the drapes, Thomas again traced the lump's outline and beyond, until he was satisfied with his exploration. "The right side, now," he said quietly, and continued, once again closing his eyes and forcing himself to concentrate only on what his fingertips could trace.

When he opened his eyes, he discovered that Mrs. Schmidt was watching his face attentively.

Chapter Six

He motioned for Carlotta to sit up again and then stepped back as Bertha Auerbach slipped the modesty wrap off the woman's shoulders. Carlotta's flush deepened perceptibly at being so openly disrobed, but she made no comment. At the same time as Bertha placed a hand between Carla's shoulder blades, Thomas said, "Shoulders back, if you please." Other than the left being minutely smaller than the right, the two breasts were from the same mold, regular, full, and healthy. He nodded at Bertha. "Thank you." By the time Mrs. Schmidt had donned her clothing and made herself presentable, some of the blush had faded from her cheeks.

Thomas sat down, giving himself time to think.

"Mrs. Parks is in the waiting room," Bertha interrupted. "Along with Dr. Hardy."

"Really?" He turned back to Mrs. Schmidt. "How fortuitous," he said. "Mrs. Schmidt, as long as you are here, might we take advantage of yet another opinion in this matter?"

"I…"

"Another physician experienced in such matters has just arrived, and I would appreciate his opinion. I know that it's an ordeal for you, but we should not let the opportunity pass in such a case."

"Such a case?" Carlotta said. "It is but a small lump."

Thomas looked down at her in deep sympathy. "Mrs. Schmidt, may I be blunt?"

"I would appreciate that, Doctor."

"For the tumor to have grown to walnut size in mere weeks, for it to have influenced the lie of skin over it, it must indeed be aggressive, perhaps even now invading the lymphatic tissues. That is my best understanding of the case. Delay is foolish. In fact, delay is *dangerous.*"

"You seem sure of this." She watched his face intently, the linen hanky pressed to her nose, her luminous eyes close to tearing.

"In matters of this nature," Thomas said carefully, "time is of the essence, Mrs. Schmidt." He paused. "Lesions of this nature are known to be highly malignant."

"It is a small imperfection," the woman said, and Thomas noted the quaver in her voice. "It has not changed in the past week."

"That's good. I don't mean to be argumentative or unpleasant, but it's also impossible to measure the tumor's size and behavior with any assurance, Mrs. Schmidt."

She dabbed at her eyes and then lowered the handkerchief. "All right. Do what you must. This is the new physician who is joining the clinic?"

"Indeed it is. Good. Good." He strode to the door and opened it to see his wife in animated but quiet discussion with a rotund man of early middle age, waistcoat drawn drum tight over an ample belly, expensive coat draped in a custom cut from square, powerful shoulders, and a face so round that he might have been drawn by a caricaturist.

Dr. Lucius Hardy turned and threw up both hands in surprise. He reached up and doffed his English-style woolen cap to reveal a shock of russet hair. "And here he is!" He stepped forward and pumped Thomas' hand, then drew him close in a bear hug. "Go ahead, say it. You've grown so bloody successful that you won't confess to recognizing an old chum!" The man beamed, his mouth splitting a perfectly manicured mustache and beard to reveal impossibly white teeth saved from perfection by looking as if they'd been inserted by a cross-eyed dentist.

"You can't imagine how good it is to see you, Lucius," Thomas said. "I'm sorry to have kept you waiting."

"Well, I think I can survive a few more moments after three weeks as an itinerant, Thomas. But let me tell you…you've been holding out on me. This young lady has absolutely captivated me for the past few moments." He beamed at Alvi, and then surveyed the waiting room with open admiration. "And here I thought you were practicing out of a small log cabin, the ocean surf pounding on your doorstep…"

Thomas laughed. "We lead the vanguard toward the twentieth century, Lucius." He clapped him on the shoulder. "You came down in the carriage from One-oh-one?" Thomas had not heard the horses, and he peered out the window, expecting to see Horace, the groundskeeper at their home at 101 Lincoln, six blocks up the hill.

"It is a gorgeous day for a stroll," Alvi allowed. "Although I must confess, we've given *sedate* a whole new definition at the rate I walk these days."

"I offered options," Hardy said. "She would hear none of them. So arm in arm we promenaded, and I'm sure we've set some of the local tongues a-wagging." He grinned at both Thomas and Alvi and held out his hands. "So here I am. And you're with a patient. I apologize if I am intruding."

"As a matter of fact, you couldn't have timed your arrival for a better moment." Thomas lowered his voice. "It is a simple enough case, I believe, but I would appreciate your opinion."

"My mind has been numbed by travel," Hardy chuckled, but rubbed his hands in anticipation. "But I would welcome such an opportunity."

"If you please, then. Alvi, will you join us?" He turned again to Hardy. "I depend on my wife's intuition, you see. If I knew a tenth of what she does, I should be a happy man."

Carlotta Schmidt straightened a bit as the three entered the examining room. Thomas saw that Bertha had already assisted the woman, the modesty drape arranged like a Roman toga.

"Mrs. Carlotta Schmidt," Thomas announced. "May I introduce Dr. Lucius Hardy? And of course you know my wife, Alvina."

Carlotta extended a hand and Lucius Hardy took it in both of his own beefy paws. He bowed his head, his direct gaze assessing her carefully.

"Mrs. Schmidt, my greetings. Give me but a moment." While Alvi engaged Carlotta in animated conversation about Alvi's condition, Thomas watched while Dr. Hardy strode for the back counter and made use of hot water and then the antiseptic drench as if he were a veteran of this very room.

"You know," Hardy said, his voice a whisper, "there are still those among us who think all this preoccupation with asepsis is a waste of time, Thomas."

"And would that they all continue to practice elsewhere," Thomas replied. Hardy held his hands up for a moment while the alcohol drench evaporated.

For the next ten minutes, Carlotta endured a repeat examination. Lucius Hardy was thorough, almost maddeningly methodical. Thomas curbed his impatience. Alvi remained at Carlotta's right shoulder, holding her hand, while Bertha stood sentry behind the left, tending the wrap.

"Indeed," the physician said at last. He straightened up, and popped his back with a stretch. When nothing else was obviously forthcoming, it was Carlotta Schmidt who demanded an answer.

"What must be done, Dr. Parks?" She directed the question to Thomas, and Hardy stepped back out of the way.

"The tumor is reasonably small, Mrs. Schmidt," Thomas said, "and its location is to our advantage. A single, simple incision allows us to enucleate the tumor from the surrounding tissue."

"And then?" Her shoulders squared a bit, her hands clenched in her lap. She did nothing to hide her left breast from the view of her audience.

"And then, we see," Dr. Hardy explained. "Careful microscopy will help us establish the tissue's malignancy."

"And then?"

"If there is reason to believe that the tumor is malignant, then the surrounding tissue must be removed as well," Hardy said gently, and Thomas nodded his agreement.

Carlotta's expression didn't change, but tears flowed unhindered down her cheek. Her eyes never wavered from Thomas'.

"You have accomplished this surgery before?"

"No. But I will have assistance." He did not add that Dr. Hardy was himself but thirty-five years old, and far from an experienced hand as a surgeon.

Carlotta was not blind, however. "Should I travel to Portland, perhaps?"

"That is your choice, of course."

"Their facilities would be more…"

"Certainly. But ours are entirely adequate and becoming more so by the day. And I would remind you that our nursing staff is superb. Your post operative care would be unfailing and attentive."

"Still…"

"The decision is yours alone, Mrs. Schmidt. You, and then with your husband. But I would counsel this. Any delay on your part merely exacerbates the dangers to you. You are young, strong, in otherwise good health. Delay is…well, I cannot emphasize enough. In this case, delay is your worst enemy."

"And if I choose to leave this in God's hands? If I do nothing?" Her eyes searched his, and he took a moment, thinking of a dozen responses.

"Don't be ridiculous," Dr. Hardy interjected, and his abrupt answer reminded Thomas of Alvi's late father, Dr. John Haines. "The prognosis of carcinoma of the breast is always most serious, Mrs. Schmidt. Treatment is not something best left to chance."

"Will you speak with my husband?" Again, she directed the question to Thomas. He noticed that, although his wife had said nothing, Alvi still held Carlotta's right hand in both of hers, a simple, consoling touch.

"I will insist on it," Thomas replied. "Regardless of what course of action the two of you might take, I wish to see you both tomorrow morning. The both of you. You and Bert. Promptly at nine o'clock, if you will. I shall interrupt whatever matter engages me at that moment to speak with you both. If you elect surgery here, I shall want to operate the following morning. That would be Saturday." He reached out a hand and pulled the drape up over her shoulder. "No delays, now. If you decide that Portland or some such is the answer, I would expect to see your departure for their facility within a day or two." He squeezed her shoulder hard. "Delay is the enemy, Mrs. Schmidt."

Carlotta turned to Alvi as if she had spent all the moments in consideration that she could afford. "And you are well?"

"Fit as can be," Alvi said.

"I keep listening for the heart beats of twins, but I doubt we shall be so fortunate," Thomas added.

Carlotta Schmidt arose carefully and accepted Bertha Auerbach's assistance behind the screen. "I shall see you tomorrow morning, then," she said as she donned her cloak.

"With your husband."

She nodded and Thomas held the door for her. After the woman had left, he turned to Lucius. "She drove herself into town today. A most resourceful woman."

"Apparently so. Her husband is a reasonable man?"

"Oh, indeed he is. At least, in the dealings I've had with him so far, most reasonable. He owns the largest mill on the coast."

"Shall I summon Howard?" Bertha asked, and Thomas regarded her with affection.

"I am in your debt, you know. As is Carlotta Schmidt."

"I think not."

"I had not noticed the lesion," he explained to Hardy, and the other physician's eyebrow shot up. Thomas couldn't tell if Hardy was reacting to his admission, or the failed observance, or his expression of gratitude to his nurse. "Nor had I looked for it. She visited for a separate issue." He hesitated and watched his nurse, who busied herself changing the rinse water.

"We depend in large part on the patient to guide us," Hardy said with a shrug.

"But I should have seen it. We can make all the excuses we like, but that's the simple truth. I have been preoccupied with other things. But I should have seen it."

"A questioning of procedure is healthy, sir," Dr. Hardy said.

"You sound just like Dr. Roberts," Thomas laughed. "So… tell me. Should she go to Portland?"

"Now that's unfair, my good man," Hardy said. "I've been inside your clinic door for what, ten minutes? What I think should hardly matter."

"Ah, but…" Thomas interrupted. "I want to know exactly… *exactly*…what you think. Always." He nodded at Berti and Alvi. "Just as I expect a frank opinion from each of you."

Bertha Auerbach took a long breath, her dark brown eyes unwavering. She folded her hands over her stomach, looked as if she wanted to speak, thought better of it, then again thought better of any reticence. "Were I Carlotta Schmidt, there would be no choice. I would have the surgery done here."

"There you have it," Hardy said, and it seemed to Thomas that he detected a slight flair of irritation in the physician's tone. Perhaps he was of the older school whose contention it was that nurses should be seen, but not heard.

"Sonny Malone might argue with you," Thomas said.

Bertha laughed abruptly, and covered her mouth with her hand as if embarrassed by the outburst. "There is no parallel with the two cases, Dr. Parks. We accept what we can do, and move on."

"Now I obviously know nothing of this Mr. Malone of whom you speak, but I'll say this…Mrs. Schmidt has but a fifty-fifty gambler's chance of surviving the surgery," Hardy said. "Fifty-fifty, here or anywhere else. And not to put too fine a point on it, without surgical intervention, she has *no* chance."

"And here we all stand, dithering." Alvi frowned. "It's Carlotta's decision, not ours." Thomas grinned at his wife, who suffered no compunction about speaking her mind.

Berti started for the door. "Shall I fetch Mr. Deaton?"

"Thank you. Yes. Dr. Hardy and I will be in the office for a few moments. I want to review my notes." He reached out and took Hardy by the elbow. "You may find that instructive as well." He turned to Alvi. Despite the walk down from 101 Lincoln, or perhaps because of it, Alvi looked radiant…and enormous.

"You shouldn't walk back up the hill," he said. "Did you leave word with Horace to fetch you, or…"

"I shall make myself useful here until you and Dr. Hardy are ready to take some refreshment. We haven't offered the poor man so much as a glass of lemonade since his arrival. And then *you* shall escort me back to One-oh-one," she said. "Is Nurse Whitman upstairs with the Snyder child?"

"The child's parents are with her, I believe."

"Then I shall ride the wonderful Otis and speak with them." She reached out and touched her husband's cheek, a familiarity that prompted an instant blush.

The office beside the main examining room was anything but Spartan, thanks in large measure to the late Dr. John Haines, Alvi's father. Thomas settled back, cradled by the enormous leather chair, the journal open on the desk in front of him.

Hardy surveyed the comfortable room, the huge bookcase, the locked cabinet that included a significant pharmacy. Thomas let him explore uninterrupted while he flipped the journal open. He traced the patient names to Howard Deaton, aged thirty-four years, compound fracture of the tibia and femur, and began to read.

Chapter Seven

"I find your wife to be a remarkable woman," Hardy said, and the unexpected comment jerked Thomas out of his reading. "My God, how studious you are," Hardy laughed at the reaction. "I understand now why both your wife and Miss Auerbach were so reticent about disturbing you during an examination. You startle so!" He made a slashing upward motion with an imaginary scalpel. "Whoops, pardon me! Sutures, please!"

"Alvi *is* remarkable," Thomas replied in self-defense. "I heartily agree. I wish you could have met her father."

"Passed rather suddenly, did he?"

"Yes. A stroke this past autumn. She misses him terribly. We both do."

"Well, of course you do."

Thomas beckoned to a chair. "Here, please. How about some brandy to wash down the dust? We haven't allowed you a moment's rest from your journey."

"I haven't seen dust since I left the Dakotas, Thomas. Wash away the *muck*, perhaps. And yes to the brandy." He watched with keen interest as Thomas poured two glasses, both with a conservative jigger or two. Accepting the glass, Lucius Hardy closed his eyes, sipped delicately, twitched his mustache, and uttered a heart-felt groan of pleasure. He smacked his lips then, and carefully placed the glass on a small table near his chair without taking a second sip.

"So," he said, eyes roaming about the office. "Look at you."
He reached for the glass again, took another minute sip with
closed eyes, and replaced it. "Alvina is charming. You're a lucky
man, Thomas. Getting on a bit, isn't she."

"Seven months."

Hardy's thick eyebrows shot up. "Really now? My soul, she's a
mountain for seven, I'll say that. What is she carrying, triplets?"

"I wouldn't care to bet."

"Surely by now you can hear the separate heart beats,
Thomas." Just a trace of reproof there, Thomas thought, the
same gentle tone he'd heard from Lucius Hardy in the laboratory at the university where Hardy had first been an anatomy
assistant, and then an instructor in microscopy.

"I can, Lucius. Two good strong hearts—mother and child."

"Well, then. There you are. That's my specialty, you know. I
left the university and indulged in Philadelphia's high life for a
couple years. Lots of very wealthy young women having lots of
stunningly beautiful babies."

"Dr. Roberts so informed me, Lucius. And in part that's why
I wrote to you, at his urging. I hardly dared believe that you
might accept my offer."

"Well, you know," Hardy said with a casual, dismissive wave
of the hand. "You've seen one stuffy parlor of the wealthy, you've
seen them all, so to speak. I've always loved the notion of the
sea…not the sea itself, mind you," he laughed. "I've discovered
that I become dreadfully seasick. But the *notion* of it. The sea
at a distance. I had been considering a post in New Haven, but
then your persuasive letter arrived. Having never been west of
Philadelphia, the lure of adventure was strong. And I have to
admit, Thomas, I half suspected you of aggrandizing the situation you have here, but my word." He looked around the room.
"This is most pleasant."

"I've tried to make it sound so, and now here we are. Dr.
Roberts says that you were the best in your class. I had to work
hard to lure you."

"The best in *any* class, my friend. Simply the best. And still am. Perhaps hampered by an overwhelming modesty, but I work to overcome that." He grinned and sipped the brandy again. "So, tell me what…" He stopped in mid-sentence, and Thomas turned to see Berti at the office doorway.

The nurse could set her narrow, pretty face into an expression of perfect neutrality, exactly what she did at that moment.

"Mr. Deaton is ready for you in the examining room, Doctor. And Mr. Malone remains unchanged. Alvina is upstairs with the Snyders."

"Thank you, Berti."

When the door closed softly behind the nurse, Hardy nodded his approval. "She'd be a beautiful young lady if she would smile more often."

"She has to feel the need," Thomas said. "The most important thing is that she has made herself indispensable, as you have no doubt noticed. Come with me? You'll have an introduction to the Clinic before you take a few hours to relax. After dinner, we can settle in for a serious chat. Alvi has made the pronouncement, and our housekeeper Gert James will have outdone herself with the preparations."

Hardy slapped his belly. "As you can see, food is of little interest to me. But lead on, Doctor."

Howard Deaton leaned on the end of the examination table, arms crossed over his chest, his thatch of eyebrows and lined face giving him an expression of vexed impatience—and at this moment, a little more than usual. He straightened as the two physicians entered the examining room.

"Howard Deaton, my man. Let me introduce you to Dr. Lucius Hardy." Howard extended a hand uncertainly, as if undecided about how deferential to be. "Dr. Hardy, Howard is the best man with horses and an ambulance on the planet, in addition to a long list of other skills."

"My pleasure," Hardy said, and then nodded another greeting at Bertha Auerbach.

"The leg troubles you some?" Thomas' question appeared to take Deaton off guard. Perhaps he'd been expecting a discussion of proposed new ambulance features, or the general health of one of the horses.

"Some days more'n others," he said. "But I'm gettin' on." His convalescence had been both exquisitely painful and complicated, and no doubt seemed interminable. That he was loath to even broach the subject of his injury was understandable.

"May I have a look?"

"Ain't no different from what it was," Deaton replied, and for a moment it looked as if he wasn't going to oblige. Then he stepped across the room and sat in one of the straight wooden chairs. "You need the boot off?" Thomas nodded. "I was afraid of that." He took his time unlacing his boot, pulling the laces wide all the way to the bottom of the tongue.

"A multiple compound fracture of the tibia and fibula a few inches above the ankle," Thomas explained to Hardy. "The result of an accident with a steel-shod freight wagon. A Stimson's fracture box was tried first, but the results were unsatisfactory. Eventually we resorted to open surgery, and I pinned the large bone fragments with silver."

Hardy's left eyebrow raised a fraction.

"Closure and healing of the wound were uneventful, except that Mr. Deaton went through hell for several weeks."

"Months," Deaton muttered morosely. "I wouldn't be the one to call it uneventful." His jaw set in determination, he eased the boot off, and let out a sigh of relief when it slipped free. The woolen stocking came next, not yet showing signs of life of its own, but certainly due for a walk in the nearest creek. Thomas patted the table, and Deaton limped across and positioned himself near the head so the he could swing his leg up. He hiked up his trouser leg, and Thomas regarded the enormous scar that marked the front of Deaton's shin for eight inches above the ankle. With the lightest of touches, he ran the index and middle fingers of each hand down the sides of the man's leg. At one point four inches above the ankle he felt Deaton's involuntary jerk.

"Tender there?"

"A mite."

Thomas repositioned himself, remembering exactly where he had pinned the shattered bones. He could feel a prominent knot on the anterior blade of the tibia where the bone was repairing itself, but as he moved his fingers laterally where he could feel the rise of the fibula, Deaton sucked air sharply through clenched teeth.

"Dr. Hardy?" Thomas nodded toward the leg.

"I'm no surgeon," Hardy allowed. He glanced up at Deaton, eyes twinkling. "In point of fact, young man, if you were several months pregnant, I'd be of considerably more use."

"I ain't that."

"Well, thank God," Hardy chuckled. "But I feel some inflammation here, some swelling, more than there should be at this stage. Surgery in September, you say?" Thomas nodded. "Then we most certainly have a little something going on here." He shut his eyes as Thomas had done, and let his fingers roam for a moment. "The silver was used here as well?"

"Yes."

"Huh. Silver. I hadn't heard of that." He straightened and held out a hand toward Bertha, who instantly passed him a clean towel. He wiped his hands thoughtfully and handed the towel back without so much as a glance her way. "What turned you away from grafting, if I might ask? Shierson has had considerable luck at our own *alma mater.*"

"The gravity of the situation, for one thing," Thomas replied. "Time was of the essence."

"Ah." Hardy looked up at the patient. "How do you describe the pain, Mr. Deaton?"

"Well, it hurts like hell sometimes."

"Sharp stabbing pain? Blunt, aching pain? A deep, burning itch? Be specific, man."

Deaton looked first at Thomas as if he wanted permission to speak, then back at Hardy. "Feels like somebody's holdin' a white hot iron poker to my leg. But deep inside."

"Ah. How does it bear weight?"

"Fair to middlin'."

"And what does that mean?"

"Well, I can walk on it all right. I mean, normally, it don't hurt none."

"But there is some discomfort, obviously. What makes it hurt at its worst?"

Deaton thought for a moment. "Seems like when I twist some, maybe carryin' a load. Like I pick up a saddle and turn… why, hurts all to hell."

"May I humbly suggest that you don't do that, then?" Hardy said.

"Amen," Thomas added, motioning to Bertha. "This is what we're going to try. I want ice for the inflammation, four times a day, fifteen minutes each session. Without fail. Follow the ice with soothing heat—not so much as to redden the skin, but enough to sooth out the chill from the ice."

"I ain't got the time…"

Thomas held up a hand to interrupt Deaton. "You *do* have the time, Howard. You do. Or to put a finer point on it, you will *make* time. Consider it part of your job. I'll *pay* you to do it."

"But I got things to tend to."

"Indeed you do. Your leg, for one. I can't afford to lose you, sir. Perhaps you recall the discomfort from your previous convalescence?" Deaton's jaw clamped. "You don't want to go through that again, I'm sure. And I can't have you lolling about in bed all day for weeks at a time. Things to do, as you say. So let's try the easy route first. Ice and heat upon first rising, then noon, at supper, and just before you retire. Without fail. You might even try a mild liniment, such as you use on the horses for sore muscles."

"And the rest of the time, favor it," Hardy added. "It wouldn't hurt to go back to the cane that you no doubt used earlier."

"Don't need no cane."

"Welllll…" and Hardy drew the word out for full effect, "yes, my good man, you do. Think how elegant you'll look. The ladies will swoon." Thomas noted with satisfaction how thoroughly at ease the physician appeared, hands thrust in the pockets of his tweed woolen trousers, completely at home though he been under the clinic's roof for less than an hour.

Chapter Eight

They left Howard Deaton to his first round of therapy with Bertha Auerbach, and Thomas escorted Hardy through the rest of the first floor of the clinic.

"You favor a sort of temperature therapy, I see," Hardy said at one point as he studied the small operating room on the north side of the building that Thomas had reserved for dissection and post-mortems. "I find that interesting."

"It seems natural to me. Cold tends to relieve inflammation as well as numbing discomfort. Heat encourages the chemical reactions of healing, as well as feeling heavenly." He leaned against the operating table. "I tell you, Lucius, during my own convalescence, I think I should have gone insane without it." He touched his right eyebrow, over which a scar arched, disappearing up into his hairline. "Fracture of the orbit." He held up his left thumb. "Fracture of the thumb." He stretched and touched ribs on his left side. "Multiple fractures." Finally, he indicated his left hip. "Dislocated. And bruises from head to toe."

"My word, man."

"Yes. Alvi was a saint during my recovery. And the ice and heat…well, I have no doubts about its use."

"You think it can actually make a difference in a difficult case such as your blown-up logger?"

"Probably not. I know nothing else to do. I *do* know it can do no harm."

"Well, there's that. You know, your surgical skills were legendary at school. I never realized *how* good you must be until I discovered how *abominable* I was." He grinned. "Although I do a damn good post—as long as the patient doesn't need to get up and walk away afterward." He surveyed the room. "I'll probably be of considerable use here for just that sort of thing. I have a question, however."

"Please ask. Anything."

"You have nothing to lose with…Mr. Malone, is it? Why not a simple exploratory surgery with him?"

"For one thing, there is no 'simple' surgery involving the brain, Lucius. I'm sure you know that as well as I. That, and I have no suggestion about where to begin. If there's an obvious wound, then I would know. But there is not. I can't very well evacuate his entire brain case, chasing shadows."

"The explosion was above him?"

Thomas nodded, and formed an umbrella of his hands over his own head. "Like so."

"And yet he didn't fall."

"They wear a climbing belt. Steel core. And most extraordinary. He cut the rope when he saw that the split would crush him."

"After the explosion?"

"Exactly. He had but a fraction of a second to make his decision and act."

"My word. And no exploratory, at least at the top of the cranium where the brunt of the explosion was taken? And here I thought you surgeons could find any excuse to use the knife."

Thomas laughed ruefully. "What this surgeon has learned is that every time the knife touches the flesh, there is an equal chance of correction or fatality. I would be less than truthful if I were to say my record in the past few months was anything but dismal."

Hardy reached out and shook him lightly by the shoulder. "Come, now. Look at the sorts of cases demanding your attention, Thomas. I suspect a goodly number of your patients are the walking dead anyway—finished before they are ever carried across your doorstep. I haven't seen much of this country in the last hour, but I've heard tales and read a good deal. Absolutely fascinating."

"My God, Lucius, the life that some of these people lead is simply amazing. We must visit the timber on the very first opportunity. You'll be astonished. And in addition, they laugh and joke about the dangers, completely heedless. I wish you could have seen Malone's rescue from the tree tops this morning. Just remarkable. And the first patient on my doorstep this morning? Hand absolutely ruined by a ridiculous *game.* And yet he laughed about it, at first refusing treatment. Finger twisted with painful fractures, dislocated thumb…my God." He took a deep breath as he saw the grin spread across the other physician's face.

"I carry on, don't I," Thomas said. "What I need right now, as I told you in our correspondence, is not just another surgeon. You see, I had the rare occasion to work with Alvi's father for just a few weeks before his untimely death this past autumn. Dr. John Haines? He had lost the sight in one eye, drank too much brandy, but still could diagnose circles around me. I am painfully aware of my inexperience, and I miss his presence terribly."

"You are somewhat removed from the rest of the world in this little island of activity you have here," Hardy said.

"But the opportunity is boundless, Lucius. To *build.* I want to show you the renovations we've accomplished upstairs for both women and children." He turned toward the hallway behind them, then stopped. "Let me tell you what I'm *not*, Lucius. I am no obstetrician. And…" He looked behind him as if someone might be eavesdropping. "I don't *want* to be. If that sounds unnatural, so be it. In my nine months here, I have delivered exactly two infants. Both successfully, I may add. But throughout the entire procedure, it was Nurse Auerbach and a competent mid-wife who orchestrated events. It would be fair to say that they *tolerated* my presence, should some kind of surgical intervention be necessary."

"Surely you exaggerate a bit," Hardy said. "But an interesting woman, your Miss Auerbach. You have other nursing staff, I understand?"

"Three others. You just missed Helen Whitman, who has gone for the day. She is a competent woman with no particular formal training, but vast experience. The other two provide coverage for us during the nighttime hours. Mrs. Crowell and Miss Stephens, both competent." He hesitated. "Well, Mrs. Crowell is competent. She has recently lost her husband and finds that working at night is somehow soothing. Miss Stephens is very young, but tried a few months at St. Mary's across the sound before returning home. She has much to learn, and I have reservations, I admit. She is somehow easily embarrassed by the human body and its functions."

"I have to say that I am impressed with Miss Auerbach," Hardy mused.

"A gem," Thomas said fervently. "She and Alvi are the only two who will tell me what I need to hear...*exactly* what I need to hear, whether I like it or not."

"How fortunate you are—I think." Hardy chuckled again. "You might disagree with Cushing's comments, then. That in all things, the physician is captain of his ship."

"If he meant that no one should be allowed to speak up and remind the physician when he's being a stubborn mule-headed pedant who is clearly *wrong* and headed toward disaster, then yes. I couldn't disagree with him more. What little experience I have has taught me that."

Hardy's eyes twinkled. "You've found yourself in that situation, have you?"

"Too many times."

"You're a remarkable man to admit it, sir."

"My convalescence had a lot to do with it. During the six months when I was a patient..." He hunched his shoulders. "Primarily I learned how very little the physician actually *knows*, without fear of debate. The moment I think I'm in control of all factors in a case, nature proves to me otherwise."

"Ah. I suppose so. You must tell me more about your own mishap when you have a moment."

Thomas stopped and gestured around the men's ward they had just entered. "Originally, this was the *only* ward. Eight beds, no provisions for women or children. No provision for extended care. No way to separate the chronically ill, or the infectiously ill, from otherwise healthy surgical patients. Now this floor is reserved for male patients, with three separate rooms toward the rear for the most challenging cases, or those that require the additional privacy. That's where we've placed Mr. Malone. so he would have complete quiet." He patted the foot rail of the first bed.

"The young man with the broken finger was here this morning. He recovered from the oxide quickly, and we saw no reason to keep him further. He left with absolute instructions about how he should take care of himself. I don't believe that he will," and the physician grinned ruefully. "But later today, I plan to ride out to the tract and check on him myself. We also have the possibility of food poisoning at the camp, and that can be fearsome. I would be remiss if I didn't investigate the situation."

Thomas gestured toward the rear of the ward, and Dr. Hardy followed him. At one point half-way down the short ward, he once again thrust his hands in his trouser pockets as if not quite trusting them to venture out unsupervised.

"I heard mention of a women's ward? You have them separate?"

"Upstairs."

"Up?" Hardy looked puzzled.

"We have an Otis," Thomas said proudly. "A pregnant woman need navigate not a single step. An absolutely remarkable machine. Hydraulic, you know."

"My word. An elevator. How cosmopolitan."

Thomas opened the doorway to one of the tiny private rooms. Sonny Malone lay insensible. His mouth hung slack, eye lids parted, breath coming in hesitant, irregular little gasps.

"So it is a general concussion, then," Hardy mused. "Very much as if a cannon shell had exploded near his skull."

"Absent the fragmentation, yes. Both eardrums are ruptured, massive internal hemorrhage showing itself in the vitreous, little or no reflex at the extremities."

"Nothing for it then, is there."

"I'm afraid not. I've instructed continued cold wraps to the shaved skull, in a vain hope that the bleeding might yet stop and be reabsorbed."

"Might I listen?" Hardy held out his hand and Thomas drew the coiled stethoscope from his jacket pocket. For a long time, the physician roamed the instrument across Sonny Malone's pale chest. "I don't think that the blast injuries are limited to the brain."

"Almost certainly not."

"It sounds as if his heart is trying to pump lard."

"It amazes me that within an hour of the event he was heard to utter a coherent sentence. And then nothing but groans and cries." Even as Thomas spoke, Hardy bent over and, placing a hand on each side of Malone's rib cage, applied compressive pressure in a number of places.

The physician straightened up and hunched his shoulders. "Will he swallow? A trickle of brandy, perhaps?"

"No. And the risk of gagging is too great. A single cough might kill him."

"As surely as he is already on the way," Hardy said softly. "We can do nothing for him that you haven't already done, Thomas."

He waited outside the room while Thomas closed the door.

"So…you have your man with a game leg, another poor man blasted to pieces…and you began your day with surgery of the digits. Now there is a delightful woman suffering a dangerous carcinoma. And it's not yet dinner time. Somehow we have avoided the constant flow of hypochondriacs who vie for a physician's time. What else has filled your day, then?" He smiled and clapped Thomas lightly on the shoulder again.

"We have our full share of the continually ill, as Alvi's father used to refer to them," Thomas said. "Bertha is most effective as captain of the guard. In real need, she schedules them for the first three days of the week. She has her techniques."

"And your lovely wife is most skillful herself, I have gathered. As she progresses along, you must miss her steadying hand. She is in her seventh month, you say?"

"I believe so."

Hardy stopped short. "You *believe* so? Dr. Parks, you surprise me." He crossed his arms over his barrel chest and rested his chin in one with his index along the side of his nose. He frowned at Thomas. "You've spoken to the local mid-wife?"

"Mrs. McLaughlin. Yes, of course."

"I mean, surely, sometime in the past nine months of your residency here, a child has been born? Didn't you mention two?"

"And many more that I never saw."

"But you attended two?"

A flush crept up Thomas' neck. "To be honest, I would have to say that I *assisted* twice."

"Assisted the mid-wife? I thought that you were just being modest when you said that earlier."

"Yes. I assisted."

Hardy regarded him with a mixture of skepticism and amusement. "How very interesting. May I ask a somewhat presumptuous question? May I presume on our past friendship at the University?"

"Certainly."

"You said that your wife is in her *seventh* month."

"Yes."

"How has that been ascertained?"

"She has been in continual conversation with Nurse Auerbach, and with Mrs. McLaughlin. That is what she wished."

"You've examined her yourself, I assume?"

"Of course. But she becomes impatient with me. It's really quite remarkable, Lucius. To feel the outline of the infant…"

Hardy nodded slowly. "How very interesting. Let us pray that all is progressing perfectly with her pregnancy, then."

"It is. In matters of this sort, Alvina has far more experience than I. As does Nurse Auerbach."

Hardy laughed. "Thomas, Thomas." He shook his head, and Thomas wasn't quite sure what was amusing the physician, who added, "The woman with the carcinoma of the breast...if she chooses to remain in Port McKinney for the surgery?"

"I shall operate Saturday morning at nine o'clock. You'll join me and administer the ether?"

"Of course. Of course. And you have a good microscope? Mine is being shipped and won't arrive for some weeks."

"I do. A new Heinnenberg with immersion."

"Good. Then we can rapidly ascertain whether the beast be benign or malignant, and have the deed be done before she awakes." He cleared his throat. "We need take no one's word for it. You know, despite the gloom of the gambler's choice we were discussing earlier, I've read of success rates as high as ninety percent for a mastectomy with axial complications."

"I will be satisfied with one hundred percent in this particular case," Thomas replied.

"Ah. We love all our patients, don't we. She is near and dear, then?"

"I would suppose that in a village the size of Port McKinney," Thomas said, "that they all are. But you force me to admit that this is my first such case."

"We must all turn a new page," Hardy said. "You know, the time will come soon enough when you'll bore all your friends and acquaintances with the sheer volume of your case experience. You'll shake your finger in the air and say things like, 'Why, in thirty years, I've seen too many cases to count.'" He looked at the long flight of stairs up which Thomas had already started. "The Otis?"

"It takes far too long," Thomas replied. "Have you performed a mastectomy, Lucius?"

"On a patient or a cadaver? I have one hundred percent on specimens in the laboratory." He grinned. "Otherwise, I've assisted in perhaps half a dozen. I told you, Thomas. I am not a surgeon." He held out his hands as he plodded up the stairs after his tour guide. "With hams like these...now, the women somehow find them reassuring. It's all in the touch, you see."

"But the cases in which you assisted?" Thomas persisted.

"I have yet to experience the pleasure of seeing one survive."

Thomas nearly missed a step and stopped, turning to look down at Hardy.

"None?"

"In three cases the carcinoma returned more vicious than before, completely inoperable. We could have saved the patients exquisite agony by not operating in the first place, leaving them to the morphine in their final months. In two others, sepsis was the villain. In another, suicide." He slapped the banister. "But we don't need to discuss those dismal statistics with your patient."

"No, indeed not," Thomas said fervently. Nurse Helen Whitman, a middle-aged, portly woman with frighteningly glacial eyes but a warm heart, met the two physicians at the top of the stairs. "Ah, Mrs. Whitman. I thought you had gone home."

"Both Nurse Auerbach and I like to be here when the other staff arrives for the night." She nodded deferentially at Lucius Hardy. At their introduction, the physician gave her the same stiff, almost dismissive nod with which he'd favored Bertha Auerbach.

"Miss Whitman," Thomas said, "I've left instructions with Berti regarding Howard Deaton."

"She explained the case to me, Doctor."

"Good. If you would help us make sure that Mr. Deaton behaves himself? I want that therapy done exactly as I've described regardless of how busy we might otherwise become."

"Certainly, Doctor."

"Not a single missed session. On no account."

"We'll do our best, Doctor. And a pleasure to meet you, sir," she added to Hardy.

Thomas saw a man and woman step briefly into the doorway of one of the private children's rooms at the end of the empty ward. "Missy's parents?"

"They've been with her all day," Helen replied. "Such good people."

His gaze swept the otherwise empty ward. "I understood that my wife is here as well? She said she would stay until I could walk her home."

"I'm afraid that she returned to One-oh-one," Mrs. Whitman said. "She tires easily nowadays." She nodded again at both of them, and bustled down the stairs.

"Matilda Snyder has had a bilateral tonsillotomy," Thomas explained. "She seems to be responding well. Somewhat at odds with the cocaine swab, but otherwise good. She'll go home tomorrow."

"Home tomorrow. That's what a patient wants to hear. Your first?"

"No, certainly not." Thomas grinned. "My *second*. John Roberts supervised the first case last spring at University."

"Well, then, there you go. A veteran."

Thomas stepped into the single room where he introduced Lucius Hardy to the child's parents, both of them looking more haggard than the little girl. Flora Snyder, tall and thin, reminded Thomas of an undernourished version of Gert James, his house-keeper—without any of the healthy bloom that Gert enjoyed. Marcus Snyder hovered silently, overly deferential as he shook Hardy's hand. His clothing carried a heavy fragrance, an odd mixture of fish and sawdust.

"May I?" Hardy indicated the patient.

"Certainly."

Hardy sat gently on the edge of the child's bed. Sharing the most unattractive traits of both parents, Matilda was thin to the point of emaciation, hair in straw-colored strands, hollow-eyed and buck-toothed. Hardy reached out and brushed a strand of hair away from her eyes with a touch so gentle the child never blinked.

"Will you face the light and open your mouth for me, my dear?" he whispered, as if sharing a secret for the child's ears only. Thomas turned up the gas lamp, and Hardy pivoted the child's head this way and that, peering into the tiny throat. "Beautiful," he announced, and glanced at the enameled pan on the small table near the bed. "You have plenty of ice, my dear?"

"Yes," the child whispered. "Miss Whitman said she was going to find me some ice cream."

"Then she shall." Hardy stroked her face once more and rose. He extended his hand to the child's parents. "A pleasure to meet you," he said. "What a delightful child. You're with the timber industry?"

Snyder looked flustered, and glanced at Thomas as if he needed permission to speak. "No, I'm a fisherman," he said. "Do some sharpening on the side."

"Well, that's good."

"My wife here works at the Clarissa," Snyder added. "She's been with them since the hotel opened, goin' on twelve years now."

"Ah, the Clarissa," Hardy said. "Well, my good people, you have a delightful child."

Feeling as if he'd just completed rounds with a senior physician, Thomas followed Lucius Hardy from the room.

"Puzzling that parents can be so blind," Hardy muttered. "Why in God's name don't they *feed* the child?"

"I have Miss Whitman putting together a prescribed diet for her," Thomas said. "I think that in this case, it's a combination of ignorance, poverty, and the mother's own constitution. As you saw, she is a wraith herself. But we'll see what we can do."

"There's a limit, I suppose."

"So I'm continually reminded."

"So…" Hardy took a deep breath as if to remove an abundance of stale air from his lungs. "You put a great emphasis on privacy," Hardy said. "That's both interesting and commendable."

"Privacy is an inexpensive enough commodity," Thomas replied. "Something else learned from the past few months." He pulled out his watch. "I'm distressed that Alvina chose to walk back to One-oh-one by herself, but that's a good example. What's the expression? She marches to her own drummer, Lucius."

"And you must love her all the more because of that."

"To be sure. And you will join Alvi and me for dinner? We don't want you ending up looking like the Snyder child, a mere shadow of your former self. Here you've just arrived, and we haven't even given you a moment to settle into your room up at the house. Did Alvi…?"

Hardy held up a hand to interrupt. "We are ahead of you," he laughed. "I am to lodge in the third floor of this marvelous clinic. I'm told it's a truly magnificent suite, with a marvelous view. Alvina has given me the key." He look upward and then back at Thomas. "I took the liberty earlier of carrying what little luggage I have to the room. I must say," and he took a deep breath, "one sight of that magnificent feather bed proved a powerful attraction."

"Anything else that you might need…"

"Ah, not a thing. Not a thing. The suggestion that I join you for dinner is wonderful. I passed by the hotel's kitchen door on the way up the hill from the coach this morning, and it smelled like they were roasting kelp. At what time shall I reappear this evening?"

"At eight, then? Unless, of course…I'm planning a ride out to one of the leases this very afternoon. If you'd care to accompany me?"

"That's a temptation, but I confess that, after twelve days of constant travel, what appeals to me right now is motionless unconsciousness. Let me join you for dinner tonight, and we'll map out a strategy for the days to come."

"Of course. How stupid of me. Eight it is, then."

He watched Hardy take the stairs two at a time toward the third floor.

When Thomas turned away, he found Bertha Auerbach regarding him.

"So, what do you think?" Despite their earlier conversation, it didn't surprise him that Berti responded only with the faintest of unreadable smiles.

Chapter Nine

Sunshine was warm on Thomas' shoulders, so warm that he could smell the sweat from the gelding as Fats plodded through the acres of slash, the hard outlines of stumpage softened by steam rising from the baked duff.

In another twenty minutes, he reached a valley rank with grasses, sedges, berry bushes and tinny saplings in soft groves. The meadow had been logged long ago, and since then the stumps had been continually hacked and trimmed for firewood until most of them now were stumps the height of a footstool.

The timber camp stretched half the length of the valley, favoring the upper end where the stream burbled out of the timber. In total, Thomas counted thirty-five structures—tents, tent-shacks, rude little cabins of slabwood.

Although he knew that timber camps came and went as cutting crews moved, this one appeared impossibly ramshackle, as if the simplest creature comforts meant nothing to the loggers. And perhaps they didn't. Home at dark from a day of danger and toil, the loggers uncorked the bottle, gambled, and then fell into bed. They rose at dawn, off for another day in the timber.

Their dwellings were ordered in loose groups. Most of them were within staggering distance of the creek, and here and there, bathing pools had been scooped and dammed.

The largest structure in the valley, tucked up close to the tree line on the far side of the meadow, had managed slabwood all the way up to the eaves, with cedar shakes on the roof. Two bent stovepipes thrust up through the shakes with no visible thimbles to prevent the hall from bursting into flames.

Fifty feet uphill from the hall, a large privy had been constructed, long enough for five or six holes, and like most of the other buildings that showed signs of carpentry, not a straight line graced its architecture.

Thomas drew out his watch and saw that it was nearly three. In another hour, the sun would be obscured by the promontory west of the camp. Between that hill and the blockade of timber to the east, days here would be short—a late dawn through the timber, and no lingering sunset.

A man emerged from the doorway of the large hall and pitched a basinful of water into the grass, then ducked back inside. A slender tendril of fragrant cedar smoke issued from one of the chimneys. Not another soul stirred in the camp, and Thomas urged the gelding forward, taking the shortest route across the meadow.

When he dismounted in front of the mess hall, he took a moment to turn and survey the camp again. Thomas recalled some meadows in Connecticut that had smelled divine—so sweet that they begged a man to lie down and stretch out, listening to the symphony of bees and birds. This meadow, home to a hundred hard working, hard playing loggers, wasn't one of those. It stank.

The privy stank. The mildew on the canvas walls stank. What should have been a bubbly, happy little brook stank in half a dozen ponds daisy-chained the length of the clearing.

"You lost, friend?"

Thomas turned and found he was being surveyed from head to toe by a stout fellow. His enormous beard perfectly mirrored the thickets of salt and pepper hair on top of his head. The usual woolen trousers and the gray top of his long johns were much mended, touched here and there with interesting stains or remnants from the kitchen.

"Good afternoon," Thomas said. "I'm Dr. Parks, from the village."

"Yep." The man retreated into the hall, apparently assuming Thomas would follow. The physician did, but stopped just inside the door. Fifty feet long, twenty wide, the structure included only two windows high on the south end, neither with glass. Twenty-four slab wood tables with benches were arranged in two rows, and the end of each was graced with a stack of tin plates and a scattering of forks and spoons, as if in tribute to the possibility of organization. Half a dozen oil lanterns hung from ceiling cross-beams.

At the opposite end of the hall, an enormous iron cook stove presided with a high table beside it. Thomas could feel the heat rolling from the cast iron stove, the cedar snapping in one of the chambers. At the table, a young man worked, and when his eyes adjusted to the dim light, Thomas saw that the lad, perhaps fourteen at most, was working his way through an enormous colander of onions, mincing them into another blackened pot. His left arm was withered, with an elbow that didn't work properly. The arm was useful enough that the clawed left hand could hold the onion steady for the flailing knife.

"You want coffee?"

"No thanks, sir. Your name?"

"Name's Lawrence."

"Actually, sir, I was looking for a young fellow. Buddy Huckla? I was wondering if you could tell me which cabin was his."

Lawrence stepped back to the doorway, and as Thomas drew closer, he almost recoiled from the man's odor—an amazing amalgam of kitchen and foul hygiene. Food poisoning was not a distant possibility.

"See the second bath?" the cook asked, pointing at the puddles where the stream had been dammed. "Just up yonder from it is where he stays."

'Up yonder' could have been any of a dozen tents. "You mean the one right by the creek?"

"Yep. He ain't there right now, though. He come back from town all distressed, and after I helped him take off that damn thing he was wearing on his hand, well, he went out to where the flume crew is workin'. That's where he's supposed to be."

"He took it off? The bandages and splint?"

"Yep."

Thomas stared at the cook in wonder. "Whatever did he—" He bit it off. "Have you seen his partner? Ben Sitzberger?"

"Saw him early this morning. Not since then." The cook turned away from the door. "I ain't looked, though. What do you want with him?" The man's large brown eyes, surrounded by abundant wrinkles that hinted at laughter when called for, gazed at Thomas without much interest.

"Early this morning, when he brought Mr. Huckla to the clinic, it appeared that he was ill. Huckla suggested it was something he ate."

"Well, that ain't strange."

"I thought to check on him while I was here. And on Mr. Huckla at the same time."

"They're out in the timber someplace. Most likely at the flume. Other than that, I couldn't tell you." Lawrence wiped his beard, drawing it together before releasing it like a tangled spring. "They'll all be here at dark, if that's what you want."

"Perhaps you can direct me."

"Direct you?"

"To the flume project. If it's not far, I'd like to visit the construction."

Lawrence frowned, and stepped to the doorway again. "Nice horse you got yourself, Doc." Thomas couldn't tell if the man was assessing the animal as transportation or for victuals. "You see right off that way? Right past Larson's tent, there. The last one? Well, right there's a trail big enough for an army. Just get on there and it'll take you where you want to go."

"How far is it?"

"Don't know. I suppose one, maybe two miles. Ain't never measured it." He turned back inside. "I got bread risin', so if you get lost, just ask somebody." Lawrence plodded off toward the stove, scratching the small of his back as he walked. Thomas shook off the nauseating image of those hands kneading the bread dough.

"Thank you, sir," Thomas muttered. He turned to his horse. "You probably know right where it is, don't you, nice horse." The gelding's ears wandered in opposite directions, and the physician laughed.

Lawrence was perfectly correct, however. The trail had been beaten into a fair road by the ebb and flow of a hundred loggers, and Thomas made rapid progress. After half an hour, he reached the bluff. In the distance, he could see the great billows of fog rising off the inlet, but the beehive of activity below him drew his astonished attention.

The skid troughs snaked here and there out of the timber, sometimes just gouges in the hillside, sometimes logs laid side by side, sometimes a corduroy roadway for mules or oxen. The wasteland where the harvest had been completed reminded Thomas of photographs taken of a Civil War battlefield after a week of unrelenting bombardment.

The flume below was nothing more than an enormous gutter, like one of the eaves troughs on his father's Connecticut house. The structure originated at a two acre holding pond, fed by waters from three creeks that spilled into the valley. Sometimes supported by sturdy trestles, sometimes running on grade, the flume was the simplest of structures—bottom planks assembled to form a shallow V, heavy timbers rising to form the sides.

The boom of logs, or what Thomas had learned the loggers were fond of referring to as 'sticks', floated in the pond, waiting their turn to be nudged through the sluice gate at the end of the pond for their ride down the flume. The sluice gate blocked the logs, but not much of the water overflow from the three eager streams. The flume, nearly full, dripped and leaked its entire length.

Far off on a hillside, he heard shouts and then the protracted roar of one of the spruce or fir giants crashing to earth. Rather than riding into the middle of the confusion, he nudged the gelding down the slope toward the holding pond where, standing near the sluice gate, he saw two men who appeared to be doing nothing other than relaxing in the sun.

One of them, his hat pushed back on his head and a big grin on his face in response to some personal joke, was Buddy Huckla. And even as Thomas watched, the man bent over the gate and slid his bandaged hand into the water.

Chapter Ten

"Hullo!" Huckla called out as Thomas approached. "You lost, Doc?"

Thomas didn't say anything until he had ridden right up to the sluice gate. The gelding swung his head down and gulped water. Thomas sat quietly, regarding Huckla and his friend, a man whose left hand was missing all the fingers at the first joint. Huckla's bright grin widened. "Damn, you got a day for it. Ain't it something?"

"Yes, it is," Thomas said. "Do you remember nurse Auerbach's instructions, Mr. Huckla? And my instructions?" A momentary look of puzzlement slipped across the young man's face. "I thought we had been quite clear when we asked you to keep that hand clean and dry."

Huckla pulled the bandaged hand out of the water. "This cold water feels mighty good," he said, "Don't see how that can hurt."

Thomas saw that the original wrappings and splint had been replaced by what appeared to be a portion of an old shirt. He looked out across the storage pond and sighed.

"Feels good, must be good," Huckla chirped. "That's what my ma always said, bless her soul."

What kind of logic was this, Thomas wondered, that replaced a perfectly good and perfectly *clean* splint and bandage with filthy flannel? Why was it necessary to look as if tending the injury was such a trifle?

The sun glinted off the water, and for a moment he had visions of the swarm of interesting things lurking there, waiting to examine Huckla's hand more closely. It would be instructive to collect a vial of the water and examine it under the microscope.

"It's all right," Huckla said, seeing the doctor's vexed expression. "It don't hurt none, Doc."

"It will, my friend," Thomas replied. "And when it does, it is going to be much more difficult—and more painful—to treat. I hope you appreciate that." The open, engaging expression on Huckla's face hinted that he didn't appreciate his danger at all. Thomas shifted in the saddle, surveying the pond and the gate structure.

"So, what happens here?"

"Well, me and Barney here are waitin'," Huckla offered. "It's a hell of a thing to be paid for just waitin' in the sun, don't you think?"

"And for what do you wait?"

Huckla withdrew his hand from the soak and stood up. "See, all them logs are comin' into the pond, here. And when the boss man is ready to start sendin' logs down the flume, all them logs you see floatin' there will go through this gate here. Me and Barney count 'em when that happens. We both know our numbers pretty good. End of the day, we write it all down." He shrugged. "Don't know just *why* we do all that, but that's what Paul Bertram wants, so that's what he gets."

"What all happened to Sonny Malone?" Barney asked. "I heard he got hung up, and that he's down at your place."

"We have him in the clinic, yes."

"He going to make it?"

"We hope so." Apparently he didn't feign sufficient optimism, because Barney's eyebrow lifted skeptically.

"Not likely, though, eh?"

"Probably not likely." He stood in the stirrups, stretching. Fats took a last guzzle, sensing that something was about to be asked of him. "The famous flume," he said. He looked down the serpentine path that the wooden flume traced through the timber, sweeping in graceful curves to avoid terrain.

"Somethin', ain't it," Huckla said. "I'm bettin' a man could straddle one of them sticks and ride it all the way down to the chute."

"Another dollar bet?" Thomas offered.

"I'm thinkin' on it." Despite the wide, silly grin, Buddy Huckla was completely serious.

Barney nodded downhill. "You follow it along for about two miles…that about right, Buddy? Follow it along and you'll come to the headlands where they got the chute project. And *that's* something to see, Doc." He angled his hand downward sharply. "Logs tip from the flume into the chute. Seventy-five degrees down for sixteen hundred and seventy-nine feet. Logs run so fast they smoke. That's what the engineers say."

"Bet a man could ride that, too," Huckla said.

"Make it for more than a dollar if you do, Mr. Huckla. Gentlemen, I'll be on my way. I don't look forward to riding off the bluff after dark."

"Good luck to you, Doc," Barney said. "Down about a mile, you'll come to a log deck, where they're workin' right along the flume. Don't go gettin' in the way. One of them sticks will smash you flat. Can't have that." He nodded at Fats, who was dozing, eyelids at half mast. "Smart horse you got yourself there."

"He doesn't spook," Thomas said. "He gives me time to think."

"Nothin' wrong in that. Look, there's a photographer workin' down at the chute this afternoon. You'll see him, too. Everybody wants their pichure took. Maybe he'll get you, too."

"Obliged," Thomas said.

"You'll find Bertram down there, if you was lookin' for him. Stick close to the trail along the flume. That's the safest way."

"I shall." Fats started to saunter down the slick slope under the flume's trestle, and Thomas called back to Buddy Huckla, "Someone will be at the clinic this evening, Mr. Huckla, should you decide to have the hand looked at."

"It's fine, Doc. You done good with it."

As he rode down hill with the flume now above his head, Thomas could hear the gentle gurgle of the water and the steady drizzle of leaks pattering on the duff under the trestle. When the sluice gates were open, the rampaging water and logs would be a sight…and he could imagine Buddy Huckla trying to find hand and toe holds on the slick spruce giant as it careened through the flume.

In a mile, the valley first narrowed and then opened up. He could see the log deck, an area where the tract of timber was close enough to the flume that logs could be dragged there by steam donkey and cable on simple skid trails.

Up above, another spar towered, rigged with cables that ran every which way on the slope. The loggers were as ants, swarming through the timber and on the hillside. For some moments, Thomas watched in fascination, then urged Fats onward. The valley narrowed again, the trees thinned, and he could see the brilliant horizon far ahead. As he rode toward the headland, it was with a sense of relief, a sense of release from the dark, rank timber behind him. Below, the waters of Jefferson Inlet were cut by half a dozen ships, and he could see far to the north, almost to the Strait of Juan de Fuca.

To the south, looking like a small wart on the end of the hook of land, Bert Schmidt's sawmill dominated the inlet, smoke from the chip burner and the various boilers a thick plume that drifted across the spit. A bluff domed just high enough to hide Port McKinney from view. Thomas started to turn away, then stopped.

He stood tall in the stirrups, squinting against the bright sun. Bert and Carlotta Schmidt lived in a comfortable two-story home on a rise above the mill.

From where Thomas sat on his horse, he could see that the plume of bluish-white smoke from the various burners drifted east, out over the water. But there were times, he assumed, when the plume drifted elsewhere…or hung over the quiet countryside like a flannel blanket. A nose not numbed to the aroma—the evergreen bouquet—would be able to identify every species of wood burned.

"Of course," Thomas said aloud. When Carlotta Schmidt had journeyed to Portland, her sinuses had finally enjoyed blissful relief from the continual smoke, flushed out by fresh sea breezes. Back home, it was only a matter of time before she was assaulted anew.

Thomas left the headland and returned to the flume, following a long curve as it skirted a series of rock ledges. He did not see the chute at first, but did see a dozen men gathered near the last sluice gate in the flume. Behind the men towered an enormous deck of logs, hundreds of sticks harvested, Thomas supposed, near at hand during the construction. In the flume itself, he could see a string of logs, nose to tail, pushing against the gate like cattle waiting to enter a pasture.

Three of the men stood on a mammoth log, so huge that Thomas couldn't imagine it floating down the flume like a great, cylindrical railroad car. The rest of the crew was gathered here and there in an interesting group as a slight fellow behind a bulky tripod and camera orchestrated them.

Dismounting, Thomas led Fats the last few yards, waiting patiently while the photographer took what appeared to be his final exposure. Finished at last, the photographer tipped his cap, and the men climbed down. One of them Thomas recognized immediately. Paul Bertram said something to the photographer, and then made his way toward the young physician.

"You're out and about." Bertram extended his hand.

"A perfect afternoon," Thomas replied.

"Givin' Kinsey here a show." The foreman nodded at the photographer. "Sometimes I think we got us more photographers in the timber than we do loggers. Could have used him this mornin', don't you think?" He started to smile, then turned serious. "You brung word about Sonny?"

"The word is not good," Thomas said. "If he survives the day, I'll be surprised. The nurses are with him constantly, but there's nothing to be done. The brain has been concussed, and there is nothing to be done for that."

"Just too damn bad."

"I rode out first to visit the camp…I was interested to chat with Buddy Huckla."

"Useless as tits on a boar hog," Bertram muttered.

"The surgery on his hand was successful, but he's in the process of undoing all the good work." Thomas waved a hand up-flume. "He's at the holding pond, soaking his hand in the filthy water."

"What did you want him to do?"

The question surprised Thomas, but he could see that the timber foreman was genuine in his curiosity.

"To keep it dry and clean, for one," the physician said. "It was splinted, and should stay that way until the bones and ligaments have a fair chance to mend. As it is, the young man is working as hard as he can to win an amputation—if infection doesn't kill him first."

Bertram frowned and looked off into the distance. "Well, he's going to do what he's going to do. I put him on count to keep him out of trouble. He'll be all right. Come on," Bertram said, beckoning. "Tie off that horse and let me show you." He led Thomas to the precipice. Beyond the last flume gate, a simple three log trough, one log contoured as the bottom, larger logs laid along the sides, plummeted with the terrain, a frightening drop to the water far below.

"You ready now?" the foreman shouted, and the photographer waved a hand. "Don't know how he's going to do it, but that's his business." The photographer had moved his bulky camera to the very lip of the bluff.

Thomas watched in astonishment as the iron sluice valve was spun open with a burst of escaping water. Loggers with heavy cant hooks urged the mammoth log along in its own gush of water. It floated until its weight tipped into the chute, and then gravity took over. With a howl of its own, the log shot away, accelerating wildly on the steep initial section, its passage slicked by the spray of water. One after another, logs tipped into the chute.

He hadn't counted the seconds, but the logs became a smoking blur, and seconds later smashed into the inlet far below, sending geysers of water high into the air. By the time they hit the water, the multi-ton logs were but tiny, black dashes against the exploding water. What the camera could record was a mystery to Thomas. Certainly nothing was holding still for the sensitive film.

"There's been talk," Bertram explained, "that you could ride a log down the flume. I hear that every day. And you know, someday some crazy youngster with more nerve than brains is going to try it."

"We can hope not," Thomas said.

Bertram adopted a thoughtful stance, one hand on his bristly jaw. "You know, a man might save himself a hell of a long hike to town by hookin' a ride down the chute. I hear a man in the Klamath tried it on the Pokagama, longer'n this." Bertram grinned at his own jest. "Schoolyard dares, Doc. That's the way I figure it. These are good boys. Work hard, play hard. Sometimes drink too much." He shrugged.

"I'm planning to talk to Mr. Schmidt about the possibility of a telephone up on the lease."

Bertram's expression went blank. "How's that?"

"I've given it a lot of thought. If we had a central location up here on the lease where a ring could summon help...imagine the time to be saved."

"A telephone..."

"Exactly. The cities have exchanges now. Both Seattle and Tacoma, and more coming every day. I spoke with an engineer from the company just a few weeks ago. It would be possible."

"I've heard of 'em," Bertram said. "Don't give it much account. You're sayin' that a man gets himself hurt somehow, and we find this telephone?"

"Exactly. In fact, this wonderful chute gives us a route up the headland for the wires. How hard could it be to run poles right up the route cleared for the chute? Much of the work has already been done."

"Somebody gets hurt, we just take care of 'em here, or find a way into town," Bertram said. "You know that."

"And that's what kills more often than not."

"You think so?"

"I do. Most certainly I do."

"Huh. The telephone wouldn't have done Sonny Malone a damn bit of good."

"Not that particular case, but useful for other things as well, I should think. Mr. Schmidt requires a fair accounting of the logs that leave the headlands, does he not? Huckla is proud to be counting, back at the pond."

"Schmidt's got himself some new accountants," Bertram said. "Always countin' things. That's what they do. Number of logs that leave the timber, number into the chute, number down at the inlet. Number at the mill. Numbers, numbers, numbers."

"Well, then. The mill would not have to wait for that information. The telephone could make short work of such."

Bertram shook his head slowly. "Used to be a man went into the woods with an axe and a cross-cut, and earned his way one tree at a time. Now we got to count this, and count that." He grimaced. "Anyways, you do what you got to do, Doc." He pointed to the north. "Don't know how you came up the hill, but you cut off that way a bit and you'll find the lease trail. Take you down to the inlet road. That's the way your driver come up earlier. Be easier going."

Thomas accepted the offered hand. "It appeared that Huckla's companion was feeling poorly this morning," he said. "Sitzberger? He's working now?"

"Suppose he is, but I couldn't put my finger on just where right at the moment." He turned at the waist, watching the flume crew work the sticks through the chute. "The kid workin' the pig there," he nodded at the last log in the chain, "that's Todd Delaney. He shares the tent with Sitzy. He'd know, if you wanted to ask."

"Well, if he feels poorly enough, he'll seek us out," Thomas allowed.

"'Spect he would be. That your man?" He pointed behind Thomas. Sure enough, a horse and rider had emerged from the timber, cutting across the open ground toward the flume. Thomas first recognized the fisherman's knit cap, and then the tight, collected posture in the saddle. Howard Deaton didn't allow the mare to slacken pace until horse and rider were nearly upon them. The mare danced to a halt, blowing hard.

"Doc, sure do needja down in town."

"I was just on my way. What is it?"

"It's Mrs. Parks, Doc."

Thomas' heart leaped. "She's fallen?"

Deaton had already turned the mare toward Port McKinney, and she danced sideways at the delay.

"She's…she's had the baby, Doc."

"My God." The mare's excitement had awakened the gelding, and Bertram caught the bridle even as Thomas stabbed a boot into the stirrup.

"You watch yourself," the timber foreman said, but Thomas had already given the heel to the gelding.

Howard Deaton and his mare certainly knew the way, and Thomas urged Fats to keep pace. Myriad questions flooded Thomas' mind, but he was caught, with nothing for it but to ride as he'd never ridden before. Reaching the village, Deaton chose one of the quiet back alleys of Port McKinney, and in a moment they burst onto Gamble Street, passing the clinic in a burst of hurled mud.

Deaton slipped off the mare and grabbed the gelding's reins as Thomas dismounted. His fingers felt like sausages as he fought with the ties that secured his medical bag and then he was flying up the front porch steps of 101 Lincoln.

Chapter Eleven

"Congratulations, old fellow," Dr. Lucius Hardy said. He put a hand on Thomas' chest, effectively blocking his way for just a moment. "You have a healthy son."

"Alvi…"

"As perfect a delivery as I've ever seen." Thomas slipped past, but as he did so, Hardy added, "Go easy, Doctor."

The room was flooded with soft light, only the fine inner curtain drawn over the window.

"She is asleep," a woman's voice said. Thomas stopped at the foot of the bed as a short, powerful figure rose from the bentwood straight chair.

"Mrs…"

"Mrs. McLaughlin." Thomas could see that the folds of her voluminous white dress and apron were blood and fluid stained. "Yes, we've met on occasion." Her voice, almost gruff, was barely a whisper. "Your wife summoned me this morning."

"I…"

Why hadn't *he* been summoned, Thomas thought in a whirl of conflictions. Those conflictions were written clearly all over his face, and Mrs. McLaughlin reached out a hand and touched Thomas' forearm. "I know."

"You *know?* What do you mean, you *know.* I talked with my wife at luncheon this very day. The child is…the child is…" and Thomas could think of nothing further to say. Alvi must have known that birth was imminent, and yet had said nothing to him. Still, such things sometimes came as a surprise, he'd been told. One moment all is fine, the next moment, the water breaks and the infant demands to meet the world.

"Your son is perfectly formed in every way," the mid-wife said with considerable satisfaction. "And he sleeps like a perfect angel."

Holding his breath, Thomas drew near. Alvi's serene expression showed no traces of the agonies that Thomas had come to associate with childbirth. His wife was so beautiful, lying against fresh white linens, her reddish-blond hair fanned around her head. The infant, in fine white muslin, lay in the crook of one arm, and Mrs. McLaughlin drew back a corner. The infant was indeed perfect, a little wash of black hair on the front of his skull.

"They must both sleep," the mid-wife said. She touched Thomas' hand to intercept as he reached out to stroke the infant's forehead. He waited for her to withdraw her hand, then with a feather-light brush of his fingers, watched the wisp of hair rise and then settle on the almost transparent skin.

"The birth was without complication, and the little boy was most prompt in joining the world. One of the quickest deliveries I've ever seen. But even so, rest is the best thing."

Thomas stood by the bed, at a loss. He surveyed the room, and saw the minimal trappings of labor—the small cart with its twin pans, an abundance of clean towels that apparently had not been used, the black rubber pad folded in a bucket on the table's lower shelf. And he had not been present.

"How has the episiotomy been managed?" he asked finally, the only thing he could think of, so flummoxed was he by this turn of events.

"The smallest amount of tearing," the mid-wife assured. "Nothing that might warrant even a single suture."

"And injury to the pelvic floor?"

"Doctor, there was none." Mrs. McLaughlin folded her hands in self-satisfaction.

"But the infant weighs…" Thomas could see the outline through the muslin, and was certain that the boy surely totaled six or seven pounds.

"A healthy, full-term infant," the mid-wife said. "What more could you wish?" *Full-term*. The impossibility of the words echoed in his brain.

"Assuredly," Thomas said, and for a moment was sure that he would pass out on the spot. "Bleeding…" He said the single word with his eyes closed, waiting for the world to steady on its axis.

"Little. And now fully subsided."

Thomas could think of nothing else to say, so Mrs. McLaughlin said it for him.

"You have a healthy wife, and a fine, healthy baby boy. You should be most pleased."

"I am…I am."

To her credit, Rachel McLaughlin did not laugh, even though Thomas was certain that she understood his consternation. She remained tactfully silent, letting the obvious speak for itself, allowing Thomas' thoughts to jumble unhindered. He started to reach out toward Alvi's right hand, curled in complete relaxation on the coverlet, but he stopped.

"She is a mountain for seven," Lucius Hardy had said.

"And how could I…" he started to whisper to himself, but stopped. "When did my wife first contact you, Mrs. McLaughlin?"

"That would be yesterday afternoon," the woman said.

"She informed you that her labor was imminent?"

"She did so." Mrs. McLaughlin leaned closer and lowered her voice until Thomas had to watch her lips to be certain. "She said that she wanted me to know, since you are so often called for emergency surgeries, Doctor. Just to be prepared." That made eminent sense, of course, and Thomas could fully imagine Alvi, in her own thoughtful way, making such a preparation.

"And today?"

"Shortly after lunch, Miss James came to fetch me."

"Gerti did?"

"Yes. It is my understanding that you had just gone up on the headlands. The moment the event seemed certain, Alvi requested that Mr. Deaton find you."

He could feel the hot flush on his cheeks. "And did it occur to you that I would certainly *not* have ridden *anywhere* had I known the birth was imminent?" He sounded petulant, he knew—but in large part it was directed at himself. As a physician he should have *known* that birth was near and not two months distant. Yet he could not shake the revelation that so much had apparently transpired behind his back. Part of him said that he had no wish to argue with this capable mid-wife, but he couldn't stop himself.

"I wouldn't presume to say, but I would suppose so, Doctor." She leaned just heavily enough on the final word that her meaning was clear. "And you know perfectly well that your wife is a woman of strong convictions."

"That's the truth," Thomas said, and let it go at that. Mrs. McLaughlin was right, of course. Alvi's independence was part of the young woman's charm. She did not ask permission to take walks, or have the old dog in the house, or arrive at the clinic whenever she pleased, or talk with patients unannounced.

He leaned over and touched his lips to Alvi's forehead, just a slight brush. "And we all love her for it, don't we." He straightened up and nodded at the mid-wife. "Thank you, Mrs. McLaughlin. I am forever in your debt." Her wide face split in a smile.

"I will attend her until evening," she announced. "And then I shall return in the morning. But there is no cause for any concern. Not even a little bit."

"Thank you." He did not bother to remind the woman that there were now two physicians in the house. Had he done so, he thought, her laughter might awaken both infant and mother. "Was it you who summoned Dr. Hardy?"

This time, Mrs. McLaughlin looked uncomfortable. "I don't know the gentleman, sir," she said. "But it is my understanding that Mr. Deaton informed the doctor before Howard rode out into the timber to fetch you."

"And Dr. Hardy assisted you?"

"Well…" she began thoughtfully, "he offered one or two notions that were certainly helpful." She looked pleased that she had managed to be so tactful.

Chapter Twelve

"What am I to do?" Thomas asked, and for a long time, Dr. Lucius Hardy let the question hang, as if unsure that the younger man actually wanted an answer. The evening was splendid, a few clouds scattered on the horizon, just enough to spread the final burst of sunlight. Thomas sat in one of the wicker rockers on the porch of 101 Lincoln, Prince curled nearby, watching. The dog had studiously ignored Hardy, instead positioning himself so that he could see through the front door to the interior of the house. Thomas knew that the animal was waiting for Alvi's appearance, fretful that he hadn't been allowed in the bedroom.

"You knew, didn't you?" Thomas prompted. *What's done is done,* he kept telling himself.

"I hadn't examined your wife before I was summoned," Hardy replied carefully. The physician's large hands were quiet in his lap, wrapped around a fragile tea cup. He had refused an offer of brandy, but Thomas had served himself a generous portion. Hardy held up a hand. "I speak as an outsider, of course, and that's easy to do. But I see a certain priority here. The child has arrived, he's safe and healthy, as is your wife."

"He cannot be mine." It was the first time Thomas had actually given voice to the thought, and he was surprised at the awful lump that it produced in his throat. His voice dropped to a whisper as he repeated himself. "He cannot be mine."

Hardy regarded his cooling tea. "How old is your wife, Thomas?"

"She will be twenty-seven in July."

"And what month did you arrive in Port McKinney?"

"My ship docked on September twelfth." He frowned and tried to clear his throat again. "Almost exactly eight months ago."

The corners of Hardy's eyes crinkled, but it was sympathy that prompted his amusement, not mockery. "You fell for Alvina immediately, I would say."

"Yes. I like to think that it was mutual."

"And you thought that the child was conceived a month or so after your arrival? That's why you so firmly believed that she was seven months along?"

"One month, perhaps two."

"Obviously not, then. I mean no insult, but Alvina was pregnant with this child some weeks before your arrival."

"Why didn't she tell me?"

"And at first, why should she? Let me play the devil's advocate with you, Thomas. Please be patient with me." Hardy stretched his legs out, and reached down to place the cup and saucer on the porch deck. "An attractive young woman, then twenty-six years old—why should she *not* have relationships? At the risk of seeming crude, my word. At twenty-six, many women—*most* women—have an entire family under their roof."

"I suppose…"

"You saw no signs during the long days you spent recuperating in this wonderful house? No one coming courting? No obvious interest in another's presence?"

"There were *some* signs that she enjoyed a friendship with her father's assistant. He shared the dinner table with the Haines family on a regular basis."

"A *friendship?*"

"Yes. That's what I thought. Even more than cordial."

Hardy chuckled softly. "Ah, Thomas. You're wonderful."

"I feel I should be offended by that."

"Please, no. At the risk of sounding like a court's advocate, let me ask this. At some later time, after the two of you had become intimate, did you *ask* her about this friendship?"

"No, of course not. On what grounds should I do that? What she did before my arrival is hardly my concern. Even *after* my arrival, I might add. But then her father passed away, and that consumed us both. The bond between us grew rapidly. And the gentleman in question had left Port McKinney shortly thereafter. Alvina seemed entirely content in my company. There seemed to be nothing between Alvina and the gentleman in question at that point, no lingering attachment, if that's the word. When it became obvious that she was with child, sometime around Christmas, I think, we were both delighted. *Both* of us. And I just assumed."

"So there you are."

"I don't know *where* I am."

"Your wife has been entirely faithful to you, Thomas. That seems obvious to me, for what my opinion is worth. *You*, somewhat blinded by love, have assumed that the child was yours all this time, despite…and I mean no offense, my dear chap…the rather obvious signs that Alvina was somewhat further along in her pregnancy than *you* suspected."

"Somewhat," Thomas said wryly. "I don't understand any of it. I don't understand why she didn't tell me when she first suspected her pregnancy."

"Put yourself in her place, Thomas. If she *had* told you, would it have affected your attraction to her?"

"I don't know. I really don't know. I would hope not."

Hardy pursed his lips. "Well, I doubt it. I say that as a newcomer, based on first impressions only. But my impression is a strong one. She would not have wanted to *lie* to you. You *do* love your wife, do you not?"

"Yes. Unequivocally."

"Then we have answered the question." Hardy leaned forward, his hands clasped over his belly. "We cannot presume to know what went through her mind when she knew for certain. So recently bereft of her father, she may have feared that you would turn from her. She may have thought that, with many months before term, that situations could change, making such an announcement unnecessary. Tragic or not, much can happen between conception and birth. It's a long nine months."

"She should have told me," Thomas insisted.

"Perhaps so. Perhaps so. We aren't privy to your wife's rationale. But again, at some risk, may I gently add that you, as a physician keen of eye and understanding in so many *other* respects, should have known. But there you are, Thomas. I can assure you, given the mother's natural propensities, that Alvina loves this perfect infant with all of her heart—and will share that love with you, my lucky fellow. It appears that the actual father is out of the equation, so to speak. He has moved far away?"

"Yes. San Francisco."

"And not apt to return to Port McKinney?"

Thomas laughed dryly. "Most likely not. There were some legal issues that would face him should he do so."

Hardy's eyebrows shot up. "An interesting fellow, it would seem. So, you see, it's up to you. I…" Hardy started to say something else, but stopped as footsteps could be heard coming down the stairs and then advancing across the wooden floor to the front door.

Prince's bedraggled ears perked but otherwise the dog remained motionless.

Thomas turned to see Gert James standing in the doorway. "Doctor, Alvina wishes to speak with you." Gert's manner was so stiff, so entirely proper, that Thomas experienced yet another lump in his throat.

She knows as well, he thought, looking at the housekeeper's wonderfully hatchet-like face. *Well, of course she does.* "Will you excuse me?" he said to Hardy, and the other physician picked up his cup and rose to his feet.

"I shall stroll back down to my grand suite at the clinic," he said. "Should you need me, there I'll be. I took the liberty of borrowing a copy of your father-in-law's book to browse through. It appears to be a fascinating tome, this *Advisor.*" He handed the cup and saucer to Gert. "And my thanks to you for the most wonderful dinner that I've enjoyed in many years." She accepted the cup and saucer without a gracious nod.

"May I ask that tomorrow morning at nine, you join me in my conversation with Carlotta Schmidt and her husband?" Thomas asked. "I think that will contribute to their peace of mind. By then, perhaps I will be able to think in something other than a muddle."

"Indeed I would. Thank you for the confidence. And please… will you pass on my very best wishes to your wife? If medical assistance is required, you know where I am." He chuckled. "The Presidential Suite atop the clinic. And I still have the pleasure of meeting the rest of the nursing staff this evening. Mrs. Crowell? Miss…"

"Stephens."

"Ah, yes. And I'll look in on both the child and Mr. Malone from time to time."

Thomas paused in the doorway and extended his hand to Lucius Hardy. "Thank you for your counsel, Lucius. And thank you for dealing with Mrs. McLaughlin. I appreciate your being there."

The physician ducked his head. "For whatever it's worth, my friend, you're very welcome. Mrs. McLaughlin is a force of nature. We're fortunate to have her in the community." As Hardy said that, Thomas saw a softening on Gert James' face, a warmth in the eyes when she looked at Lucius Hardy. "Good night, then. Miss James, good night to you, too. What an adventure to have a child in the house again, eh?"

Gert James brightened a bit more. "Not a moment's peace and quiet, I fear." She managed a smile, and the expression reminded Thomas of a cracked porcelain cup. She stuck out a well-worn shoe, moving to block Prince's determined advance over the threshold. "You don't need to come inside, you wretched beast," she said.

"Oh, yes," Thomas said. "For a few minutes, it will be fine."

"Honestly," Gert muttered, her generalized comment on most things of which she disapproved. "Mrs. McLaughlin said that she will call at nine o'clock this evening for a few minutes."

"That will be fine," Thomas said. "Unless Alvi is asleep, in which case we shall not awaken her."

Gert nodded and closed the front door firmly, glancing after Prince, who had already started up the long stairway, one slow, careful step at a time as if he were a hundred years old. "You watch him," she added sharply. "There's never any way to predict how such a monster will behave around infants."

"He'll be fine," Thomas said. He also took the stairs methodically, more to give himself time to think than as a means of favoring his now fully-healed hip.

The master bedroom's drapes and curtains were drawn wide to let in the soft glow of late evening. Alvi looked lovely as she cradled the infant, and even from across the room, Thomas could hear the tiny, greedy sounds of the baby's feeding. The physician drew closer, astonished at the color blooming across his wife's cheeks.

"You are astonishingly beautiful," he said softly. The dog's tail thumped the side of the bed, and Thomas frowned at him. "She's fine, hound. Find a quiet corner now."

"He frets," Alvi said.

"Yes, he does. But we don't need dog hair fretted all over the room." Thomas drew the infant's blanket down a trifle. The baby's eyes were closed, one tiny hand clutching breast as he suckled, the other wadded up under his chin. "You're beautiful, and so is he."

"You were in earlier," Alvi whispered. "You should have awakened me."

"Mrs. McLaughlin would have taken an axe to me had I done so. She leaves word that she will be back at exactly nine this evening to check on you. I told Gert that if you're asleep at the time, you are not to be disturbed."

"I shall sleep *a lot,*" Alvi said with a sigh. "And if we're lucky, so will he. He's even decided that he can eat while asleep. Such talent."

Thomas touched his little finger to the curled hand, and smiled with delight at the tiny grip. "How much did he weigh?"

"Just under eight pounds."

"My word."

"And you know, he must have a name other than '*he.*'"

Thomas sat down on the bed beside Alvi, and she clamped his hand in a ferocious grip with her free right hand.

"You're upset," she said.

"No."

"And now, you're fibbing. I can see it in your eyes, Dr. Thomas. I can always tell when you are cast adrift."

He covered her hand with both of his. "Will you explain to me why you didn't tell me from the very beginning?"

She didn't reply for a very long moment. "May I tell you right now what is the most important thing to me, Dr. Thomas?" He smiled at her perpetual use of her private nickname for him, one that she had settled on the first time she'd spoken with him—while standing at *his* bedside.

"I hope so."

"Twenty-five years from now, I want to be able to look at one of those wonderful framed photographs that will be standing on the mantle above the fireplace in the library," she said. "Perhaps we can hire the wonderfully adventurous Mr. Kinsey to produce it for us. It will show Dr. Thomas Parks," and she reached up to run her fingers through his thick locks, "touches of gray beginning to enhance his already distinguished appearance, his wife Alvina Haines Parks, perhaps a bit matronly by now in *her* appearance, and the fifteen Parks children arranged around us. One of them will be this child, and I want nothing more… *nothing* more…than for him to be a Parks, Dr. Thomas. That's what I want. That's the whole and substance of it."

For a moment he couldn't speak. His wife had presented the "whole and substance" of it in a way that brooked no misunderstanding. The baby shifted and gave his finger another squeeze, as if prompting him for an answer.

"Fifteen," Thomas said in wonder.

"That's in the *first* twenty-five years."

"I should have been here for his birth, Alvi."

"Bosh," Alvi said. "There is no way to predict such things. You know, in the past few months, several of the town's more adept gossips have made *sure* that I heard an endless litany of gruesome tales about the birth process. '*Why, when Millie Jones had* her *baby,*'" Alvi mimicked, "'*the labor went on for thirty hours!*' And so on. You can imagine, I'm sure. They made sure I heard *all* the tales."

"I can imagine."

"It's going to disappoint all the wagging tongues to hear that the arrival was so prompt and free of complications."

"I'm sure they'll find other things to wag about. I really don't care what they think."

"It gives me joy to hear that, Dr. Thomas. Let them wag. I know what *I* want, and I hope you do as well. I don't care what the wags say."

A loud thump drew Thomas' attention. Prince had allowed his remarkably bony, gangly carcass to slump to the floor, knees akimbo, front paws stretched out, head lowered to them, eyes sleepily fixed on the doorway.

"You won't be late tonight, I hope?" Alvi said.

"I have some reading that I must do for tomorrow," Thomas said. "The Schmidts are coming to the clinic to make arrangements for her surgery. If they decide to have it done here."

"Anything else would be unfortunate."

"Bertha Auerbach is in agreement with you."

"Then the Schmidts should heed her advice, Dr. Thomas. And yours." She squeezed his hand again. "I felt an immediate affection for Dr. Hardy. When he arrived, I was so taken with his manner. He could have been most impatient with Mrs. McLaughlin, you see. But he wasn't. He could have made an enemy of her, but he didn't. It is my belief that he understood her skills from the moment he met her. I hope he'll stay with us."

"As do I. I think we will make a good team, Alvi."

She drew in a deep breath, careful not to disturb the infant who had dozed off still affixed to her breast. She enjoyed an enormous yawn.

"He makes me sleepy just looking at him." She reached out and patted the bed gently. "Tonight."

"I'll be just across the hall," Thomas replied. "An instant away."

"Absolutely not," Alvi responded. "Too far away. The loneliness would be unbearable." She patted the bed again. "I shall move over a bit. I want you here. There's ample room, Dr. Thomas. For the three of us." She yawned again. "Bring your book up here. The light will not disturb us."

"Do you know what Mrs. McLaughlin is going to say about all this?" Thomas laughed.

"I love her to death, Dr. Thomas. But in this, I don't suppose I care one little bit what she says," Alvi said sweetly. "We have much to discuss, anyway. *He* should not awaken in the morning without a name. We must see to that."

"He'll awaken many times before then, demanding attention," Thomas observed. He stepped back a bit and almost planted a boot on the dog. "Let me take the beast outside for the night. Then I'll be back."

"He's fine where he is, don't you think?"

"You wish to smell damp dog all night?"

"I find him soothing," Alvi replied. "And now that I've had sufficient time to consider it, before you come to bed, would you inform Gert that I don't wish to see Mrs. McLaughlin until morning? I want the uninterrupted time with you and *him.*"

Thomas walked back down the stairs, enjoying the jolt of each tread, each shift of weight. It was hard to imagine how many of those steps there might be before the photographer squeezed the bulb, capturing the Parks family that now lived only in Alvi's imagination. *He,* the infant without a name, would be grown up, a young man in his twenties. Perhaps *he* would be in medical school. Perhaps *he* would be writing letters home about his adventures elsewhere on the globe.

Thomas reached the bottom of the stairway even as the decision coalesced in his mind. Never again would he bring up the issue of the infant's lineage. Little *He* would be a Parks. John Thomas Parks.

Chapter Thirteen

Thomas heard the bare feet padding up the stairs, and hoped that Gert James would pass by their bedroom door. That was a wasted hope, however. Gert did not venture to the second floor, did not disturb their privacy, without compelling reason. Her own suite was on the first floor on the northwest side of the house, and more often than not, it was she who answered knocks to the front door at all hours of the day or night.

And sure enough, the knuckles on the bedroom door were light and tentative. Thomas sat up, mindful of Alvi and the infant, both of whom had been quiet for the past hour.

He listened, wondering if he had imagined the sound, but in seconds the rapping came again. A hand slid under the covers, strong fingers gripping his flank.

"Go see, and then hurry back," Alvi whispered.

Loath to leave the bed, loath to give up the comforting smells of wife and newborn, Thomas swung his legs out from under the bedding. Below him in the dark, Prince huffed once, deep in the chest, enough to let them know that he was awake, and that he had recognized the footfalls on the stairway and then the knuckles on the door. Thomas had never known him to bark at a visitor. A rap on the door might prompt a ragged perk of the ears, but beyond that, the dog merely waited for developments. What would happen should someone burst in on them was, happily, untried.

Slipping into his robe, Thomas made his way to the door. Gert waited in the hallway, a small lantern in hand.

"What time is it?" Thomas asked, out of habit wanting to establish the *when* of things in his mind.

"Just after two," Gert whispered. She didn't apologize for disturbing him—in a house of physicians, there was nothing sacrosanct about any hour of the day. "Mother and child?"

"They're fine," he said abruptly, one hand still on the door knob. "What is it, Gert?"

"Mr. Deaton has brought word, Doctor. Dr. Hardy requests that you come to the clinic immediately."

"Dr. Hardy requests?"

"Yes. Mr. Deaton did not explain beyond that." She turned toward the stairway.

"I'll be dressed in a moment," Thomas said. "You need not concern yourself any further, Gert. Thank you." But Gert James ignored his suggestion and headed down the stairs toward the kitchen.

Thomas moved stealthily, not creaking a single floor board. Still, Alvi's soft whisper floated to him as he shrugged into his shirt and trousers.

"What is it?"

"I have no idea. Dr. Hardy is at the clinic and sends for me."

"He can't manage by himself?" She chuckled a little bubble of amusement. "I mean, after all, he has been a Port McKinney resident for some twelve hours now."

"I have no idea what he wants. But if he sends for me, then it's something that he or the nurses can't contend with." He bent over the bed, and Alvi's arm circled his neck. Her kiss was enough to tempt him to send word that Dr. Lucius Hardy was on his own. The baby fussed softly, and Alvi's reply was a brief wash of sweet breath on Thomas' face. She shifted position.

"If John Thomas continues to eat this much," she whispered, "he will be a giant."

"Is there anything you need? What may I bring you?"

"Yourself, Dr. Thomas." She kissed him again. "I want John Thomas to greet his first dawn with both of us under his command."

He left the bedroom, but Prince showed no inclination to get up. Even the attraction of his various canine mistresses around Port McKinney couldn't dislodge the dog from his assumed post.

Well aware of Thomas' habits by this time, Gert James managed to delay his departure for a few seconds. His heavy medical bag in one hand left one hand free for the inch-thick piece of warm bread, smeared richly with butter and huckleberry jam. He set the bag down and accepted a cup of coffee, taking thirty seconds as the fragrant warmth plunged all the way to his toes.

"You're a gem, Gert," he said, talking around a mouthful of bread and jam. "And by the way, we've named the child John Thomas. John Thomas Parks."

"You're a fortunate man, Doctor."

"Yes I am." He set down the empty cup and hefted his medical bag. "Alvi informs me that John Thomas is the first of a brood of fifteen." He grinned at the blush that touched Gert's cheeks. "Can you imagine this house with fifteen urchins?"

"Mrs. Jorgenson has thirteen," Gert allowed.

"I don't know her. Was Ralph of the broken wrist one of hers?"

"Her eldest."

"Ah. Well, with fifteen, we shall have to erect some tents out behind the house." He leaned forward and bussed Gert on the cheek, a familiarity that she both cherished and protested. "Thank you. I'll see what trouble Dr. Hardy has gotten himself into."

Thomas had hoped for a canopy of stars when he stepped outside, but the drizzle was fine and cold. Whether it was thick fog or thin rain, he couldn't tell. He pulled his hat down hard on his head, hunched his shoulders, and headed toward the clinic six blocks away, mindful of his footing on the slick boardwalk.

Every gas lamp on the clinic's first floor was blazing, the light pouring into the mud of Gamble Street. An oil lantern burned out in the barn, and Thomas could see the outline of one of the ambulances and the slightly stooped, slow-paced figure of Howard Deaton.

"Dr. Hardy is in your office, Dr. Parks," Adelaide Crowell said as he stepped through the clinic's front door. The nurse had appeared from the dispensary, and headed for the stairway without another word.

The door of his office was open, and the gas lamps burned high both there and in the small laboratory. That room, added during the clinic's renovation the past winter, was nothing more than a small addition with a bay window looking out on the empty field beside the clinic. Despite the dispensary's modest size, six gas sconces flared, shadows like a kaleidoscope about the room.

Dr. Lucius Hardy was in the process of screwing the door closures shut on the gas-fired incubator, and he turned as Thomas entered.

"Good morning," he said, but without his usual good humor. He glanced over at the small wall clock. "Rather an unpleasant interlude, and I find myself all thumbs in a strange dispensary. I spend so much time searching for things that I trip over myself."

He beckoned. "Come with me, will you?" He left the tiny room. Thomas followed as Hardy strode through the waiting room and then took the stairway up to the women's ward two steps at a time.

A single patient rested in the first bed on the right. In the back of the ward, the door to little Matilda Snyder's room was closed, but Thomas could see a faint sliver of light as if the gas light had been turned to its lowest flicker.

"This is Miss Lucy Levine," Hardy said. He stood by the woman's bedside, the tips of his fingers in his vest pockets. "She is twenty-three years old, and until only recently, in excellent health."

Nurse Crowell waited off to one side, her hands wrapped in her apron. Her gaze flitted from Miss Levine, who appeared ready to roll herself into a ball, to the two physicians.

"I know Miss Levine," Thomas said, but he was ready to argue that the patient in the bed could not be the bouncy, ebullient young lady with a comical cackle that reminded Thomas of a turkey's call. He had seen her from time to time at the Clarissa Hotel and at the clinic, including less than a month ago when he had extracted an abscessed molar for her. Although the young woman's eyes watched him in a singularly unfocused way, there was little life there. Her cheek bones stood out from a sunken face, her eyes dry and hollow. Thomas touched the back of his hand to her face and felt the cool, dry skin. He had expected to feel the rages of an interior furnace of infection, and was startled at the chill.

"What was her temperature the last time you checked, Miss Crowell?"

"Ninety-four degrees, doctor. That was at two on the clock."

"Ninety-four? You're certain?"

"Indeed so."

Miss Levine jerked, a feeble hiccough that recurred several times in rapid succession. An unintelligible murmur passed her lips. Thomas lifted away the light blanket, hesitated, then pulled it entirely off the narrow bed. The linen was foul over the rubber pad, but fresh elsewhere. Mrs. Crowell had been attentive, trying her best to keep up with the evacuations. She now used towels as one would diaper an infant.

The patient's legs worked feebly, and Thomas knelt to listen to the shrunken chest with his stethoscope. Even Lucy's breasts, normally so buxom and enticing for her logger clientele, were shriveled in on themselves, as if sucked to desiccation from within. Thomas closed his eyes and concentrated, hearing a laboring heart beat with a feeble second stroke. He tried to rest his hand on her abdomen, but the woman uttered a cry so piteous, so heart-rending, that Thomas flinched. Her gut was hard and he could see every striation between the muscles, the skin drum-tight and dusky.

What had been the body of a healthy, robust young woman now lay as a pathetic creature, all the life shrunken out of her.

Thomas was about to ask Nurse Crowell to remove the bedding when the patient evacuated again, so violently that it caught Thomas by surprise.

The nurse moved quickly with towels, and Thomas stood back, stunned. Perhaps two quarts of light straw colored fluid issued from the now frail body, looking as if someone had upended a cauldron of rice water.

"She looses fluid faster than it can replaced," Hardy said. "We're seeing dehydration to the point of desiccation. Look there," and he touched the corner of a listless eye. "She has not a tear remaining."

"She is able to hold water given by mouth?" Thomas could see that, although Lucy might be so ill that she couldn't bear to speak, she was *hearing* the conversation, and the fear in her eyes stabbed his heart. "Anything at all?"

"Not a drop," Mrs. Crowell said. A robust, determined woman with the heavy foot tread of a laborer, her face was grim. "The poor thing wastes before our eyes," she whispered. Thomas saw the pan on the next table, the black tubing and bulb coiled in the solution. He nodded at it, and Mrs. Crowell said, "Twice now, at least four liters. So little good."

"My God. Food poisoning, you think?" he asked, turning to Hardy. Bad fish could be lethal, he knew, but he had never seen a case as violent as this. "How did she come to us? To your attention, Lucius?"

"A friend of hers came to the clinic, and Mrs. Crowell roused Howard. He went and fetched the girl in the ambulance. And a good thing he did, too. That's been nearly three hours ago, now." He turned his back to the bed and lowered his voice. "We are losing ground, Thomas."

"You should have called me earlier. She is alone in this? No others are ill?"

"Apparently not, and frankly, that surprises me." Hardy turned and regarded the girl. "She managed to tell me that she was taken ill the night before." He consulted his watch. "Some thirty hours."

"Poisoned shell fish?" Thomas said, meaning it more as a thought than to be expressed aloud. Hardy inclined his head in skepticism, and Thomas answered for himself. "I see no respiratory spasms, and no paralysis. What else do we know that attacks so suddenly, Lucius? And with sub-grade temperature. She became ill Wednesday evening?"

"It would seem so. She complained of an odd malaise for several hours, but professed to no serious distress until the early morning hours yesterday. And in that short time…" He nodded at the girl's pathetic figure, and reached down to gently spread the light blanket across her upper body. "Come downstairs for a moment. But first…Mrs. Crowell?" Hardy asked, and she nodded. "I want that stripped linen out of this room. If it cannot be properly washed, then it must be burned in the incinerator." He turned to Thomas. "You have such?"

"Behind the clinic. Of course. But *burned*? You're speaking of something that is highly contagious. Surely, with something like food poisoning…"

"We are beyond that," Hardy said cryptically. "We have contagion, of the worst sort."

Thomas stared at Hardy, and then at Lucy Levine. "Mrs. Crowell," he said softly, "I know that Eleanor Stephens was not planning to work tonight, but now it is imperative that she do so."

Hardy interrupted before Thomas could continue. "If the laundry room is not adequate in some way, you must tell us immediately. If the linen has not been soiled, it may be laundered with lye soap, otherwise burned. At all times, this woman must be on clean linen. I don't care if it is changed ten times a night. Your use of towels is commendable. Continue to do so."

"Yes, Doctor."

"And be mindful of your own hygiene, always. Repeated cleansing of the hands is an absolute necessity. Finish with alcohol."

"You are thinking…" Thomas asked, since it seemed to him that Hardy clearly had a diagnosis in mind.

"Let me show you, with the culture," Hardy said. He turned away from the bed, beckoning Thomas. "It's best we be in accord with this."

"I'll have Howard fetch Miss Stephens," Thomas said to Mrs. Crowell. "He's in the barn still?"

"I believe so," the nurse replied.

"Good." He turned to Hardy. "When I arrived, I saw you at the incubator?"

"Indeed. I want to be sure. A culture gives us something to examine in patient detail. In the meantime, I have made a crude suspension for you, taken from the evacuations. I want you to view the slide immediately."

"This very moment," Thomas said, and he felt not foreboding but incredible excitement driving his pulse skyward. "Wait…Miss Crowell, stay with the patient. Make sure she remains dry, clean, and warm. If she will take no fluids, then we must try something else…perhaps by injection. Warm wraps over her abdomen may provide some relief. If the pain is great, a single injection of morphine now may be of some help. Begin with a quarter grain."

He knelt by the head of the bed, looking Miss Levine directly in the face, eye to eye, a hand on her forehead. "We're with you now, Lucy. Keep your courage. Do you understand me?" Perhaps she did, perhaps not, but Thomas was galvanized by the chill of her breath. "If the cramps in her legs become severe, an inhalation of chloroform may be of help," he added. "We'll be right back. I shall alert Mr. Deaton myself."

Hardy turned away, and then stopped. His tone was sharply commanding. "And nurse—every time, and I mean *every* time you handle her linens when they become soiled, *every* time you handle the patient in any way, you must cleanse your hands and arms as thoroughly as if you were about to assist Dr. Parks or myself in surgery. Do you understand that? *Every* time. With no hesitation, no delay. That is an absolute instruction that *will* not be debated. You will make whatever arrangements are necessary for fresh, clean clothing as well." He nodded at her soiled apron. "Get rid of that immediately."

He spun around before she could reply, and made for the stairway, with Thomas on his heels. Behind the clinic, Howard Deaton was cleaning the inside of the ambulance, and Thomas stared at the soiled blankets. "My God," he whispered. "All to be burned, Howard. Not laundered."

"You can't burn all of them," Deaton said automatically.

"Oh, yes, we can. And liberal coal oil to make the fire instant and hot. In fact, before the night is finished, we'll be burning a good deal. If one incinerator is inadequate, fashion another. Lindeman must have something you can use. Wake him, if necessary." He held up his hand, lifting a finger. "First, tend to the blankets you have there. Second, wash your hands all the way to your elbows with strong soap and hot water, disinfect after that with corrosive sublimate. You'll find the bottle of that in the dispensary, marked as a solution. Ask Mrs. Crowell to assist you. Keep it away from your eyes. A witch hazel or brandy splash afterward may make it more agreeable. And *then*…and *then*…go fetch Nurse Stephens. Understood?"

Deaton looked at Thomas askance. "What hit her?"

"We're about to find out, Howard." Thomas returned to the clinic, and in the laboratory, Hardy straightened up. Gas light flinted off the polished brass barrel of the Heinnenberg.

"See for yourself, Thomas." Hardy offered his place at the microscope. "While you're looking, I'll see if Mrs. Crowell knows what she is about. The evacuations are so frequent that if she is capable with the tube and bulb, so much the better. I'll be back in a moment to speak with you about a strategy." He dropped his hand on Thomas' shoulder and then was gone before Thomas could frame a single question.

After some finagling, Thomas forced the image into startling clarity under the Heinnenberg's big lens. At his elbow, a volume of Fellow's *The Theory and Practice of Medicine* had been opened and marked. Although the poor rendition in the textbook paled in comparison with the brilliant image in the Heinnenberg microscope, Thomas could see the deadly similarities.

"*From one half to two-thirds the size of the tubercule bacillus,*" he read quickly. "*Thicker and somewhat curved, resembling a crescent or comma in shape, sometimes occurring in a double S. Length of the bacillus rarely exceeds a micron, with most half that. Frequently aggregated in small groups, perhaps even a spiral.*" He went back to the microscope, shifting the slide this way and that to observe the entire specimen. "My God," he whispered, and sat back.

When Thomas had been at University, it had been fashionable among the medical students to discuss various careers paths. One popular notion had been to serve the wealthy and healthy, earning a sumptuous living. A second, favored by the most altruistic, was to journey to the far reaches of the globe, waging war against the dangerous diseases that decimated entire populations, diseases that preyed most commonly on the poverty-stricken and down-trodden. In between the two extremes were the majority, doctors-to-be who wanted a quiet life in modest private practice, whether in the congested cities or in the country.

In his class, Thomas had been alone in his fascination with the trauma that both war and peace could inflict on the human body.

But in deference to the second group, those who wished to confront the major scourges of the world, professors were fond of pontificating on what young physicians should do when serving in India, Burma, or China, fighting an epidemic.

"Exactly," Thomas said aloud. This very bacillus had been the subject of discussion on more than one occasion, and Thomas could now freely admit—when he most needed for circumstances to be otherwise—that he hadn't listened to the professors as well as he might now wish. He took a deep breath, and readjusted the instrument and the objectives, seeking more power. When his eye started to water with the concentration, he sat back again, referring again to the text.

"*The bacillus thrives in foul water, especially briny water, and Koch considers the Delta of the Ganges to be its natural home,*" the book's passage reported. *The good Dr. Koch*, Thomas thought, a man who knew more about the 'wee beasties' than anyone else on the planet—and still didn't know very much. "Such tiny things," Thomas murmured. He looked up at heavy bootsteps. Hardy reappeared, this time rubbing his hands, the smell of strong chemicals permeating the tiny room. "You've started a culture?" Thomas asked.

"Two, actually," Hardy replied. "Peptone and beef broth. And by the way, Mrs. Crowell is *most* adept around the patient, although she had never performed this particular procedure. She appeared to feel somewhat more relieved when I admitted that I had never done it myself…but that you had instructed me carefully." He grinned. "A small untruth, but a useful one. We're a pair, aren't we. Of course, by the time this night is finished, we'll be seasoned veterans."

"And the patient took how much?"

"The better part of a liter the first time." Hardy grimaced. "And then promptly evacuated again. We repeat and repeat, whatever is necessary." He reached over Thomas' shoulder and turned several pages in the text. "I have followed this compound," he said. "I don't know what else to do." Thomas read the mercifully brief list of preparations—boiled water with an infusion of chamomile, a few grains of tannin, a generous allowance of laudanum, and fifty grains of powdered gum arabic. On the counter across the room, he saw the pitifully inadequate supply of gum arabic.

"Do we have enough of *anything* for this? I mean to accomplish a continuing treatment?"

"I don't know." Hardy nodded at the clutter of chemical bottles on the counter. "I hope you'll excuse my rummaging about."

Thomas shook his head impatiently. "The clinic is yours, Lucius. Do as you see fit, always."

"Well," Hardy continued, "We have a great sufficiency of laudanum and morphine, somewhat less so of cocaine, should pain become unbearable." He reached out and tapped the book. "This?" Thomas scanned the indicated paragraph. "We have chloride of sodium and sodium carbonate. If she continues to evacuate in such volumes, then we should not hesitate. You've done hypodermoclysis?"

"Never. Not even the bulb…"

"Before this night, anyway," Hardy said. "We must hydrate, or we lose her. I believe it's that simple." When Thomas didn't reply, he reached out again to tap the book. "So. Am I correct about this?"

"I fear so. I would never have believed it, but the symptoms leave no question. I don't see *how* you could be wrong." He sat back. "And if it's some lesser thing, we can only be successful by treating for the worst possibility." He took a deep breath. "And this is certainly the worst, Lucius. We must act on the supposition." He patted the barrel of the expensive microscope. "Were the proof not in front of my own eyes, I would think a silly mistake has been made. This is hardly cholera country." He patted the open pages of the text. "We are far, far from the Ganges River."

"*Any* country may be cholera country, if the conditions are right," Hardy replied. "You might recall the scourge in England and Wales half a century ago that killed fifty thousand. And as recently as '73, when cholera rampaged through portions of New York City." He heaved a sigh. "But the *immediate* question is simple, so simple. How are we to save Miss Levine's life?" He lowered his voice. "And how to prevent the progression of what is now an isolated case? How many live in this village?"

"I've been told nearly eleven hundred if one includes the various small establishments on the periphery, along with the logging camps."

Hardy's expression was grim. "Fifty thousand in Egypt eight years ago, Thomas. This disease can be traced into every dark corner of the globe." The muscles of his cheek clenched, and for the first time, Thomas saw some of Lucius Hardy's confidence drain away.

"Not much frightens me, Thomas." He nodded at the microscope. "This does."

"Indeed," Thomas said quietly. "This text instructs us. The cholera is no shrinking violet, Lucius. It will not be content in taking but one life. *Someone* brought the condition to Port McKinney, and Miss Levine is the first case brought to our attention. We can guarantee that she will not be the last. But how did this specter come under the Clarissa's roof? According to this," and Thomas nodded at the text, "there has been no generalized epidemic of cholera since that reported in 1873 in New York. Only isolated cases since. We can hope that's true."

"We must discover the origin. But we're fortunate in one aspect, if only one. The thinking now is that cholera is not spread by the innocent exhalation," Hardy said. "The bacillus thrives in the gut, and is then expelled, as we are now seeing all too clearly. Those who are in touch with unclean waters, infected food, the feces, the vomitus…"

"Both Mr. Deaton and Nurse Crowell must be the focus of our attentions," Thomas said, standing up abruptly. "They are in jeopardy from this."

"Mrs. Snyder as well, Thomas. In the process of admitting Miss Levine to our care, the good woman felt compelled to assist. She apparently knows Miss Levine."

"She works at the Clarissa, Lucius," Thomas said with alarm. "So of course she does. She…her husband…the child."

"And you and I," Hardy added gently. They stood in the small laboratory in silence for a dozen heartbeats. "Port McKinney has a newspaper?"

"We do. If you stand on the front boardwalk by the telegraph office on Lincoln, you can see the sign a block south on the little side street. The *McKinney Sentinel*. Frederick Garrison manages its publication."

"If this is truly cholera, we shall have to court his cooperation, then. You know him well?"

"Well enough to call him by name. Nothing more. But before that…"

"Two things," Hardy said, as if reading his mind. "First, we must protect ourselves and our families, and our patients. The environs of the clinic must be spotless—aseptic. In that, we are ahead. But the staff, each and every one, must be educated this very night…this very moment. And then, we must know with a certainty what still hides in the Clarissa. The patient's room must be purged, the contents burned. We must know with whom she has had contact. We must trace the origins of this so we clearly understand the scope and magnitude of this threat." He looked up at Thomas. "You agree?"

"Of course."

Hardy turned the book toward the light. "What's the incubation period on this fearsome beast?" He read quickly, his face scrunching in a frown of impatience. "This is useful. I now read: '*The incubation between first infection and the development of symptoms is not known with any certainty, perhaps as brief as a day, or as long as a fortnight.*'" He looked up at Thomas. "Helpful, yes? As brief as a day, Thomas. As brief as a day. We must find out who she has been with, who has shared her bed."

The room fell silent, the ticking of the wall clock loud and insistent.

"Perhaps this is not a good time to remind you that you have a discussion with Mr. and Mrs. Schmidt this morning at nine?" Hardy asked.

"She must go to Portland," Thomas said without hesitation. He looked at the clock again just as the minute hand jerked to thirteen minutes after three. "To remain here would be irresponsible. She must leave. There is no question about that."

Hardy nodded slowly. "And your own wife and child?"

Thomas felt as if someone had stuffed a cotton swab down his throat. "I'll speak with Alvina," he replied. "But the quarantine must be complete."

Chapter Fourteen

"I erred on the side of caution." Thomas caught Lucius Hardy during an increasingly rare quiet moment. "I should have sent the Snyder child home yesterday. She was running a mild fever, and I wanted to be certain that her recovery would be uneventful."

"What's done is done," Hardy replied. "But the mother, now..."

"She complains of enormous headache, cramps in the gut, and voids like a geyser. I have Mrs. Crowell with her in the third bed in the ward. But she couldn't contract the disease and then run its course in just hours, Thomas. She must have been exposed at the Clarissa."

"Her husband?"

"He shows no signs yet. Nor the child. But now I fear sending them home, Lucius. There are four other Snyder children at home as well. I have the child isolated in her room, and Mr. Snyder spends time with both. He is with his wife now, and I have given him the most thorough instructions." He held out his hands. "Husband and wife refuse to remain apart, but at least this way, we can keep track of them."

"Better that they be here," Hardy said. "It appears that your wife's father was a believer in Salol. I have made a preparation with it. I'm not optimistic, but it's something else to try." He pulled his watch out and regarded it with some disbelief, as if the hands were moving backward. "A Miss Eleanor Stephens has arrived. We met on the stairway, and I introduced myself." He looked at Thomas skeptically. "Were I to hazard a guess, this is the last place she wants to be, Thomas."

"A tender violet," Thomas allowed. "But she has been of some use in the past. She suffers a squeamish stomach."

"And yet wants to be a nurse?"

"Well, with time, maybe. She is the one I told you about who spent a few months across the sound at St. Mary's. I hired her in the first place as a favor to Gert James, who thinks highly of the girl's step-father, Pastor Roland Patterson. The good pastor is frustrated by his step-daughter's…what's the word Gert used? Her *inclinations*."

"Toward what?"

Thomas grinned at Lucius Hardy's blunt question. "I did not press the point. I have found it a good policy to accept Gert's word at face value and let it go at that."

"The girl is attractive, I must say," Lucius said.

"She is that. I'll go speak with her. It will be dawn in a bit. Will you be able to break away to visit the Clarissa with me? We must know, Lucius. If others are ill there, they must be brought here without delay."

"Give me an hour. Howard Deaton and I are organizing the laundry and incinerator." He nodded toward the door ajar behind him. "And the dispensary. I want the potions near at hand, the compounds already prepared, the cultures from each patient carefully recorded." Hardy rested his hands on his hips. "This is really quite remarkable, Thomas. I had never supposed that I would cross paths with the cholera in this lifetime. The journals will be interested."

"An hour, then," Thomas said, and took the stairs back to the women's ward. Lucius Hardy was right. Eleanor Stephens was attractive—tall and willowy with a face so pale that she looked carved from alabaster. Mrs. Crowell, so completely opposite in stature, was lecturing the girl about something, and Eleanor Stephens stood with her right hand's index knuckle caught in her teeth, as if trying to stifle a cry.

"Ah, thank you for coming in," Thomas said as he approached.

"I was reminding Miss Stephens of the need for absolute asepsis," Mrs. Crowell said.

"You understand the nurse, Miss Stephens? In all matters?"

"I do, sir."

"Good. Let me tell you that *symptoms* are of singular importance to us at this point, Miss Stephens. We will be admitting more patients this day, and that is a certainty. We must know the symptoms of each with absolute accuracy. On the clock. If you don't know already, Mrs. Crowell will show you how I want each documented. Is that clear?"

"Yes, sir."

"And that," Thomas said, lowering his voice a bit but making no other effort to be tactful, "is a habit you would do well to break." He reached out and pointed at the girl's hand, whose knuckle still hovered near her mouth. "I would remind you, *again,* for I'm sure Mrs. Crowell has already spoken of it. The cholera bacillus is more vicious than anything we have ever treated. And it passes from soiled bedding, from soiled patients, from soiled *anything,* into the unlucky gut of the next victim. If you introduce the bacillus into your mouth from your hands, *you* will be taking up one of our beds." He smiled briefly. "I'd hate to see that. So would you, my dear."

Her voice quavered. "Yes, sir." She dropped her hand away from her face.

"What we ask of you is complete vigilance, every moment you are in the ward. Do not hesitate to consult with Mrs. Crowell when you have questions. She will be your guide in all things. Understood? During the day, Miss Auerbach or Mrs. Whitman."

"Yes, sir."

He turned to the older woman. "It seems to me that Mr. Malone's pulse is somewhat easier. Is that my imagination?"

Adelaide Crowell's eyebrows flickered upward a bit at the unexpected consultation from a physician.

"The last time I applied the ice, I thought that one of his eye lids flickered ever so slightly, Doctor."

"He must think he's fallen head first from the tree into a frozen pond," Thomas said. "In all of our rushing about, we must not forget him."

"We can hope that he *is* thinking," Mrs. Crowell said, and Thomas laughed in agreement.

"We'll see what the new day brings for him. It's quite amazing, really." He turned again to Eleanor Stephens. "You have any questions?"

"No, sir."

"That in itself is remarkable," Thomas replied, not unkindly. "I have dozens and dozens." He looked toward the back of the ward where Marcus Snyder stood in the doorway of his daughter's small room, leaning against the jamb so he could keep a vigil on both his daughter and his wife, the two separated by half the length of the ward.

Thomas lowered his voice. "Keep a close watch on him," he whispered. "The more removed he remains…"

"I'm keeping my eye on him," Mrs. Crowell replied. "And we are using a frightful amount of the carbolic, the alcohol, and the witch hazel."

"We shall find more. There are several bottles of brandy down stairs in the dispensary and more in my office, should the need arise." He smiled. "For the hands, that is."

A piteous groan arose from Mrs. Snyder, and Nurse Crowell turned without another word and made for the woman's bedside. "Do what you can to be useful," Thomas said to Miss Stephens. "Miss Auerbach will be here no later than six. I would ask that you plan on each night until this crisis has passed. Perhaps some hours during the day as well."

The girl nodded. Thomas watched her move away, stopping first at Lucy Levine's bedside, and then, at a summons with the snap of fingers, to Mrs. Crowell's assistance. Thomas checked his watch again, and then knelt beside Lucy Levine. Whether or not the girl was conscious was hard to tell. With his thumb, Thomas ever so gently lifted the corner of one eye lid, and saw with astonishment how dry, how tearless, the girl's eyes were.

"Eye drops of the mildest saline," he said loud enough for Mrs. Crowell to hear. "The same for all patients." He rose and found a small bulbed pipette in the dispensary cart in the corner of the ward, and pulled ten milliliters of saline solution. Five drops in each eye prompted a feeble blink, and the fluid ran down Lucy's sunken cheeks.

"Mrs. Crowell, Dr. Hardy has prepared some powder of Salol in the dispensary. I think it may be warranted with each session of the enteroclysis. Perhaps five grains each time."

"I am not familiar with its use," Mrs. Crowell said.

"Nor I," Thomas replied. "But at this stage, we'll try anything. Salol is but phenyl salicylate, and in the gut releases some percentage of phenol—we may gain something from its antiseptic properties."

"I see."

"Perhaps five grains each time. Anything we can do to make the gut inhospitable for the bacilli, we'll do." Back at the cart, he found a single length of sterile tubing, together with its bulb. "The clave must be kept busy." He held up the tube. "We have but the one?"

"We'll see to it, Doctor Parks."

"Because I'm going to use this one," Thomas added. "I see it's been nearly thirty minutes since Lucy's last evacuation."

"She was sleeping...I did not wish to disturb her," Mrs. Crowell said.

"Well, the bacilli are not sleeping," he replied.

"Eleanor," Mrs. Crowell instructed when she saw the girl hesitate. The elder nurse nodded toward Thomas, and Eleanor approached Lucy Levine's bedside. Even as Thomas looked up at her, he saw her index knuckle start its ascent toward her mouth.

"Don't," he snapped. "Go cleanse your hands and then give me some assistance here. Do not use a towel. Let your hands dry in the air." Even as he said that, he heard the loud grumblings from Lucy Levine's gut, and the girl writhed into a tight ball. In a couple minutes, Miss Stephens returned, hands dripping. Thomas drew away the towels that had diapered the patient. "Two clean towels, quickly now." He had exactly enough time to reposition the bedding and towels before Miss Levine's gut released. Even as the patient whimpered, Miss Stephens backed away.

"More towels," he instructed. "She is finished, I think. And each time, we must fight the sepsis, Miss Stephens. The tube and bulb must be clean, the patient must be clean. It would certainly be counterproductive for us to reintroduce the contagion into her gut. Now," he added, satisfied that the patient was as ready as she could be. "The tube I've prepared. And we must be generous with the petroleum gel." For the next few moments, he concentrated on the simple procedure, all the while watching Lucy's face. The girl lay as if pole-axed. Whether the infusion of two liters of fluid, salts and the Salol into the colon did any good at all was impossible to tell.

At one point he glanced up, and saw that Eleanor Stephens had backed away from the bed again, her already pale face now pasty white.

"Are you all right?"

The girl nodded and looked away.

"Do you know Miss Levine?" The question brought a slight nod. "You are personally acquainted?"

"She lives at the Clarissa."

Thomas pointed at the blanket. "The corner of that, please." She pulled the covering within his reach, and he draped the patient for some small semblance of modesty. "Do you know with whom she rooms there?"

"A girl name Missy. I think her last name is Buchanan."

"She knows of Lucy's illness?"

"I would not think so, Doctor. She has traveled to Seattle with a boyfriend."

"How long ago?"

"Some days."

"Some?"

"It has been a week."

"Had you spoken with Miss Levine recently?"

"Not long ago. Earlier in the week."

Thomas turned and looked at her quizzically. "But days ago, only? Was she ill then?"

"No, sir. Not that I could tell."

"Do you know her well enough to know with whom she associates?"

Eleanor Stephens hesitated. "I suppose…I suppose that I do."

Thomas emptied the last of the bulb, and as delicately as he could, removed the black rubber tube, wrapping the whole thing in a clean towel. "This must be rinsed and then claved immediately," he said. "Has Mrs. Crowell showed you how?"

"I can do that now," the older nurse said as she came up to the bed.

"Mrs. Snyder?"

"Resting easy for a moment. Let me do this now while I have the chance, and while you are in the ward, Doctor."

Thomas stood up. "Miss Stephens, I would like a list of all of Miss Levine's associates…all that you can remember."

"Ben…" the single word came from the patient's lips as a mere exhalation of breath, and had Thomas not been standing immediately beside her, he would not have heard it.

He knelt down and placed his hand on Lucy's chilled forehead. "Who is Ben, Lucy?"

"His sister…his sister has died." Lucy Levine eyes drifted almost closed, and the next sound from her was a faint, muted cry of pain.

"The turpentine stupes might help now." Twisting at the waist, Thomas looked back at Eleanor Stephens. "Do you know who she means?"

"The man she would marry," Eleanor murmured.

"And that would be…" he prompted.

"Ben Sitzberger," the girl whispered, as if somehow a young lady's beau was the world's biggest and darkest secret.

Thomas stared at her, dumbfounded. "She associates with the logger, you mean?" He could remember Ben Sitzberger's pale face, hand pressed to his gut as he bent over his horse's saddle horn early that morning, when he had accompanied Buddy

Huckla to the clinic. Spoiled salmon, indeed—only if the young man was most fortunate, Thomas thought.

"Yes. He spends a great deal…a great deal of time with her."

"How do you come to know this?"

Eleanor Stephens looked down at the floor, and her voice was a whisper. "Lucy invited me to share her room at the Clarissa. After her friend moved to Seattle."

For a long moment, Thomas regarded the young nurse, unsure of what to say. "That would make a gay party," he said finally, and immediately knew that the attempt at levity was exactly the *wrong* thing to say. "We must find him, this young Mr. Sitzberger. I saw him this morning, and he was not well. His companion, a young chap named Buddy Huckla…you know him?"

Eleanor nodded slightly, the knuckle starting to stray toward her mouth.

Thomas snapped his fingers and pointed, and the young girl jerked her hand away as if stung.

"Fetch the stupes now," he ordered. "I want to talk with Mr. Snyder for a few moments, and then Dr. Hardy and I shall be visiting the Clarissa…as soon as Nurse Auerbach and Nurse Whitman have arrived for the day."

Adjusting a warm blanket over Lucy, and then doing the same at Mrs. Snyder's bed, he made his way to the back of the ward after another session at the nurse's cart to sterilize his hands. Marcus Snyder had slumped in a straight-backed chair by the doorway, and his face was pale, creased with worry.

"She sleeps." Milly's father pushed himself upright, at the same time tipping the door more widely open so Thomas could slip past. The little girl lay in peaceful rest, her face relaxed. Thomas touched the back of his hand to her forehead and was relieved to find her cool. As he moved his fingers to the side of her neck, one small hand curled up and grasped his wrist. He smiled as he counted the strong beats, an even sixty-five in a minute.

Thomas disengaged himself and tip-toed away from the bed. "Any coughing?"

"She's been quiet."

"No distress of any kind?"

"None but the worry for her mother," Mr. Snyder allowed. "The child cries when she's awake. I'm afraid I haven't been much comfort."

"Your wife works at the Clarissa regularly?"

"She's been managing six days a week." He managed a faint smile. "Not havin' infants in the house helps some."

"Matilda is the youngest?"

"She is that."

"And the oldest?"

"That's Robert. He's seventeen, now. Works out to the mill. Gwendolyn—she's sixteen. She's to home."

"Dr. Hardy has talked to you? That it would be best if you and Matilda were to remain here for the duration of this?"

"Doc, I can't do that. I mean, a man has to make a livin'."

"This disease is a frightful thing, Mr. Snyder. Until we're certain, I would hate to send the child home, running the risk of infection for the others. And you, sir, have been just as exposed, perhaps more so. Until we are sure, observation must be conscientious."

"Don't guess I'm going to expose nobody out in a fishing skiff."

"But you handle the fish, and then pass them along to the markets. We really must insist, Mr. Snyder."

The man regarded Thomas for a moment, and then shrugged helplessly. "I guess it's up to me. Don't see no bars on the windows."

"No, you don't, sir. But I appeal to your good sense." He saw Dr. Lucius Hardy appear in the ward, and reached out a hand to Snyder's shoulder. "We'll be gone but for a few minutes," Thomas said. "Should you need anything, Mrs. Crowell is at your beck and call. And Bertha Auerbach will be here in a few minutes."

"Well, I'm just going to sit right here and watch my two women sleep," Snyder said, and he slid down into the chair with a sigh.

Chapter Fifteen

"I had him," Thomas groaned. "Yesterday morning, I had him. The young man from the timber camp." The fine drizzle had turned sideways as the two physicians left the clinic and walked down Gamble Street. Wind lashed from inland, driving the droplets like fired pellets. By the clock, it was dawn, but the sun was so reluctant to greet this day that the inlet lay black and featureless beyond the fringe of trees.

"We'll find him," Hardy said with far more assurance than Thomas Parks felt.

A single light flowed yellow from the tiny slab-wood cabin that served as the Port McKinney constable's home, office and lock-up. Thomas rapped hard on the door, and was rewarded by the prompt response, bellowed in Constable George Aldrich's thick German accent.

"The coffee is fresh," he called and opened the door. "So, look at you two." He stood to one side, taking Thomas' hand in a hard grip as the physician entered the cabin. The rush of warm air carried a powerful mix of sweat, whiskey, tobacco smoke, and freshly toasted bread.

"Constable, this is Dr. Lucius Hardy. He arrived just yesterday to join the Clinic." Aldrich's alert blue eyes inventoried Hardy from head to toe.

"And where are you from, sir?" the constable asked.

"Most recently from Philadelphia," Hardy replied. "More or less."

"Ah, again the east comes to us." The constable hauled out a large pocket watch. "You're both early risers." He then started to hand Thomas a metal cup, but the young physician shook his head.

"There's no time, Constable."

"Really?" Aldrich sounded skeptical, as if, no matter the gravity of the situation, there was always time for coffee. "So… what may I do for you?"

"We have a serious outbreak of cholera in the village, constable."

Aldrich stopped with his coffee cup halfway to his mouth, then set it carefully on the edge of the stove. "Cholera? The summer cholera?"

"No. Asiatic cholera, constable. The worst."

"How is that possible?"

"We don't know yet," Thomas said. "But we have Lucy Levine at the clinic, desperately ill. And Flora Snyder."

"Really, now."

"You know Miss Levine?" Hardy asked, and Aldrich almost smiled.

"Of course." He reached out for the coffee cup, hesitated, and then picked it up. "How would this happen?"

"That is exactly what we must discover. We must know with whom Lucy Levine was in contact most recently. We know that Mrs. Snyder works at the hotel. We know that Miss Levine associates on a regular basis with one of the loggers—young Ben Sitzberger."

Aldrich smiled. "*Associates*. I like that."

"Sitzberger isn't yet at the clinic, but I know he is ill, and should be treated. I'm certain of it. And equally important, the Clarissa must be quarantined until we know for certain that the risk has passed."

"You cannot quarantine the entire hotel," Aldrich said.

"If it comes to that, we can, and we will—with your help, if necessary. We're on the way there now, and I wanted you to accompany us. We can use all the assistance we might muster. The gravity of your office is no small resource."

Aldrich smiled again. "The *gravity* of my office, eh? If it's gravity you want, then you should talk with the Reverend Patterson. He preaches to me on a daily basis. *Close the Clarissa*, he says. *Close the Clarissa*."

"For different reasons, I would imagine," Thomas knew Patterson as a rigid, stern man who had consented to having a painful boil on his buttocks treated, and then raged against Thomas later—after the boil had healed perfectly—for exposing his undraped behind to the nursing staff while the boil's owner was unconscious during the surgery.

"Well," Aldrich said philosophically, "Let us go see, then." He turned to Hardy. "Yesterday was *your* first day?" He chuckled as Hardy nodded. "Something of a tradition, this man has going." He patted Thomas' shoulder. "He arrives and within minutes is his own patient. You arrive, and step right into the middle of this cow pie." He glanced at Thomas. "Lucy came to you? How did you discover her illness?"

"A friend at the hotel summoned help. Not soon enough, it would seem. Will you accompany us?" Thomas persisted.

"Of course." Aldrich set the cup down, reached for his oil slicker and shrugged into it as he held the door, following the physicians out into the rain. He made no effort to avoid even the deepest of puddles, but stomped along between the two men. By the time they had reached Lincoln Street, a phalanx of four dogs had joined them.

"How is your wife?" Aldrich asked, aiming a kick at one small mongrel who appeared intent on biting his boot heel while the other three, larger and potentially more formidable, kept their respectful distance.

"She gave birth yesterday. A healthy boy. Mother and child are fine."

"Well, well," Aldrich said. "That's something." He skirted a particularly large puddle, and then they reached the narrow boardwalk in front of the hotel. Aldrich took hold of one of the uprights and whacked each boot in turn against the edge of the planks.

The lobby made an effort at elegance, with furniture so overstuffed it appeared bloated in its blue and gold velvet, light from the gas chandelier turned low enough that the dust didn't show. A single gas light was turned on behind the registration counter, with no one in attendance. Beside the bank of pigeon hole mail boxes, a grandfather clock's pendulum hung motionless, the hands frozen.

"Someone's in the kitchen," Aldrich said, but before they had the chance to follow the aromas, an enormous woman appeared. Her improbably golden hair was curled upward into a bun that nestled squarely on top of her skull. She wore a white muslin dress whose fringes swept the floor—not the garish gown that Thomas had imagined might be appropriate for a woman in her position. A kitchen towel was slung over one arm, and one hand held a large butcher knife.

"Gloriosa, you three are out early," she said. "We got breakfast ready for you, and coffee, and a dry place to set yourselves…" For the first time, she noticed the grim expressions, and her heavy face glowered. "How's my girl? First thing *I* was going to do this morning was march up to that grand clinic of yours and see what's what." She pointed the knife at Thomas. "But here you are. Saves me a trip."

"Mrs. Jules, we have urgent business," Thomas interrupted. "Miss Levine is desperately ill. We need to visit her room, and speak with the girl who first found her ill."

"Some of the others say that she took ill. She didn't tell *me,* so it couldn't be all that bad. She's a strong girl, and I suppose whatever it is will pass soon enough. She sent you down to fetch something for her?"

"Mrs. Jules," Aldrich said, his voice easy but firm, "we must see the room. I do not wish to argue with you."

"I am *not* arguing," the big woman bristled. "The east garret on the third floor, as you well know, constable."

"Mrs. Jules, one more thing," Thomas said. "Mrs. Snyder works each day, does she not?"

"Of course she does. Don't know what we'd do without her, the poor thing."

"Poor thing? How is that?"

"Well, nothing that a little meat on those bones wouldn't cure," the massive woman said. "Such a tiny thing she is. And here she had five children of her own." She frowned at Thomas. "She's not…"

"Taken ill? Yes. She has. So in point of fact, you will have to find a way to do without her."

"Oh, my soul." Her head swiveled from one to the next.

"We must see the room," Thomas said. The woman pointed at the staircase. With each step on the stair treads, Thomas could smell the mildew on the narrow carpet runner. He had never explored the bowels of the hotel. He knew that its owner, mentioned only as a Mr. Eggleston, lived in Portland, visited rarely, and left the daily running of the establishment to Fred and Viola Jules.

The long, carpeted stairway ran up one brocaded wall on the north side of the lobby, and passed through the ceiling to a warren of dark hallways. The farther back in the building they progressed, the darker and stuffier it became.

A single window at the end of the longest hallway looked out on the inlet. Smells other than mildew thickened the atmosphere of the building. In an alcove just before the window, a pot-bellied stove stood on a pad of bricks, its stovepipe thrusting through a blackened tin wall thimble. The stove was cold and stank, and Thomas opened the isinglass door to see that the firebox was full of all sorts of unmentionables, awaiting a blaze.

"Charming. Another floor?" Hardy asked, and they thudded up another flight of stairs to the Clarissa's third floor. The rough fir flooring creaked under their boots, and the darkness closed in, bounded by the slope of the building's gambrel roof . The stairway landing provided access to at least four small rooms, Thomas could see. No gas sconces marked the walls, and Hardy stopped and struck a match.

"Over here," Aldrich said, and Hardy lit a single candle that nestled in a great bouquet of melted wax in its tin sconce. The single small flame danced in the abundant drafts, adding no cheer. Thomas held his hand over his nose as he stepped up onto the third floor landing.

"My God," he whispered.

"This one," Aldrich directed. The door was neither numbered nor locked. Across the landing, another door opened, and Thomas turned toward it, the light so faint that he couldn't distinguish shape or form. The door closed.

Hardy nudged the door to Lucy Levine's garret room with his elbow, and turned his head at the stench. Coat sleeve across his face, Thomas pushed past, struck another match and searched for a candle, finding a two-inch stub waxed onto the corner of a battered dresser. On the floor, a small coal-oil lantern rested on its side, a dark puddle of oil sinking into the rough wood flooring. Righting it, Thomas struck another match, turning the lantern's wick high both for the light and the blast of chemical aroma from the oil.

A wire hung from a beam in the center of the room, and he looped it through the lantern's handle.

Two single beds crowded the room, a steamer chest at the foot of one, and a single, roughly hewn armoire angled into a corner. The blankets of one bed were pulled into some semblance of order, but the other prompted a shiver up Thomas' spine. And this was the place that somehow attracted Eleanor Stephens?

For who knew how many hours, Lucy Levine had laid in her own mess as the room closed around her. There was no sign of succor—no glassware, no bottles of elixir or any of the other patent medicines that people turned to for the ague or the grip, or when spoiled food turned their guts inside out. The disease that had struck Lucy had done so with brutal rapidity, destroying her strength and resistance, even her ability to stagger across the hallway for help. And for hours, no one had thought to look in on her. Were they so acclimated to the stench of this place that they hadn't noticed?

Had she initially had the strength to reach the chamber pot, that strength had quickly failed her until she lay exhausted, quarts and quarts of evacuations soaking the bed, the horsehair mattress, even the floor. The enameled pot, lid in place, rested on the floor in the corner, just beyond the end of the bed. Thomas touched it with the toe of his boot, feeling the weight of a full container.

"You and Howard lifted her out of this quagmire?" Thomas turned and asked Lucius Hardy, fearing for the physician's own welfare.

"No, not me. Howard and two of the girls here," Hardy replied. "It appeared that they used one of the blankets off the other bed as a sling. She weighed next to nothing, I might add."

"So little left," Thomas said. Aldrich had stepped inside the room, but had then retreated quickly and now waited out in the landing. He had opened a tiny window and stood in the blast of wet air banking in off the inlet.

"By the time I completed the preliminary clean-up at the clinic, I was imagining that a full bath in sublimate would be welcome," Hardy said. "As it is, your supply of phenol and alcohol have been severely depleted."

"Everything in this room must be burned," Thomas said, and even as he uttered the words, he heard rapid boot falls on the stairway behind them, a flood of light blooming in the stairwell. Fred Jules appeared with a lantern held high.

"Aldrich, what are you after?" he snapped at the constable, and then saw the other two men. "My wife said there is a problem with Miss Levine."

Thomas had met Fred Jules only once, and at that time, had thought that nothing could perturb the man's good nature. His ruddy face was haloed by a ruff of white hair, and even though almost a head shorter than his imposing wife, still Fred Jules was a burly, powerful man, portly of belly with shirtsleeves rolled up as if he'd been interrupted with his arms elbow deep in a vat of something. He advanced across the landing toward Thomas. It was not humor on his lively face this time, but concern.

"Dr. Parks, how is my girl? Why didn't someone tell me about all this?"

"Your girl, sir, is gravely ill. She is being treated at the clinic, but whether she will survive the day is open to question."

"As I came up the stairs, I heard what you said," Jules bleated. "Burn?"

"Everything," Thomas said. "All the bedding. This awful bed itself. All the clothing. Everything."

"Now see here, it can all be washed as new."

"No, it can't," Lucius Hardy interrupted. "Look here, man. Even the room must be thoroughly disinfected, the walls and floor washed down with corrosive sublimate solution."

"But..." Fred held out both hands beseechingly. "Just who is going to do all that? You said that Lucy is dreadfully ill. Who called you to fetch her?"

"I heard her name once...Winston?"

"Bessie Mae Winston?"

"Surely so. We'll need to speak with her."

"She is downstairs with..." Jules bit off the rest. "Everything washed?"

"Yes. Your hotel staff shall do that," Hardy said coldly. "With the exception of Mrs. Snyder, who herself is at the clinic, dreadfully ill." He stepped closer, glaring at Jules. "Sir, do you *smell* the condition of this room? Suppose I were to ask *you* to spend the night in this foul bed?"

"I..."

"Indeed," Hardy snapped. "The room must be absolutely clean before anyone else may use it. And that brings us to a further issue." He unhooked the coal oil lantern from the ceiling hook and stepped back out into the landing. "I see three other rooms," he said. "They must all be evacuated and quarantined. We must examine each person thoroughly. The more we can isolate this incident, the better off we will all be."

His jaw clamped shut, Fred Jules looked from door to door, as if an answer would pop out from one of them.

"What is the disease?" he asked. "You have not said."

"Cholera."

"My God!" He stepped back as if punched.

"It can be managed with intelligence and due diligence," Thomas added, not sure that he believed what he was saying. "First, while we are aggressively treating the stricken patients, every effort must be made to render these rooms as sterile as possible. And the rooms around it. If the entire hotel must be quarantined until that is completed, then so be it."

"That is *not* possible," Jules said.

"Well, it is," Aldrich spoke up. "If it must be done, if these two men order that it must be done, then it must be done, yes?"

"You have no authority." The hotel manager's voice hardened.

"Oh, I do," Aldrich said easily. "You know, Fred, I have never looked to put my nose in your business, but we both know it *is* a business, and we both know what the statutes say about that, eh? Heaven knows I do. Pastor Patterson reminds me often enough."

Fred Jules glared at the constable for a moment, then turned to Thomas.

"Just what do you want of us?"

"We shall begin with absolute cleanliness," Thomas said. "At this point, we have but the two cases, but the character of the disease makes that most unusual. As this room is cleaned, along with the others on this floor, we must also determine who was in intimate contact with Miss Levine."

"If the town hears of this," Jules said softly.

"The town *will* hear of this," Thomas said quickly. "Of that, I'm certain. We will make sure that the town hears of it. If we don't act with accord to stop this thing, Port McKinney will be decimated." He surveyed the landing. "When the residents of this floor must use the toilet, and don't want to use the chamber pot, where do they go?"

"The privy is on the north side of the building," Jules offered.

"And who is charged with emptying the chamber pots from the rooms?"

"The guests are not expected," Jules said. "But you said that Mrs. Snyder…are you sure? She is ill?"

"She is. She cleaned for you?"

"Well, in addition to many other things," Jules said.

"I would guess that Lucy Levine was not considered a *guest*, however. Am I correct in that?" Hardy asked. "She would have emptied her own, were she up to the task?"

"Yes."

"And for the other rooms? For the guests on the second floor?"

"One of the maids."

"Would Lucy have done that, perhaps? Both she and Mrs. Snyder?"

"She works thus from time to time. We have many rooms that must be attended to."

"When she is not otherwise engaged," the constable said dryly.

"The girl who rooms with Lucy?" Thomas asked.

"She has traveled to Seattle. She has family there."

"When did she leave?"

"It has been a week. She…how does my good wife say it… Missy found her man. One of the loggers took her from us."

"We will want to speak with her. She must be found."

"She was well when she left," Jules said.

"When was the last moment that you saw Lucy, by the way?"

Jules frowned, taking his time. "She was having dinner with a favorite of hers, and that would have been just a day or so ago."

"A gentleman named Ben Sitzberger?"

Jules nodded. "Is he…"

"We must know for certain when you saw her last."

The manager watched the sputtering flame in the lantern for a moment. "It would have been Wednesday at supper."

"And she was well?"

"She appeared to be so. She was enjoying herself and her company. She's showing favor toward him, you know," Jules said. "And we like to see that. When the girls can leave here and find contentment and build a home of their own, then my wife and I feel a sense of accomplishment."

"I'm sure you do," Hardy said.

"Sitzberger. Ben Sitzberger," Jules said, confirming. "A promising young man who works for Mr. Schmidt."

"Sitzberger spent the night?"

"I would think so," Jules said, then quickly added, with an uneasy glance toward Lucy's pathetic room, "but not here, of course."

"Of course not," Hardy said with considerable acid. "Where, man?"

"I would have to ask my wife, but certainly it would be one of the guest rooms on the second floor." He scratched his scalp. "The girls do not host in their private quarters." He said it as if that was a policy of enormous distinction, Thomas thought.

Thomas drew Hardy to one side. "The disease struck in just hours, Lucius. Just hours. One moment, Lucy was enjoying the company of her beau, and the next, the cholera had laid her low."

"That's the way of it. Who works for you that you trust?" Hardy asked Fred Jules. "I mean trust with your life, sir? Because that's to whom you must entrust this task at hand. You must make sure that your employees do your bidding in the most meticulous, thorough fashion. This room must be cleaned, as must all the others. As we said, all the bedding and soft things burned. Everything else be washed down thoroughly with strong disinfectant. The best is the corrosive sublimate that you can purchase by the bagful at Lindeman's. And then," and he reached out a hand to grasp the hotel manager's shoulder to make sure he was listening, "once clean, everything must remain clean, sir. Fully aired and clean. Fully disinfected. Make sure every employee scrubs her hands to perfection. And scrubs often. *Every* time something from one of the rooms is handled."

"Do you know what you ask, sir?" Jules bleated.

Hardy barked out one of his short, hard laughs. "Well, then, think of it this way. This is Friday, is it not? Do you wish to see the sunrise on Monday? You and your wife? Every one of your hotel staff? Your guests? Because *that,* good sir, is the choice the cholera gives you. You are a marked man, Mr. Jules. We who have come into contact with this contagion…we are *all* marked."

"I'll tend to it," Jules said, and sounded as if he meant it.

"Today," Hardy added, and Jules nodded. "The hotel will be under strict quarantine until we are satisfied that all is well. Constable Aldrich will enforce the quarantine. No one must leave until either Dr. Parks or myself can confirm that the risk has been abated. Only when we're sure that you are doing all that we ask can we attend to other matters more difficult."

"My God, man," Jules exclaimed, looking quickly at Aldrich as if he held the answers. The constable remained silent. "What matters do you refer to?"

"Staying alive, for one," Hardy said. "When a cholera epidemic breaks out, the dead are counted in thousands, sir. How many live in Port McKinney? Five hundred?" He squeezed Jules' shoulder once again as he turned toward the other rooms. "Now, show us these rooms."

Chapter Sixteen

Thomas' hopes rose as they visited first one room and then another on the third floor. All save one were empty, and showed no tell-tale signs of illness. All reeked of various amounts of perfumes and incense, but not the wretched, putrid miasma from the cholera.

Aldrich's knock on the door farthest from Lucy's and the stairway was answered by Letitia Moore, a large young woman no doubt capable of smothering the fittest lumberjack in a close hug. She opened her door despite being attired in the thinnest of undergarments.

"Three at once?" she announced cheerfully, then turned as Aldrich stepped into view. "Well, make it four, then." She held a towel under her chin as a drape, looping a finger through one of the golden ringlets that cascaded down beside her face. She could have been Flora Jules' daughter.

"Miss Moore," Jules said, and he couldn't seem to bring himself to look at her face, "Miss Levine has been taken ill."

"Oh, I'm so sorry," the woman said with what sounded like genuine sympathy and affection. "But I'm otherwise engaged, Freddy. I have a gentleman downstairs."

Fred Jules colored at the familiarity. "No, these gentlemen…"

"The *handsome* good doctor," Letitia said, beaming with perfect white teeth. "I've told Alvina on several occasions that we all need stars as lucky as hers." She reached out a hand to Lucius Hardy. "And who are you, kind sir?" She even curtsied slightly.

"Dr. Lucius Hardy," the physician replied, and bowed stiffly without taking the proffered hand.

"Well, my." She rolled her eyes. "Two doctors in one visit. I wish I were ill."

"Did you speak with Lucy at all during the day yesterday?" Thomas asked. "Did you see her?"

"I confess not. We have been unusually busy, and I'm sure I don't know why. Perhaps some phase of the moon. Is she desperate?"

Thomas ignored the question. "Did you happen to encounter Mrs. Snyder at any time in the past few days?"

"Encounter? What*ever* do you mean by that?"

"Did you see her? Speak with her? She is ill as well, and we need to know with whom she associated."

"She's ill? Heavens. And she is *such* a jewel, you know. But, one gets sick now and again, don't we. You know," Miss Moore said, and she pursed her lips judiciously. "I just don't recall things like that. Some of the older employees of the hotel…" She swept a hand around to include the walls as if that's where the older employees resided. "I'm certainly aggrieved to learn she is unwell."

Remarkable, Thomas thought. "Listen, these are your closest friends, your associates we're talking about. Discretion is one thing, but this is absurd. A woman a doorway removed is ill to death, and no one notices? My God."

Before the girl could answer, Hardy turned to Thomas and Jules. "We'll want to talk with everyone. It will only take a few moments to ascertain the state of things." He lowered his voice and said to Thomas, "There is yet a chance, my friend. If the contagion can be limited to this floor, to the one room…"

"There is that chance." Thomas looked critically at Letitia Moore, who appeared to be, in all ways, in the prime of health. "You have been well, Miss? You have any complaints, however trivial?"

"Only that you're happily married," she laughed, and touched Thomas' cheek with two fingers, bubbling a laugh as he recoiled back.

"Should you feel any distress in the bowels, any sudden vomiting, you must come to the clinic immediately," Hardy said. "You will not leave the Clarissa until you are told you may do so."

"My." The girl was obviously not entirely used to taking orders. "We are to be quarantined?"

"Indeed you are. Just so we understand each other." Both beds in the room were empty, and Thomas surveyed the tiny confines as he stepped past Letitia. With the toe of his boot, he touched the chamber pot, and it rocked easily.

"My, you are a curious one." Letitia's expression of amused affection was replaced by concern. "Will Lucy recover? You have not said what the malady is."

"She may, she may not. Who shares this room with you?"

"That would be Constance," Jules offered quickly. "A young woman from Portland. She was so taken with the village that she decided to stay."

"*So* taken," Letitia said sarcastically. "Had she the money for fare farther up the coast, away she would go."

"Where is she?"

"Now? I believe she is with a gentleman who prefers to awaken in the company of a pretty girl," Letitia replied. "The first mate of the *Willis Head*, so she may yet find her ticket up the coast. She has been in his company since Thursday." Letitia suddenly reached out a hand, again making contact with Thomas' arm. "Now *she* said Lucy was taken ill with the grippe. She was making some broth for her. I was busy and didn't really pay attention. Constance seemed not to worry."

Thomas glanced at Jules, then said to the young woman, "It is not the grippe, Miss Moore. Would that it were so. Miss Levine suffers from cholera."

Letitia Moore's face lost the rosy hue of playful banter, and her eyes went cold and watchful. "The cholera?"

"Yes."

"However…"

"We don't know," Hardy said abruptly. "Now if you'll excuse us."

It took an hour to prowl every remaining room of the Clarissa, and Thomas let his nose guide his suspicions. The victims didn't mope about for days, feeling off their feed. The avalanche of symptoms crashed down, destroying any will, laying waste to any inclination for self-defense. As untidy, dark and dank as the Clarissa might be, once they were clear of the third floor, the potpourri of other odors—odors less lethal—greeted them whenever a door was opened.

No one professed to be ill, although the first mate of the *Willis Head* greeted the four men with less than good cheer. As Thomas held up the oil lantern, he saw the man recoil away from the light as if someone had thrust a dagger in his eyes.

"Jesus and all the saints." The man held up his hand. "What are you about? What do you want?" He held a straight razor in his hand, but the lather soaking under his full, red beard indicated he'd been razoring his own neck at the moment of the knock, not someone else's.

Jules touched Thomas' elbow. "That's Constance," he whispered. "She shares the room with Miss Moore. Constance DeJohn."

"Sir, may I speak with your companion?" Thomas asked.

The man stood rooted, looking from one face to another. "And just who the hell are you?" he asked Thomas. Had he wanted to bar the door, he certainly would have had no trouble, Thomas thought. With his cordage-like muscles graced with enough tattoos for ten men, the man's decorations also included a fair selection of scars inflicted with something more dangerous than an artist's needle.

"Dr. Thomas Parks. I need to speak with Miss DeJohn on a matter of the greatest urgency."

The figure still occupying the bed sat up, holding the sheet to her chin.

"Miss DeJohn?" Fred Jules called, and the sailor glared at him and then saw the constable for the first time, the small brass badge on his vest now visible as was the revolver at his waist. "These men need to talk with you."

"I ain't decent," she replied. "Is that the doctor?"

"Dr. Parks," Thomas announced. "Excuse me," he said to the sailor, and stepped past into the room. "Miss DeJohn, we are concerned about Lucy Levine."

"All I done was make her some chicken stock broth. She had an upset tummy."

"When was this?"

The girl pulled the sheet up so that the lower half of her face was covered. The bedding fell away enough to reveal one shapely shoulder. "I guess it was yesterday morning. Something like that. I brought her the soup for lunch. I don't think she liked it."

"Thursday noon."

"She was in a bad way. She said that Benny was not feeling so good either."

"Benny? This would be the Sitzberger boy?"

Constance nodded, and smiled broadly, ducking her face into the sheet once again. "Almost every night, he comes down from the camp. Sometimes he don't spend the whole night. Sometimes he does."

"Did you manage Miss Levine's bedding? Anything like that?"

"I helped her change it." The girl made a face. "She had an accident, she said. But I did that and then she said she was feeling better, and I had things to do. The other girl said she'd help some before she had to leave."

Thomas sighed. "The *other* girl?"

"Eleanor. The mean guy's daughter. Or step-daughter, I guess she is."

For a moment, Thomas could not find the words. "*Eleanor* was here? Eleanor Stephens?" Constance DeJohn seemed puzzled at the physician's stupefaction.

"She ain't no stranger to the Clarissa, Doctor Parks. I woulda thought you knew that."

"My God," he whispered, and looked at Hardy. "And this Sitzberger…we must find him." He paused, looking at the sailor. "Where's your captain, sir?"

"I'm the first mate. I ain't in charge of him," the sailor replied.

"He's not here at the hotel?"

"Nope. He's got his own roost." He flicked the razor closed then open again. "You boys found out what you needed to know?"

"I'll need to speak with him," Thomas said.

"Then you'll find him out at Schmidt's mill. The *Head's* carrying Schmidt's tonnage, mostly. It'll be unloaded today, if there's room at the wharf down the way. We're waitin' on that. He's got three square-riggers in at the same time, and there ain't room for us. We're to make headway for Bellingham, so he'd best find a spot for us soon."

"How many remain on board now?"

The first mate looked at Thomas with curiosity. He wiped the drying soap off his neck with the small towel, and passed it across the razor. "Two remain," he said. "Why does that concern you?"

"The rest are here?"

"No. There's only three others, and they got their own digs."

"Here in town?"

"One of 'em has a brother working the timber. Where there's a good card game, that's where Luke is sure to be. He took Cy and the Murray kid with him."

Once entertaining hopes that this outbreak might be easily contained, Thomas felt a wave of hopelessness. Somewhere off in one of the other rooms, he heard a whoop of delight, and for a moment he imagined that the cholera was laughing at him.

It took them just moments to find Bessie Mae Winston in one of the second floor's front rooms. Miss Winston's paying companion had already left, apparently paying her sufficiently to allow her some moments of peaceful slumber by herself. Groggy and sleepy-eyed, Miss Winston's tale was grim. She'd wanted to borrow an article of clothing from Lucy, and had found the girl comatose. A girl with great common sense, Bessie Mae had not wished to awaken the Jules, both of whom had terrible tempers. Knowing that a nurse could always be found at the clinic, she had hurried there. Self-reliant, quick thinking—*I should hire this girl*, Thomas thought.

"Did Miss Levine tell you when she first experienced symptoms?" Thomas asked, and Bessie Mae frowned. She was a tiny thing, the pillow she clutched as she sat in bed more than adequate for her modesty.

"It's been a couple of days," Bessie Mae said. "She was havin' dinner with Benny a couple days ago, and I know she didn't feel up to snuff then. I remember her sayin', 'sometimes you gotta just paint on a good face.'" Bessie Mae managed a brave smile. "Can I come up and see her?"

"Indeed," Thomas replied. "That would be important."

"She's like to die?"

Thomas hesitated. "Come see her today." Bessie Mae understood his meaning, and pressed her face into her pillow.

Chapter Seventeen

"A moment," Constable Aldrich said as they walked out of the Clarissa. "Come. Let me show you something." They walked along the inlet trail for a hundred feet, and the constable stepped out onto the broad wharf. The *Willis Head,* a small steamer showing Canadian colors, was moored on the south side of the wharf, riding easy in the gentle waters.

Aldrich's boot heels were loud on the resonant wood planking.

"We taking an early morning dip?" Hardy said to Thomas. "It might not be a bad idea, filthy as I feel right now."

Short and stocky, the constable walked briskly, his hands thrust into the pockets of his coat and his chin tucked low. The two physicians had to hustle to keep pace. Eventually, Aldrich stopped ten feet from the end of the wharf. He walked to the north edge, and slapped a hand on top of one of the pilings. Behind them, the dark shape of the *Willis Head* towered over them. The Clarissa Hotel, her detailing just now beginning to sharpen in the early dawn light, looked like a giant box rising out of the glassy calm of Jefferson Inlet.

From his walks, Thomas knew that at low tide, there was a strip of shoreline between the hotel's water-side pilings and the inlet, littered with the remains of the inlet's flora and fauna—and the varied detritus of human endeavor—little of it pleasant. A guest standing in one of the windows facing Jefferson Inlet had a wonderful view when the rains lifted and the sun touched the country. That same guest could lean forward from the window a bit and look down at the collected garbage and filth.

"Now, you can see." The constable's sweeping gesture included the Clarissa in all its black, rank glory. "Where do they throw the garbage, yes? Where does the sewage go?"

Thomas stepped closer to the edge of the wharf, the water eight feet below. Ten hotel windows faced the inlet—four on the ground floor and four more on the second, capped by two garret windows high above. One of those uppermost windows, Thomas knew, was less than a dozen steps from Lucy Levine's door.

"You see?" Aldrich asked. "You see where it all goes?"

Below each window, the raw cedar planking was streaked and splotched, but only partly from the constant run-off of rain and mist.

"When I see the young lady's room, I start to think," the constable said. "I used to fish from time to time out here, and I see them. *Whoosh,* out the window it goes, you know. Slops the side of the building, even. They just toss out the pots. A lot easier than walking down to the privy, yes?"

"That's a fine thing, isn't it," Hardy muttered. "That cedar cladding makes a rather effective sponge, I would think."

Thomas stood quietly, hands in his pockets, gazing at the looming structure. "And how do we deal with that?" he asked.

"The literature says that it's unlikely that the contagion is spread through the air," Hardy pointed out. "With the bouquet down here, I keep reminding myself of that. If that's actually correct, then it really doesn't matter what the place *smells* like, hard as that is to believe. I would worry more about children of the village playing along the shore, perhaps exploring among the pilings that support the rear of the building. We know that contaminated water certainly *is* an issue, Thomas."

"We can hope that the constant rain and storms beating against the back of the building mitigate for us, but that only adds to the danger down below."

"Remind me to fish elsewhere," Aldrich muttered.

"Indeed. But it would seem that this is behavior easily changed." Thomas shook his head in disgust. "The entire building is such that it's impossible to engineer anything that might pass as sanitary. The privies can be limed, but this?"

Hardy clapped his hands. "Well, we have work to do. Perhaps we can influence Jules to fence the area behind his building."

"I will speak to him," Aldrich said. "And remind him that there is an ordinance on the books that addresses public nuisance. He is going to have to train his patrons and his staff, I think, yes? If this hotel must be quarantined, I will do so."

"Are the eminent town fathers going to help us or hinder?" Hardy asked, and Aldrich laughed dryly.

"Town fathers?"

"The good men who pay your salary, sir."

"This," and Aldrich placed a hand over his modest badge, "comes from the county sheriff. The village has no force."

"Ah. No mayor? No village council?"

"That is right. And that is why no one bothers the Clarissa. It is a manageable thing."

Thomas turned and gazed at the *Willis Head*. "The ship must not leave until we know. The first mate is in the hotel, at risk. Three of the sailors have apparently gone to the logging camp, since that's where the gambling is." He turned to look at Lucius. "We must find out what Eleanor Stephens has been up to...the whole arrangement is most curious."

"I find it pretty obvious," Hardy said. "I've not met the girl's father, but it would appear that she has interests that the Clarissa serves really quite well. At the very least, Miss Levine is a dear friend of hers."

"If Sitzberger is ill with the cholera, he's taken it to the camp." He held up his hands hopelessly. "My God, Lucius, this thing is going to tear us in every direction. Even to Seattle, where Miss Levine's roommate has gone."

"A telegram to the authorities in Seattle, giving them her name, and a caution about her condition and what we having going on here," Hardy said. "That's paramount. They must be alerted. And here, cultures. Every last person. We must know the extent of all this. If this chap Sitzberger is now ill, then we open another front. Whoever *he* has associated with, who *he* lives with."

They left the wharf, with Aldrich returning to the Clarissa.

"Can he be trusted to follow through for us?" Hardy asked as the constable disappeared through the front door of the hotel.

"I trust him," Thomas said. "He is intelligent enough to understand the gravity of this."

Behind the clinic, smoke was billowing up from the incinerator, and as he stepped inside the building, Thomas could smell the cloying aroma of the various disinfectants. He heard urgent voices. Bertha Auerbach walked out of the examining room and stopped short when she saw Thomas.

"Miss Stephens has left us," the nurse announced.

"Left us? What do you mean?" Out of habit, Thomas looked at the Seth Thomas clock. "Not yet seven in the morning, and she is gone?"

"She has left our employ," Bertha said icily.

"I would have predicted that," Hardy said. "We have a replacement? For her and about ten more?"

"We'll see," Bertha replied. "But if you have a moment, Doctor?"

"What is it?"

"Upstairs with Miss Levine. Her step-father has made himself a nuisance."

"Miss Levine's *step-father?*"

Bertha held up an impatient, shushing hand. "No, Doctor. Eleanor *Stephens'* step-father. Pastor Roland Patterson."

"I beg your pardon?"

"Pastor Roland Patterson is with Miss Levine now."

"A little prayer might help as much as anything," the physician replied. "Is there any change in her condition?"

"We have been able to administer nearly four liters…nearly that much evacuated, I fear. But I sense some small relief in the cramping. It may be my imagination. Her temperature has stabilized at ninety-six."

"What does Patterson want?"

"I will let you talk with him, Doctor." Thomas watched Bertha's eyes as she talked, and saw the characteristic narrowing that said her patience was running thin.

"Talking with the good pastor is the last thing on my mind just now," Thomas said. "Can we spare Howard Deaton this morning?" Thomas said. "He needs to ride out to the Dutch Tract camp and find a logger named Ben Sitzberger. The lad who was with Huckla yesterday. He needs to bring both of them to the clinic immediately."

"I believe Howard was looking for a few moments sleep," Bertha said.

"He can sleep while the team takes him to the camp," Thomas said. "The horses surely know the way." He nodded at Hardy. "Join me? You haven't had the pleasure of meeting the good pastor. I lanced a boil on his bottom, and he's never forgiven me."

"I would certainly prefer the lancing to the boil," Hardy answered, "but then again, it was his posterior, not mine." He followed Thomas to the examination room, where they scrubbed and disinfected as if they were headed for deep surgery. Finally, jackets removed and shirtsleeves rolled up to the elbow, they mounted the stairs to the second floor, hands still dripping alcohol.

Roland Patterson was immensely tall, slender and graceful, almost theatrical in his movements, his posture ram-rod straight. Various patients during the past few months had reported that *they* attended services at Patterson's church to enjoy the pastor's performances, implying that the young physician and his bride should do the same.

But Thomas had not been able to banish the writing of Geoffrey Chaucer from his mind whenever Patterson dominated the room. The pastor's clothing was not the rude cloth of a poor cleric. His black suit fitted his body to perfection. He somehow managed to appear as if he rose above the muck and grime of Port McKinney and its earthly industries, from his brushed, flawlessly blocked narrow brimmed hat down to his expensive, polished boots. Well aware of his commanding appearance, Patterson kept his sharp tongue on no leash at all.

"Pastor," Thomas greeted, and he managed a smile—not from any affection for the man, but at the memory of Patterson trying to instruct him in the boil's treatment even as the pastor sank under the ether. "Let me introduce Dr. Lucius Hardy. He has joined our staff."

The chubby Hardy clamped Patterson's elegant hand in one of his paws, and Thomas caught the fleeting expression of distaste and discomfort on the pastor's face. "How do you do." Patterson didn't wait for a response. "Eleanor tells me that you claim the cholera has struck." He took a deep breath, as if preparing for a difficult lecture. "I've examined Miss Levine myself, and find myself truly puzzled by your diagnosis, young man."

Thomas felt the damned blush rise on his neck and cheeks.

"I'm sorry you're puzzled, sir. But there is no doubt. None whatsoever."

"And how do you know this?"

"It's our business to know it," Hardy said. He had first grinned at Patterson's pomposity, but the grin soon vanished and his voice took on an edge. "You have a microscope at your disposal, Pastor?"

"I do not *need* a microscope," Patterson announced. "Let me instruct you." He sucked in a breath and regarded the ceiling through half-lidded eyes. "Cholera is a disease of the fetid east, sir. I have had the dubious honor of traveling extensively in that very land, spending more time in Calcutta than I would have liked. I have seen the filth of the Ganges, I have seen the degradation of the people." He leveled his eyes on Thomas to make sure that the physician was listening.

"I have seen how those filthy heathen live, with their filthy heathen ways, and I can see plainly that the scourge of disease is their birthright. Now, to imply that such a disease—that *cholera*—has somehow been cast loose in this tiny village, where *good* people make their honest living, where the principles of cleanly living are embraced…"

He was interrupted by a loud laugh. Hardy threw back his head and bellowed, then just as quickly recovered.

"Sorry," Hardy said to Thomas and then glanced at Lucy Levine, who didn't appear to care if the world collapsed around her. "Sir, with all due respect, you spout nonsense from a century ago. It is absurd to say, *'this is where a disease may occur, and no where else.'* Perhaps a hundred years ago, or two, the ignorant believed that myth. And if you wish to broach the topic of filth, perhaps you would like to visit this young lady's room at the Clarissa? Perhaps you would like to gaze upon the very back wall of that fine establishment, where offal is routinely tossed out the windows, to foul the waters of the inlet…where children of all these fine people play and where fishing is a routine pastime."

"Now listen to me," Patterson started to say, and a long, slender forefinger pointed at the heavens, a finger of discipline and temper. But Hardy wasn't impressed or intimidated.

"No, I don't think we have the time for such nonsense," Hardy continued. "You may believe what you wish, sir. You are not the one charged with treating this patient."

"When I arrived," Patterson said, drawing himself to his full height, "these women were violating this young woman's privacy. I saw that with my own eyes."

"These women?" Thomas asked quietly. "Are you referring to the nurses, sir?"

"You call them so," Patterson said smugly.

Thomas turned and saw Bertha Auerbach standing by the stairway, arms folded. Her eyes were dangerously black, and he could see the outline of a jaw that was clenched so tightly she was in danger of chipped teeth.

"And kindly inform me," Hardy continued, "how they were violating her privacy? And while you're at it, tell me why you felt the need to watch? You are no relative of Miss Levine's. You have no business in this ward."

"You see the instruments there." Patterson nodded toward an enameled pan that held a freshly sterilized bulb and rectal tube.

"I have no time for this idiocy," Hardy snapped. "My God, man, you give ignorance a whole new portrait. I will take thirty seconds with you, and then you will leave this establishment…or by God, I'll carry you out." He stepped so close that Patterson had to retreat a step to avoid being bowled over. "The patient can hold no food or liquid. She vomits and evacuates astonishing volumes of fluids, and were the nurses not able to replenish that fluid rectally, the patient would soon expire from dehydration. That is how cholera kills, my friend. *Cholera.* You hear me?"

Patterson had started to reply, but Hardy gave him no chance. "The bacilli infest the intestinal tract—and I'll use whatever term your overly sensitive nature prefers. The *gut,* the *bowel,* the *colon,* her *person.* It infests and turns its *environs* into loathsome, rotten tissue. There are cases where in final stages patients evacuate the very lining of their gut. So, *these women* you so easily insult with your own peculiar brand of ignorance, *these women* risk their own safety and replace the liquid in the only way we know how."

He took a deep breath. "The last major epidemic of cholera—and it killed some three thousands of people—occurred in New York City but nineteen years ago, not Calcutta. That's along the Hudson River, should you have forgotten, not the Ganges. There have been smaller, sporadic outbreaks now and then, and in *every* case, the outbreaks can be traced to unsanitary conditions. Now, just how Miss Levine came to be infected, we don't know. We are going to find out. We will use every measure at our disposal, although those measures are regrettably few. You can help but I will not allow you to hinder."

Patterson's tone sunk to a dangerous whisper. "You claim cholera, yet you admit that you have no notion of its origin." A disdainful curl of the lip remained. Hardy took no notice.

"Not yet, sir. And the longer you stand in our way, the longer that discovery will take. If you want to be useful, you could convince your daughter, Miss Stephens, that our shortage of nursing staff is acute, especially if the epidemic grows, as it no doubt will do. Why she left us, I couldn't say, but I can't say that I blame her. Fighting cholera is a fearsome task, and she is young and inexperienced. Perhaps she might benefit from your good counsel, since every pair of hands is so badly needed." He flashed a thin smile. "And now, if you'll excuse us?"

Patterson's eyes narrowed, and he regarded Hardy for a long moment. "Where are you from, *Doctor?*"

"Where I or you or anyone else is from doesn't matter one whit," Hardy snapped. "Excuse us."

It appeared to take Patterson a moment to reach a conclusion. "Very well. But I can promise you that if Miss Levine fails to recover, we shall speak again. In the meantime, I *forbid* you to spread the rumor of cholera in this community."

"*You* forbid? How very interesting," Hardy replied. "I readily admit ignorance, since I've just arrived. But Thomas, does this fellow hold a position in this community of which I am unaware? Perhaps even a medical degree that he has kept hidden from us?"

"He heads a small parish. His church is down the hill from us, on Angeles Street."

"I'm impressed that you know of our existence," Patterson said. "I have not seen you celebrating the Sabbath with any congregation, and certainly not ours. I understand that your wife has given birth. Perhaps you understand the importance of baptism."

"I'm sure I do," Thomas said. *But not from you.* "Fred Jules and his wife need considerable assistance at the Clarissa, should your flock care to pitch in, Pastor. I'm sure you'll lead them in that effort."

"*That* den of…*that* abominable place…" Patterson tried and then clamped his jaw shut. He glanced once more at Lucy Levine, and then turned away from the bed. As he passed Bertha, he didn't pause in his step, but said tersely, "I shall speak with Eleanor."

They listened to his steps on the stairway for a second, and then Thomas knelt at Lucy Levine's bedside. Her skin was dry, her eyes appearing collapsed into her skull. With the stethoscope, he listened to her lungs and heart, then stood up thoughtfully, folding the instrument. "My, my," he breathed. "If she just has the strength to hold on. How long has it been since she vomited?"

"I would say an hour," Bertha replied. "But a feeble attempt at best."

"Then a tiny amount of stimulant," Thomas said. "A few drops of brandy, perhaps, if she'll tolerate it."

"Now is when I would attempt hypodermoclysis," Hardy said. "If you have the instruments."

"Have or can fashion them," Thomas said. "Have you done such?"

"No."

"Nor I."

"We have little to lose," Hardy said. "I will see what I can scavenge."

Hardy left and Thomas beckoned Bertha Auerbach. "Dr. Hardy is suggesting that we actually inject fluid beneath the skin for absorption into the blood vessels and lymphatic system," he said, and bent to touch Lucy's flank through the blanket, between the ribs and the hip bone. "A fine canula positioned carefully, between the skin and fascia." He glanced up at the nurse, who listened without comment. "It must not penetrate the fascia, Berti." He shifted the blanket and lifted a fold of skin, so pathetically desiccated that it remained pinched after he removed his fingers. "Just under the skin. It demands a fine touch, since the canula's bore is large. And then with a fountain syringe, we allow a liter or two of fluid over at least twenty minutes." He made a face. "Should we *have* twenty minutes."

"And the solution?" Bertha asked.

"Chloride of sodium and sodium bicarbonate, I should think. Dr. Hardy will instruct you further. But she is so cold, so emaciated, that it may be the only way."

"Conditions at the Clarissa are grave?" A note of worry had crept into her voice.

"Impossible," Thomas replied. "So much to do, and to be done immediately. On top of that, we must find the young man who spent his time with this young lady. He is at risk, along with everyone he meets. If he's still alive. Howard was willing to go?"

"Of course. And if I may say so…" The uncharacteristic hesitation turned Thomas' head. "You must take time to look in on your wife and son," Bertha said.

"Ah," Thomas replied ruefully, "but not in this condition."
He took a deep breath. "Berti, I want everyone turned away
from the clinic today. We must be prepared to dose our effort
as well as our medications. Nothing but the direst emergencies
until this has passed."

"I understand. You were to meet with the Schmidts this morning."

"I *was*. I have business with him, anyway. And I must also
stop by the newspaper and make sure that Mr. Garrison is
entirely on our side."

"The whole community must know?"

"Indeed. Must know what to *do*, idiots like Roland Patterson
not withstanding."

"He may yet understand," Bertha said. "He is not used to
having his authority questioned in such a blunt fashion."

Thomas laughed. "Refreshing, this Dr. Hardy. But Patterson?
You are a believer in miracles, my dear." The familiarity prompted
a raised eyebrow. "And Berti," he said as he started to turn away,
"make absolutely certain that you, Mrs. Whitman and Mrs.
Crowell are taking care of yourselves. It is the nurses who are
always most at risk in cases like this, handling bedding and such."

In cases like this, he thought with a twinge of self-conscious
doubt. This was his first, and he felt completely at sea. He looked
toward the back of the ward. The door of the child's room was
closed, and Mrs. Snyder's tiny figure two beds down lay quietly.
"The Snyders?"

"The same. Marcus is with the child just now. His wife is so
frail." He nodded. "I'll scrub, and have a look at her before I leave."

A few moments later, as he returned to the second floor ward
from the dispensary, he saw Lucius Hardy kneeling beside Lucy
Levine's bedside, in close conference with Bertha Auerbach.

"Now, ever so gently," Thomas heard Dr. Lucius Hardy say
as he approached. "The object here is to inject the liquid *just*
under the skin, like so," and despite his large hands, he handled
the razor-sharp canula deftly. "And then sterile padding to seal
the wound." He motioned with his head, and Bertha bandaged

the instrument and the first six inches of the rubber tubing with clean linen saturated with carbolic acid.

"Let gravity do the work," he instructed. "And as the fluid flows under the skin ever so slowly, a little gentle massage will help distribute it to the surrounding tissues for absorption."

"If we see no reaction almost immediately," Thomas added, "then the process should be repeated." *That's what the book says,* he considered adding. His sleeves were still rolled up, and he held his hands with the fingers spread, allowing the antiseptic to dry.

"Exactly so," Hardy agreed. "I am optimistic." He had some reason to be, since Lucy Levine had been quiet for some moments, her skin temperature elevated a bit, her pulse ever so slightly pronounced.

"Mrs. Crowell is with us on this?" Thomas asked, and Bertha nodded without looking up.

"She's downstairs with Mr. Malone at the moment."

Thomas leaned over and looked closely at Lucy, whose eyelids flickered. Thomas thought he saw the ghost of a feeble smile—perhaps not.

"You know everyone in this village, Berti. If there is someone who might assist us, I'd like to know today." He started to reach out, to place a soothing palm on Lucy's forehead, then stopped. "There is so much to do," he said, drawing back.

He strode back through the empty ward, wondering what the storm would be like when it actually struck.

Chapter Eighteen

Thomas stopped just inside the door of 101 Lincoln, astonished. Dressed in an elegant purple robe, Alvina stood in the doorway to the spacious library, the infant swaddled in blue linen and cradled in her arms. John Thomas Parks was suckling a fashionably late breakfast.

"You're up," Thomas said, and realized how foolish he sounded. "I mean, *should* you be up?"

"John Thomas needs to see the world, although I admit, those ravishing blue eyes of his haven't done much looking." She frowned at her husband's clothes. "You didn't leave this morning looking so ill fitted, even early as the hour was."

"Ah. I needed to change at the clinic," he said. He drew near to her and she wrinkled her nose. "It's the disinfectant," he said. "My skin is pickled."

"Word is spreading through town," she said. "I believe Gert has had half a dozen visitors in the past hour, early as it is."

"So you know."

"That we have cholera? Yes, I know." She leaned forward and kissed him, but kept her hands on the infant.

"I feel as if I should take a hot bath for about a week."

"Or a long swim in the inlet," Alvi suggested.

"Ah…no. That was a nasty little discovery we made just after dawn, Dr. Hardy, Constable Aldrich, and I. The Clarissa is dumping offal directly into the Jefferson behind the hotel."

"But children *play* down there." She pulled a corner of the blanket over her son's face as if he needed protection from the awful idea.

"Indeed they do. Or *did*."

"The girl who is infected…"

"Lucy Levine."

"She is a dear, sweet thing. Will she survive?"

"I don't…I *wish* that I could say yes." He shrugged off his cloak. "There are signs that she may. But I have never seen a disease so vicious, Alvi. It is as if she is being devoured from within, as if her entire gut is held by some strange, raging beast. Her room at the Clarissa was a sight to behold. That it can even be sufficiently cleaned is open to question. It seems to me that the entire building is fashioned from cedar, so porous that it soaks up the effluent like a sponge." He shook his head. "They dump the chamber pots out the windows, into the inlet."

"Father once dealt with an outbreak of cholera at one of the fishing villages to the northwest."

"Mortalities?"

"Some two hundred from a village of two hundred fifty. He managed to avoid contracting the disease, but one of his nurses didn't."

"And she…"

"Died. Mild symptoms at first, then more severe. She arose from bed one afternoon, convinced that she was on the mend, took ten steps, and fell as dead as a stone."

"My heavens. I was thinking it might be best if you were able to travel to Seattle for a few days, Alvi. The trip by water would not be arduous for you. Just until this outbreak has passed."

One of Alvi's shapely eyebrows rose. "I think not, Doctor Thomas."

"But the risk."

"There is no risk for us," she said, sounding as if she knew with absolute certainty the location of every cholera bacillus on the peninsula.

"There is always risk, Alvina."

"And the trip itself would be," she said. "In this house, we are as safe as we can be. The water is hot and endless, thanks to the Victor down in the basement. I am eating lightly from only the best foods, properly prepared. John Thomas here is eating *only* the best, I assure you." She smiled and gently jostled the feeding infant, who released his toothless gums and offered Thomas a wide smile of satisfaction.

"I could be jealous," he grinned.

"You came for lunch, sir?" She looked down at her full breast and the infant's face that was once again buried against it, then laughed at her husband's expression. "Do not worry yourself about me," she said.

"That's easily said."

"You have enough clothing at the clinic for a frequent change?"

"I came to fetch more," he said.

"And the kitchen there?"

"Stocked," he said. The kitchen had also been a recent addition, dominated by an ungodly expensive Acme coal-fired cooking range that had taken six men to lift from the freight wagon.

"And who is doing the cooking?"

"That will be an issue," Thomas said. "Bertha *was,* during the day, with Mrs. Crowell doing her best at night. But both are so consumed now." He sighed and sat down on the foyer bench. "With but four patients. My God."

"Four with the cholera?"

"No. Mr. Malone, the high rigger, lingers in a coma. The Snyder child is healing nicely, but must be quarantined, along with her father. Mrs. Snyder and Lucy Levine are ill with the cholera."

"You suspect there will be more?"

"I know so. There is every probability of one at the logging camp on the Dutch Tract."

Alvi frowned. "Gert could assist you."

"No. I don't want her down there."

"How can there be danger in the kitchen, Doctor Thomas?"

"With this disease, there is no safe haven. I will speak with Bertha about it. She knows everyone. Miss Stephens left us this morning."

"That is no surprise."

"I suppose not. I was thinking of asking her to work the kitchen, but I doubt that she can cook, either."

"Be kind, Doctor Thomas."

"She's been down to the Clarissa—apparently she is a friend of Miss Levine. I don't know what the relationship is." He looked sideways at Alvi. "Do they share a beau?"

"I have no idea. Lucy's current beau is a handsome, randy, sweet-talking youngster. What Ben Sitzberger has been able to arrange with the ladies is anyone's guess. But Lucy is in no condition for idle conversation, and I doubt that Eleanor could manage such a discussion." Alvi pivoted and glanced at the clock. "You were to talk with the Schmidts at nine?"

"Was. I sent word for them not to come today. She should go to Seattle herself. She can have the surgery there, and proper post-operative care."

"The delay is dangerous."

"No more so than our circumstances, Alvi. I'll find a moment to speak with Schmidt and encourage them not to delay departure."

"And if Carlotta refuses?"

"That would be foolish. But I cannot force her."

With deft movements, she tucked the infant into the wrap and pulled her own robe to cover herself. "You want to carry him upstairs for me?"

He hesitated and held out his hands as if they were coated with the most vile of muck. "I would, most certainly, but I shouldn't."

"Oh, for Heaven's sakes, Doctor Thomas. You smell like the inside of an antiseptic bottle. And we'll change his wrap after he's made his statement."

He accepted the infant, finding himself absurdly clumsy with the small bundle.

"Like so," Alvi instructed, adjusting until John Thomas rode easy in the cradle of Thomas' arm. "It's not so difficult after all, is it."

"Are the stairways too much for you?"

She guffawed in a most unladylike manner. "You are *such* an old lady, Doctor Thomas. The exercise is good for me. You yourself have said as much countless times." Even so, Thomas noticed the care with which she placed each step on the wide staircase, left hand guiding up the rail. He followed, amused with the puzzled expression on John Thomas' face as the infant tried to make sense of this person looming just out of his range of focus. Alvi stopped halfway up and took several deep breaths before continuing.

"Earlier today I had to stop three times," she confided. "Tomorrow I shall take to the high-wheel with John Thomas strapped to my back."

"The wheel has been stolen," Thomas fibbed. "I made sure of that."

"Then I shall buy a new one. Mr. Lindeman has two in the store now." She turned at the landing and held out her arms. He maneuvered the infant as if the child was a stiff stick of firewood.

"The Sitzberger boy is ill?" Alvi asked. "Is he the one who worries you at camp?"

"I believe so. Perhaps others as well. How do you come to know him?"

"Sometimes, the employees at the Clarissa want a woman's touch for their medical needs, Doctor Thomas. I make it a point to visit now and then."

"I never knew that."

Her gentle chuckle told him that there might be much that he didn't know.

Alvi saw the nonplussed expression on her husband's face. "You forget sometimes that I was *born* in this town, Thomas. Well, not exactly that. But since I was a year old. It's easy to come to know just about everyone."

"I suppose it is."

"And I have mentioned to you on occasion about working with Viola Jules to keep the girls healthy. It's no mystery. My father wouldn't spend much time down there, but there's a need, Doctor Thomas."

He watched her deft movements as she changed the infant's cotton diaper and despite his best intentions recoiled back an involuntary step at the odor.

"Nature's little factory," Alvi laughed. "You've smelled worse."

"Indeed. We had another visitor at the clinic this morning. Apparently he felt the need to confirm Miss Levine's condition for himself. The good Pastor Patterson?"

"Oh? Be careful of Roland Patterson, husband."

"You've heard a lot for one confined."

"I've been up since five, sir," she said. "And just moments after Miss Stephens quit your employ, Gert began to funnel all the best gossip from Port McKinney to my eager ears. You'd be amazed how efficient we all are. Miss Stephens lost no time in embellishing her tales of the dread conditions at the clinic."

"Patterson barged right in, first announcing that the disease could *not* be cholera. Lucius took him to task quite handily, though. The pastor is an idiot, Alvi."

"I would not call him that. But he sees what he wants to see." She held both hands to the sides of her head, mimicking a horse's blinders. "On several occasions in years past, he ranted and raved at me when I would go to the Clarissa to tend a sick girl. Did he use the expression 'the devil's hovel' with you?"

"No."

"I'm surprised. That's one of his favorites. But it *doesn't* surprise me that his step-daughter, with all her young and tender years, found tending cholera patients beyond her bearing."

"Yet she visits the Clarissa?"

Alvi's expression was quizzical. "I suspect that every soul in town has visited the Clarissa at one time or another. At the best of times, their cuisine can be tolerable. And Eleanor is of an age, Doctor Thomas. She would find friendship with the young women there. And their beaus."

Gert James appeared in the doorway. "Howard Deaton is here for you, Doctor."

"On what cause? He was to go to the logging camp without delay."

"He didn't say, Doctor."

Alvi caught his arm and turned him just enough to plant a kiss. "Write when you have the time," she said cheerfully, but he marked the deep concern in her eyes.

Chapter Nineteen

Marcus Snyder sat on the edge of the bed, arms wrapped around his mid-section. Stripped of his clothing, he wore only a loose cotton night shirt that reached his knees.

"Lie down, man," Thomas said, taking Snyder by the shoulders.

"I…bloody…can't," Snyder groaned through gritted teeth.

"Laudanum," Thomas snapped at Bertha.

"Dr. Hardy has just given him a quarter grain."

"Then again. Do we have Salol? If we do, that as well."

"Dr. Hardy is in the dispensary making preparations for Mrs. Snyder."

A violent shiver raced through Snyder's frame. "Warm blankets, now," Thomas said. "And hot stupes for his gut." Again he took Snyder by the shoulders, feeling the trembling in the man's thin body. "You must help us, Marcus. We know how to fight this thing."

"Feels like I'm bein' cut in half," Snyder managed, and he almost panted, so difficult was it for him to breathe. "What the hell…Flora?"

"She's upstairs, man. She'll be fine. Now lie back. You must do that." To Bertha, he said, "I'll try the morphine by injection instead of the laudanum. The relief must be quicker." With linens above the Kelly pad, Snyder finally stretched out in the bed, and Thomas watched as the nurse spread blankets across the quaking body.

"Shit," Snyder said as the chemical flame from the morphine burned into his leg. And then his gut exploded, the geyser of diarrhea soaking night shirt and bedding. Thomas marveled at

Bertha Auerbach's aggressive efficiency as in a moment Snyder was cleaned, and the soiled bedding and nightshirt thrust into a covered enameled bucket. He lay back, cursing roundly, the morphine slurring his words.

Bertha glanced up at the ceiling, indicating the women's ward upstairs, as Thomas turned away from Snyder. She whispered, "I fear that she is worse. We must find someone for the child to stay with."

"The child is the least of our problems," Thomas said. Marcus Snyder's eyes were closed, and Thomas could see the spastic contractions of his gut. "I'll see to the Salol," he said. "If he hasn't yet begun to vomit, it may be of some use. We have caught this thing early."

Back in the dispensary, he blessed the memory of Dr. John Haines, Alvi's father. The fat stoppered glass jar was two-thirds full of the large .06 gram tablets of phenyl salicylate, and he pulverized two, then added two more for good measure, and dissolved the powder in water, along with a dose of laudanum.

"Four Salol with laudanum, every hour as long as he tolerates it without nausea," Thomas said to Bertha, who had just positioned one of the mustard stupes to Snyder's abdomen. He handed her the glass. Looking toward the rear of the ward as if for inspiration, he saw the single rooms and remembered his first patient of the day, a man nearly forgotten.

"Mr. Malone?" he asked.

"As before," Bertha said. "He has survived the night."

"Remarkable. Have you tested his reaction to stimulant?"

"I have checked him on the hour, Doctor. There is no change. Although I thought that perhaps there was slight movement when I held the ammonia caplet under his nose. My imagination, I suspect." She assisted Snyder with the small glass, and he held one hand on his gut, the tears streaming down his face in agony. "If you can keep this down, it will help," she soothed.

He turned at footsteps and caught a glimpse of Lucius Hardy walking past the ward.

"A moment," he said, and Bertha nodded.

He entered the dispensary to see Hardy at the mortar and pestle, the heavy jar of Salol on the counter.

"So," Hardy muttered. "You managed to spend five minutes at home." He watched as Thomas industriously scrubbed his hands under the flow of hot water from the French table, a wheeled device that carried two five-gallon glass jars, one for hot and one for cold. Rinsed, Thomas submerged his hands in a pan of dilute carbolic acid. With a pick that had been in the carbolic bath, he cleaned under his fingernails, and then plunged his hands into a second pan of methyl alcohol. "And Snyder?"

"He will fight," Thomas said. "He has taken the Salol and laudanum. His stages are the earliest, and he is strong. His wife?"

"We'll see," Hardy said, with none of his characteristic optimism. "There is so much pain that she cannot see. She cannot think." He glanced up at Thomas. "I am constantly fascinated by the aggressive nature of this bacillus. I have never seen anything like it." He took a deep breath. "All is well at home?"

"Yes. All is well. I brought a bale of clothing so that I might change frequently."

"I have what I have, with more at what's his name? Lindeman's?"

"The same. The clinic has an account, of course."

"I shall find time to visit him."

"Did Bertha tell you, by the way? Malone still lives. She may have seen a reaction in the eyes."

"And *that's* remarkable," Hardy said. "Oh," and he held up a hand sharply. "I have had to speak with Mrs. Crowell more than once." As he spoke, he rolled up his own sleeves. "She understands *aseptic* only in the most general terms, Thomas. The motions are there, but not the accomplishment. At one point, she removed the soiled linen from Miss Levine's bed, and then returned with fresh—without a thought to her hands. I instructed her, but she bridles in her true matronly fashion."

"She washed, however?"

"I fear I mortified her. I escorted her to the upstairs station and supervised the procedure. I'll apologize if I have to, but she must be with us on this."

Thomas nodded, but after hearing the confrontation with Pastor Patterson, he could imagine the blunt Dr. Hardy's choice of words with Adelaide Crowell. "Stephens has left. We can't afford to lose Mrs. Crowell," he said tactfully, and Hardy's smile was edgy.

"I'd rather her feelings suffered than have her become the cholera's accomplice," he said. "Or a victim herself, which is more likely."

"I agree. I'll speak to her as well. And I think a telegram to St. Mary's is certainly in order. They may be able to lend us staff."

"The Whitman woman?"

"She will come in this evening. A veteran and a jewell."

"That's good. I keep thinking about how this contagion is encouraged," Hardy mused and shrugged heavily. "It seems logical that our source of contagion is the Clarissa."

"Brought by ship, do you suppose?"

"Perhaps, and had the *Willis Head* been at dock for a week or more, I would suspect so, but she's but a day or two in, I'm told." Hardy looked hard at Thomas. "Gut cultures. That's the only way. In every case. The Snyder child, the missing logger… if they are clear, fine. But I doubt that optimism."

Thomas looked heavenward. "I have sent Howard to fetch the young man. With a culture from him, we'll know…" He turned as Mrs. Crowell appeared in the doorway.

"Doctor," she whispered, "Mrs. Snyder has passed…"

Hardy reacted as if stung, bursting past the wide-eyed woman and racing for the stairway, Thomas hard on his heels. They reached the upstairs ward to see the Snyder child, little nine year-old Matilda, prostrate over her mother's chest, arms encircling a body that no longer responded.

The child wailed as Thomas took her gently in his arms. The child could have weighed no more than forty pounds, but her skinny arms were surprisingly strong.

"Let me," Bertha Auerbach said behind Thomas, and he turned, handing the child to her. With the stethoscope, he roamed Flora Snyder's chest, but the heart was silent. One foot twitched in the cholera's oddly characteristic post-mortem response, and the child saw her mother move.

"She lives," Matilda cried hysterically.

"No, child," Bertha soothed. Thomas blocked out their voices, listening for any tell-tale sounds from the patient. No blood pushed through the carotids on the emaciated neck, no whispers from lungs. Flora Snyder lay flat, deflated, eyes glazed, jaw slack. Thomas reached out and gently touched the unprotected left eye, with no response. He looped the stethoscope around his neck and consulted his watch.

"Mr. Snyder must be informed," he said. "A sad, sad thing."

The child's tiny body shook with sobs. Thomas lowered his voice. "The child must be washed." He turned to look at Bertha. "Will you do that? And then she must remain isolated." He reached out and took Matilda's hand. "I'm sorry, Tilly."

"There are four other children in the Snyder home," Bertha said.

Thomas stared at her blankly. Lucius Hardy pulled the linen up over Mrs. Snyder's face.

"We must ascertain that they are well," Bertha said. She had not released the child, but hugged her against her clean apron. "Marcus has a brother living over in Carter. We must send a message to him. I will have Mr. Deaton tend to that. If all is well, Gwendolyn…that's the oldest daughter…is perfectly capable of keeping things together. I will have Mr. Deaton fetch her so that she may have ample instructions about what must be done."

"Howard has driven to the logging camp, Berti."

"Then…"

"We have but three patients, Thomas. If you will examine the Snyder children, I will watch over the clinic," Hardy said. "I will want cultures of all of them. And from the residents of the Clarissa. And from the loggers at the camp. Cultures, cultures, cultures." He punched a fist into the palm of his hand. "All. It will be simplest if you have them come to the clinic. By morning, we shall have answers. Pray that will be early enough."

Chapter Twenty

Thomas bridled and saddled the gelding, and felt as if he should don blinders so that he might finish *one* errand without interruption. He swung onto the horse with a keen sense of foreboding, hating the thought of leaving the clinic, hating the thought of what he might find…and strangely excited at the same time by the whole challenge that consumed his world.

The gelding, freshly groomed and looking as magnificent as his shaggy personality allowed, stepped out smartly. The rain had stopped, and once more sunshine threatened to break through the clouds. A few more days of such weather, and some local wag would refer to the past fortnight as a "dry spell."

Thomas had spent a privileged childhood and youth in Connecticut neighborhoods of neatly groomed village streets, white houses in neat rows with their white fences fronting the by-ways, meticulous stone walls at property lines, and overflowing flower beds. In medical school, claustrophobia had been his companion during the years spent in the teeming, dark city.

But here, as the gelding made his way through the slop and the rocks and the muck, Port McKinney reminded him of some of the hand-tinted engravings of carbuncles in the medical texts, an ugly little growth on damaged skin.

At one point in the village's development, an attempt had been made at uniformity. A three block area bordered by Lincoln, Gamble and Lewis Streets actually looked village-like, with the doctor's grand, Victorian house at 101 Lincoln overlooking the town, with the new brick bank—soon to go bankrupt and become the home of the Clinic—and a scattering of other buildings that appeared stout enough to survive a generation. But then folks became impatient as the timber industry boomed. The favored structures became slabwood shacks built from mill scroungings, often with canvas providing the roofs, the structure thrown up in record time. When a shack's owner died or moved on, the materials in his little hovel were appropriated by another.

Marcus and Flora Snyder, along with their five children, had managed better. Thomas found their home a mile north along the inlet on a rise a stone's throw from the water. Snyder had built first a one-room cabin, tight and pert of line, with steeply pitched roof and generous overhang. Two additions had been added over the years as the family grew and as Marcus could afford the mill boards.

As he approached, Thomas saw that the privy was a hundred paces from the house, slightly downhill, obscured by a grove of cedar saplings. It was as neat as the rest of the homestead. A tall young woman appeared at the front door as Thomas swung down from the horse, and his first thought was one of relief, that a neighbor lady had come to the Snyder home to help with the children. She took a moment to lean her broom against the side of the cabin as if the broom's precise position somehow mattered.

"Good morning," Thomas said. "I'm Dr. Parks, from the clinic. I'm looking for Gwendolyn." It never occurred to him that this young woman might be the child, barely sixteen years old.

"Yes, sir. I recognize you. I'm Gwen." Stepping closer, Thomas saw that indeed she was younger than she first appeared, but so thin and angular that no bloom favored her. Pale face, thin hair, prominent teeth, nothing about Gwendolyn Snyder shouted the vitality of healthy childhood blooming into adulthood, or the romantic idyll suggested by her Arthurian name.

Thomas took his time as he tied the gelding's reins to a small stump beside the cabin, running through his mind the names of the Snyder children that Bertha Auerbach had supplied.

"Gwendolyn, my nurse, Bertha Auerbach, is tending little Matilda. The child is healing nicely." A smile touched the young woman's face and shed a layer of years.

"She was so frightened," Gwendolyn said, her voice a soft, gentle alto. "I was going to take some bread pudding to her today. Would she like that?"

"I'm sure." Thomas regarded the ground for a moment, searching for some heartfelt way to continue. He could feel Gwendolyn's deep green eyes on him, waiting. Did she know why he'd come?

"Gwendolyn, your mother has died." When she didn't respond, he added, "Just moments ago." The girl lost her balance, appearing to trip over her own feet as she pivoted back toward the doorway. She fell against the door jamb, both hands on the wood. Pushing herself erect, she leaned her forearm against the door frame and buried her face in the crook of her arm.

Thomas quickly reached her side, and with a hand on each shoulder, could feel the shuddering of her body.

"The illness was too much for her," he whispered. "She passed quickly, with little pain."

"I visited for a few moments last night," the girl whispered. "So ill…my father?"

"We will do everything that we can, Gwendolyn."

She pushed herself away from the door frame and grasped the broom handle, at the same time taking several steps away from the house. Holding the broom as if it might be a rifle of use to defend the homestead, she looked off across the inlet, the tears coursing unchecked down her cheeks.

"What are we to do now?" she whispered.

"The welfare of the others is at stake," Thomas said. He stood beside her, a hand on her bony right shoulder. "I wish to have Matilda remain at the clinic so that her condition might be watched, Gwendolyn. There is some evidence at hand that if this contagion is stopped at its earliest stages, there is yet hope." The child said nothing, eyes still locked far off in the distance.

"The other children?" he asked. "Frank, Mary, and Florence?"

For a time, he wasn't sure if his words had registered. The broom wavered a bit, and she lifted it enough to rest the tip of the handle on the toe of her shoe, movements painfully slow and precise.

"Frank works at the mill, Doctor. He does not live here now. Mary and Flo are at school," she said. Thomas heard her clearly, but for a moment, the possibilities overwhelmed his ability to reply. "At school," he managed finally. Of course they were. Bertha Auerbach had spoken of the thirteen year-old Mary who might become the beauty of the family and ten year-old Florence, who was as likely to skip school to investigate the tidal pools as not.

They would be in the tidy frame schoolhouse a mile to the southwest, inland from the cove that arced around to the saw-mill, on a promontory above one of the largest neighborhoods of tents and tent-shacks.

And if the contagion had spread through the family, the Snyder children might yet be well enough to share the bacilli with every other child in the tiny school.

"How many students attend the school?" Thomas asked. Gwendolyn rubbed her nose on her sleeve.

"Sometimes as many as eighteen," she said. "Each day, perhaps ten. Mr. Whitman is not strict." *Mr. Whitman.* Nurse Helen Whitman's elderly husband, a former ship's captain was now so crippled in the knees that he spent his days comfortable in a chair as school master.

Thomas grasped the young woman by both shoulders and turned her to face him. He could feel the outline of her bones.

"It is a dreadful disease, and highly contagious, Gwendolyn. I think that your mother contracted her illness while working at the Clarissa." He could feel the girl flinch at that. "Do you work there yourself at times?"

"No. Only sometimes."

No, only sometimes. "Have you worked there recently?" She shook her head once. "Listen to me, Gwendolyn. In your mother's case, the disease seems to have made itself known in a matter of hours, and through some weakness in her constitution, she was not able to fight it to a successful conclusion. And now your father is also ill, but it is too early to know the course of his illness." He shook her shoulders gently. "I fear for the children, Gwendolyn. Can you answer some questions for me?" She nodded.

"Have any of your siblings complained of illness of any sort in the past week?"

"No. Only Matilda."

"But the others are hale and hearty? No headache, no upset of the stomach or gut?"

"No."

"Yourself?"

"I am well."

Thomas looked at her critically, seeing a child who would be helped considerably by abundant meals rich in fat. Seeing Gwendolyn Snyder, Gert James would throw up her hands in despair and head right for the kitchen.

"When I first saw your mother at the clinic, she along with your father and the child Matilda, your mother seemed well enough. She was prostrated just hours later. While home, did she complain of illness? Disturbances? Weakness?" Her answer was another slow shake of the head, and Thomas felt a surge of elation.

"Gwendolyn, I would ask you to go now to the clinic. Your father will only benefit from seeing you, but I also want you to talk with Dr. Lucius Hardy. He is new with us. You know Miss Auerbach?"

"Yes."

"Find her and have her take you to Dr. Hardy. He will want a culture from you." At the puzzled expression that showed through the tears, Thomas added quickly, "it is a painless, quick examination of little consequence, and yet it allows us to be certain that no one in your household has contacted the cholera. Will you do that for me?"

"When should I go?"

"This very instant. I shall go to the school, and make a similar request there." *The school,* Thomas thought with urgency. After securing another promise that Gwendolyn would immediately make her way to the clinic, the physician awoke Fats and forced the horse to jog through the streets and allies of Port McKinney. As he rode up the long slope, past the village of tents and shacks and a myriad of dogs all of whom Fats ignored, he could see the mill burners far to the south, one looking like a giant mushroom, spewing smoke across the countryside. Just inland from the original mill, a new structure had been erected—Schmidt's new shingle factory, with its banks of saws, splitters, and drying kilns.

Still several hundred yards from the school, a shrill whistle attracted his attention, and he looked toward the inlet. Two horsemen were cutting across toward him, riding from the trail that bounded the shoreline.

Loath to pause for even a moment, Thomas did not pull the gelding to a halt until he recognized the broad figure of Bert Schmidt. The second man was a stranger, both to Thomas and to the horse that did its best to accommodate the man's clumsy, uncollected efforts. Heavily clothed, with a bulky woolen coat, the man rode with his elbows nearly perpendicular to his body, bouncing in the saddle.

"Doctor, wait a moment, if you will," Bert Schmidt called. He rode a stocky, close-coupled mare the same color as the sea otters that romped everywhere along the coast, and unlike his companion, Schmidt was completely at home in the saddle.

"My wife sends me to speak with you," Schmidt said. He grinned. "She wishes that I return to her with the result of our conversation."

"The result?"

Schmidt laughed. "Her words exactly, young man. 'I don't wish the two of you regarding me like some piece of sausage,' she says. So her fate is in our hands. She's in a curious frame of mind, sir. I don't understand her." He turned in his saddle. "Doctor, this is Captain Jacques Beaumont."

"With the *Willis Head?*"

"The same. She's moored at the village wharf."

Beaumont waited while Thomas urged Fats to flank him, then extended a beefy hand. "My pleasure," he said.

"I can do nothing about your wife at this time," Thomas said, and Schmidt frowned. As quickly as he could, he recited the events of the past evening and dawn. When he finished, it was Beaumont who found his tongue first.

"Saints be," he murmured. "Cholera. For certain?"

"As certain as I am sitting here. Mr. Schmidt, the last thing I want is for your wife to be exposed to the contagion. Far away," and he nodded at the house in the distance. "That's the safest thing right now. Seattle would be better. Portland, better still. There should be no delay, sir."

"Cholera frightens me as much as it should any man with half a brain," Schmidt said. "It isn't a *question* of delay, my young friend. What's your best, educated guess that my wife's…what did you call it? A lesion? What's the guess that it's the cancer?"

"Better than fifty percent."

"Does the new fellow…Hardy? Does he agree?"

"Yes."

Schmidt had been packing his pipe thoughtfully, and now he touched a match to the pipe until it billowed. "I haven't met your new partner yet. Hope to hell he isn't another Zachary Riggs." The reference to his late father-in-law's errant scallywag of a partner prompted a flinch.

"He is no Riggs, sir. A fine fellow. And brilliant. And hard-working. You will like him."

"And you're certain it's cholera?"

"I'm certain, sir. And that's why you and your wife should be on the next packet to Seattle. I shall not be able to accomplish such surgery on her while we're with the cholera. The risk is simply too great."

"Cholera." Schmidt rolled the word through a cloud of pipe smoke. "Unusual, isn't it?"

"Highly."

"You know, in the far East, cholera kills a lot of people."

"Indeed it does, sir. Here as well. Mrs. Snyder has just expired."

Schmidt looked hard at Thomas. "Flora Snyder? Dead?"

"Yes. The same. And Marcus is in the battle."

"Son of a bitch. You know he's one of my best filers. When the lure of the sea doesn't kidnap him. The little girl of theirs ill recently? Tilly? I suggested…no, I *told* him…to take her to you."

"She is well. A small surgery. But she is in danger, Bert."

"She has the cholera as well, you mean?"

"No, but she is exposed. At first, my thought was to send her home. But we can't do that now. If she were to bring the contagion into the house with the others? Or if they have caught the contagion from their parents, then…"

"So what's to be done?"

"Bertha knows of a Snyder brother in Carter. I haven't been there. I don't know where it is. But in the meantime, I am headed to the school. If the Snyder children are at risk, so too is every other child in that building. They must all be tested."

"You can do that?"

"Of course." *I sound as if I do this on a daily basis,* Thomas thought.

"A boy rode out to the mill not long ago," Beaumont said. "He informed me that I was to return to the *Willis* on summons from my first mate. This is why?"

"Indeed, sir. Your crew is in jeopardy as well."

"Then best we be on our way."

"I ask you not to do that, sir. The Clarissa is quarantined, including some of your crew, your first mate as well. For another thing, several of your crew have gone to the Dutch Tract camp. There is poker there, I'm told."

"Oh, you betcha," Schmidt laughed. "That's what keeps my crews poor and working."

"One of those loggers has been exposed to the cholera, sir. Ben Sitzberger?"

"Sitzy? Really? How is that possible?"

"I don't know. I have sent Howard Deaton to fetch him. If he is ill, then his companions are in danger as well."

Schmidt grimaced as his pipe gurgled. "I don't understand all there is to understand," he said after a moment, "but by the look on your face, I know desperation when I see it. What do you need from me, Doctor? I can't imagine you having many resources at your disposal."

"Who alerted you?"

Schmidt turned his pipe this way and that, regarding the handsome burl. "The boy, as Captain Beaumont reports. And Horace James took it upon himself, Doctor, early this morning, at urging from his sister. And with other news as well." He reached across, extending his hand. Thomas grasped it, and for a moment, Schmidt held on, then pumped twice and released him.

"Congratulations. The infant is thriving?"

"Indeed he is."

"And Alvina?"

"An amazing woman. She was up and about, walking with the infant, when I was able to return home early this morning for a few moments."

Schmidt nodded with satisfaction. "So…how may we help? When all is under control, we'll worry about the surgery. My wife wants no one else to touch her, and now that our minds are made up, there is no changing it."

"To remain is a dangerous decision, sir."

"We don't think so. What do you need? You must have needs, sir. If this thing catches fire, you'll be overwhelmed."

"I have a list, I'm afraid," Thomas said. "First and foremost, a cook to work the kitchen, and to work with the Victor and the laundry. One of my nurses has already quit." He grimaced. "She took one look at the cholera and ran home. I can't say that I'm surprised."

"That would be the young woman? The step-daughter of the man with Presbyterian knees?"

Thomas laughed, once again finding himself amazed how everyone in this small community knew the slightest stir of a neighbor. "The same."

"And that's all?"

"Most urgent is to find this young man, Sitzberger. Howard is about that at this very moment. We have every reason to believe that Sitzberger spent the night at the Clarissa with one of our patients before she was stricken."

"At the Clarissa. He was with the buxom Miss Levine? Or was it the Patterson girl this time? Well, not Patterson. The step-daughter, Miss Stephens."

"I don't know."

Schmidt shrugged. "I may be mistaken. I have a lot of employees, but they're a talkative bunch, you know. When the machinery is idle, the mouths aren't." He took another long inhale of smoke. "What else?" Schmidt regarded Thomas with interest as the young man put both hands to the side of his head, forcing the thoughts into some sort of order.

"Do you have a water pump? The sort of thing that one uses for quenching fires?"

"After a fashion. It's a hand pump, with an inch line."

"Does it draw from a tank?"

"It *could,* but the tank is but a hundred gallons, Doctor. We usually just drop the feeder hose in the inlet."

"It must be from a tank." Thomas quickly described the back side of the Clarissa as it faced the inlet. "That is contagion just waiting," he said. "I envision mixing sublimate in a rich mixture and hosing the back wall thoroughly, right down to the water line."

Schmidt's eyes narrowed. "And that would work?"

"It might."

"Let me think on that, Thomas. Jules understands the need?"

"He does…I think. But George Aldrich *certainly* does, and he is at the Clarissa to enforce the quarantine."

"And he will do just that. Let me talk it over with my mill foreman. He's a creative man, is Jean Paul."

"Thank you, sir. And your wife? She must be distressed."

"Of course. But patient."

Thomas pointed off toward the mill. "The smoke is a nuisance, I think. Your new shake mill is often upwind of your home. I wouldn't be surprised if there is an irritant there that causes her distress. The mill is new, is it not?"

"Just months."

"As is her sinus distress." He pulled up his own sleeve. "This is a simple test that you should employ. It is cedar used for the mill, is it not?"

"For the most part."

"I thought so. Even I could smell it in the village now and then. So try this. Take some aromatic cedar scraps, then, finely chipped. The pungent saw dust is even better. Rub them on her forearm, here." He indicated the soft underside of arm. "When you do that, you may well see a reddening, an irritation. The faster the reaction, then the more of an irritant the cedar is. If that's the case, then we certainly know that she suffers from the wood essence somehow."

The mill owner sat silently for a moment, gazing off toward the plumes of smoke. "Move the house, the mill, or the wife," he said, and smiled. "Is that the choice?"

"I would think so."

"Life is never simple, is it." He touched his cap. "You're a busy man, Doctor. I'll keep you no longer. If your man Deaton doesn't find young Sitzberger, we will. He'll be on your doorstep, impressed with the urgency of the matter. And I'll see what I can do about a couple of hands to lend for the clinic staff. No one is going to want to work around cholera, you know."

"Including myself," Thomas said.

Chapter Twenty-one

Nels Whitman was no stern taskmaster. He sat on a banker's swivel chair on the crude raised dais at the front of the classroom, a book in one hand held open to place with his thumb, the other hand held high in the air, fingers pointing down at one of the older students as if Whitman were the conductor and the student his first violinist waiting for a cue.

"Think on this now," he was saying. "*Innocent stealing.* A marvelous concept, don't you think? And one that might stir young Huck's conscience. I search for one example." Without changing his position, he swiveled the chair with a toe, the raised hand drifting across the fourteen eager faces. "Just one." He drifted far enough that he could see the door behind the students, and Dr. Thomas Parks standing in silhouette.

"Page two hundred and fifty, chapter twenty-nine. And while Samuel reads, follow along." Whitman pushed himself out of the chair and frowned great mock thunderclouds at a stumpy, powerful youngster who sat near one of the three windows. "And Samuel…when you come to it, the third word is *fetching.*" He fired off a quick smile. "I thought you'd want to know."

The boy rose, thumped across the rough board floor and mounted the dais, obviously with great pride. He settled into the swivel chair with a great creaking of the springs. At least half of the faces, watching Samuel's enthronement, shone with delighted envy, as if to say, "*Oh, if only I could sit there!*"

Whitman extended a hand as he limped up to Thomas. "What a pleasure," he said, and beckoned toward the steps. He gently eased the door shut behind him. "We're exploring the intricacies of a new book by this Twain fellow. Remarkable, really. There are at least two students who know what I'm talking about. And equally remarkable...I hear such tales from my wife." He held both hands over his head, and Thomas caught the strong aroma of a much-used pipe, the stem of which protruded from the breast pocket of Whitman's frock coat. "A man caught high in a tree, hands smashed in an unrelenting grip." He rolled the R's theatrically. "How is the poor soul doing?"

"He still lives, which is remarkable in itself," Thomas said. "But I come on an urgent matter that will affect us all, Mr. Whitman." He reached out and made sure the door was tightly shut. "We have cholera in the village. Right now, it is a limited outbreak."

"Merciful heavens, I hadn't heard. Helen has said nothing about it."

"Have you noticed any illness among your students, sir?"

"Of those who attend, none."

"Lethargy? Discomfort of the gut? Vomiting? Frightful headaches?"

"Believe me, Doctor, I would know. These children are as my own...would that I could adopt about half of them."

It appeared that the schoolmaster was about to embark on a litany of how wonderful his students were, each and every one—and indeed Thomas could hear the boy Samuel's fluent, theatrical job of reading chapter twenty-nine, with no tittering or horseplay. But Thomas cut him off.

"This is what I ask, and it is an immediate thing, sir. We can readily identify the bacillus that is reputed to accompany the cholera. We can actually *culture* the dreaded thing in our laboratory, humble as it is. We must have culture samples from each child."

"Culture samples?"

"With a sample of the fecal matter, we can establish if the bacillus is harbored in the gut, sir. If we *know* it is there, then we can act aggressively."

"My word."

"I can't exaggerate the danger of this," Thomas said, growing impatient. "In such an epidemic of the cholera, we can expect to lose eighty percent. That is eight of ten." He nodded toward the door. "Neither of us can imagine losing so many." He saw anguish in Whitman's eyes.

"The entire town must know of this," Whitman said.

"Indeed. But even more urgent is to establish a culture for each student. It will take but a moment for each child."

"You've come to do that this morning?"

"No. I cannot do it here. But at the clinic, it is a simple matter. This is what I propose."

And fifteen minutes later, trading a reading of the new *Huckleberry Finn* for an adventure of another kind, the fourteen children paraded in a military line, Mr. Whitman limping along in the back, Samuel Pinkston in front like a teen-aged Ulysses Grant, the youngsters arranged by height from great to small. The least of all clasped Mr. Whitman's free hand with both of hers. Not singled out in any way, the two Snyder children were among the rank and file.

The school was half a mile from the clinic, and Thomas pushed the gelding hard through the streets, reaching the clinic in time to warn Lucius Hardy that his laboratory was going to be busy indeed. Hardy and Bertha Auerbach quickly arranged the examination room.

"Aldrich will do what he can for us at the Clarissa," Hardy said, "but I doubt that he'll achieve the equal of this…like the pied piper." They could see the line of children as the parade reached Gamble Street. But it wasn't the fourteen children and their teacher who reached the clinic first.

It was Adelaide Crowell who saw the young man as he lashed the reins against the flanks of his mule. "Dr. Parks?" she said, and pointed. Reaching the clinic, the young man slid off the mule, snatched his hat from his head, and presented himself at the door, hat rolled in his hands along with the reins of his mule.

"Mr. Schmidt sent me to ask you," the man blurted. The sun now broiled the hard clay of the street, and the young logger's cloths actually steamed.

"And what am I to be asked, sir?" Thomas glanced up the street at the advancing parade.

"We got five down with the grippe," the lad said. "Mr. Schmidt wants to know if you're comin' out there, or we should herd 'em all in here. Mr. Deaton, he don't know what to do. He said you should bring the other ambulance out if you can."

"Your name?"

"Fran Nolan." He said it as if he wished that he weren't. "Ain't never seen nothing like it."

The grippe. Maybe that was the best tactic, Thomas thought. Such a common complaint, especially as the summer months closed in. Working men, tight quarters, food prepared in the most casual way—it could be the grippe.

"Sitzberger?"

The logger nodded. "He ain't good. His girl is with him, even. Sick something awful. Him and the Dane, and three others. Maybe more."

"Wait for me," Thomas said. "The men must be brought here, but there is preliminary treatment that we shall undertake out at the camp. You understand me? *Wait* for me. While you wait, think of the most expeditious route for the ambulance. I've only been to the camp on horseback. The ridge trail is far too rough."

Nolan frowned. "I can get you there, Doc."

"Then take your ease for a few minutes," Thomas said, his mind spinning. "Wait. Do you know how to drive a team?"

"Sure do, Doc."

"Then you shall." He turned and dashed back into the clinic, to be met by Bertha Auerbach as she came down the stairs. "At the camp," he said. "We'll need both ambulances," he said. "The young man out front will drive the second. I'll take the gelding. We'll want a supply of clean blankets, laudanum, morphine, the Salol, turpentine…you know what we need, if you would help me assemble the kit. And at least a half dozen sterile syringes."

The words burst from him in a flood, and the unflappable Berti waited patiently until he had finished.

"You will bring them all here?" She nodded at the doorway, where Mr. Whitman now stood, the urchins behind him.

"We must," Thomas replied. "You will be long finished with the cultures before we return." Hardy appeared, his hands dripping. "I must to the camp," Thomas said. "At least five, maybe more. If we leave them there, there is no way to provide continuing treatment. Remaining there, they might as well not be treated at all."

"I was not arguing against it," Bertha said. "But we must be prepared. We will see to that."

"But the children first. Include Matilda Snyder in the procedure."

"I believe Dr. Hardy has accomplished that already."

"Gwendolyn is here? I ordered her to come."

"She is, and rests upstairs with the little girl. Mrs. Whitman is with them."

"And cultured," Hardy added.

"Thank God." He started first toward the door and the expectant Mr. Whitman, interrupted himself to turn toward the dispensary, then stopped again. "Mr. Schmidt will find us help," he said. "We talked." He started to say something else, and Hardy held up a hand.

"You're needed at the camp. We'll tend to the children, prepare for the arrival of the ambulances, and if we have the time, confer with Mr. Aldrich about progress at the Clarissa."

In twenty minutes, the second white ambulance pulled out of the clinic driveway, the horses tossing their heads with excitement at the new hands on their reins. From a quartering view from the rear, Thomas watched young Nolan half standing, half seated as if he were driving a Roman chariot. Howard Deaton would have blistered the air at such treatment of his pampered team and polished rig. The two horses would be blowing and lathered in ten minutes.

The route Nolan chose was a wide trail, and Thomas could see from the hard edged ruts that the freight wagons favored the road, cutting around several bluffs before reaching the end of the valley, at the head of one of the tributaries was the Dutch Camp.

As they broke out of the third growth timber, the camp shimmered in a fog of insects under the fresh sunshine. It took but a moment for the flying hordes to discover the approaching feast. Horse tails and men's hands were in constant motion, swatting and flailing. The deer flies, with what seemed like teeth to rival Prince's, were particularly aggressive, and seemed attracted first to the tender neck. Thomas pulled his collar high and scrunched his hat down hard, but the force of insects, including minute no-see-ums, mosquitoes, deer and horse flies, was maddening.

Reaching the Dutch, Nolan led them on a narrow path along the east side of the encampment. Across the valley, Thomas saw the burly figure of the cook appear in the doorway of the lodge. They stopped at a small encampment with half a dozen structures circled around a central fire pit. Howard Deaton's ambulance was parked on a grassy flat, but Thomas saw no sign of Howard or Bert Schmidt and Jacques Beaumont, the ship's captain.

Chapter Twenty-two

From yards away, Thomas could smell the illness. Half a dozen men milled about, and two were tending a roaring fire in the pit, an enormous iron cauldron suspended over the flames. He recognized Jake Tate, the young sawyer who had masterminded the renovations to the clinic while on loan from Schmidt.

"It's bad, Doc. Just real bad," Tate called as Thomas dismounted. He had a mound of blankets clamped between two sticks, and with a fearful grimace, deposited the blankets in the cauldron, poking them down into the boiling water. As the physician approached, Tate added, "Don't guess that you really want to go in there." He nodded at the nearest large tent-shack.

"All five?"

"Four," Tate replied. "Dick Bonner up and crapped out on us. Three hours ago he was riggin' a spar line just over the hill." He shook his head in wonder. "Shat all the way down the tree, and then couldn't walk a straight line once on the ground."

"He's dead? Just like that? In three hours?"

"Deader'n shit," Jake said. "He felt the shits comin' again, made for the trees, and wouldn't you know, he slipped and fell under one of the freight wagons. Popped his skull like a punkin." It sounded casual and logger-tough, but Thomas could see the fear in the young man's eyes. "We got three of 'em in here." He pointed off into the timber with one of the sticks. "Sitzberger's about two hundred yards that way. They found him lyin' out there. Girl's about to go crazy. You need to fetch her out of here, Doc."

"The Stephens girl?"

"She's with him." But he nodded toward the timber, not at any of the shacks. "Mr. Schmidt and Deaton's over there, too. I ain't never seen nothin' like it, Doc. Sitsy, he's in a bad way. But one of the boys saw the Stephens girl headin' in toward the camp, and he went and told Sitsy. 'Don't want her to see me like this,' he says, and off he goes."

"It's a desperate illness, Jake."

"You ain't lyin' there. How long we got to boil the blankets?"

"Fifteen minutes. Then to dry in the sun. When you're finished, you'll clean your hands thoroughly. I have alcohol."

"Believe me, Doc, I ain't touched *nothing* inside there. " He nodded at the nearest shack.

"You'll still wash," Thomas said, and strode toward the cabins, both the crudest construction with bark-covered slab wood hammered together for walls, with canvas stretched over slender rafters of spruce limb wood. The slab wood door was a scant five feet high, held in the frame with leather hinges not quite stout enough to properly hold the door's weight. That was all right, since the cabin would be used for only a few months, and then abandoned as the crews moved on. Thomas turned up the two lanterns that hung from the ceiling.

"My God," he muttered. The cabin included four bunks, just slab wood with rounds of spruce for legs. A small table jutted out from the wall opposite the door, and the cheap sheet metal pot-bellied stove that Lindeman's mercantile sold by the schooner-load at $4.70 each stood in the small space dead center in the room. A washbasin rested on the table, full of water that no doubt Hardy could culture in the incubator.

The physician stepped past the shipping chest at the end of one cot. The logger, young, pale, hollow-eyed, and unfocused, stared up at him.

"You got somethin' for me?" the man whispered. "God, it hurts all to beat hell."

"In the gut?"

In reply, the man lifted his hand just enough to lay it down again on his belly.

Thomas turned at the sound of a thud on the ground behind him. One of the enormous medical bags rested there, and Howard Deaton nodded at him gratefully. "Good to see you, Doc." He limped back toward the ambulance for the other bags.

"Let's ease the pain first," Thomas said, and quickly prepared a large syringe of morphine. "What's your name, son?"

"That's Herb Bonner," Tate said behind him. "Dick's little brother."

"That going to hurt more?" the man asked piteously, and Thomas wondered if the logger even knew that his brother had expired.

"Yes. But then you'll feel better. How long since your last bowel movement? Since the last bout?"

"Five minutes, maybe," Bonner said, and heaved his head back. "God, that hurts." A glance at the rough board floor under the bed was sufficient to explain where the bulk of the effluent had gone, flooding through the cracks to the earth underneath.

"When did you take ill, son?"

The young man closed his eyes while he pondered that. "Hit me yesterday afternoon."

"Jake, there's a clean copper bucket in the first ambulance," Thomas said. "Get it, and then half-fill with fresh water from *above* the camp. And then brought here." Making his way around the cabin, Thomas quickly assessed each patient. Bonner was the only one of the three conscious enough to be coherent. The physician turned to an angular man standing just inside the door.

"Who is this?"

"Gunnar Bloedel. The other fella there is Carl, his brother. He's been in the timber a week."

"Family is common out in the timber," Thomas said, more to himself than the logger.

"Sure enough. Hell, over on the east side of the Dutch, all five Bohannon brothers are workin', right along with the old man."

"Where are the blankets coming from?"

"Well, sick as they are, we all chipped in. Loaned one here and there. Been boilin' the ones we could save."

Thomas grimaced on hearing that. "Shared blankets," he muttered. "That's bloody wonderful. Now listen…there's nothing I can do here for these men. But back at the clinic, we can tend them and get them through this. Who has been working here with them?"

"Oh, we got a couple nurse maids," the logger said. "You know."

"I need them here, right now. Anyone who has been in this cabin, or who has helped to tend the men."

"They going to get sick?"

"We would hope not." He looked toward the empty bunk. "Where is this man?"

"That's Dick's. He got crushed."

"Ah, the corpse outside. Your name, sir?"

"Name's Pope. Dud Pope."

"Where do *you* stay?"

"My digs is across the way a little." The man gestured vaguely.

"Well, Mr. Pope, this is what is going to happen." And in short order, Thomas gathered together the five men who would admit to being in the cabin with the stricken loggers. Jake Tate returned with the bucket, and Thomas emptied a box of corrosive-sublimate into the water. "First, wash your hands, each one of you. Thoroughly. Then clean clothes." He saw the look of astonishment on their faces. "Sleeves up to the elbow, and wash. If you have no clean clothes, then borrow some. Then wash again. Jake, you're first, because you're going to help me." He started off toward the ambulance, and the men stood stock still, staring after him. Thomas spun around and glared at them. "You have one dead already, gentlemen. How many do you want?"

"Hell, Doc, we ain't sick," Pope replied.

Thomas laughed humorlessly. "But you *will* be, if you don't follow my instructions. And believe me, cholera isn't the way you want to choose to go."

"Cholera?" the logger gasped.

"So do as I say, and things will turn out all right. Wash first, then change your clothes, then wash again. If you have alcohol, rinse with that when you're finished. It will calm the sublimate a bit."

"Rather drink it."

"As you choose." Thomas gathered four clean blankets from the ambulance. "Let me," Howard Deaton said, reaching for the blankets. "The kid and the girl are right over there?" He pointed at the timber. "Head for that rock outcrop. They're just past that."

"Sitzberger's?" Thomas pointed at the second structure.

"Yep. And Delaney and Huckla are out at the flume," Deaton added.

"That's a good place for them to be," Thomas said. "But someone needs to fetch them. This very instant." He pulled the floppy door to one side and peered in.

"The girl is sick?" He turned back to Deaton.

"Just up here," Deaton said, tapping his own skull. "If he ain't yet, Sitzberger is near dead. Damnedest thing *I've* ever seen, I'll tell you that."

"We need all the sick in the ambulances, Howard. If you'll help me with that. You and Jake? And Mr. Pope. He seems to know what he's doing. And then we'll tend to the girl."

Eleanor Stephens, Thomas whispered to himself, his thoughts in a whirl. What did the girl think she was doing?

Only one of the sick men cried out as he was moved. The others were like sacks of flour. One by one, the four were transferred to the two ambulances. When he was satisfied that he'd done all he could, Thomas regarded the cabin and the wash-up operation.

"They must be burned," he said. "When you're finished, burn them both." He looked across at Dick Bonner's corpse, wrapped in a woolen blanket. "And you might as well put him inside and let him go with it. It's the safest thing to do."

A large man with deeply lined face turned to confront Thomas. "Now see here. Bertram sees us settin' fire here in the timber, we'll be skinned alive. And that's if the old man don't do it first. You'd better talk to Mr. Schmidt about that."

"Then I shall. But make preparations, because it *will* burn, gentlemen. If you don't do it, I shall."

"It ain't proper," the big man said.

"Your name, sir?"

"Name's William Farley," the logger said, and Thomas saw none of the flippancy toward injury or illness that some of the younger men embraced—men like Buddy Huckla with his hideously smashed fingers. Farley was older, perhaps even forty, and Thomas saw the muscles of his jaw clench with anger. "Those of us here ain't in the timber cuttin' today because there's God-fearin' men sick in camp. But we ain't about to just burn Dick Bonner to ashes without proper services. He deserves better'n that."

"Maybe he does," Thomas said. "If you know a few words, I'm sure that will make his passing easier. What you must understand, Mr. Farley, is that the longer that corpse lingers as it is, the more risk there is that others will be taken as well. And then you'll have a grave big enough to fit this whole camp."

"Burnin' just ain't right."

"Just don't stand in the smoke, sir," Thomas said, and immediately regretted the off-hand remark. He saw Farley's eyes narrow. "Look, Mr. Farley, if you want to drive into town and fetch quick lime and coffins while others are digging proper graves, then that's up to you. I'm telling you how to protect the *living*…and quickly."

Farley didn't reply, and Thomas turned back to the others. "Gentleman, if you suffer *any* symptoms of illness—the slightest cough, the slightest sniffle, the least belly ache, or pain when you piss, you must come to the clinic immediately. Is that understood? Not tomorrow morning, or tomorrow after work, because you'll be dead by then." The men gazed at him as if he were speaking a foreign language. "And keep yourselves so clean that you'd think you were on your way to Sunday Mass."

Voices drifted down from the timber and Thomas hefted his medical bag. "I must see about Sitzberger." He set out through the rank grass and the berry bushes that tore at his trousers. The mystery still gnawed at him. The Clarissa was filthy enough, and even though Port McKinney was no metropolis of international trade, ships from anywhere in the world visited port on a regular basis. It was not unlikely that a passenger might have brought the bacillus to land in clothing, even on his person. Thomas had read of cases when a person might actually carry a disease such as typhoid or typhus without suffering from it himself—happy only to pass it on. He understood no reason why cholera might be different.

He reached the timber and saw a large mound of soil and roots from a dead fall. Bert Schmidt appeared, hands on his hips, and when he saw Thomas he beckoned impatiently.

"You tell me what to do with *this* one," he whispered. On the other side of the root mound in a small clearing ringed by spruce and fir saplings, curled up on the duff, was Ben Sitzberger. The young man lay on his right side in a tight fetal position. Within easy reach, Eleanor Stephens sat with her back to a smaller stump, legs drawn up under her skirt, head resting on her arms. She ignored all, and for a moment, Thomas thought that she might either be asleep, or expired where she sat.

Captain Jacques Beaumont knelt near the young couple, and Thomas could see that the sailor was talking urgently to Eleanor—who offered no response.

Thomas placed his medical bag down gently, as if loath to make any sudden noises. Beaumont glanced up at him, said something else to Eleanor, and patted her shoulder. That small display of sympathy also drew no response.

"Eleanor? It's Dr. Parks." Thomas placed a hand on her forehead, feeling the flush on her velvet skin. He let his hand slip down until he could find the carotid. Her pulse was strong but so fast he had to count twice to be sure. The flutter of beats reminded him of what he had felt once when holding a stunned bird that had crashed against a window.

But about Ben Sitzberger, there was no question. His eyes were half-lidded, staring blindly at the earth, the surfaces gone dry and dull. Thomas reached across and felt the already cooling skin. Not a trace of pulse echoed in the arteries. Once a hale, hearty, and amorous fellow, all that remained of Ben Sitzberger was the drained husk, so dehydrated that his joints thrust at his soiled clothing, his face a grim mask of gray skin stretched over the facial bones.

"Eleanor," Thomas whispered directly in her left ear. "You must come away now. He's gone."

"He's *not* dead," she cried. Her voice was muffled in the folds of her dress.

Thomas looked up at Schmidt. "How long has she been here?"

"Don't know. A couple of the men say that she came out early this morning. Been here all this time."

Thomas reached across and lifted the corpse's hand. Rigor had already begun.

"He sleeps now," Eleanor said, her voice muffled. "So tired."

"Then you should come away," Thomas tried to ease her left shoulder back so that she would look at him, but her muscles were tight as steel bands. "Let him sleep, girl. I need to talk with you."

"You'll save him?"

Thomas took a few seconds to ponder how he might maneuver around that.

"Eleanor, you must help me. You must tell me what happened so I know what to do." He stroked her forehead as if she were a child. For the first time, he noticed how exquisitely porcelain her skin was. She dug her face even harder into her arms. "Help us, Eleanor." He glanced up at Captain Beaumont. "Your men?"

"Gone back to the ship. I sent 'em packing."

"Before that ship moves an inch," Thomas said, "your entire crew must be examined to make sure they are free of the contagion."

"All right. You just tell me what to do."

"Help me with her," Thomas instructed. He felt some compliancy in Eleanor's arms, and she arose like an ancient woman, her legs shaking. She leaned against Thomas, and he could feel her pulse pounding. For the first time, she seemed to actually *see* Ben Sitzberger as he really was—a withered corpse, teeth bared in death, eyes without any trace of passion or fear or life.

"I'm sorry, Eleanor."

She buried her face in her hands and crumpled backward into his arms, turning as she did so to dig her face into his coat.

"He's dead, Dr. Parks."

"Yes."

She tipped her head back, flooded eyes searching his face.

"There are so many others who need our help, Eleanor." He looked at her face, a canvas of conflicting emotions, and wondered what bacilli were running rampant in her system. That unromantic thought wasn't what Eleanor was searching for, apparently. As if reading his mind, she thumped a sharp little fist into his chest, coming dangerously close to the tender scar over his mended ribs.

"He's *dead,* Dr. Parks." She turned away. Trying to square her shoulders, she nevertheless stumbled as she marched out of the timber, still talking to herself. Stepping quickly, Thomas caught up with her, taking her by the elbow.

"Eleanor, you must help me with this. I need you to come back to the clinic. I don't want you riding back alone."

Her shoulders slumped in submission.

"At least ride in company with the ambulances. Back at the clinic, Miss Auerbach will guide you." He lowered his voice and squeezed her shoulders. "Mr. Schmidt and I will take care of Ben."

She nodded mutely, and he walked her back to the ambulance, keeping the team of horses between them and the terrible image of the shacks. He beckoned Howard Deaton.

"She will ride beside the ambulance," he said. "That's her horse, I think." The black mare grazed fifty yards away, her reins dragging between her front feet.

"Will Hardy want a culture?" Deaton asked, and Thomas looked at him in surprise, impressed.

"Indeed he will." He ushered the girl toward Deaton. "And thanks. Take good care of this young lady."

As he trudged back to where Sitzberger's corpse lay, Schmidt and Captain Beaumont looked at Thomas as if he had all the answers. "I've told the men that the tent must be burned. The bodies as well."

He saw Schmidt turn and gaze across the clearing, and then toward the timber, as if gauging the distance of tree from flame. "It has to be done," Thomas said. "For the dead, there are only two choices. The bodies can be burned along with the tent, or they can be buried with thorough sterilization with corrosive sublimate. I recommend the former, since there is less contact, even casual, with the living."

"Some of the men aren't going to like that," Schmidt said.

"I don't care what they like," Thomas said abruptly. "We *can't* care," he added to soften his tone. "I've spoken with your man Farley, and he has made his reservations clear. But this is no time for ceremony. I don't know if he can be made to understand that, but you have seen how fast the cholera can progress through a camp."

"Indeed I have. And the camp is not all that worries me, Doctor. The children at school? They're tested now?"

"They arrived at the clinic with Mr. Whitman just as I left to come out here. I trust that Dr. Hardy has made quick work of the process."

"Then let's do the same," Schmidt said.

"Two more to be found," Thomas said suddenly. "Huckla and his friend. Delaney, I think it is."

"He'll be found," Schmidt said. "To the clinic?"

"Yes."

"Are we going to have to put the torch to this entire valley?"

Thomas hesitated. "I don't know. I don't understand the path of the contagion's spread. But I've been told that the men regularly gather in the dining hall for evening recreation. The gambling is what attracted the sailors. If the cholera spread from the soiled bedding, from the poor sanitation, then yes…it could involve the whole camp. What is the dining hall's water supply?"

"A roof cistern, but many take water from the creek, of course. It's clear, most of the time, especially higher up."

"But do they bother going 'higher up' for the casual drink? I saw the baths that they've excavated right in the middle of the community…I intend to culture those. I would not be surprised at what we find."

"You cannot test everyone or everything," Schmidt said.

"No, I can't. But I can speak with the men and explain to them what they must do to save themselves. Vigilance is sometimes worth more than anything else." And once again, the young physician felt the familiar twang of inexperience raising its ugly head, since he did not know for certain that vigilance was worth *anything* with this disease.

Chapter Twenty-three

Thomas re-entered the rough tent-shack nearest the stream and looked at the cot that had been Sitzberger's. A carved tree limb had been nailed to the wall, with an irregular scrap of flat slabwood nailed to it. Folded upon it were three shirts and two pairs of trousers, along with three pairs of long johns. Five pairs of socks, none of them particularly clean, rested under the cot, next to a single pair of boots.

The fetid cot painted the awful picture of a terminal cholera patient. In retrospect, Thomas was surprised that the young man had been able to sit a mule for the ride into town with Huckla. The disease obviously struck with unrelenting rapidity—it was conceivable that when the decision to ride into town before the day's work truly began, Sitzberger had felt well enough to accompany his friend. Perhaps he had spent the night in Port McKinney, with the fair Lucy Levine—herself on borrowed time. Thomas could not imagine the young man, sick as he might be, actually asking a doctor for help. That didn't appear to be part of the code of the timber.

Thomas skidded a small sea-chest to one side and opened the hasp. Inside he found a well-thumbed Bible, a clean shirt and trousers that Sitzberger might well have worn when visiting Lucy Levine—or Eleanor Stephens, or both—three dime novels, and a large Colt revolver still in its cardboard box. Tucked in the corner of the chest was a bulky package, loosely wrapped in butcher's paper, the string tied in a clumsy bow, along with a collection of several dozen letters, tied together with a bit of ribbon.

Thomas hefted the letters and turned one them toward the light. The heavily canceled postage stamps were British, and the handwriting was obviously feminine, a full, flowing script. He stared in fascination. The return address announced the Convent St. James, Burdwan, Bengal, India. Fanning out the letters, he searched through the postmarks until he came to the most recent, postmarked in late December, 1891. The handwriting was angular, even shaky, as if penned by someone too elderly to hold the pen steady.

Feeling like an intruder, Thomas slid the single page missive from its envelope.

> *My Dear Mr. Sitzberger, it is my sad duty to inform you of the death of your sister, Sister St. Ignatius, on the Fifth of December, 1891, of the cholura. She went to her Lord with a full heart, and love for you. I have sent, by separate mailing, her personal effects, though they be few.*

The letter was signed by Sister St. Denis, the Mother Superior of the Convent St. James.

Heart racing, he stood with the pack of letters, holding them as if they might themselves be the most lethal of poisons. "Other effects," he whispered, scanning the trunk. Unless the aging Mother Superior had mailed off a Colt revolver from India, there didn't appear to be much of interest. He bent down and retrieved the bundle and unwrapped it. Inside was a simple black garment, what appeared to be a nun's habit.

"Why ever…" Thomas whispered. He tried to imagine Sister St. Denis mourning over a favorite associate, a woman who had only her deeds and precious little else to mark her passage through the world. Maybe it made sense to the Mother Superior to send the habit back home to the remaining family, little realizing that she was sending something else as well.

"Mr. Tate?" He held up the packet of letters and the package containing the habit. "I'm sure you gentlemen will arrange to do with the men's possessions as you will, but I must take these. They will be at the clinic, should someone ask." He started toward the gelding that now grazed behind the second ambulance, but stopped. "And Mr. Tate? The cabin and its contents… and the two men…*must* be burned immediately. I've spoken with Mr. Schmidt, and he agrees. This clearing is large, there is little wind, so there is little danger to the surrounding timber. Will you take care of that?"

"I'll do it," Jake Tate said, but Thomas saw him glance toward William Farley. "We got someone here in camp who can say a few words," he added, but Farley didn't look mollified.

It's the three in the ambulances who need the words, Thomas thought, but kept the thought to himself. "Thank you. And remember what I said about washing your hands thoroughly. More often than not. When you're finished, I want to see you at the clinic." At Tate's apprehensive expression, Thomas added, "It will take but a moment. All the men who have been helping us here today. I need to see them all."

An hour later, the two ambulances rolled under the clinic's portico in Port McKinney. Pulled off to one side was Coroner Ted Winchell's black hearse, and Thomas dismounted quickly as Winchell trudged over to him.

"Well, this ain't no fun," Winchell observed. Townsfolk would grow used to seeing his black hearse. Winchell, dressed in a flannel shirt and laborer's trousers, made no effort to look his role—no black frock coat, no black top hat, no dour saturnine expression.

"What did the autopsy show you?"

"Autopsy?"

"Doc Hardy said that you wanted to do an autopsy on Flora Snyder before we tend to her."

"I haven't had a chance. And I don't think I *will* have the chance, Ted. I should, I know. I am derelict if I don't. But…" and he shrugged hopelessly. "You'll go ahead and take her? As you can see, we have an outbreak at the Dutch camp."

"Well, shit," Winchell said succinctly. "How many?"

"We have three with us now. We left two at the camp for cremation. I fear there will be many more." He took a deep breath, watching as Howard Deaton ushered Eleanor Stephens into the clinic. "We work in haste," Thomas said ruefully. "It is so important to our understanding of the disease, but the time…" He shook his head in frustration. "We should take time to do a post on the two at camp, but…"

"I'd offer to help, but hell, *I* sure as hell don't know enough."

"And I don't want you out there, Ted." A pitiful cry issued from the front ambulance, bringing Bertha Auerbach from the clinic, along with Lucius Hardy. The physician looked quizzically at Thomas, who held up a finger. "A moment," Thomas called. "Please. Give me a moment." He turned back to the coroner. "I've never seen the case, but I can imagine that were I to do a post mortem on a man who died of thirst in the Sahara, I'd find much the same condition. Cholera manages the dehydration with considerably more rapidity, sadly enough."

"Some seem effected less than others," Winchell observed. "Marcus Snyder seems to be doin' all right."

"Some do, I've read. And now I believe it. Some might *wallow* in the contagion and never take ill. Some may never take ill, but carry the disease to others." He held up his hands helplessly. "There is no understanding it. All we know for a certainty is that the disease is unbelievably rapid in its genesis."

"Got some nervous folks in town, Doc."

"As well they might be," Thomas said. "There is no such thing as too much prophylaxis. I have sent detailed list to Mr. Garrison of what steps each family might take. I hope his publication is prompt, and widely read."

Winchell coughed a little chuckle. "You're really asking for a miracle now, Doc. I should go ahead and take the Snyder woman's remains?"

"Yes."

"What else?"

"If you would find George Aldrich? He is down at the Clarissa, the last I knew. We need to find every person who might be ill. It's as simple as that. They must come to the clinic, and we will do what we can."

"I'll use the white rig," Winchell said. "As soon as Howard's free, him and me will take Mrs. Snyder. Someone taking care of the family matters?"

"I think so."

One by one, the sick were transferred from the ambulances to the first floor men's ward. In the flurry of urgent activity, Thomas noticed that Eleanor Stephens had left.

Chapter Twenty-four

Thomas closed the door of his office, sank into the chair, and opened his journal to the page he had reserved for the cholera outbreak. The names of the dead were followed by the date and time of their passing—Dick Bonner, Benjamin Sitzberger, Flora Snyder, and now Herb Bonner, who had survived the ambulance ride down off the bluff, the transfer into the clinic, and the first session of enteroclysis before gasping for breath through blue lips and then expiring.

Marcus Snyder had taken to sitting on the edge of his ward bed, hands clasped between his knees, too sick to stand without assistance. With sad, hollow eyes, Snyder watched the ministrations to the prostrate loggers, unable to help or even offer encouragement.

He had been too ill to accompany his wife's body when Ted Winchell and Howard Deaton had carried the pathetically light wicker casket from the clinic. Flora Snyder's remains would go to the Port McKinney cemetery up behind the Congregational Church, buried without delay and a thorough blanket of lime to keep any contagion at bay should ground water seep beyond the grave.

If the practice of either cremation or immediate burial offended some of the tough loggers, Thomas reflected, it was sure to offend the more tender spirits in the village…no doubt he'd hear from Pastor Patterson at some completely inconvenient time. Let that be, he thought. If the pastor wanted to conduct graveside services, fine. A *covered graveside.* But to allow a coffin bearing cholera inside a crowded church bordered on stupidity.

Thomas turned the page and added another note under the remarkable entry for Sonny Malone, who still rested by himself in the small room at the rear of the ward, oblivious to what was transpiring around him. Malone's system concentrated on one shallow breath at a time as his damaged brain tried to defend itself from the seepage of blood within his skull.

Closing the journal, he entered the tiny laboratory and checked the gas incubator. Inside, the bottom shelf was full of glass culture dishes, and Thomas was quite sure that their technique could be called into question. With a finite supply of the glassware, Dr. Hardy had divided each smooth culture surface into quadrants, one patient to a quadrant, the name printed in red wax on the lid. Fifteen cultures from the school now brewed, along with Gwendolyn and Tilly Snyder's, and now twelve from the Clarissa. Two cultures had come from the India letters, and two that contained tiny snippets from what appeared to be the nun's habit—an odd farewell memento send to a brother in the United States. The final cultures had been drawn from Eleanor Stephens and the rest of the nursing staff—and one each from the two physicians.

"I'm not sure I want to know," Thomas had said as he saw his own name printed on top of the glassware.

"A sentiment shared, I'm sure," the other physician had replied.

Still skeptical that such a possibility was possible, Thomas had searched through the textbooks for hints, but had found only the one—the cryptic and unexplained comment in Dr. Fellow's *Theory and Practice of Medicine: "(Cholera) has been communicated through the medium of the mails."* If Dr. Fellow's report was accurate, this would be amazing confirmation.

A matter of hours will tell the tale, Thomas thought.

"You're musing," Lucius Hardy said behind him, and Thomas turned. Hardy's pleasant face was marked by dark shadows under each eye, his lively step now heavy and plodding.

"And you need rest. Let me suggest that you retire upstairs for the remainder of the day, sir."

"In due time. By the way, while you were occupied, I…" He twisted to look past the physician at another figure who appeared in the doorway.

"Ah, my God…Miss Stephens," Thomas blurted. The Seth Thomas said that it was nearly five in the afternoon. Eleanor Stephens had walked off hours before, and wandered who knows where, spreading who knows what. She had changed her ruined clothes and now wore pristine white. The girl was really quite attractive in a wan sort of way, her hair nearly raven black, but her skin so pale and flawless that even a single fetching freckle would appear out of place. She was dressed in the whites of a nurse, perhaps the very dress she had been wearing when she left the clinic in tears the first time. Her hands were clasped at her narrow waist.

"Pardon, sir. I did not mean to intrude, but the door was open, and with both of you here…"

"What may we do for you, young lady?" Thomas kept his tone neutral. He knew not what to think with this girl, and the quiet reservation in the eyes gave little hint. Somehow, at least to outward appearances, she had now managed to pull herself together, and seeing her dress and manner, his first assumption was that Eleanor Stephens was seeking employment once again, or bringing yet another complaint from her step-father. Perhaps Patterson had been standing down below, on the corner of Gamble and Angeles Streets, and had seen Ted Winchell's hearse leave the Clinic's portico, headed out to the cemetery.

"My mother is ill, sir. I have come to ask if you might…"

"She is with you?" Thomas interrupted, rising quickly. "Have you taken her to the ward?"

"No. She is home. My step-father will not allow…he does not want her to be brought here."

"Where is Pastor Patterson now?"

"He is at the church, sir. They are planning evening services for those afflicted, and for those who have…passed." Thomas saw moisture in the corners of the girl's eyes.

"And you say that the Pastor knows your mother to be ill?"

"Yes. And that my sister and I tend her."

"Tell me how your mother is suffering," he demanded, glancing at Dr. Hardy, who had remained silent but attentive.

"She…" and her face flushed.

"You must tell me, Eleanor," Thomas said kindly, but his mounting impatience gave the words an edge. "You know perfectly well what we face here—and at the Clarissa, and out at the camp. We must know what we face. We must have a culture."

"She has pain," and Miss Stephens touched her stomach. "Such pain as is unbearable."

"Diarrhea? Vomiting?"

"Yes. Most distressing and fearsome," the girl said, and she raised her hand and placed the back of it to her forehead most theatrically. "Just as you have here. I fear for her."

"I'll go to the home with her," Hardy said immediately, but Thomas shook his head.

"No, let me. This may require some discussion with the good pastor, and I'm the one who should do that."

"With a club," Hardy said, and Thomas glanced at the girl. She hadn't reacted to the insult…perhaps she agreed.

"Her bedding is clean? The room is immaculate? Her toilet attended to?" The flush shot up Miss Stephens fine cheeks like flame. How could this wilting damsel be the same girl who had huddled a corpse just hours before, bedded down on the damp duff of the forest?

"I have instructed my sisters in what must be done."

"Your sisters? How many of you are there?" Thomas knew that at one time or another, Gert James had told him who was who. That was one of his housekeeper's hobbies, it seemed.

"I have two sisters and a brother," Miss Stephens said.

"Younger, I assume?" Thomas walked toward the door without waiting for an answer, beckoning the girl to follow. In the dispensary, he quickly assembled a small kit, including a sterile rubber tubing from the clave, and a spare bulb. It had been that very procedure, he remembered, that had driven the blush from

Miss Stephen's face and sent her from the room before a dead faint sent her to the floor.

Thomas paused for a moment, looking at his inventory.

"Syringes," Hardy prompted. "And you accuse *me* of being weary, old man."

Thomas added three freshly claved hypodermics to his kit. "All right. Lead on, Miss Stephens. And by the way…" He turned back to Hardy. "I left Jake Tate at the logging camp. He is a most resourceful young man. But I would expect there to be more cases from there. And now, with this, who knows." He smiled sympathetically at the older physician. "I was told that someone saw smoke over the trees, coming from the Dutch camp. We may yet stop this thing."

Chapter Twenty-five

Thomas followed the girl down Gamble Street, past the constable's log cabin office, beyond the partially completed Post Office building, to the intersection with Angeles Street—as narrow, rutted, and unfinished as all the others. Nevertheless, the walk felt good, the late afternoon sun hot on his shoulders.

The sunshine had been one of the few blessings this day. Without it, the sodden linens, the blankets, the mattresses—all things washed would remain soaked and unusable. But all day, the sun had roasted the laundry, and they had kept the cycle of wash, rinse, boil, and hang to dry at a frantic pace.

Eleanor said not a word as they walked. She didn't refer to the episode at the camp, or offer an explanation of her relationship with Ben Sitzberger. Thomas didn't press her. He could imagine the girl, smitten by the logger—perhaps smitten for the first time in her life. What Eleanor's relationship with Lucy Levine might have been, Thomas could only guess. Perhaps Ben Sitzberger, in his own offhand, carefree way, had enjoyed both girls equally. None of it mattered now, and Thomas left it alone.

The impressive church steeple rose high to overlook the town, and by the time Thomas had mounted the long hill to the church, he was breathing heavily.

The Pastor's home was a large frame structure set well back from the church, its cedar clapboards painted so white that in the sunshine it hurt the eyes. With its frilled porch and endless variations in roof line, with its bumped out windows and dark cedar shakes on the roof, it looked as if it had been transported with the stroke of a sorcerer's wand from a New England village.

Thomas glanced at the grounds in front of the church where the buggies, horses and mules of a fair-sized congregation would assemble for Sabbath…with all those people at risk. Off the side of the church, a long, low-roofed hall had been built for gatherings other than worship.

"You'll fetch your step-father for me?"

"He will be in the church hall," Miss Stephens repeated, "and then he was to go to town. I believe he was seeking out Mr. Garrison."

"I see." *While his wife lies dying,* he thought. They mounted the white steps and entered the house. Instantly, the repugnant odor struck his nose, the impact heightened after the walk through cleansing sunshine and inlet breezes.

"She is upstairs," Miss Stephens said.

"Where are your sisters?"

"Elaine is upstairs with mother. The two youngest children are accompanying their father."

Their father. An interesting distinction, Thomas thought.

"You know that, having been exposed, that is exactly the wrong thing for them to do?" Eleanor didn't respond. She functioned as if hollow inside. "Were they in school today? Were they among those tested?"

"They are too young for school."

"At least there's that," he said, and followed Eleanor upstairs, and straight back to the rear of the house. The bedroom door was closed, and Eleanor Stephens knocked discreetly, then pushed it open without waiting. Mrs. Patterson lay curled on her side, one hand listlessly over the side of the bed. In a chair beside her, a teen-aged girl sat sideways, both hands enclosing her mother's. She looked up as her sister as Thomas entered, and placed her mother's hand back on the linen.

At the foot of the bed a large chamber pot rested, the lid slightly askew.

"Empty that immediately," he instructed, and it was the younger girl who leaped to obey. "You are Elaine, young lady?" He didn't recall seeing the girl at the school.

"Yes." Her voice was strong, with just the trace of a lisp. She shared her sister's black hair and pale face, but with more prominent cheekbones and a forthright chin. She would play hell with the schoolyard boys, Thomas reflected.

"You weren't at the school today."

"No, sir. I have tended mother all day."

"When did she take ill?"

"Early this morning, just as we finished breakfast, sir. We supposed it was something that she ate."

"The chamber pot, then." Thomas fought down a surge of temper, refusing to snap at the girl, who certainly knew no better. He glanced at Eleanor, who certainly *did* know better, but who now stood infuriatingly mute. "You didn't see the similarities between your mother's illness and the cases at the clinic?" The physician moved to the side of the bed.

"Mrs. Patterson?"

Her eyes had been staring at the linen beside her face, and they shifted without the least movement of her head, having trouble focusing. Her forehead felt dry and cold. He took her hand in his. "Can you squeeze my hand?" The response was slight. A nearly full glass stood on the nightstand. For a healthy woman, the glass would have been near at hand. For Mrs. Patterson, it might as well have been a mile distant.

"Have you been able to hold down water?"

"No," the woman whispered. Her voice tapered off to just the movement of her lips. "So thirsty."

"When were you…" Thomas started to ask, and was startled as the woman drew her legs up sharply with a cry of distress. Eleanor moved forward with a towel, but her ministrations were slow and awkward, as if she wanted to accomplish her task from a dozen feet away. The girl's face was so pale that Thomas could see the network of capillaries under the skin, and Eleanor's lips trembled.

With a yank, Thomas threw the bedding to one side, but the gush fountained, most of the release caught by several layers of rough towels. "A deep wash basin first," he commanded. "Where are you putting the soiled linen?"

"We have a Morgan washer," the girl said.

"These must either boil or be burned," Thomas instructed. "And replaced the moment they are soiled. The towels are good, but there must be more of them, and clean." He turned back to the woman, who now lay panting, mouth dry. Eleanor backed out of the room, the linen wadded in her hands. "At first we thought...I mean, at first, the symptoms seemed a mild grippe only."

"I'm sure," Thomas snapped. As Eleanor started to turn away, he added, "And change that apron." With swift movements, he listened with the stethoscope, hesitated and then listened again, frowning. He moved the instrument down the side of the woman's thin back, pausing several times just below the tip of her shoulder blade. "Can you manage a deeper breath, Mrs. Patterson. Just ever so?" If she heard, there was little response. He leaned closer, pushing the left earpiece in tightly, trying to catch the slightest irregularity. Closing his eyes, he sat quietly, listening far longer than need be. The cholera had joined with an old ally. The rales of lungs ruined by tuberculosis were distinctive. Mrs. Patterson's heart beat like a butterfly flitting from flower to flower, tripping beats of little force or regularity. As he listened, she writhed in agony.

"Now," Thomas said as the younger daughter, Emily, returned. "How old are you, young lady?"

"Fourteen, sir."

And soon to be much older. "I want a large pan filled with the hottest water you can find," he said. "Lots and lots of hot water. *Clean* hot water. Do you understand me?"

"Yes, sir." The lass frowned as if offended by his blunt question.

"Good. From where do you fetch your water?"

"We have a good well, sir."

"Even better, then. Hot, hot, hot. And clean towels. We must do half a dozen things at once." The child's eyes grew large as he retrieved one of the syringes from the kit. He pulled a half grain dose of morphine from the tiny brown bottle and injected it into the woman's thigh. She jerked and moaned.

"The morphine will help with some of the gut pain. We must be able to force her to relax. That's the first thing." He placed the used syringe into a small enameled pan from his bag. "Mrs. Patterson, listen to me," he said, moving to the head of the huge bed. "You're going to be all right, do you hear me? Your daughters are angels, and they're going to help me. *You* are going to help me."

Again, that prompted little reaction, but just as Thomas turned toward his medical bag, the woman vomited an enormous geyser that splashed across the bed, spattered the fashionable chest of drawers, and flooded onto the floor. Her eyes closed, and she rolled away.

Elaine nearly pounced across the room to dab at the mess with yet another towel.

"Hot, hot water," Thomas repeated. "And we need it now, girl."

Elaine nodded and vanished holding the fetid towels. Eleanor had yet to return, and from her expression on backing out of the room, Thomas wasn't surprised.

Thomas snapped one of the towels from the small pile at the end of the bed, opened the bottle of carbolic acid, and splashed it liberally over his hands.

"Doctor?" The single word came clearly, if only a whisper.

Thomas bent down, keeping his dripping hands well back.

"Am I to die?" Mrs. Patterson whispered, so little breath that Thomas was forced to read her lips.

"Most certainly not." Thomas forced the lie to sound like an optimistic promise. He knelt at the bedside, and her eyes, sunken and listless though they were, locked on his. He did not need to tell her that her tuberculosis, itself untreated for who knew how long, had ruined her otherwise sturdy constitution.

"Listen to me." He kept his own voice just above a whisper. "I have given you an injection to dull the pain and quiet the spasms. We must replace the fluids that you have lost. That is the main thing right now. Do you understand me?" She blinked. "You will help me with that."

To his surprise, Eleanor reappeared, carrying linens, towels, and a large basin.

"In my bag, you will find a box marked corrosive sublimate." He pointed at the bottle of carbolic acid on the bureau top. "Mix approximately…" and he stopped, holding out his hand. She handed him the box, and he shook perhaps a gram into the pan. "That much. Fill with hot water, which your sister is fetching. Then wash your hands first with that, then a drench with the carbolic acid. Then you will help me." He paused. "And I instructed you to change that apron as soon as you have the chance. The contagion is spread by just that sort of thing." She started to turn away. "But not until you have sterilized your hands. That first, then change, then sterilize again."

While he waited for the water, Thomas removed the black rubber tube and bulb from their sterile linen wrap, along with another small pan. The tube and bulb went into more disinfectant.

Elaine returned with the water, more tepid than hot.

"This is the best you have?"

"I have more on the stove. It will be some minutes."

"We do with what we have. But the instant it boils, please fetch it. Now, she must be on her side," Thomas said, "facing away from the edge of the bed." The girls managed that, and at the moans from their mother, Eleanor blanched, her breath panting as she fought her own nausea.

Elaine, however, had no such difficulties. Surprisingly strong and deft, she cooed to her mother at each step of the process, and when Thomas instructed her in her mother's positioning, the girl obeyed perfectly.

"We must replace all the liquid that her body has lost," Thomas explained. "There is no point in trying to force her to swallow, since her stomach will simply eject the fluid instantly." He glanced at Elaine, who was listening with complete concentration. "So we are going to replace the fluid directly to her gut,

Elaine." The girl's attention was so complete, so rapt, that despite the urgency, he found a pleasure in instructing her.

And clearly knowing that his actions must be dictated by that urgency, since for every moment that the patient's system was deprived of fluid, her chances dwindled, Thomas nevertheless took care with the preparations. Sweeping the linens to one side, using one towel after another, he cleaned the woman, explaining each step to the girl. There was no consideration of drapes to address modesty.

"The contagion that poisons her resides in the gut, Elaine. If we are not careful, we run the considerable risk of reintroducing it to her body once again. Do you understand me?"

"Yes, sir."

"We can't have that." He continued talking as he worked, an almost conversational dialogue that the young girl neither replied to nor questioned. He noticed that Eleanor hovered near the doorway now, hands clasped, her face ghostly pale.

"Upward pressure here and here," Thomas said, positioning Elaine's hands on Mrs. Patterson's hip and buttocks. "The linen, if you please." She understood his intent, and with one hand flipped the clean linen over as much of the woman's body as she could without interfering with Thomas' work. She watched as he lubricated the flexible black rubber rectal tube. "Merely a foot or two is enough," he said, and was astonished that, as much as he would have wished for Bertha Auerbach's calm, utterly competent assistance at that moment, this fourteen year-old child was herself a wonder.

He filled the bulb with their standard brew of chamomile infusion, tannin, laudanum, and gum arabic and then opened the small clamp ring to secure the bulb to the black tube. "This must be done after *every* evacuation, Elaine. The goal is to replace the fluid that she loses. Even more if we can. One must be diligent, for it is a battle between us and the disease." He looked up at her, and saw that her eyes were locked on his right hand, now gradually squeezing the bulb.

"How much?" the girl asked, the first time she had spoken in many minutes.

"The goal is two liters," Thomas replied, then when he saw the puckered eyebrows, turned just a bit and nodded at the bottle that he had brought with him. "That much. *Each* time."

"But you have no more."

"No, I don't. That means we must take your mother to the clinic where she can be treated. Twenty-four hours a day. That is the only hope."

He refilled the bulb and continued. The liberal dose of laudanum would have a quieting effect on the gut, he hoped. Without interrupting the infusion, he turned and looked at Eleanor. "Had Dr. Haines treated your mother for tuberculosis?"

"No, Doctor."

"Why ever not? Her condition is advanced." But the girl didn't answer, her attention drawn elsewhere. At the same time, Thomas heard the heavy footfalls on the stairway, and a moment later, Pastor Roland Patterson's dapper figure appeared in the bedroom doorway.

For a few heartbeats, Patterson didn't speak, his eyes taking in the scene on the bed. "Elaine, this instant," he said, one slender finger pointing out of the room. His voice was little more than a hiss, his face white. For a fleeting moment, he reminded Thomas of one of the professors at the university whose volatile temper was legendary. The elderly physician had once hurled a scalpel across the operating theater, where it stuck into the molding around the doorway. There it had remained for weeks as a grim reminder not to try Dr. Bolhman's patience. Despite the tone that defied any contradiction, Patterson's step-daughter didn't move. Instead, she looked across at Thomas, who hadn't changed his grip on the bulb or the rubber tube.

"Sir," Thomas said quietly, "your wife is fighting the cholera. If we don't do something to replace…" and that was as far as he got. Patterson crossed the room in two strides, and with one hand reached out and grabbed the child, practically snapping her small, lithe form off the bed and onto the floor. With the other hand, Patterson reached out and grabbed the rubber tube. His action was so unexpected that Thomas was caught completely off guard. Apparently not knowing where the other end of the tube actually *was,* Patterson jerked it hard from Thomas' hand. The clamp ripped open from the bulb and the tube was yanked from its position, solution splattering.

"Get *out* of my house," Patterson snarled, and he bent over and jerked the linens across his wife's exposed body. "What kind of man are you?"

Flabbergasted, Thomas reached for the dislodged tube and bulb. "Good God, man, listen to me. If we don't replace fluids…"

"Good God, indeed," Patterson shouted, his face livid. As he spoke, Elaine pushed herself to her feet, coming into her father's view. "And my *daughter,* for the love of God." His anger soared to a point where he enunciated only spittle and his eyes bulged, and he turned his fury on his step-daughter. "Elaine, you will leave this room. This is no place for you." He swept an arm wide, jabbing his finger toward the door.

"Sir, do you have any idea, any idea at all, what this is?" Thomas reached out and retrieved the tube, standing as he did so.

"You will leave my house." Patterson spat each word, fists clenched. Thomas could see the pulse throbbing at the man's temples. Would he actually lash out? Surely, no one could be so unreasonable, Thomas thought—especially with a loved one so frightfully ill. But the young physician was in no mood to negotiate.

"I don't think so, Pastor." He took a deep breath and shifted his weight, hands ready to defend himself. But he made no move from the end of the bed. "To do so will certainly jeopardize your wife's life. She needs constant treatment, sir. She must be taken to the clinic where the nurses may deal with her distress day and night." He held up the tube. "She cannot retain food or fluids, sir. She vomits them immediately. The unrelenting diarrhea drains her body. If that fluid is not replaced, then she dies." He shook the tube again. "If not replaced via the mouth, then via the rectum. It is as simple as that."

Patterson didn't reply but stood rooted in place, eyes huge and glaring, lips pressed to a white line. What was the source of this odd man's anger, Thomas wondered. Did Patterson really believe that *his* biding was the *only* biding? Apparently so. Thomas dropped the soiled black tube and bulb into the carbolic acid bath.

"What is she doing here?" Patterson managed, and Thomas looked down at Elaine. The last thing he wished to see was the transfer of the distraught man's anger to the young girl…the only person so far to have showed the least modicum of nerve in the Patterson household.

"I need help, Pastor. That's what your step-daughter is *doing*. If anything saves her mother's life, it will be her brave, steadfast labors on her behalf…at considerable risk to her own safety, I might add. Many people cannot face…"

At that moment Mrs. Patterson let out a piteous cry, spasmed double, and ejected the latest assault on her gut. The geyser was so violent that it spattered the pastor's perfectly creased trousers and highly polished shoes. Elaine darted into action with towels, at the same time catching her sister's eye.

"Hot water now, Eli," she ordered, and in any other circumstances the commanding tone in her little voice would have been comical. Eleanor left to do as she was told, commanded by a fourteen year-old girl.

Thomas drew the bulb and tube from the sterilization bath. "You'll allow me to work?"

"What are you doing with that?" As the fires of temper died, Patterson appeared to wilt, losing an inch of stature. His tone managed to continue imperious, however.

"Essentially, what we are doing is providing hydration to your wife's gut in the only way open to us, pastor. She cannot swallow, so she cannot drink. We provide liquid to her system. It is no cure, sir. But it is the only avenue open to us. Once we do that, it is up to God to do with it as he wills."

"I never entertained the impression that you spoke with God," Patterson said, his tone oddly neutral, neither sarcastic nor jocular.

"In my own fashion," Thomas said, taking advantage of the lessening of tension. "Just as last fall, your wife tended to *you* following surgery when you could not fend for yourself, so the same is expected of you now." Thomas saw the flare of temper rise again at the suggestion that Patterson might have been helpless.

"At least have the decency to cover her, young man."

Thomas hesitated while he fought his own temper. "I cannot work with the task concealed in the dark," he replied sharply. "If the sight of a human buttocks so offends you, then leave the work to Elaine and me. I'm sure, should your wife survive, that she will forgive the indiscretions. And she might even forgive those who allowed her to lie untended for so long. First the tuberculosis, and now this."

The pastor's face went from purple to ashen, but Thomas was in no mood to trade further barbs. The tussle of tempers was gaining them nothing, and only wasting time. He turned away from Patterson and prepared the bulb and tube. As he worked, he was conscious of the pastor standing immediately behind him. He could hear the man's breath. And as he worked, he was aware that Elaine's concentration on the task at hand was absolute, as if her step-father were absent from the room.

With the bulb emptying, Thomas let his breath ease out in relief.

"You are in a position to be of invaluable help," he said, but earned no response from the pastor. "You can organize those in town who are most in danger. With the ability to culture the bacillus, we are able to…" The response was hearing Patterson's boots on the floor as the man turned toward the door.

"Pastor Patterson?" When the man did not reply, he twisted around and looked at him. Patterson's face was glacial.

"Your wife must be taken to the clinic. I have neither the supplies nor facilities to care for her here. We must have laboratory cultures from all who live in this house, even those who as yet show no signs of illness. And just as important, the contagion must be cleared from this dwelling." He heard no reply. "It is not just your wife at risk, sir. It's you and your children. It is every member of your congregation with whom *you* come in contact." He glanced at the man's stained trousers and shoes. "Even yourself, sir."

Thomas turned back to his patient, continuing his gentle pressure on the bulb. He could feel that Pastor Patterson's dark eyes were smoldering twin holes through the back of his skull, but the man offered not a word.

In a moment, his boot-steps receded and Thomas let out a long sigh of relief. Elaine's attention had never wavered. If she had noticed that her step-father was beyond lifting a finger to help his wife, whether from incapability or fear, she gave no hint.

Chapter Twenty-six

Thomas felt a surge of triumph so strong that he let out a yelp. He held in his hand a population of the very demons that besieged Port McKinney, and he knew their origin. He had scraped a tiny sample of the culture to a slide and examined it under the Hiennenberg with extraordinary care. And there they were, the minute, lethal curls of bacilli. Both pages from the Mother Superior's brief letter and the souvenir of linen habit had produced active cultures, the 'wee beasties' having traveled from India half way around the world in the little, protective pouch, protected from sun, perhaps dampened now and then from squall, mist, or ocean spray…just enough to keep them alive and hopeful.

He wondered if any sisters of the convent in India still lived, or if even as she penned the brief words, the Mother Superior had been feeling the first roiling in her own gut. He could imagine Ben Sitzberger weeks later, stricken with grief, reading the final, sad and stained letter over and over again, clasping the scrap of his sister's clothing, perhaps bringing it to his nose for a final trace of her scent…the only worldly possession the nun might leave behind—that and the bacilli, who had responded with an astonishing reproductive virulence.

Thomas slid the glass culture dish back into the incubator and closed it securely. His cry of triumphant discovery was short lived, replaced with a morose sense of helplessness. He knew what the bacilli were, and now he had a good guess about where they had originated. That would make, come some peaceful day, a fine report for one of the scientific journals. Learned physicians the world over would read the Parks-Hardy article and shake their heads in wonder. But that pipe-dream was a distant one. First, one had to survive the onslaught, and there was no triumph yet to be had in this battle.

The cultures taken and prepared earlier in the day showed a sobering reality under the microscope. The warm, moist climate of the incubator would produce rapid, aggressive growth in those culture dishes, Thomas knew, but there was no point in waiting until that growth flourished. A quick survey showed infection in two other loggers, in addition to those evacuated. The cholera was also deeply entrenched in the Clarissa. Two of the sailors, including the first mate of the *Willis Head,* hosted the infection.

Not a single school child—including the two Snyder children—produced a positive culture.

The two loggers, testing positive but neither showing outward symptoms of the illness, had protested quarantine, Buddy Huckla more so because it had been Dr. Lucius Hardy who had cleaned his hand, then rebandaged and resplinted it, and done so with somewhat less patience and sympathy than Huckla might have liked. Both he and Todd Delaney grudgingly downed their Salol brew, but the clinic could offer little else. It was a matter of waiting.

In the second floor ward, two of the three young women, Mary Gates and Bessie Mae Winston, suffered in the earliest stages of cholera, and of the two, Mary's less robust constitution collapsed at an astounding rate. They had roomed together on the third floor, directly across the hall from Letitia Moore. The robust Letitia had become the most pathetic advertisement for what cholera could do in short order to an otherwise healthy person. She deflated with astounding rapidity, the ferocious intensity of her headache reducing her ebullient nature to quiet gasps and whimpers. At the same time, she wept without end, her tears driven by the terrible depression and feeling of dread, despite now being too ill to afford giving up a single extra drop of moisture.

Mildred Patterson, the pastor's failing wife, rested quietly in the rearmost bed of the ward, lying on her right side, eyes turned away from the world and the rest of the ward. Elaine had drawn a chair close to her bed and tended her mother with unflagging intensity.

Thomas had taken a few moments to visit with Sonny Malone, a one-way conversation that he carried out as he listened to the man's heart and lungs, peered into his unresponsive eyes, and with the fine needle tested the various reflexes. Although showing little improvement, still Malone held his own, and that was something of a victory.

Leaving Malone, this time with a warm wrap around the bald, polished skull, Thomas returned to the dispensary and washed his hands again, grimacing at the red, tender skin. Enjoying the soothing lanolin, he walked to the clinic's front door and stood on the step, breathing the sweet air deeply. Evening was approaching, the sun just ready to hide behind the hills that bordered the inlet. The afternoon had settled into a litany of desperate treatment, but had been interrupted by no new patients. Thomas knew it was too early to believe that they had made real progress toward stopping the epidemic.

In the timber, hundreds of loggers who had not yet consented to give culture, might be breeding the bacilli, might be spreading it far and wide.

To the north, several blocks down the hill toward the church and then the inlet, Thomas saw a plume of smoke. He had left instructions with Eleanor Patterson that included burning the bedding and the mattress, and he felt a surge of hope that the girl had managed the task.

But three important individual cultures remained uncollected, and that infuriated Thomas. Roland Patterson would be the last person on earth to consent to having a culture swabbed from his royal behind. The physician understood that, and short of wrestling the arrogant preacher to the floor and taking the culture by force, there was no practical way to force the issue. Patterson would take his chances.

But the two children, hopefully innocent of their father's boneheaded stubbornness, had yet to be examined, let alone tested. While at the Patterson's earlier, Thomas had requested the examination, and had been refused. Argument had been to no avail—ignored, in fact. Thomas had considered medicine at gunpoint.

Perhaps, in her own quiet, ineffectual way, Eleanor would prevail.

He found himself wishing he understood the inoculation procedures so effectively employed against diseases like smallpox. Would they work against cholera? Lowenthal reportedly had seen immunization results with attenuated cultures injected into certain animals, but the text was vague about methodology.

Still pondering that notion, Thomas turned away from the evening and trudged up the long flight of stairs to the clinic's second floor. He found fourteen-year-old Elaine Patterson in intense, quiet conversation with Nurses Helen Whitman and Bertha Auerbach—and his wife Alvi—all gathered around Elaine's mother. Mrs. Patterson, tiny, shrunken, febrile, was still able to move her lips for silent conversations with her daughter.

Alvi looked up and saw Thomas, no doubt correctly reading the flabbergasted expression on his face that quickly turned to angry impatience. She stepped away from the confab and walked the length of the ward to where her husband stood by the stairway.

"Do you have *any* idea what you're doing?" Thomas whispered. "My God, Alvi…"

Reaching up, she curled her hand around the nape of his neck, her affectionate grasp ensuring that he paid attention to her. He flinched at her icy cold fingers, and smelled the antiseptic.

"I'm the delivery lady," she explained. "I was mad for some exercise, and mad to be of some use. I brought a bottle of champagne from the house, and another small parcel of ice from Mr. Lindeman."

"There are a hundred people who could do that," Thomas snapped, and he saw the stubborn veil that settled over her expression.

"A *hundred*. My." She turned and regarded the two nurses and the young girl. "Elaine tends her mother like a veteran, Doctor Thomas. And Berti has been *most* strict in not only explaining procedures to promote asepsis, but making sure that she follows those procedures to the letter. Elaine understands fully."

"I'm not concerned with that. I am concerned with *you*, Alvi. You visit this place of contagion, and now risk its spread with you. You put yourself at risk, and you put the infant at risk... not to mention anyone else with whom you come in contact."

"As do you, Doctor Thomas—if that is indeed the character of cholera. And your text is not the least bit supportive of that notion."

"There is *always* a risk, the text be damned." Thomas immediately wished he had curbed his tongue. The harsh words with Patterson rang too clearly in his memory, and he had no wish to add nonsense of his own. "I..." he started to say, but Alvi shushed him with an amused chuckle.

"Now *that's* an interesting scientific position," she said. "But precautions have been taken," Alvi said. "Berti has given the girl the whites. She looks wonderful, does she not?"

He turned and saw that indeed Elaine looked crisp, clean, and professional in her starched whites, complete with a small nurse's cap pinned to her raven hair.

"She will remain here," Alvi continued. "Until her mother passes the crisis. She has no wish to go back to the house while her mother is here, but worries about the others."

"I have given instructions. Eleanor knows that at the least hint of symptoms, the family is to come here. I need a culture from Patterson himself, but there is little hope of reasoning with him. In the meantime, they are disinfecting the home. I saw smoke from the fires just now."

"And while all are at risk here, and there, and yonder, you think that I should become a clam with my shell snapped shut at One-oh-one, hiding my face?"

"Don't be ridiculous. But you take needless risks, Alvina. You shouldn't be here. For one thing, the walk itself may be too strenuous, merely a day after."

"Well," and she shrugged, giving Thomas' neck another squeeze. "The walk was intoxicating, and here I am. I was musing through my father's books in the library, and remember him talking about the use of champagne—how when iced it is an effective salve for the dry mouth."

"Surely," Thomas said. "I think we have used so much of it that we might be taken for drunkards. We thank you. Now… will you go home?"

"I think that I will do what I can here for a little while," Alvi said.

Thomas took a long, slow breath. "Alvi—this is one time when your stubbornness is most exasperating. And dangerous, I might add. Needlessly so. There is nothing for you to do here that Nurse Auerbach or Nurse Whitman or Nurse Crowell can't do. It is enough that Elaine is put at risk."

"And yourself," she said. "And Dr. Hardy, who is down at the Clarissa, by the way. I saw him go down the hill."

"I know he's there. We were loath for him to leave the building—heaven knows there is enough to do for all of us, but we had a few quiet moments, and he took the time." He bent until his forehead touched hers. "For us, there is no choice, Alvi. For you, there is all the choice in the world. That's my point. The baby…"

She looked askance at him. "You're really angry, aren't you."

"Yes, a little. But more worried than angry."

"May I work in your office for a while? Perhaps only an hour? John Thomas is fed to fatness, and sleeps like a satiated puppy. Gert was glad for the opportunity to rock the little angel. One hour. Would that satisfy you?"

"Doing what?"

"Well, the accounts lag behind. I'm certain of that."

"Accounts?"

Alvi's laugh was one of pure delight. She pulled his head down toward her own and kissed him so passionately that he could hardly fail to respond. Drawing back, she shook her head in mock exasperation. "Who do you suppose pays for all of this?" she said. "The procedures, the drugs, the care…Miss Auerbach's salary, Miss Whitman's and Mrs. Crowell's, eventually perhaps even your own?"

"That is not an issue just now," Thomas replied.

"Indeed not?" She patted his arm, rolling the fabric of his waist-coat between thumb and finger as if testing the quality of the weave. "In the coming weeks, it would be nice not to have to try and remember every procedure, every dose of drugs, every step along the way for a patient's billing. I'll set about making sense of all that. It's what *I* do well, isn't it?"

"My office, only," Thomas said. "And only an hour."

"Until I can no longer stand the smell," Alvi said. "Then you can walk me home. Berti tells me that it's been…how did she describe it…'desperately quiet' this afternoon. Like a war with little cannon fire."

"The situation can change in a heartbeat, Alvi. But so far, we hold on. And Mrs. Patterson continues to fight. I believe it is seeing the child at her side that helps as much as anything."

"But you don't tell that little angel to go home, now, do you."

Thomas sighed. "She will, when she can do no more to help."

"As will I. With you on my arm." She patted his cheek and turned to the stairs.

Chapter Twenty-seven

As the cool and dry breeze touched his face, Thomas enjoyed the warm pressure of Alvi's arm through his, enjoyed the slow pace up the rough boardwalk of Gamble Street, finally content that she had walked to the clinic to accompany him home. Almost. After an initial scrub, he had changed clothes, then had scrubbed with a vengeance, even more than usual, scrubbed and scrubbed and cleaned and then disinfected with a final alcohol wash. He had insisted that Alvi do the same, and she had taken her time about it, not missing a fingernail or crease in the skin.

Despite the rigid disinfection, Thomas felt the crawling on his skin, as if the bacilli had somehow leaped from the culture dish and now wandered freely on the backs of his hands, seeking a doorway inside. He knew that was absurd. If one could *feel* bacilli, then one could swat them away. His hands and forearms had been so soaked in alcohol that surely they were hostile landscapes for life.

"What are you thinking?" Alvi asked as they reached the end of the porch that circled around 101 Lincoln.

"How lucky we are," Thomas replied immediately. "How very, very lucky."

"You mean us personally, or the village?"

"Yes," he laughed. "That's exactly right." He guided her up onto the porch, and they stood for a few minutes, looking down the hill at the few, scattered lights of Port McKinney. "If we can get through the night—with no further outbreaks or without losing the patients we have, there is a chance."

"Incubation of cholera may be two weeks or more," she reminded him, and smiled almost self-defensively. "I have the time to read, you know."

He sighed heavily. "Call it wishful thinking. But I want to believe that all this is an isolated outbreak. Our beloved textbooks tell me that despite its lethal nature, the cholera bacillus is remarkably frail—when confronted with a head-on assault, the contagion can be defeated. I know it can be."

He followed her inside, the door closing behind him with a satisfying thunk. For a few moments, anyway, the rest of the world could fend for itself.

Prince appeared from underneath the first floor stairway, his ratty tail thumping once or twice before hanging at half mast.

"Gert must love her escort," Thomas said.

"No, Gert doesn't," their housekeeper said. She appeared in the doorway of the library with the infant in her arms. The dog's tail thumped again at the sight of them. "He stinks to high heaven, that creature does. But I can't convince him to go outside."

"Some things are not open to negotiation," Alvi said. "Prince has decided that John Thomas is his charge, and he takes the task very seriously." She knelt, and Thomas saw that she did so effortlessly. She ruffled the dog's unkempt headpiece and gently scratched the back of his torn ears. His eyes closed to half mast.

"And now your hands will smell like dog," Gert groused. "If it isn't one thing, it's another." She frowned at Alvi as she said to Thomas, "I tried to talk this young lady out of walking to the clinic, but you know the success of that. And now the pastor's wife has been stricken?"

"Mrs. Patterson manages to cling to life," Thomas replied, and Gert's angular face softened. "Elaine is still with her. And of course Dr. Hardy…within mere steps, should there be a crisis."

"Eleanor is with her, you mean."

Thomas shook his head. "No, just Elaine. Eleanor has enough to do at home, although I confess that nursing is not one of her talents. The episode with her up at the logging camp set me to wondering just what her mental state might be."

"She is a girl who suffers the flights of fancy," Gert said. "I have known her for years, the poor child."

"I have to say that without her sister, the outcome might have been in doubt."

"Elaine is but fourteen," Gert protested. She handed John Thomas and his cocoon of blankets to Alvi.

"And a most intelligent, calm young woman with the common sense of someone twice her age. She would not go home with her mother so in jeopardy, so this may be the next best thing. She stays at the clinic. You should have seen her assisting me. Completely unflappable."

"What does the pastor say about that?"

"I'm not sure what choice he had in the matter. And we haven't spoken with him since, which is just as well. He's an ass."

Gert frowned disapproval. "Come now. He is highly thought of in the community, Doctor. And his family is threatened. It is a difficult time for him."

"For many. You know him better than I do, Gerti, but it appeared to me that he was content to let his wife lie there and die."

"Oh, pshaw," Gerti sniffed. "His faith lies in prayer. That's what we all turn to when we don't know what else to do."

"Listening to advice would be a start for him," Thomas replied. "What is the logic of not allowing himself to be tested for the cholera? A culture swab is so simple. But he refuses—in fact, refuses to actually acknowledge that the outbreak *is* cholera in the first place. But he neither likes nor trusts me. That much is obvious. He is furious that Winchell takes corpses directly from the clinic to the cemetery, without public funeral." He shrugged. "So we'll work around him. I left instructions with Eleanor about cleaning the household, and not long ago I saw smoke rising, so at least they've made a start. That house should be quarantined, and so should the church."

"The entire church?" Gerti asked.

"I would think so. The pastor goes from house to church, from house to church, from house to church…even if he doesn't lift a finger for his wife, with the changing of linens and such, he is at risk, just like the others. And then he carries it to the church. To the congregation."

"And the little ones? Are they in danger?"

"Of course."

"But what's to be done?"

"Once their home has been cleaned and aired, only vigilance. Cleanliness and vigilance, Gert. A bright, airy home, good food, cleanliness. And if we can keep other people away, that will only help."

"And Eleanor understands that? She understands that clearly?"

"I believe that she does, Gert. I certainly hope so. It was my intent to return there later this evening. I must see the children again."

"And the pastor? You've explained all this to Pastor Patterson?"

Thomas held up his hands. "What *he* believes is a mystery to me, Gert."

"Perhaps in the morning," Gert said, without adding what she foresaw for the morrow. She reached out and folded back the baby's blanket, revealing a snoozing face with two tiny fists clenched. "Everyone needs a good night's sleep. That's the secret." She raised an eyebrow at Thomas. "Dr. Hardy? How is he fitting in?"

"Like an old slipper, Gerti. It's as if he's always been with us. I don't know what we'd do without him."

"We must have him to dinner, Thomas. It's not right that such a gentleman is marooned down there in that monstrosity."

"Most certainly. I look forward to it. But right now, he is where he is needed."

"Of course." Her breath whistled out of her impossibly spare frame. "You will take time for breakfast in the morning?"

"I cannot remain for the night," he said. "There is…"

"Yes, he will," Alvi interrupted. "That will be my mission." She smiled at Thomas. "They'll come to fetch you if there is a need, Doctor Thomas."

With no will to argue, and knowing that his mind was in a fog of fatigue already, Thomas spent an hour eating dinner and enjoying entertainment provided by little John Thomas. Then, an exquisite, long hot bath followed by ferociously laundered night clothes touched with lavender water welcomed them to bed, and where the night went, Thomas had no idea. He awoke to a silent house and an empty bed. For a moment he lay still, disoriented.

"Alvi?" he said, and his voice, though a whisper, sounded thunderous in the empty bedroom. With no response, he threw off the bedding and slid out. Only the dog's fragrance lingered, and Thomas made his way quickly in the dark to the stairway. He had padded half-way down when he smelled the coffee and bacon, and then heard the tiny *eh, eh, eh* of his son fretting in his wicker bassinette. The towering clock in the hallway clicked to 4:12 a.m. as he passed.

The kitchen was bright from four gas lights, and the coal-fired Newark kitchen range chased out the dampness. Prince lay like a large unkempt rug just inside the kitchen door and rose as Thomas appeared, stepping deferentially to one side. Alvi worked at the range, and the bacon in the frying pan snapped even as she turned at his approach.

"Go get dressed," she said. "By that time I shall be finished here."

"I could have slept another ten hours," Thomas said, then saw the tight expression on Alvi's face. "What is it?"

"Gert has gone down to the Pattersons' to see if she can help," Alvi said gently. "Mrs. Patterson passed last night. Not long after midnight." Thomas felt as if every benefit of a solid night's sleep had been snatched from him. His first thought was of Elaine. He could not imagine the Patterson child's heartbreak. She had tried so hard.

"Horace has gone down to help with the horses."

"I'm sure Pastor Patterson needs little help with his horses," Thomas said, but Alvi's withering glance told him that wasn't the case at all.

"*Our* horses, Thomas. Howard Deaton is ill."

"My God," Thomas said. "I'll be but a moment." He charged back up the stairs, cursing in desperation, first at those who had not awakened him, and then at himself. Why had he left the clinic? Those critical hours spent pleasuring himself...those very hours could easily have meant the difference for a patient. Lucius Hardy was competent—more than competent—in every way, but still...

He dressing quickly, then selected a clean pair of boots from the armoire. Back downstairs, he was ready to shrug into his coat when Alvi called from the kitchen.

"Come here, Doctor Thomas."

"Please, Alvi. There is no time. How could you let me lie abed like some sluggard while the whole world comes a flinders."

"Proper nutrition," she snapped. "I read the same books as you, Doctor Thomas. The foundations of health are proper nutrition, adequate rest, and fresh air." As she talked, she slid a mound of scrambled eggs onto a plate, hemmed in with a half dozen slices of thick bacon and a generous slice of the plain brown bread that Gert favored over the "high-fallutin' white." The coffee gurgled into the cup, forming a slick of rich bubbles around the rim. "Take five minutes, Thomas. It will make a world of difference to you, and to the patients you treat. This day will be one for your journal."

As he gobbled the food without argument, she rolled an apple across the table toward him. "Take that with you."

"Really Howard?" he asked between mouthfuls. "Who came to the house last night to awake you?"

"Elaine, that dear, sweet child."

"What? *Elaine* did? But her mother..."

"Just so." Thomas saw a tear in the corner of her eye, and stopped. For Alvi to cry, to be overwhelmed, meant that basically the world had stopped turning. She was touched easily, Alvi was, but her usual reaction was a warm smile or gentle touch. "I tried to comfort her, but do you know what she said to me?"

"I can't imagine her grief, Alvi. She is but a child. To lose her mother so?"

"'I will cry later,' the child said. And remember, Thomas, this *is* a child speaking. 'I will cry later.' she said. 'Right now there is too much to do.'"

The flavor of eggs, bacon, and buttered toast blended together into a tasteless lump in his mouth. "What time did the child come to the door?"

"Shortly after three," Alvi replied. "Dr. Hardy sent for you on hearing about Howard's illness. Should the ambulance be needed for others, he wanted a driver. Jake Tate is out at the Dutch camp still."

"How do you know that?"

"Because he is not *here*, Doctor Thomas." Having come to know Jake Tate over the past months, Thomas understood exactly what she meant. The man had been given a job to do, and would stay until he was satisfied. It was that simple. When finished, he would come to the clinic to report.

Rising from the table, Thomas drained the last of the coffee. He stood still a moment, staring down into the small swirl of grounds in the bottom of the cup. "Howard was diligent with his hygiene," he said. "I don't understand. This contagion is so virulent, so pervasive." He looked across at Alvi. "That is why I'm going to plead with you, Alvi. Despite our best intentions, our best efforts, it is obvious that this contagion can spread with an ease that baffles us. Please stay away from the clinic." His wife started to reply, but he interrupted her. "And now Gert has done *exactly* what she shouldn't."

"It is a shared thing, Doctor Thomas."

"Of course it is, but…"

"One person's worth is no greater or no lesser than another's. If Gerti knows that she can be of assistance, then you cannot tell her *not* to be so."

"I can if she endangers others," Thomas snapped.

"She is well aware of the dangers," his wife said. "As am I. As are your nurses. Even the child—even little Elaine." She held up a hand as if caught in mid-thought. "There is another issue as well."

"What do you mean?"

"Mr. Patterson has become an issue."

"What has he done? Does he not know that his wife has died? Did no one tell him?"

"Elaine did," Alvi said. "And then returned to the clinic, despite harsh words from her step-father. I would guess that the combination of grief and anger stirred the good pastor's mind beyond reason, Thomas. He went to the clinic and took the body home. He tried to drag Elaine with him, but she would not go. Finally, Dr. Hardy had to interfere."

"My God. Has Patterson no idea…"

"That is absolutely right, Dr. Thomas. He has no idea." A hint of impatience touched her voice. "He took his wife home. The body will be prepared, and then I suppose he plans a proper funeral in the church."

Thomas looked heavenward. "And all the neighbors in," he muttered. "Has this man not a single, solitary brain cell in his head? I'm surprised Dr. Hardy allowed this."

"He struck Dr. Hardy, Thomas."

The young physician stared at his wife. "He *struck* him?"

"That is what Horace said. He escorted Elaine here, and that was the story I was able to pry out of him. Dr. Hardy refused to release the body to him, and Pastor Patterson rose up against him. Cut his face, I'm told."

"I must go." He started for the door, heart pounding in his chest.

Close behind him, Alvi said, "Show them exactly what they must do, Doctor Thomas. Whatever towns people gather? I'm sure they will listen to you. Explain, and then *demand* that all precautions be foremost in their minds. And then trust them do their part, just as you trust me. That is really all you can do." A faint smile touched her mouth. "And then maybe Roland Patterson's prayers will do the rest."

"Would that were a comfort now to Elaine," Thomas said.

"Perhaps it is. We don't know." She ushered him out of the kitchen. As he picked up his heavy medical bag, Alvi's strong fingers locked the back of his neck . Her voice was a whisper in his ear, her breath warm. "How often do you disinfect the grip of your medical bag, Doctor?"

He turned to her with astonishment. "I…" and suddenly the bag, with its familiar and comforting black leather and brass fittings, felt like a lethal thing in his hand.

"You see how easy it is," Alvi said. "But you drip with alcohol most of the day, so I can't imagine a bacillus living on the grip for long." She pushed him toward the door and the darkness of dawn beyond. "Give Elaine *much* to do today, my love. She needs it."

Chapter Twenty-eight

"I found him halfway between the back door of the barn and the outhouse beyond," Dr. Lucius Hardy said. He dabbed at his swollen lip with a fresh gauze sponge and flinched at the sting of alcohol. "I had stepped out for a breath of fresh air just before midnight, and first saw his lantern on the ground."

Thomas knelt beside Howard Deaton's bedside. The man lay curled in a tight ball, the pillow wrapped around his head the way a child might who was afraid of the night's creatures. "The head hurts?" he asked, and Deaton grunted something unintelligible, then pulled the pillow away from his face.

"It's comin' apart, Doc. Holy Christ, it hurts."

"Let me listen." Thomas pulled the blankets aside and roamed with the stethoscope. The man's pulse was rapid and strong, flailing away against his own anxiety. It was one thing, Thomas thought, to be blind-sided by a disease without knowledge of the most likely outcome. But Howard Deaton had watched what cholera could do, had watched it kill the strongest and fittest.

"Can you roll more on your back, Howard?" Deaton did so with a groan.

"This is killin' me, Doc."

"You're too tough to kill, my friend." Thomas listened while the man's gut rebelled. The gurgling and splashing in Deaton's lower gut, the characteristic borborygmi, practically bellowed through the instrument. "How often has he evacuated?"

"Since I found him?" Hardy looked up at Bertha Auerbach, who stood at the foot of the bed watching the teamster with the deepest sympathy.

"Eight," she said, always the meticulous keeper of statistics.

"Howard, when did the symptoms strike for the first time?"

"Christ, I don't know," he muttered. "Didn't feel so great after I ate my supper."

"What did you eat?"

"Some of that stew that Gert James sent down."

"There can be no fault there. To drink?"

"Still workin' on a jug of wine."

"And the vomiting?"

Deaton groaned, gritting his teeth. His hands dropped down to his lower gut, and he curled onto his side once more. "This is it, Doc. This is it. It's gonna take me."

"Nonsense, Howard. Work with us now."

"He has vomited everything we've given him," Berti said.

"Enteroclysis?"

"Four times," Bertha replied. "And we have been aggressive with the stupes and the laudanum."

"I'm thinkin' of becomin' a dope addict," Howard whispered, and tried to laugh. "You got any more, Berti?"

"All you want," she promised.

"His temperature?"

"An hour ago it was just under ninety-seven. Still, he has been able to hold some iced champagne long enough to sooth the mouth."

"We're giving Deaton champagne?" Hardy burst out loudly in mock protest, sounding as if he'd known Howard Deaton for a decade as best friend. He toed the door of the small room closed. "The staff is coddled thus?" he added when he saw the teamster try for a smile. He turned to Thomas. "We will need more Salol," he said quietly. "In fact, we'll need more of everything. The nearest source?"

"Someone will go to St. Mary's," Thomas said. "It's thirty miles down the inlet. Or to Seattle. Someone must set out this morning. The pharmaceutical salesman won't be through until the end of the month. We could wire the firm, but at least a month, nevertheless."

"My brother will go," Bertha Auerbach. "He can be back by Monday. I will arrange a list. And by the way…" She laid a hand on Thomas' elbow. "Mr. Malone *swallowed* last night. He actually *swallowed*." He looked at her for a moment, taking time to catch up.

"My word," he said. "All of this, and Mr. Malone sails along in the middle of the battle, untouched and unaware."

"Elaine is with him at the moment," Bertha said. "Although there is no response, I think a tender touch and conversation must be helpful. The poor child needs much to do."

"I wish I knew," Thomas said, still thinking about the blasted brain of Sonny Malone. "But a swallow…that's a good sign." He turned to Hardy. "You've had a chance to look in on him?"

"I have. His body continues while his brain has simply ceded from the union, so to speak." Hardy reached out and rested a hand on Thomas' shoulder, steering him away from Deaton's bedside.

"You heard about this?" And he dabbed his lip once more. Thomas cocked his head to look at the laceration. "It's really nothing," Hardy said. "My own tooth is the villain, and cut the inside of my lip. I would never have guessed that man was so quick."

"I'm surprised you didn't cut his throat, Lucius."

"Had I a scalpel in my hand, I would have," the physician chuckled, then the amusement left his face. "Patterson was obdurate, Thomas. Most eloquent for a man in such a rage." He raised a forefinger to the heavens, imitating Patterson. "'You shall not dump my wife into unconsecrated ground like so much offal,' he shouts. 'She is a Christian, and by heaven will go to her God as befits…' and so on." He sighed deeply. "I let him take her, Thomas. Maybe Winchell and the constable can talk sense to him."

He lowered his voice. "With the child standing there, tears streaming down her face, I was not about to enter into a fisticuffs with this man, the two of us tearing at the mother's remains like a couple of jackels. Berti and I made sure the corpse was wrapped in a sterile blanket and then…" He held up both hands. "Off he went, carrying her downstairs without benefit of the Otis, out into the night, sobbing and muttering to himself." Hardy turned and looked toward the back of the ward. "Off into the night without a thought for his step-daughter." He turned back to Thomas. "My friend, it's as if the girl has ceased to exist in his mind."

"We must watch over her, then," Thomas said. "I was astonished to learn that Gert James went to the Pattersons' as well, earlier this morning. What she can do for them, I don't know. But during the night, she made off to the Pattersons' home, just after Elaine brought word. Gerti fears for the two remaining children, I'm sure."

"That's not good. Look what she might be walking into, Thomas."

"We must collect Constable Aldrich and Ted Winchell. With his wife's remains, Mr. Patterson has just delivered the cholera to the church, if he hadn't done so already. There must be no gathering for a funeral. If the children are ill, they must be brought here. If not, it would be wise to find less dangerous lodging for them."

"Easily said, my friend."

"We must make every effort, this very dawn. How are the others?"

Hardy dabbed his lip again. "Mr. Snyder will live, I am sure of it. In its own capricious way, the cholera has paid him little heed. What killed his wife in but a day or two is going to leave him just as surely, I believe. There will be a period of prostration, during which we will have to be vigilant." He beckoned Thomas to follow him through the ward.

"Snyder sleeps, a bit fitfully, but sleeps nevertheless. The diarrhea has stopped, and he tolerated the iced champagne well, nearly five ounces of it. Even the borborygmi have settled. It no longer sounds as if there's warfare going on in his gut." He heaved a deep breath, holding up his ample belly for a moment, and then relaxed. "The brothers Bloedel present considerably more of a challenge, Thomas. And I see no lessening in the others. It's to be a fearful day."

Thomas scanned the ward. Gunnar and Carl Bloedel, in neighboring beds, were tended at the moment by Adelaide Crowell.

"I hold little hope for Ira Johnson," he whispered. "The first mate of the *Head?* While his skin feels cold to the touch, we have recorded an internal temperature several degrees above the norm. The cyanosis worries me. Truly remarkable, Thomas. It's as if every last vestige of water has been withdrawn, leaving his blood as thick as mud. We have been aggressive with infusions—more than aggressive, I think." They turned at the clank of a glass and saw Bertha Auerbach still fretting with Howard Deaton.

Hardy dropped his voice even lower. "She works like a demon, Thomas. She has stayed, you know. The whole evening and now night. When Mrs. Crowell came in, I was able to convince Helen Whitman to go home for some hours rest. But not Bertha. At first, she came to be with Elaine, whom she obviously cherishes. And then with Howard. She takes the condition of each patient as a personal crusade. Simply wonderful. A lesson for those of us who might tend to sloth." He patted his gut again. "If any of our patients survive, it will be a testament to your nurses."

"I don't think we can accuse you of sloth, sir."

"I hope not." He turned back and nodded at Buddy Huckla, in the first ward bed, who lay curled in a small, childlike ball. "Huckla would make a gambler nervous," he said. "At first, I thought he would escape, despite the presence of the bacilli in his gut. There seemed to be no reaction. And then, in what seemed like a matter of minutes, he became thus." Hardy shook his head in wonder. "So fast, Thomas. So fast. The same with Delaney. There is some sign that the infusions are easing the…what might we call it…the debt of dehydration that grows so savagely. We are hard pressed to keep the equipment claved. It is a constant thing."

"And I slept through it all," Thomas growled.

Hardy laughed grimly and slapped him on the shoulder. "You'll need it, sir. Not to worry. Now that Mr. Patterson has joined the opposition, the battle is about to become pitched, I'm afraid. You know," and he swept a hand theatrically through the ward, "when I first saw this—eight beds here, three small private chambers to the rear, and the same upstairs—I thought that your dreams may be exceeding the reality of this tiny village. And now I see the opposite."

Thomas pulled out his watch. "We must confront Patterson. May I ask that you remain here?"

"You should not confront him by yourself," Hardy replied, correctly guessing Thomas' intent.

"Indeed not. I'll have Constable Aldrich with me. And Ted Winchell. Two more stout men would be hard to find." He tried to smile. "And Gert James is there. She's worth any ten men. If nothing else, I must protect her if I can."

Hardy nodded. "You'll need them. I fear for the good pastor's sanity, Thomas."

"We have far more to fear from the cholera. Patterson is but words."

"Uh huh." Hardy dabbed at his lip again, amused.

"Two things," Thomas said. "I will go to the church, and have Aldrich nail it shut. I fear for Eleanor and the other two Patterson children who remain in the house, not to mention the pastor himself. And then I want to visit the Clarissa. I don't know why people are so slow to come to us at the first sign of the disease, but they appear content to just curl up into a ball and wait for death."

"They work like slaves to clean the place," Hardy offered. "Although burning it to the ground would be a good thing. I'm not sure I've experienced a filthier place since a visit to the Paris slums." One of the sailors, Cyrus Collins, uttered a loud groan, and Hardy turned toward his bedside. Thomas caught his arm.

"While I am gone, if Alvi should come to the clinic…"

The sympathy in Hardy's eyes was immediate.

"With Gert at the Patterson's, Alvi will be with the child," Thomas said. "If she is tempted…"

"If she comes here, I have an enormous favor to ask of her," Hardy said. "From the moment she arrives, she will be busy in your office, preparing a copious list of supplies for Miss Auerbach's brother. We need that, Thomas." He regarded the gauze sponge. "And then someone must speak with Mr. Lindeman about a supply of fresh fruit, and certainly more champagne. More this, more that. Your lovely wife won't have a moment for anything else."

"Thank you, Lucius."

As he stepped away from Thomas, Hardy added, "Be careful, my friend." His eyebrows shot up then, and he nodded toward the front of the ward.

Horace James, looking as an undertaker should, stood deferentially in the door of the ward. How long he had been there was anyone's guess. His enormous, knotted hands were folded at his chest as if caught in prayer. He took a half step forward as Thomas approached.

"Sir, Jake Tate was askin' for the ambulances. Both of 'em."

"Both, Horace?" His heart sank.

The man nodded. "I'll drive one, him the other? That's what I was thinking."

"He's here right now?"

"Yes, sir. Out in the stable."

Thomas darted past Gert's brother and sprinted to the side door of the clinic, where Jake Tate waited under the portico, smoking a cigarette.

"How many are ill, Jake?"

"Got five. Probably four by the time we get back out there. They sure need you, Doc."

Thomas almost spun in a circle, trying to marshal his thoughts. "Listen, I'm going to give you syringes. Can you manage those?"

"Guess so. Seen you do it enough times."

"Morphine to keep them quiet for the trip," Thomas instructed. "Take fresh blankets for each. Mrs. Crowell will make sure you have the proper ones. Then get them back here as quickly as possible."

"You ain't comin' out?"

"We have a problem at the church," Thomas said. *And Gert has walked into the middle of it.* "The loggers must be treated here anyway. There's nothing we can do for them out in the timber other than the morphine to keep them quiet. I'm depending on you, Jake. Horace is going back with you in the second ambulance."

"All right." The young man sounded resigned.

"And Jake…while you're there, while you're tending the men? Talk to them in the most cheerful terms if you can. Cholera is a fearsome thing, and it's important that the men have hope. And if you can discover *how* the men came into contact with the others—that would be important for us to know."

"Well, hell, I can guess at that, Doc. Come an evening, most of 'em gather in that chow hall. Biggest damn poker games you ever saw."

Thomas closed his eyes, imagining the whiskey jug passing around the table, the spittle, the cards passing from hand to hand, the back-slapping, the card players wiping hands through their beards and dabbing at eyes irritated by the smoke, using shirt cuffs as napkins. "How many gather there on a night? I know there were but three from the *Head*."

Tate shrugged. "I've been there when there was thirty, Doc. Smoke in the hall so thick you didn't need no pipe to smoke. 'Course, I don't get up there much, work at the mill bein' what it is."

"And thank God for that."

"Yep. Schmidt's up there right now, too. He's fixin' to move the men maybe today. He's going to burn the camp to the ground. Took care of the two shacks yesterday after you left."

"Would that had been done before," Thomas said. But before *when,* he thought ruefully. He saw Horace leading one of the teams out of the barn. "Not a moment to lose now, Jake. If any of the others are beginning to feel the first signs—vomiting, the running shits, pain in head or gut—they must come here immediately."

"Might have a houseful," Tate remarked.

"We already have that," Thomas replied.

Jake pinched out the butt of his cigarette. A tightly knit, powerful man, Jake looked haggard. He forced a grin. "I'm going to be a popular guy, pushin' all that dope."

"If they hurt, give the injection. It quiets the gut. And waste no time coming back."

Tate nodded and strode back toward the barn where the ambulances waited.

Thomas returned to the clinic, catching Hardy for just long enough to inform him about what was coming. "The beds may be pushed together," he said. "There are more frames and mattresses in storage behind, where we keep the linens and blankets." And then he grabbed his medical bag and headed out into the pre-dawn to find the constable and the coroner.

Chapter Twenty-nine

The gelding enjoyed his stall, since it was dark, quiet, and well-tended with food, while the night was so often wet, slippery of foot, and filled with all manner of odd sights, sounds, and smells. When Thomas swung open the stall door, the big horse stood quietly, his rump backed into one corner.

Still saddled and bridled, the animal took a deep breath as Thomas tugged at the cinch.

"Stop that." The young man slapped the back of his hand against the sleek flank. Quickly lashing the medical bag, Thomas mounted in the barn, and then urged Fats out into the pre-dawn darkness.

Mist sifted against his face, but it was too early to forecast the day. Constable Aldrich was already up, his suspenders hanging off his shoulders. His affable greeting turned to resignation as he listened to the urgent request.

"You fetch Winchell, then," Aldrich said. "We'll meet at the church."

Winchell was well into his day as well, stacking a load of select spruce planking in the shed behind his mortuary.

"You'll need your rig," Thomas said, and when he explained to Winchell where they were going, the undertaker shook his head in disbelief.

"He's off his nut." Winchell let his comment go at that. Thomas waited while he rigged the ambulance, and the two of them set out through the back ways to Angeles Street, paralleling the inlet. A quarter mile ahead, the church stood tall and dark, the slender steeple outlined against the sky, the first spot in Port McKinney to see the sun on those rare dawns when the gold burst over the inlet. Thomas saw no light in the church itself, although the dawn could play tricks.

"I saw that they started cleaning the back wall of the *Clarissa*," Winchell called across to Thomas. The physician urged his mount closer to the hearse.

"And more than that," he replied. "Schmidt's pump is working, then?"

"After a fashion. A dozen times the pressure would be helpful, but we do with what we have." The church loomed, and Thomas could imagine it packed with towns folks, all hugging and weeping, spreading contagion.

"How does the pastor handle funerals?" Thomas asked Winchell just as they started up the last grade. "You know him better than I. What will he intend with his wife?" When Alvi's father had died, the ceremony had been a simple graveside service...without Roland Patterson officiating.

"Well, now." Winchell relaxed the reins and allowed his team to pull without interference. "I don't know what he plans now. In normal times, when he puts on his full funeral performance, he wants the customer right up front, ahead of the front row of pews. Even if it's just a simple box." He waved a hand toward the church. "That's what most folks around here can afford. Nothing fancy. It works for me, since I do a good business with that. Once in a while, somebody gets all cushy and orders a proper casket from the city, but generally it's the spruce box. Or fir. Sometimes cedar. That smells pretty good." He grimaced. "Sometimes that's important. The pastor puts the casket right at the head of the aisle. Then he can command the view from the pulpit." He leaned toward Thomas, lowering his voice to a conspiratorial, gruff whisper. "Nobody gets to God without going through him."

Thomas glanced at the undertaker, always surprised by Ted Winchell's blunt manner of speech. Winchell saw the reaction.

"Yep, I'm a bloody heathen," he said. "But you don't need to spread *that* around. Patterson puts up with me. You get a job nobody else wants, what can they say, right?"

He pulled the horses to a halt in front of the Patterson's house. The constable stood by the front gate, waiting. Lamps blazed inside, and as they approached, Thomas had seen a shadow pass in front of the window. The constable reached out and grasped the gelding's bridle.

"You sure that Dr. Hardy doesn't want to sign out a complaint?" Aldrich sounded almost hopeful.

"No. I can't say I'd be as generous." Thomas unlatched the gate, and it opened on well-oiled and properly adjusted hinges. A figure appeared in the doorway, and Thomas saw that it was Gert James. She wore black, with one of her starched white aprons—and even in the poor light, Thomas could see that the apron was splotched dark.

"You shouldn't come in, gentlemen," Gert said when they were close enough to hear her hoarse whisper. She held out a hand toward Winchell and Aldrich. "The little ones are ill, and I fear for the Pastor himself. But he's in a fury. If he catches sight of you, constable…"

Aldrich settled his rump against the short porch railing and dug his pipe out of his pocket. "If he takes a swing at anybody, he goes to jail, Gerti. And that's that."

"He won't strike me." Thomas sounded more certain than he was. "Wait for me."

Gert reached out a hand for Thomas as he passed through the door, then thought better of it, and clasped her hands together at her waist. "The children need to be at the clinic," she said. "He won't let them go."

Thomas stopped short. "Good God, Gert, why ever not? What kind of madness is this?"

"He has his reasons."

"Do you know them? The reasons?" Even as he spoke, he opened his medical bag and handed her a brown bottle of carbolic acid and another of alcohol. "Clean your hands, Gert. They must be disinfected often."

She accepted the bottles. "The pastor and Dr. Haines did not see eye to eye," she whispered. "Nor with Alvi, either. But that's a grudge that should be long gone." Gert lowered her voice even more, and Thomas had to watch her lips to catch what she said. "His first wife, you see."

"Patterson's first wife?"

She nodded, but before she had time to answer, Roland Patterson appeared from a back room, a stout cane in his hand. The cane was not intended as a weapon, Thomas could see. Patterson did not stride with his usual iron-backed posture, but sidled into the room, moving as if he'd aged half a century. One hand was thrust into his trousers at the gut. His eyes were bright, and locked on Thomas.

"What do you want?"

"The children are ill. Will you let me tend them? They should be taken to the clinic immediately."

"My wife has died," Patterson said, his voice surprisingly soft. "A good, strong woman." He pushed himself up a bit, keeping most of his weight braced by the cane. "She died within a day after you began your barbaric treatment."

"Barbaric?"

"Those are my words, young man. Your intrusions, your narcotics, your potions…"

"You consider modern medicine *barbaric?*"

"I do. And you took Elaine. You took her after I expressly forbade it."

"Elaine came to the clinic of her own free will, Mr. Patterson."

"She *has* no free will, young man. She is but fourteen."

"Mr. Patterson, if you remain in this house, it is more than likely that you will all die." He took a breath, and the odor came to him, making his skin crawl. "Is that what you want? Gert says that the two little ones are ill. And it's obvious that you are suffering, sir. There is no way of knowing how many of your congregation have been infected by the cholera. When it strikes, few are spared. You've witnessed that yourself."

"And I say again—it is ridiculous to think that this is *cholera,* the scourge of the filthy, the Godless…"

"This is nonsense," Thomas interrupted, and he turned toward Gert. "Where are the children?"

"This is *my* house, and this is *my* family. I will *not* have a man who lives in sin telling *me* what I must do!" Patterson roared, a show of his former strength. He thumped the cane hard on the floor, but didn't lift it to threaten Thomas.

"I neither know nor care about what you imply," Thomas said. "But I *do* know that human ignorance opens the way for such plagues as the cholera. If you had half a wit, you would understand that. Now, you struck my associate." Thomas stepped closer to Patterson. He could see the darkness under the eyes, the weariness that sapped the pastor's strong physique. The once neatly pressed clothing hung wrinkled and rank. "That's all the striking you will do. Threaten me, and Constable Aldrich will arrest you. He awaits outside. Three things must happen, sir, and *will* happen. You have your wife's corpse." The harsh word jolted Patterson. "That must be buried immediately. The sick must go to the clinic for proper treatment, and this house cleaned from top to bottom, purged of the contagion. No one must be allowed back inside for at least two weeks. And the church as well. The church shall be quarantined…cleaned from top to bottom, and locked for two weeks."

"You compare my home and my church to the rude streets of Calcutta? And you think to *lock* the house of God?" Patterson gasped.

"That's exactly what I think."

"The Lord has been my *life,*" Patterson cried. "You think I am to turn my back on the very place where…" He didn't finish, but glared at Thomas. "My children are recovering, thanks be to God. The good Miss James has come to offer her assistance." He held up both hands, palms toward himself as if inspecting his fingers. "I shall fashion a final resting place for my wife with these hands. Thomas heard a grunt outside from Ted Winchell, who along with the constable was certainly listening to the exchange. "And then she will have a proper service in *her* church, and be prepared to meet the Lord."

"She's already there, sir. And you're more ill than you know."

"Don't you dare preach to me," Patterson said. "There is such a swelling of gratitude for the gift of health to my children that it actually brings some upset. It is nothing and will soon pass."

"May I look in on them?"

"They rest now, after a troubling night. To disturb them is the sort of foolishness at which you are apparently so adept."

For a moment, Thomas was too angry to reply. "Gert, are the children resting comfortably?" *Comfort* was not a word easily associated with the cholera.

"I am afraid for them," she whispered.

"The Lord will assuage your fears," Patterson said, and coughed loudly.

"When was the last time either took nourishment or fluids?"

"I have been here since three," Gert said. "They have managed nothing since then. I cannot speak for the time earlier."

"Sir," Thomas said, "This disease is an issue of very public health. A single case puts the entire community at risk. I must insist. I will examine the children, with your leave or not." He hefted the massive medical bag, so heavy that a single swipe with it would flatten Roland Patterson.

"If only to satisfy you, a single look. And then you will leave the house."

Gert had moved toward the hallway, and when Thomas looked at her, she shook her head in despair. For a moment he wondered what sort of comforting message someone with the common sense of Gert James found in Roland Patterson's sermons.

"Where are they?"

Patterson extended a hand, and Thomas followed him from the vestibule. In the parlor, the sheeted form of Patterson's wife lay on a long table, the linen covering drawn so flawlessly, so neatly, that he assumed that had been Gert's first task that night.

He cringed, thinking of the risk to her. They passed down a short hallway, and Patterson stopped at the first doorway, turned the knob, and held it open. In the dark, it was impossible to make out who might be inside.

"A lantern, if you please?"

It was Gert who appeared behind him with a coal oil lantern, its wick turned high. Thomas took it and entered the bedroom. A tiny girl lay curled on one narrow bed, obviously sleeping. Though the small bed was tidy and clean, Thomas could smell the cholera's foul presence. The child's breathing was quick and shallow. Thomas looked at her sunken eyes, hollow cheeks, and pallid skin. Touching the back of his hand to her cold cheek, he turned to Patterson.

"When were the first symptoms?"

"I told you...she sleeps easily now. With the morrow, she will be well."

Thomas sighed and pushed himself erect. "Do you care for this child, sir?"

"You have no right to ask that. I care for my children as for life itself."

For a moment, Thomas simply stood and gazed at the man. "You *care* for them? Then tell me when the first symptoms were."

"Perhaps sometime yesterday."

"Perhaps." Across the room, another child lay in bed, flat on his back, head turned toward the wall. Thomas raised the lantern and groaned. Hoping that he was wrong, he placed a finger to the side of the child's neck. "Gert?"

"Yes, Doctor?"

"This child is dead." He turned to look at the older woman. "Was he dead when you arrived earlier this morning?"

"Just, I think." She let out an odd little groan. "The dear, dear little boy."

"My God. So fast?"

"Todd was not a hale and hearty little soul," Gert whispered. "His heart was frail. More than once, Dr. Haines suggested..."

"I do not care what a man who has given his soul to the needle and the bottle suggests," Patterson spat. "And the child is not *dead.*"

"And what do you call it, sir? When the heart stops and the brain ceases to function and the cold blood settles to the lowest points of the body?" He could see that his words stung, but he couldn't stop. "And when decay begins the process of taking the body back to dust? Just what do you call *that,* sir?"

Patterson tried to bleat something, his eyes tortured, but Thomas had stopped listening to him. "Gert, where is Eleanor? Have you been able to speak with her?"

"Across the hall, Doctor."

"She is ill?"

"In a manner." She touched her own temple.

"Show me."

Following close behind, he entered a small room and saw a figure sitting by the window. It was Eleanor, wrapped in a shawl that was pulled tightly around her shoulders. Thomas knelt beside her. The back of her free hand, listless on her lap, was cool. He reached up and laid two fingers to her neck. The pulse was listless.

"Eleanor?" The girl didn't respond. She sat much as she had in the timber, beside Ben Sitzberger's body. "Eleanor, it's Doctor Parks."

She ignored him, lost somewhere over the spread of the inlet outside her window.

"I fear for her," Gert whispered in Thomas' ear.

"For them all," he replied. "Eleanor, can you stand for me?" The girl remained inert, focused far, far away. He rose to leave the room and was confronted by Patterson, who had sagged against the wall in the hallway. "Get out of my way, sir," Thomas snapped, and to his surprise, the man did.

Outside, the air tasted so wonderfully fresh that he paused for a moment to drink in half a dozen breaths.

"Bad?" Winchell asked.

"Indeed. He has laid out his wife's corpse in the parlor, awaiting a proper funeral. His son is dead. The smallest child…she looks but five or six…is alive but desperately ill. Eleanor has collapsed in a state."

"This does not surprise me," Aldrich said. "I saw her earlier. A desperate young woman. For a time, she was wandering down at the hotel. It looked like she wanted to help in some way, but couldn't. Piteous, I think. What about Patterson?"

"He is also ill, although still ambulatory. It won't be long."

"What must we do?" the constable asked.

"First of all, the three of them must be taken to the clinic—the surviving child, Eleanor, and the pastor. There is nothing for it but that."

"You'll hog-tie him?" Aldrich asked, only half in jest. "He will not listen to you."

"Then he can stew in his own juices until he is too ill to complain," Thomas said. "The wife and son must be buried with all dispatch. A deep grave, heavily treated with corrosive sublimate, as you've been doing." He held out his hands. "That's what must be done. Whether the Pastor approves or not."

"And if he stands in the way? This is the man's home, after all," Aldrich said.

"We must do what must be done." Thomas looked off toward the rest of the village. "When news spreads of Mrs. Patterson and the child, half the village will be trooping down here to offer condolences. They'll hear Patterson's nonsense that the disease is not exactly what it is, and bolstered by that, they'll bring food." He lowered his voice so Gert couldn't hear. "That's what people do. And we'll have hands mixing and kneading and feeding and being oh, so helpful. The bacilli will have a grand old time. The cholera will not have to find them. They will come to it."

Chapter Thirty

"My suggestion was permanganate of potash," Ted Winchell said. He regarded Thomas with his habitual amused expression. How he could find the light-hearted aspect of each dreadful situation, Thomas could not fathom, but he appreciated the undertaker all the more for it. "See, I thought that would give the hotel's cedar siding a nice purple hue, don't you know. Damn fashionable."

He yawned and glanced at the wall clock. Much of the morning had fled since their visit to Patterson's, and the time had been a blur. "We don't have much permanganate," Winchell continued, "but Lindeman's got sacks of Perlman's Privy Purifier, and that'll sure as hell work. Mostly chloride of lime, if I remember right."

The undertaker lounged in the doorway of the clinic's dispensary, watching Thomas compound yet another supply of what had come to be called "gut brew", the concoction of chamomile infusion, tannin, laudanum, and gum arabic. From his demeanor, one might guess that the man had spent a day of complete leisure, rather than behind the hammer, saw, and then shovel.

"Schmidt says it's going to ruin his pump, but he says that's okay," Winchell added. "What's the count now?"

"Four more brought in from the camp," Thomas said, decanting the brew carefully into the large amber bottle.

"Will they live?"

"You want an honest answer, or a hopeful one?"

"Hopeful doesn't help me any," Winchell replied.

"Continue your carpentry and your digging, then," Thomas said. "Of the four, I am willing to gamble that two will survive." He glanced at Winchell. "We have four more from the Clarissa—a fisherman and three of the ladies. But you knew that already."

"Yes." Winchell's face went sober and tired.

Thomas stopped pouring and closed his eyes. "Mary and..." He shook his head in despair. "God, she was taken ill, died, and I can't even remember her name."

"Constance."

"You knew her, then?"

"If I say yes, you'll wonder about me," Winchell replied. "But yes...a delightful young lady. Both she and Ida Jorgenson."

"Ida is hanging on," Thomas said. "My understanding is that she worked in the kitchen."

"Yes. That's not good, is it."

"No," Thomas said. "It's not good. In fact, it's as bad as it gets. And Ted, this is what irks me." He inserted the bottle's stopper and brought down the wire bale. "I am convinced that had they received treatment from the first sign of discomfort, the prognosis could be entirely favorable. As advanced as their condition is now, they *must* have been suffering symptoms at the very moment when you and I and the Constable were at the Clarissa. Their rooms were empty. When we found them downstairs and spoke with them, they confessed to no ill feelings."

"Yet Lucy is still with us."

"Lucy Levine is a remarkable young lady." Thomas glanced up at Winchell. "She sleeps most of the time now, and that's good. The trick is to keep the vital systems fortified. We can do that even as she sleeps."

"Little Janie Patterson?"

Thomas grimaced. "She is a tiny thing, Ted, without the natural resiliency." He straightened and rubbed his back. "I fear for her. She has little more resilience than her brother. The autopsy on the boy was hurried, but enough to show that he had a damaged valve in the heart, you know. I'm surprised that he reached his fifth birthday, Ted."

"Damn shame." The undertaker stretched, joints popping, and patted his gut.

"And how are you, by the way?" Thomas regarded the undertaker critically.

"Sound as oak," Winchell said, expelling a loud breath.

As Thomas turned, he caught a characteristic bouquet from Winchell's clothing. The undertaker saw the wrinkled nose and chuckled.

"They have pots of sulfur smoking in all the rooms, just like Doc Hardy told 'em. Most God-awful thing I ever smelled. Couple hours of that and I wouldn't think there'd be a thing alive on that floor…man, rat, or bacilli."

"You'd be surprised, my friend. The sulfur is good for this," and he tapped his head. "People are encouraged to see such a thing. But the smoke cannot reach into the fabrics, the rugs, the furniture, into every crack and cranny. That must be tackled by hand. As long as everyone who works on the hotel understands the dangers and takes appropriate precautions."

"Eleanor still wanders?"

"Most puzzling." Thomas sighed. "She lies in bed, staring at the ceiling." He shrugged. "Perhaps she will find the answers there. I don't know. Her sister tends her, as Elaine does so many others." He started to pass Winchell, who stepped to one side.

"What else can I do?" the undertaker asked.

Thomas smiled ruefully. "Keep up with us. Who works with you?"

"Jake has assigned four from the mill to me," Winchell replied. "They work the laundry with him, and for me when I need them. Everyone works without question or complaint. Well, not exactly without complaint, to be honest. The last thing those brawny boys want right now is to be digging holes in the ground. But they do it. And that's all I can ask."

Thomas nodded. "Did you see this?" He stepped across the dispensary and picked up a poster printed on rough, brown paper. Winchell took it and nodded.

"Aldrich has posted these all over town," he said. "You can't turn around without seeing them." In enormous, florid print, the poster announced:

Instructions for the Cholera!

Until further notice from the Medical Authority:
1. Seek medical assistance at the First sign of illness!
2. Clean the Dwelling and lime the privy!
3. Boil all cistern water, or even that from deep wells!
4. Boil all soiled clothing and bedding!
5. Report contagion and avoid the ill!

Constable George Aldrich's name had been added to the bottom of the poster, underneath Thomas' own.

"Do I always speak in exclamation points?" Thomas mused, and Winchell laughed.

"Maybe it attracts attention that way. By nightfall, there won't be a single person in Port McKinney who doesn't know of the cholera. We will know who is ill, and who is not. And of course," Winchell added, "there won't be a ship that stops, or a coach that approaches within fifty miles."

It all sounded so optimistic, Thomas thought. Still, he always felt better after talking to the gregarious undertaker, and when Winchell left the clinic, the young physician took a moment with his notes. Scientific journals would demand an accounting report, and he set about the work with diligence.

If Thomas' mood had been buoyed by Winchell's visit, it was dashed shortly after seven that evening.

Chapter Thirty-one

No threat of disease prevented Maurice Frye from pounding on the door of the clinic. Adelaide Crowell happened to be passing through the men's ward when the ruckus began, and she opened the front door to find Maurice wide-eyed and panicky, hopping from one foot to the other, face so drained of color that the nurse's first thought was that another victim of the cholera had made it to their doorstep.

The dirty towel wadded around his wrist was thick with blood. "I don't think it's too damn bad," he said without any assurance, and Mrs. Crowell let him in, ushering him straight to the surgery.

Thomas, who had heard the man, joined them just as Mrs. Crowell turned the gas jets up so high that they sputtered. The twenty-year-old shrank back at the physician's touch.

"The bandage, young man," Thomas coaxed, and he lifted an end to see that the wrap was nothing but a piece of filthy, grease-laden rag. The moment the rag was released, blood flooded across the man's hand and into the basin that Mrs. Crowell had anticipated. "Your name, son?" He hadn't seen this fellow out at the camp or in the timber.

"Name's Frye," the young fellow groaned.

"Well, Mr. Frye, what have you done to yourself?" Thomas pushed the flannel sleeve out of the way, and shifted so that the light from the nearest gas sconce illuminated the wrist. The jagged slash started on the swell of muscle below the right thumb and sliced in a nasty fashion down into the tendons of the wrist. Three inches of undamaged tissue marked where the tool had then skipped before inflicting a final slash on the man's underarm.

"How did you manage this?"

Between clenched teeth, trying to look away from his own arm but inexorably attracted to the sight, Maurice Frye whispered, "Fell on the damn thing."

"The thing being?"

"I was just sharpening the saw. That's all I was doing. Got up to stoke the stove so I could make some coffee, and damn."

"Off with the shirt, sir," Thomas said. He slapped a clean linen bandage over the wrist. "Hold this now. Hard." Then he helped Mrs. Crowell with Frye's damp woolen shirt. The wound was more frightening in appearance than reality, with no major vessels lacerated, and no tendons cut. But the flesh gaped enough that the moment Thomas removed the pad, young Frye's eyes rolled up and he collapsed backward.

"Quickly, now," Thomas said, and he scrubbed out the wound thoroughly, nearly finishing before Frye groaned back into consciousness.

"Will you want an injection?" Mrs. Crowell asked. The question was asked with more than a hint of weariness, as if she didn't care whether he wanted the needle or not, and he glanced up at her. *Too tired,* he thought. *Everyone is too tired.*

"Indeed. Morphine, half a grain. Otherwise he won't enjoy the stitching."

He finished cleaning the wound and frowned at the counter behind him. "We are lacking in dressings," he said. "We must rectify that tonight. We have been fortunate these past few days." As Mrs. Crowell handed him the sterile, charged syringe, Thomas leaned sideways a bit, looking the blanched Frye in the eye. "You're going to be fine, young fellow. A few stitches, and you'll be on your way. No serious…" He jerked his head around at the sound, a deep, prolonged borborygmus from Mrs. Crowell's gut.

"Oh, pardon me," she said, but this time, looking closer, he saw more than mild embarrassment on the woman's face.

"Where is Doctor Hardy?" he asked gently even as he gave the young man the injection in the heavy muscle of his upper arm.

"He is with the women's ward," she replied. "I saw him there last."

"You will go there immediately," he ordered, straightening up.

"Oh, but…"

"Mrs. Crowell, I will *not* be debated on this. You will take the Otis and find Dr. Hardy this instant. I will finish here. If your distress is a mild gas bubble, he will ascertain that soon enough. If it is more than that, well, then." He felt a wash of sympathy as he saw the fear creep across her face. "Right now, Mrs. Crowell."

"Really, Doctor…"

"Mrs. Crowell," he said again. "Please." He dropped the empty syringe in the pan. "I can manage here. And then I'll be to the ward." The nurse stood as if her shoes had been nailed to the floor. What a terrible thing to face, he thought as he watched the range of emotions play across Mrs. Crowell's lined face.

"As you wish, Doctor," she said finally, and Thomas watched her leave the surgery, her step with none of her characteristic bustle.

"She sick, Doc?"

"We would hope not. Now, the morphine burns?"

"Like hell, Doc."

"Does the arm hurt?"

"No."

"Well, it will, Mr. Frye." The logger winced with alarm. "But not that much. The worst has been done while you were away." With the wound spritzed with ether, he began with the sutures, and after the second, Maurice Frye cooperated by fainting again. The remaining ten closed the wound. By the time the logger was alert and could focus his eyes, the arm was bandaged and the thumb splinted immobile.

"Now, sir," Thomas said, and stopped when Bertha Auerbach entered the surgery. "Mrs. Crowell has reported to Dr. Hardy?"

"She has, Doctor. She denies feeling ill."

"Don't they all, early on. I hope that I'm wrong. If I am, then nothing is lost beyond a little peaceful sleep. If I'm correct, all might be gained."

"Will you need assistance here?"

"We're finished," he said, slapping Frye's bare shoulder. "Dr. Hardy will need you, Berti, without doubt. Elaine hardly has the experience." He realized what he'd said, and added, "She has two *days* experience, in fact. I've come to think of her as part of the medical staff."

Bertha helped the young man don his shirt. "Keep it absolutely clean, Mr. Frye," Thomas said. "You will do well to avoid the sort of activity that might reopen the wound. I want to see you…" He turned to Berti. "What day is this?"

"Still Saturday, Doctor."

"Ah. Perfect. You won't work tomorrow in any case. I want to see you on Wednesday next, then, Mr. Frye. Do not allow this to become wet, do not take off the bandage and pick at the wound." The image of one logger who'd prematurely taken out his own stitches with a skinning knife came to mind. "Do not play with the stitches, even should they itch."

"I can't work with this thing on," Frye complained, holding up the wooden splint that projected beyond his fingers.

"Indeed you can't, unless you find one-handed work. The wound must be allowed to heal, sir. If not, we cut it off first here," and he made a sawing motion across Frye's wrist, "and then here," and moved his hand to the young man's elbow, "and finally here," and he touched Frye's shoulder. He frowned severely at the ghastly expression on the logger's face. "I'm not making sport with you, Mr. Frye. Keep it clean and dry, keep it immobile, and come to see me on Wednesday. That's simple enough. You can manage it." *Perhaps,* Thomas thought. Buddy Huckla had managed an hour before tugging off his wrap—but scarce difference that made to him now.

"Man's got to earn a livin'. Can't do that sittin' on my ass, Doc. How much is this going to cost me?"

Thomas tipped his head judiciously. "This part is ten dollars, sir. If there are no complications, that's all it will cost. If you don't do as I say, it may well cost you more than you ever want to pay. Amputations start at thirty. Beyond that, I don't recall what Mr. Winchell charges. You understand my meaning?"

The logger swore, then realized Bertha Auerbach was standing at his side, and he blushed. "Sorry, ma'am."

"Where are you living, Mr. Frye?"

"Got me a camp up on Tillis Creek."

"You and a crew?"

"I work by myself."

"Well, good for you. That's commendable. How did you get here tonight?"

"My mule."

"Ride carefully going home, then. And good luck to you." He kept a hand on Frye's elbow as the man slid off the table. "Wednesday next."

They watched Frye walk a bit unsteadily out of the surgery. "And don't bother stopping at the Clarissa for a whiskey," Thomas called after him. The man paused halfway across the waiting room. "They're closed until further notice."

"How'd you know I was going to do that?" Frye asked.

Thomas tapped his own skull. "I am a soothsayer, Mr. Frye. Promise me that you will go home and collapse into your own bed. You have a bottle for the pain?"

"Nope. That's what I was going to get."

"Then here." Thomas stooped and opened one of the cabinet doors. He found the bottle he wanted and handed it to Frye. "It's not bad," he said. "Wrap yourself around it tonight."

"Thanks, Doc." Frye managed a smile and headed out the front door.

Thomas gazed at the tray of surgical implements wistfully. "It feels as if it's been years since I tended something as simple as that," Thomas said. "A few stitches, and there we are. I'm afraid our world has become one of rectal tubes and other unpleasantries."

Bertha didn't offer a smile. "Janie Patterson has passed, Doctor."

He felt as if she had punched him, and he could think of nothing to say.

"She awakened, feeling cold. The last evacuation had been nearly two hours, with little gut distress. But she complained of chill, and said that her back ached terribly. We drew a hot bath, and Elaine was tending her. She simply closed her eyes and stopped breathing."

"Elaine is with her now?"

"Yes. We lifted her out of the tub and wrapped her in clean linen…such a wisp of a thing. I don't think the child weighed twenty-five pounds." Bertha's mouth pursed, and Thomas could see the lines of every muscle in her jaw. "I don't know why, Doctor. I don't know why she died."

"Nor I. There must be at least a cursory post mortem to discover the answer."

Bertha sighed. "I dread that."

"It must be done."

"I know, Doctor. I know. It just seems like the final insult to such a wonderful little creature."

He reached out a hand and rested it on the nurse's shoulder. "If it can save another wonderful little creature, it's worth doing, Berti."

"Oh," she said, shaking her head in dismissal. "I agree with you completely, Thomas. It's just so…so *sad.*" He realized with a start that this was the first time that Bertha Auerbach had addressed him by his given name.

"Indeed it is. Eleanor is aware of her passing?"

"Elaine and I told her as best we could. Poor Elaine—she is such a rock, but I fear there is so very little left of her reserve." Bertha put a hand on either side of her head, rocking it from side to side. "And Eleanor has just gone somewhere, Thomas. I mean her thoughts have flown away, and where we don't know. When told of her sister's death, she simply nodded. Just a little nod. Nothing else."

"I'll talk with her," Thomas said. "You'll assist Dr. Hardy with Adelaide? If there's a way to stop the contagion…that is what baffles us, isn't it." He followed her out of the room and around to the stairway. "That's what baffles us," he repeated. "It is as if the cholera bacilli have their sport with us."

Half way up the stairs, they paused when they saw Eleanor Stephens appear on the landing. She was dressed in her night-gown, with a robe drawn close. Her arms were wrapped around her middle.

"You shouldn't be up," Berti said, but Eleanor just smiled at her and took her time with the stairs.

"Eleanor, I'd like to talk with you if I may," Thomas said. He intentionally blocked the stairway so that the girl would have to make some sort of decision. She stopped and moved her hand to the railing.

"I must inform Pastor Patterson about Janie," she said, her voice little more than a whisper. "He will want to know."

"Of course he must know. But I don't want you walking down there by yourself, Eleanor."

"Am I ill?"

"I don't…you have no gastric symptoms? None whatsoever?"

"No."

"Gert James is with your step-father. You mean to help her with the house and church?"

"I will do what I can," Eleanor said. She gazed at Thomas with an expression of complete resignation, as if in her mental travels during the past few hours, she'd seen something far worse than what now gripped Port McKinney, and had returned to take on the lesser of two evils.

"You'll do what you must," he said finally. "Might I suggest proper clothing if you're going out?"

"Of course."

He stepped to one side to let her pass, then hurried after Bertha, who waited for him at the top of the stairs.

"She shouldn't be allowed to leave the clinic," she whispered.

"How can I stop her?" Thomas said, holding out his hands. "She answers now as if all rationale has returned. She is well, I think. And after all, Berti, she is not a child. We have other matters to attend to. In a few minutes, I will walk down and check on her. And on Gert." He hesitated. "And on Roland Patterson. Would that *his* rationale would return."

Chapter Thirty-two

Thomas entered the men's ward and stopped short. The magnitude of the problem was now painfully clear. Every bed was filled, now including four young men recently brought from the camp. True to the perverse nature of the disease, there was no predicting the path the contagion would choose.

Two of the new cases were in the second stage of cholera, their evacuations like rice water, a gushing torrent that literally carried with it the lining of their gut.

Young, hearty loggers, proud of their ability to conquer the big timber, now lay as emaciated old men. Restless, anxious, in the fight of their lives with no ability to do anything about it, the men simply sank away. The cold perspiration soaked them until there was no more perspiration to be had. Their mouths were too parched to form words.

One of the loggers recently arrived showed only the lightest symptoms—a nagging stomach upset, painful gut, vomiting and diarrhea that he could managed well enough with the chamber pot without soiling his bed. There was no reason Mike Tierney should have been more resistant, but he was, healthy enough to curse his fate in the most vocal terms.

The ambulance ride to the clinic had all but killed the fourth logger, who had been in the third stage of cholera, his face sunken and unresponsive, eyes half-closed, pulse a mere flutter. He had been a big man, but now had shrunken to a pathetic marionette, as easy for Nurse Auerbach to arrange on the bed as a child. His oral temperature had fallen to 91 degrees, and at first, Thomas did not believe Bertha's recording. He took the temperature himself, and the mercury rose sluggishly, stopping at 90.5.

Through all this, in his private chambers at the back of the men's ward, Sonny Malone slept on, his shaved head encased in ice with periodic respites for warm wraps. He now took tiny amounts of brandy, amounts small enough that they evaporated in his mouth. The swallow reflex managed what few drops lingered on the back of his tongue.

"We must be as patient as he is," Lucius Hardy had observed at one point.

When he had a moment, Thomas dashed up to the women's ward, where he found Hardy now just leaving Adelaide Crowell's bedside.

"How is she?"

"Desperate, Thomas. I have never seen such a thing."

"And the young women?"

"I wish I could be optimistic." His voice dropped to a whisper. "It is as if, by being so close to the initial outbreak, the virulence is somehow more intense. I don't think that can be possible, but so it seems. If even one survives, I will be surprised."

"And Lucy?"

Hardy gazed toward the front of the ward. "She lingers. And I suppose I could say that her struggle is remarkable in all respects. The disease has reduced her to a mere shadow, yet a stout heart drives her on. We continue to support her system as best we can. If she lives, it may be weeks before she has convalesced sufficiently to rise from her bed. And that's without the rather lengthy list of sequelae that might impede her course of recovery." He took a deep breath and looked at his watch. "I ramble on. I'm sorry. I'm tired. I'm hungry…but with no appetite." He grinned. "Make sense of that, if you can, Doctor."

"We must find help for Bertha," Thomas said. "She has worked without pause since yesterday."

"She is adept," Hardy said. "I have walked through the ward more than once and seen her on the bed toward the back of the ward, sound asleep. Yet she stirs and wakes at the smallest moan from a patient. My grandfather used to call those 'wolf naps.'"

"If this continues, she'll need more than a wolf nap," Thomas said.

"She spends a lot of time with the girl…with Elaine."

"I can't even imagine," Thomas said. "I confess I don't know what to say to the child. It is easy to accept her as a nurse-in-training, without dwelling on the collapse of her world. I don't know how to help her deal with that."

"That may be all we can do right now." Hardy smiled gently. "Have you yet noticed that not very much of what we do here was ever discussed in the quiet, secure halls of the medical college?"

Thomas laughed. "I have noticed that, Lucius."

"Old Roberts will see our article in the journals and say, 'My God, those two were but pups who didn't know one end of a scalpel from the other just a bit ago.'"

"Should we live to see it," Thomas said philosophically. "I admit to always listening with half an ear for my own borborygmi."

Hardy's own laugh was quick and loud. "You must remember what we called the 'students' syndrome.' With each new disease that we studied, we began to show symptoms. We died a thousand dread deaths, Thomas. We're invulnerable now."

"Would that were so. Eleanor has left the clinic. Did you know she was going to do that?"

"No."

"I need to find the time later tonight to visit the Pattersons. She will be at the house, with Gerti." He pulled out his watch. "And now, a few moments with the tiny child. I must know what killed her."

Back downstairs, he ducked into his office to fetch his journal. The place was a sanctuary, although the smells of the wards touched each corner and cranny of the clinic. He entered and was struck by a new aroma, a bouquet that lingered, this one altogether lovely. Alvina had come to the clinic? Surely she had not brought their son into the wards. Had she done so, another presence would have followed her…the dog would not leave Alvi and the infant.

Thomas removed his shirt and dropped it in the lidded brass bucket that served as a hamper, then donned a fresh one from the ornate armoire. He had long since given up wearing a jacket, and once refreshed, he rolled up his sleeves and spent a long time disinfecting his hands, washing and rewashing, and then drenching his hands in brandy, letting the liquid drip from his fingers into the new porcelain sink.

He glanced in the men's ward and saw that Hardy had come downstairs, now making his way from bed to bed. Taking the stairs two at a time, Thomas returned to the women's ward and saw Bertha Auerbach tending one of the Clarissa girls. Five of the beds were occupied, and in the far corner of the ward, little Elaine Stephens sat on the end of the very last bed. Alvi knelt in front of her, both forearms resting on the girl's thighs, both hands holding Elaine's locked together.

As he drew closer, Thomas saw that Elaine wore a spotless new white dress, and an apron obviously fresh from under the iron. Alvi and Elaine were locked in intense conversation, eye to eye, Elaine's head bowed so that her face were less than six inches from Alvi's.

A hand touched his elbow, and he turned to Bertha. "Mrs. Whitman will be coming in for the rest of the night," she whispered. "Her son stopped by to tell us. If we are able to convince four or five nurses to come from St. Mary's, it would be a great help. We are falling behind with the laundry."

"With a lot of things," Thomas replied. "You are holding up?"

"After a fashion," she said.

"You must take the time for rest," he said. "Nothing is more important than that."

"As she is doing at this moment," the nurse said, nodding toward Alvina. "She shouldn't be here, but she is."

"Indeed she shouldn't. Where is the infant?"

"I did not presume to ask," Bertha said in that cold, neutral tone that she could use with such effect.

"Then I shall," Thomas said. "Excuse me."

"Certainly, Doctor."

At his approach, Elaine looked up, and it was clear that the tears had been abundant. Alvi ignored her husband, but reached up with both hands to cradle Elaine's face. She whispered something that Thomas couldn't hear and Elaine nodded quickly in response. Alvi stood up, releasing her hold on the child only at the last moment.

She turned and slipped her arm through Thomas' as they walked back through the ward. "You look refreshed, Doctor Thomas," she said. "The brandy wears well on you."

"Fortunately, Lindeman has an adequate supply, Alvi. Where is John Thomas?"

"Carlotta Schmidt stopped by the house. She is with him."

"Really? How wonderful. Is that wise, though?"

"Wise? Why ever would it not be wise? She wanted to be of help. And perhaps she is lonely, Doctor Thomas. Her husband rode out to the camps again, and is still there. His operation is as much in jeopardy as anyone else with this thing that has come among us. Carlotta said that he would close the West Dutch Tract camp."

"Jake told me so."

"And if it rains, he will burn all of it."

"And Elaine?"

"She has lost too much," Alvi said, looking down at her hands. "She worries about her step-father, I know she does. And even more, she worries about Eleanor. She wants to go home, Thomas."

"It would be better to remain here where we might keep her under observation. It is no safer there than here. Less so by a good deal."

"She understands that. I told her that I would do all that I can, now and later."

"And in the meantime?"

"There is no meantime, Doctor Thomas. First I must go down the hill. I'm sure that Gert has found neighbors to assist her with the Pattersons, but I want to be sure. She has been there all day. And then I shall return here to do what I can."

Alvi started down the stairs but then stopped and turned when Thomas didn't follow immediately. "You expect something else of me?"

The single syllable would not come for a moment. Finally he managed. "No."

"Fine, then," she said. "I will return with a full report. I will offer whatever assistance Gert needs. If the pastor isn't ill, that will make things easier."

"I think he is," Thomas said with considerable resignation. "He fights it, but he is ill. He should be here."

"Then we shall see, won't we." She reached out and stroked his cheek, and they walked arm in arm down the long stairway. When Thomas opened the front door of the clinic, the wash of fresh air was welcome. The late evening sky hung low, the lights of the village reflecting off the bottom of the clouds.

"Don't worry about me," Alvi said, and reached up to kiss his cheek. "And I shall not worry about you. All easily said, is it not?"

She laughed gently and then held up a finger, frowning. Now they could hear it, shouts in the distance, shouts so far away that the words had no meaning, just sounds floating on the air, punctuated by a symphony of dogs barking in frantic rhythm.

Lights played on the clouds, more than any lantern could throw, more even than a raging bonfire. A dull *whump* thudded, and more voices. Thomas stepped out onto Gambel Street, looking through the runty trees toward the southwest. Off in the distance, a bell began to ring frantically and then just as suddenly stopped.

"What…" Thomas started, and then another explosion, this one much louder, sent flaming debris skyward, above the trees, above the village, a cascade of burning embers.

"My God, it's the Clarissa."

Chapter Thirty-three

The weathered cedar siding of the Clarissa Hotel fed a giant fan of flame, a torrent that rose up the north side of the building, gaining momentum to the eaves, roaring into the night sky. Loathe to leave the clinic, but drawn by the conflagration whose flames he could see through the trees and over the rooftops, Thomas Parks cut through the alley to Lincoln Street, two blocks above the waterfront.

A dozen people milled in the street, unable to approach the burning building. The wall of flames already curled over the roof, igniting the cedar shingles. The privy on the north side of the building, a six-holer built on a cement foundation, was entirely consumed in flames, and a constant rain of embers and slivers of burning wood speared into the shallow water behind the hotel, each sending up a plume of smoke as it quenched.

Four men were attempting to operate Bert Schmidt's small wagon-mounted pump, but their efforts were comically ineffectual. They could approach the south side of the building where the flames had not yet curled, but the intense heat kept them away from the actual fire itself.

Thomas stopped in the middle of Lincoln Street, dumbstruck. Certainly, the blaze had begun in the outhouse, but from something far more intense than a carelessly knocked pipe. The entire structure roared with flame, from foundation to shed roof and beyond. He saw Fred Jules, a silly little bucket in his hands, trying to scoop water from the inlet.

The night breeze fanned in from the north, driving the fire up the siding and over the roof to the south side.

Several of the people in the street were dressed in night clothing, ripped from their slumbers after an interminable day of cleaning and worrying. As Thomas hustled down Lincoln, he recognized Viola Jules in a billowing gown. She screamed at Fred, who abandoned his one-man bucket brigade. He embraced Viola in a helpless hug as they watched the contents of their life go up in flames. Thomas came up behind the couple and put his arm around Viola's shoulders.

"Is everyone out?"

The stout woman nodded.

"We think so." Fred's bellow was drowned by the roar. He didn't look at the growing crowd around them, instead mesmerized by the sight of the three story hotel being reduced to ash. The heat was fierce on their faces, and as the north wall began to sag inward, the eaves above it curled down as the roof timbers under the shakes ignited. George Aldrich and two others pressed through the crowd, shouting for people to move back.

The four men who had been trying to operate the hand pump had retreated to the wharf, perhaps thinking to send a thin stream of water onto the backside of the hotel. Thomas could see that their efforts were useless. As the flames swept around from the north side and from the roof, the light played on both the wharf and the steam bark *Willis Head.* On board the ship, two men stood at the bow, directly at the base of the bowsprit, shouting something at the four firemen.

If they didn't understand the problem then, everyone did in a moment, when the fire flashed across the Clarissa's rear wall above the inlet, rolling up under the eaves and around to the south side. As it burned, the cedar split and shredded, the tiny explosions of sap driving the embers out into the wind that the fire itself generated. When the first curtain of embers fell on the wharf, the jeopardy was clear.

Tarred timbers first smoked and then exploded in flame, and Thomas watched in growing amazement as the wharf ignited, the fire racing up the three cedar sides of the wharf warehouse. The pumpers directed a feeble stream at the timbers, then hastily retreated. But there was nowhere for the *Willis Head* to retreat, other than to the open water of Jefferson Inlet. Her boilers were cold, and her hundred and ten feet of hull lay heavy in the water.

The ship's bowsprit rose a dozen feet above the inlet, a full two hundred feet from the back wall of the hotel, and by the time the threat to the ship became obvious, it was too late. Converted to steam, the *Head* carried a light rig of canvas, all of it tightly furled, but as the wharf's burning warehouse blossomed into flame and sent its own fountain of sparks into the air, the jibs caught first, the flame running up the lines.

The men on board—and Thomas could see two—faced an impossible task, but it became immediately obvious what they had elected to do. He recognized the power figure of Jacques Beaumont as the captain, ignoring the blaze, bounded down onto the wharf and cast off both bow and stern lines, and at the same time, the four men who had given up on the pumper realized the problem. Covering their faces, they charged along the very edge, racing down the far side of the wharf away from the burning structures, dancing through the flaming timbers.

As quickly as they ran out on the wharf, the fire cut off their escape, roaring between them and any return to the boardwalk on shore. The roof of the warehouse fed flames to the south side of the Clarissa, and Thomas shielded his face. The light was mid-day bright, the sound an enormous rolling thunder of flames and small explosions from coal gas, coal dust, and a vast store of flammable liquids in the bowels of the Clarissa.

At first, it appeared that the six men could make no progress with the *Willis Head*, and as much as others might have wanted to join the effort, the fire had spread across the wharf and cut off the ship and crew. Flaming pitch melted off the structure and speared into the water. Because the wharf lay just off east-west, the wind worked in the men's favor, and even as the fires danced in the ship's exposed rigging, Thomas could see the gap between ship and wharf widen inch by inch.

The race to save the *Head* was agony. All the men were needed to push and heave, leaving none to fight the growing fires now in both her rigging and the canvas-covered cargo on her deck.

Quartering against her bulk, the wind both fanned the spot flames and helped to ease the ship backward, away from the wharf.

Something exploded with a tremendous roar in the last room of the wharf warehouse, sending debris rocketing far out into the water and across the *Head's* decking. At the same time, flames reached out from the ship's rigging like golden pennants, pointing down the inlet.

The first signs of smoke emerged from her single stack and Thomas realized that at least one seaman had stayed below in the ship, frantically trying to fire her boiler.

As the stern of the ship floated far beyond the end of the wharf, the effort of the six men and the persistent push of the wind sweeping down from the north gained purchase on the slab sides of the *Willis Head*.

"They ain't going to make it," George Aldrich yelled in Thomas' ear. "And they're going to have to take a plunge!" It was obvious that the six men on the wharf had two choices… clamber back on board the *Head* as soon as she cleared the wharf, or dive into the inlet and swim south, heading for shore well down reach from the fire.

The constable prodded Thomas in the ribs. "You seen the girl?"

"Who?" Thomas bent his head close to the Constable's in an effort to hear.

"The Patterson girl. Eleanor."

"Eleanor?" He shook his head, flinching from the heat. By now, the crowd of onlookers gawked at the race. Flames curled around the bowsprit where a curtain of burning, furled sail slumped off the lines and draped around the bow. Inch by inch, the ship drifted and pivoted, but with every inch, the fires at the bow raced and bloomed up into rigging, now even feeding on the marine varnish of the forward mast and running down the gunwales.

The black smoke from the stack billowed thicker now. As the *Willis Head* drifted far enough beyond the corner of the wharf and the reach of the men pushing her, all six scrambled on board. Had they had Schmidt's hand-cranked water pump now, they might have accomplished something. Fire aft of the bowsprit formed a halo of bright flame around the foremast, running up the varnished wood like a mad thing.

A blast of hot air swatted Thomas' face and he staggered backward, along with the hundred onlookers. The *Clarissa* erupted as the north side of the roof crashed inward, followed almost immediately as the inlet side of the building slumped, buckled, and then spewed out into the water, taking the south wall with it. Flaming timbers seemed to dance across the water, showering the burning wharf where fires raced along the trails of pitch toward the retreating ship.

Flames and sparks from the *Clarissa*, feeding on all four walls now and joined with the conflagration from the long wharf and warehouse, arced hundreds of feet into the air, actually curling over the *Willis Head* as she drifted out into the inlet. The six men on board now tried to concentrate their efforts on the ship, but buckets of water hauled on lines up from the inlet provided only enough water to cool their own blistering hides. The flames grew from the bow and reached another wrap of tarpaulin stretched over deck cargo.

One of the men ran forward toward the flames but was forced back. Now that the ship had drifted beyond reach from the wharf, her bow yawned away from the blaze on shore. For a moment it appeared that she would swing windward until her bow headed south, offering her stern to the conflagration, but Jacques Beaumont spun the wheel hard to keep the bark's slab sided hull broadside to the wind so she'd make full advantage of the push. Had she been able to gain even a little headway from her engines, she might have managed, but the rudder drifted as listlessly as the rest of the ship, at the mercy of the flames and the wind.

By the time she had swung abeam the wind, her stern was fifty feet from the wharf. The smoke from her stack wisped up into the night to be swept away. With her bow now engulfed and the fires spread the length of her rigging, the men retreated to the stern, and a hundred souls on shore shouted and waved at them to dive into the inlet. A seventh man—Thomas imagined him to be the intrepid fireman who had made such a valiant effort to fire the boilers—joined the group, and one by one, shed of heavy clothing and boots, they leaped for their lives into the inky waters of the inlet. It appeared to Thomas that two of them hesitated until pushed over the side by Captain Beaumont.

The captain stood on the fantail of the *Head,* both hands on the railing, watching the swimmers.

"Don't do it," Thomas heard himself shout. Jacques Beaumont could do nothing about his blazing ship, and to remain on board to be reduced to a cinder was pointless.

With another roar, the *Clarissa* collapsed in on itself, and Beaumont made his decision. Turning from a final, long look at his ship, the captain spread his arms and executed a magnificent swan dive into the harbor.

All seven men from the *Willis Head* reached shore, greeted by dozens of helping hands. Beaumont swam rapidly with a powerful crawl, then stood in water to his knees, trying to make himself heard.

Thomas heard the word "oil" shouted, and the captain gesticulated urgently down the inlet. The crowd fell silent as if stunned man by man. Now well away from the wharf and the fire, the *Willis Head* drifted unhindered, wallowing before the winds that blew her southward. Thomas saw that the ship's course, without power to drive her out into open water and safety, would carry her directly down the inlet, her hulk burning to the waterline.

One of the men who had swum ashore sat down abruptly in the shallow water with a cry of pain, clutching his left foot. Another explosion rocked the giant bonfire that had been the *Clarissa*, and Thomas hunched against the rain of sparks. Beaumont helped the injured swimmer out of the water. The captain spotted Thomas and beckoned.

With plenty of light, Thomas had no difficulty seeing what the injured man had done. The bottom of the inlet was littered with every conceivable sort of junk, and it appeared that a broken bottle or some such had slashed the man's heal to the bone, a nasty gash that circled up into the in-step.

With a discarded shirt, he bound the foot tightly and then shouted at the men, "To the clinic! Take him there now." Turning to Jacques Beaumont, he bellowed to make himself heard. "What's she carrying?"

The captain pointed with both hands. "That pallet up at the bow is two thousand gallons of coal oil, but she's got more in the hold. Dynamite, too. Lime, cordage, ninety tons of logging chain…she's sitting heavy."

"It'll all go to the bottom here in a minute," Thomas shouted back.

"God damn well better." Beaumont gesticulated toward the southwest. "If she don't, she'll run aground down yonder." As long as the *Willis Head* remained far enough out in the inlet to avoid grounding in the shallows, she would drift along unhindered as the fires raged on board, burning themselves out.

But in another mile—curtained now by the darkness—the shoreline began its slow curve toward the east, hooking out into Jefferson Inlet to form the spit where the wharfs of Bert Schmidt's gigantic saw mill complex jutted out into the waters—the saw mill, with its endless ricks of the seasoning spruce and fir—and just beyond, the new shingle mill with hundreds of pallets of fine-grained, explosively thin cedar.

A shout just behind him drew his attention back to the *Clarissa,* but it wasn't the fire there that had prompted the cry of alarm. To the north, high-lighting the dirt streets and scattering of buildings that rose inland from the hotel, light flickered against the clouds, and even as he watched, a sheet of flames rose high enough to tower over the village.

Chapter Thirty-four

Had the circumstances been different, Thomas might have laughed. The crowd surged first one way and then another, trying to decide which catastrophe to watch. On the one hand, a burning ship loaded with chains and dynamite drifted toward the life blood of the community. On the other, *something* large was burning on the north end of the village, behind their backs, ready to mow through the village itself.

A handful chose the latter, including Thomas. From the *Clarissa,* Front Street rutted north, two carriages wide through the muck when the inlet spumed over the rude breakwater. Three narrow streets ran up the hill from Front Street into the village, and then Thomas reached the intersection with Gamble.

Without benefit of a lantern, but following a few flickering lights from others, Thomas tried to avoid most of the deepest, ankle-breaking ruts. By the time he reached Gamble, he was panting hard. Jogging inland up Gamble, he reached Angeles Street and saw the fires dead ahead, beyond where Angeles snaked up the low hill toward Patterson's church.

By that time, Thomas needed no lantern. Flames towered above the church, feeding off the cedar siding, the shakes on the steeply pitched roof, the filigreed cedar trim around the tall steeple. It appeared that the fire had started in the rear of the church, behind the meeting hall, towering now to silhouette the building.

Thomas ducked as an explosion rocked the rear of the church, a sheet of flame and black smoke jetting high above the roof. Something whizzed over his head, and he heard shouts from others.

"The house!" someone screamed above the din. Sure enough, the pastor's two-story frame house, with its cedar shakes and cedar siding, had become its own conflagration. Thomas scrambled up the trail, skirting the church. Nothing could be done about that structure, and everyone knew it.

Figures were silhouetted in front of the house, and as he plunged across the yard, he saw the front door open. He recognized his wife's full figure, struggling with something. Thomas bounded up onto the small front porch, and saw that Alvi was trying to manage one end of a narrow cot, with Gert at the other. The flames swept up and over the house, the cedar shakes overhead exploding small bombs of flaming pitch-laden wood that showered over the house.

Something that sounded very like a heavy shotgun banged inside the house, perhaps a tin of oil or a gallon of liquor. With it, the roar of flames redoubled.

"Get the other end!" Thomas shouted in Alvi's ear. She ducked around and joined Gert, and at the same time Thomas realized that the high keening wail that he heard came from Pastor Roland Patterson, now lying curled on the cot in that characteristic posture, like a small child with knees drawn up and hands clasped at his face.

No sooner had they cleared the doorway than more hands crowded to take the cot. Hands freed, Thomas reached out and grabbed Alvi by both arms when it appeared that she was headed back into the house. "No!" he cried, and as if to punctuate his shout, a portion of the roof cascaded flames and sparks that fountained down on the front porch. Through the front door, he could see nothing but the thick billows of flame-danced smoke.

"Eleanor is with her mother!" Alvi shouted, and she fought Thomas with amazing strength. Struggling to hold her, he wrapped both arms around her. From his left, George Aldrich appeared and grabbed Alvi from the front so that the two men sandwiched her in their arms.

Men with water buckets tried with a few ineffectual attempts and then gave up, the crowd backing away from the heat. As Alvi stopped struggling, Aldrich released his hold, and she sank back into Thomas' arms, then to her knees, staring hopeless into the flames.

"He must go to the clinic," Thomas shouted above the din. A corner of the blanket over Patterson smoked where a cedar ember had landed, and Aldrich smacked it away.

"Anyone else in there?" the constable bellowed, but Alvi ignored him, eyes locked on the burning door as if she could will a figure to appear there. A portion of the roof caved in, sending another geyser of sparks up into the heavens. Behind them, the back wall of the church buckled.

Several men with buckets now scampered back and forth from the well, concentrating their efforts on the small spot fires that bloomed in the grass and shrubbery behind the house.

Aldrich and two others trundled the pastor's cot away from the fire, and Thomas lifted Alvi to her feet.

"You're all right?"

She nodded numbly and reached out a hand to Gert James.

"Did Eleanor do this?" Thomas asked.

"I think so," Alvi said, and he could hardly hear her. George Aldrich stepped close and looked her hard in the face.

"Eleanor Stephens was seen at the *Clarissa* just a few minutes ago," he said.

"She is inside," Alvi said, and they had to bend close to make out her words. She looked beseechingly at Thomas. "She asked me if her mother and the children were now safe."

"She knew that they were all dead," he replied.

"The part of her mind that still worked knew that," Alvi said dully. She turned to Aldrich. "We heard the fire at the church. We went outside, right here, and saw that there was nothing to be done. And as we turned around, the rear of the house burst into flames."

"We'll find what she used," Aldrich said.

"We dashed inside, and the fire spread so fast."

Alvi's face was illuminated with white light as if every lantern in Port McKinney had been turned on her, and a second later the blast hit them, followed immediately by a flat, deep-throated boom from out in the inlet. Thomas instinctively ducked, taking Alvi with him. Gert James sat down on her rump as if pushed. Off to the south, the sky bloomed noon-day bright, and as quickly faded. For a moment, Thomas saw lazy strands arcing up and out, etched against the sky, to dive back into the water like long, curling worms.

"The ship!" he cried, for that's all it could have been. The *Willis Head*'s dynamite had exploded just before the waters of the inlet flooded over her low-riding, burning gunwales, sending ninety tons of logging chain rocketing in all directions.

"How…" Gert cried.

"She's exploded!" Thomas said in wonder.

"Thank God," Aldrich said, his voice surprisingly calm. Thomas looked at him in astonishment. "I better go down and see," Aldrich said. "But she wouldn't have had the time to drift to the spit, and right now, that's all that matters, eh?" He looked first at Alvi and then Gert. "You two are all right, now?"

Alvi nodded.

"There is no one else inside but Eleanor and her mother… you're sure of that?"

"I'm sure."

"You'll be at the clinic?" Aldrich asked Thomas, as if to say, "You're not needed here."

"Yes."

"There are going to be some hurt, you know."

"We're ready," Thomas said, even though he knew they were clearly anything but ready. He looked at the two women. "I can bring the carriage down," he said.

"I want to walk," Alvi said. "Walk with me, Doctor Thomas."

She slid her arm through his, and Thomas turned and held out his hand to Gert, who joined them. When they were far enough from the fire that she could speak without shouting, Alvi leaned her head sideways until it touched Thomas' shoulder.

"She fought us," she said.

"How do you mean?"

"Gert had arranged Mr. Patterson on one of the single cots, and was just on her way to fetch the ambulance from the clinic when the church fire started, and then, the house. When we started to move the pastor to safety, Eleanor blocked our way."

"Actually physically blocked your path?"

"She demanded it," Alvi said. "I tried to ignore her, and when I picked up the end of the cot, she pushed me away." She held out her left arm and turned it, showing the rip at the elbow. "I could hear the fire, and knew we had no time to discuss matters with the girl."

"What did you do?"

"I struck her, Thomas. God forgive me, I struck her, as hard as I could."

He felt Gert's arm tighten around his.

"She stumbled across the room, and then behind her, the glass in the window burst inward, and the room was on fire. Gert and I managed the small cot like a stretcher, and then it seemed as if everything conspired against us. At first we could not pass through the bedroom door, a thing so simple when one is not in a panic. And then we almost became stuck fast in the hallway, with the smoke billowing around us. I was terrified, Thomas. And I confess that I did not think about the girl until we were outside. And then it was too late."

"There is not a thing more that you could have done, Alvi. It appears that Eleanor set fire to the *Clarissa* as well. From what I could see, it started in the privies on the north side. It spread as if the whole building was covered in nothing but pitch. I don't know what she used…coal oil, I suppose."

"And now I have traded her life for her step-father's, and he is surely a dying man," Alvi moaned. For the remainder of the walk to the clinic, not another word was spoken, and Thomas found himself cursing his tied tongue, cursing his ability to find just the right thing to say to his wife.

"We were lucky down at the waterfront," he said as they reached the front steps of the clinic. "I saw only a man with a badly gashed foot. I believe all were able to escape the hotel, and it appeared that the crew was off the ship as well," Thomas said. "There was nothing to be done. It was a fire well and truly stoked from the very beginning."

When they reached the clinic, it appeared as if Gert was ready to continue on up Gamble to the house, but Thomas ushered her inside. "At least the hands and forearms, Gert. And if we can find you a clean dress, that too. Take your time, now. Carlotta Schmidt is at the house with John Thomas. She won't want to give him up."

Lucius Hardy peered around the ward door, saw them, and stepped into the waiting room, closing the door behind him.

"The pastor is in a coma," he said softly. "I fear that there is little we can do for him. Had he come to us a day ago…" He shrugged. "Perhaps not even then. His step-daughter is with him."

"I must talk to her," Alvi said, starting toward the ward, but Thomas caught her by the arm.

"Not in the ward thus," he said. "In any event, the girl will need a few moments alone with her step-father."

"She does not know about her sister," Alvi said. "I'm the one to tell her."

"After you clean up, Alvi."

"Elaine's sister?" Hardy asked.

"Eleanor has perished in the house fire," Thomas said, watching Alvi and Gert mount the stairway to the second floor.

"My God, she couldn't simply walk out the door? The mad girl stayed in the burning house until it fell down around her?" Hardy asked, flabbergasted.

"I would guess her fate was intentional," Thomas said quietly.

"Ah…that's most unfortunate. And yet a bedridden man, one lapsed into a final coma, is saved. The world is a curious place, sometimes." He brightened. "And Thomas?" Hardy nodded toward the ward. "While the town was burning down around our ears—another monumental occasion. Mr. Malone took a tablespoon or two of broth."

"Surely he's not conscious?"

"Well, no. But he managed a feeble swallow, which considering his state is a remarkable success."

"I'm ready to hear of success," Thomas said fervently.

Chapter Thirty-five

By midnight, the fires and the shouting had died. The three-story *Clarissa* had been reduced to a pile of embers and smoking rubble no taller than the average man. The wharf and warehouse had burned to the waterline, leaving blackened stubs projecting out of the water. The *Willis Head* had simply vanished, but talk had begun to circulate that men would be able to dive into the shallow, tea-colored waters of the inlet and salvage some of the expensive chain that had been part of her cargo. She had exploded more than a half mile from Schmidt's lumber mill.

Both the church and the Patterson home had burned with a swiftness and totality that took the breath away. On the front porch of the clinic, Thomas could hear, when the breeze was just right, voices from here and there, voices filled with wonder at the disaster.

Despite the fury of the conflagration, injuries had been few and relatively minor. No one had been trapped in the *Clarissa*. The explosion that had ripped apart the *Willis Head* had lit the skies and hurled chain for hundreds of yards, but harmed no one. A dozen stitches closed the badly cut foot of the sailor who'd stepped on a broken bottle in ankle-deep waters.

Roland Patterson proved more of a challenge. Not a vestige of his temper or his umbrage were left to fight the cholera. If he knew that he had lost his entire family, including the step-daughter who had first brought the disease into his home, and then destroyed the both home and church, he gave no sign.

When Thomas checked on him shortly after midnight, he lay as if already dead, breath coming in shallow gasps, eyes dull and unfocused, body twitching in irregular spasms. Neither the tube and bulb nor the infusion through the canula appeared to make any difference to his condition. Fluid replaced in the man's body simply was evacuated again in double, and Patterson's body shrank and collapsed.

As Patterson sank deeper into a coma, Thomas sent word up to the women's ward that Elaine should attend her father…that the end was imminent. To his surprise, Bertha Auerbach came down stairs instead, her step slow and tired.

"She will not leave the ward," Berti said.

"And yet she understands the gravity?"

"Certainly she must, Doctor." The nurse looked pained.

Thomas sighed. "She has no one left."

"Elaine has the ward," Berti replied. "And for the moment, it is well that she has something so consuming. I know that Alvi wishes to speak with you about her."

"About Elaine?"

Berti nodded. "Your wife had planned to return to the clinic at dawn."

"She can't," Thomas said automatically, and then realized how absurd that must have sounded to Berti Auerbach. He leaned back against the wall. "Dr. Hardy has taken a few hours. And you should too, Berti."

"We have no one else," the nurse said quietly. "It is Mrs. Whitman and myself for two wards. With help from the child."

"And you?" Thomas' eyes roamed the nurse's face, a visage ten years older than the day before.

"I nap," Bertha said cryptically. "That will have to do."

For the next two hours, Thomas worked his way from one patient to another, his routine by now automatic. Shortly after two in the morning, Marcus Snyder whispered his name as Thomas rose from tending Howard Deaton.

"Doc, you got one gone," Snyder managed. "He sat up, and then just went." And sure enough, in the bed beside Snyder,

Gunnar Bloedel, one of Sitzberger's cabinmates at the logging camp, had expired, lips blue, eyes staring at the ceiling.

"He was havin' trouble breathin'," Snyder offered as he watched Thomas. "Breaths comin' all kind of chirpy-like. Then he sat up, sucked it in, let it out, and that was that."

"It seeks out the weak of heart," Thomas replied. He pulled the linen up over Bloedel's face.

"You need a hand, Doc?"

"I need for you to lie quietly," Thomas said quickly.

"I ain't got the strength of a mouse," Snyder murmured. "But you ain't got much help, do you."

"Not much, no. But we'll manage." He knew that the last thing the patients needed to see was a sheeted corpse being wheeled from the ward, but perhaps they were used to it by now. The hard rubber wheels whispered on the wooden flooring as Thomas pushed the bed and its cargo from the ward.

He worked methodically, leaving the sheeted corpse on the hard surface of the operating table in the back room, to await a post mortem. Using the harshest of disinfectants, he washed down the frame of the bed and removed the rubber mattress pad, cleaning it with sublimate. The soiled linen went into the soak barrel with five percent carbolic acid, with a little crude hydrochloric acid added for good measure, to await a boiling wash outside come dawn.

Thomas disinfected his own hands for the umpteenth time, then found clean linen and remade the bed before wheeling it back into the ward. Snyder was asleep, and Thomas knelt by Patterson's bed, examining the pastor's face.

Patterson was neither awake nor asleep, but caught in some terrible twilight place. Thomas listened to the pulse and heard the laboring of thick blood. The flesh of Patterson's face had shrunken around the bones, and even as Thomas watched, the man trembled as if a great cold had passed through his innards.

In a back cabinet, he found two rubber water bottles, and filled them both, nestling one in each of the patient's armpits. A hot mustard stupe on the belly seemed to produce some relaxation, and Thomas took advantage of that to administer yet another round of hypodermoclysis, introducing more than a liter of fluids into Patterson's system, this time with an added quarter grain of opiate.

Working thus, Thomas Parks spent the night going from bed to bed, with occasional trips to the women's ward where he conferred with Bertha Auerbach. During those excursions, he watched Elaine carefully. The girl worked as if in a trance.

Shortly before five, he met Lucius Hardy as Hardy descended from his quarters on the third floor.

"You managed some sleep?" Thomas asked. Hardy looked rumpled and a little pasty, and he smelled strongly of wine.

"Well," and Hardy waved a hand in dismissal. "A little burgundy to kick the system, and if I can find a coffee pot, I shall be entirely happy. You, on the other hand, look a wreck, Doctor."

"If you're going to be up for a bit, I want to go up to One-oh-one for a few minutes," Thomas replied. "Bloedel, from the camp? He died earlier. I want a post, but I suspect heart failure."

"Isn't it always, when we get right down to it." Hardy said. "Patterson?"

"He hangs on. He took a liter of salt solution at three. Perhaps another is called for now. Both Mrs. Whitman and Bertha are managing."

"Then we are content," Hardy said. "And my regards to your brave wife, Thomas. We are going to benefit from her steadying hand within these walls. Take good care of her."

"Exactly my purpose at this moment, Lucius."

Walking the six blocks, Thomas caught the strong fragrance of scorched cedar as the light wind shifted this way and that. He entered One-oh-one and to his surprise found the kitchen bright with light and activity. Gert James, smelling of fresh lilacs, worked in her long robe at the stove. The dark circles under her eyes were the only hint of what the previous evening had brought. At the sideboard, she was slicing ham paper thin. A basket of fresh eggs stood near at hand.

"Alvina is feeding the child, Doctor," she greeted. "She is in the library."

"What time did Carlotta go home?"

"I would suppose it was sometime after midnight. Her husband returned from the camps, and fetched her home."

"All went well? At the camps, I mean?"

Gert glanced at him. "I did not hear the conversation, Doctor. I would suppose so. I did hear him say that he would visit down at the clinic, but there was still work to be done in the timber." She regarded the ham critically. "Breakfast will be in just a few minutes. You will join us." It wasn't an invitation or query, but a flat command, and Thomas smiled.

"Yes, ma'am."

"How is Mrs. Crowell?"

"Grave."

"And Howard?"

"He is resting at the moment. But this disease is persistent. It retreats, and then attacks with renewed ferocity."

"Dr. Hardy?"

"He is with Howard as we speak."

"Good. I will be sending a basket down with you when you and Alvi return. The Pastor?"

"I'm am surprised that Roland Patterson is still alive at this hour, Gert. He is desperately ill. He is beyond anything I can do for him."

Gert's eyebrows rose ever so slightly. "We'll see, then, won't we."

Thomas wasn't sure what she meant, and added, "If we can force enough fluids, maybe. If his heart will support it. We lost one of the loggers this morning. The Dutchman."

"You know..." Gert began, then Thomas saw her lips clamp tightly. She turned to face him. "When Dr. Haines...Alvi's father...worked an epidemic at one of the Indian camps, everyone here in town was so afraid that he would bring the savages back to the clinic to treat them. That wasn't so many years ago."

"Everyone...meaning Pastor Patterson?"

Gert hesitated, and Thomas found himself wondering how her loyalties and beliefs must have torn her. "He tried to force the issue with Dr. Haines, to prevent…from that moment until Dr. Haines' passing last year, they had not spoken."

"People are easily frightened, I think."

"I suppose they are."

"And Alvi should remain here, Gert," Thomas said as he turned toward the kitchen door. "It's not a question of fear. It's a question of common sense. But I have been unsuccessful in my attempts to convince her."

The older woman shrugged as if to add, "I've said all I can say."

Thomas hesitated. "Gert—you did a brave thing. Thanks for last night."

A shoulder lifted a fraction. "Sometimes help has to be forced on people," she said. "They don't see it in time. Roland Patterson is a bit…starched, Thomas. If he survives, and by Heaven's grace he will, it will be interesting to see if the collar loosens a bit." She favored Thomas with a brittle smile.

In the library, Alvi sat in front of a fire just large enough to temper the dampness, the only light to break the dim of pre-dawn. She wore a hugely voluminous robe, the infant lost somewhere in its folds. As Thomas entered, she was gazing into the bright yellow fire. She looked up at him and smiled.

"It would seem that flame is the last thing I would want to see," Thomas said. "But it's soothing, isn't it. John Thomas enjoys it, I suppose."

"He eats so much," she said. "I feel as if he's turning me inside out."

"I have only a few minutes," Thomas said. "Gert demands that I have breakfast before I go back."

"You can't keep this up, Doctor Thomas."

"I know. We should have some response from St. Mary's today. Perhaps staff from there by mid-week."

"No one can wait that long," she said. "You least of all."

"I trade off with Lucius. It is the nurses who suffer the most."

"I saw that," Alvi said. "I am so sorry that Mrs. Crowell has fallen ill. You have hope for her?"

"There is always that," Thomas replied. "Always hope."

Alvi nodded and adjusted her son's position. "Carlotta will return regularly as long as we need her. That way I may go down to the clinic for short periods."

"I suppose it's a waste of breath for me to ask that you not do that."

"Why ever shouldn't I? I am as skilled, as trained, as any—and more than most. A few hours each day won't hurt me, and will provide some much needed relief."

"Berti said that you were with Elaine last night."

"Yes. I told her what had happened. I held her for more than an hour. And then she was finally able to cry, Thomas. She could not bear to look on her step-father, ill as he might be. And now she has no one."

"Patterson might yet live," Thomas said.

Alvi's smile was thin. "As I said, she has no one." She shifted the swathed infant, drawing him away from her breast. "My arms are paralyzed," she said. "He's a heavy brute." She held him toward Thomas, who took John Thomas with nervous care. "You need practice, you see."

"Precious little time for that."

"You shall have the time, when all this is past. I want Elaine to live with us, if she'll have us."

The statement came so unexpectedly that for a moment Thomas wasn't sure he had heard her correctly. "Pastor Patterson may have something to say about that, Alvi. Should he survive the night, that is. And if not, then surely she has other relatives, does she not?"

"None on this side of the continent, but that's a choice for her to make," Alvi said. "As you know, I can be most persuasive. We can. . and *should*. . .provide a home for her, Dr. Thomas. She can go to school, and then continue her medical studies. She must be encouraged in that direction."

"*Medical* studies?"

"Of a certainty. Have you ever known someone of her tender years with such skills? Such *sympathy* for the work of the clinic? It is what she wants. We must provide the opportunity."

"She has told you this?"

"In all ways but words. In any event, she must remain with us for some time. She has no home, after all. Should her step-father survive, we shall have *both* of them under our room for some time. We can't just turn them out."

"We'll have to see, then, won't we."

"You sound unconvinced," Alvi said.

"But you will see to that," Thomas laughed. He rocked John Thomas from side to side, enchanted with the tiny face and miniature hands, and then handed him back to Alvi. "If Elaine joins us, then it's but thirteen more, Alvi. You'll have your mantle photograph yet."

She smiled brilliantly. "Because she will join us not as a guest, but as a member of the family, Doctor Thomas. And what a marvelous thing that will be."

"First, we do what we can for Roland Patterson and all the others." He frowned in thought. "And what an *odd* thing."

"Odd?"

"Eleanor's madness. In some ways, most calculating. She has removed the seat of contagion from the village with massive, bold strokes. Some one—I've forgotten who—told me a day or two ago that the best solution to the *Clarissa's* problems would be the torch. We certainly expected no one to seriously entertain the idea."

"Come!" A commanding voice snapped from the library doorway. "A hot breakfast, and then you two can do what you must."

Chapter Thirty-six

With the capriciousness so characteristic of the disease, the cholera outbreak in Port McKinney killed twenty-three before burning out. The last six deaths directly attributable to the outbreak occurred on May 17th and the morning of May 19th, 1892.

At seventeen minutes after six on May 17th, Pastor Roland Patterson died after abruptly sitting up in bed, gesticulating and shouting, although no words issued from his parched mouth before he pitched back, senseless.

Later that same day, the twenty-six-year-old logger Herb Bonner received two liters of mild salt solution to ease the thickening of his blood from dehydration, asked for a drink of iced champagne, and died before he had the chance to swallow.

Hours later, logger Carl Curran suffocated after inhaling his own vomit.

Of the young women from the *Clarissa*, three suffered long and complicated recoveries, and as soon as they were ambulatory, left Port McKinney for Seattle. Letitia Moore struggled until the early morning hours of May 19th, and then passed away after telling Bertha Auerbach that she felt well enough to walk home.

At 8:12 a.m. on May 19th, fifty-two-year-old veteran nurse Adelaide Crowell died in her sleep after what appeared to be a restful and recuperative night.

Four days later, sixteen-year-old villager Bennie Tuttle drowned while diving for the trove of logging chain flung into Jefferson Inlet by the explosion of the *Willis Head*.

Thirty-nine-year-old ambulance driver and family friend Howard Deaton recovered fully, but fought a recurring infection in his leg. It killed him two years later, on Christmas Day, 1894.

Lucy Levine, twenty-two, the first to be struck in the epidemic, survived the cholera, left Port McKinney never to return, and married a saw-mill operator north of Bellingham, Washington.

Carlotta Schmidt underwent surgery for breast cancer at the Port McKinney Clinic on May 28th, 1892, and died of recurring cancer three years later.

Sonny Malone awoke from his month-long coma in June, 1892, to ask Dr. Thomas Parks what had caused the loss of all of his hair. Never returning to the big timber, Malone became a fixture around Port McKinney, although reportedly suffering from "mental aberrations."

Elaine Stephens, who had lost her entire family, lived with Thomas and Alvina Parks for six years, eventually completing her studies toward a medical degree. After completing University in Portland, she returned to Port McKinney to practice at the Parks-Hardy Clinic.

By that time, the family portrait on the mantle at 101 Lincoln showed considerable progress toward Alvi's goal.

To receive a free catalog of Poisoned Pen Press titles, please contact us in one of the following ways:

Phone: 1-800-421-3976
Facsimile: 1-480-949-1707
Email: info@poisonedpenpress.com
Website: www.poisonedpenpress.com

Poisoned Pen Press
6962 E. First Ave. Ste. 103
Scottsdale, AZ 85251